I've travelled the world twice over,
Met the famous: saints and sinners,
Poets and artists, kings and queens,
Old stars and hopeful beginners,
I've been where no-one's been before,
Learned secrets from writers and cooks
All with one library ticket
To the wonderful world of books.

ANIMAL FARM

The world famous satire upon dictatorship. The history of a revolution that went wrong. The animals on a farm drive out the master and take over the farm. The experiment is successful except for the fact that someone has to take the deposed farmer's place. Leadership devolves upon the pigs because of their higher intellectual level. Unhappily their character is not equal to their intelligence, and out of this fact springs the main development of the story.

Books by George Orwell in the
Charnwood Library Series:

NINETEEN EIGHTY-FOUR
ANIMAL FARM

GEORGE ORWELL

ANIMAL FARM

Complete and Unabridged

CHARNWOOD
Leicester

First published in Great Britain 1945 by
Secker & Warburg Ltd.
London

First Charnwood Edition
published July 1984
by arrangement with
Martin Secker & Warburg Ltd.
London
and
Harcourt Brace Jovanovich, Inc.,
New York

Reprinted 1989

British Library CIP Data

Orwell, George
   Animal farm.—Large print ed.—
(Charnwood library series)
Rn: Eric Blair   I. Title
823′.912 [F]   PR6029.R8

ISBN 0-7089-8200-X

Published by
F. A. Thorpe (Publishing) Ltd.
Anstey, Leicestershire

Printed and bound in Great Britain by
T. J. Press (Padstow) Ltd., Padstow, Cornwall

1

M R. JONES, of the Manor Farm, had locked the henhouses for the night, but was too drunk to remember to shut the pop-holes. With the ring of light from his lantern dancing from side to side, he lurched across the yard, kicked off his boots at the back door, drew himself a last glass of beer from the barrel in the scullery, and made his way up to bed, where Mrs. Jones was already snoring.

As soon as the light in the bedroom went out there was a stirring and a fluttering all through the farm buildings. Word had gone round during the day that old Major, the prize Middle White boar, had had a strange dream on the previous night and wished to communicate it to the other animals. It had been agreed that they should all meet in the big barn as soon as Mr. Jones was safely out of the way. Old Major (so he was always called, though the name under which he had been exhibited was Willingdon Beauty) was so highly regarded on the farm that everyone was quite ready to lose an hour's sleep in order to hear what he had to say.

At one end of the big barn, on a sort of raised platform, Major was already ensconced on his bed of straw, under a lantern which hung from a beam. He was twelve years old and had lately grown rather stout, but he was still a majestic-looking pig, with a wise and benevolent appearance in spite of the fact that his tushes had never been cut. Before long the other animals began to arrive and make themselves comfortable after their different fashions. First came the three dogs, Bluebell, Jessie, and Pincher, and then the pigs, who settled down in the straw immediately in front of the platform. The hens perched themselves on the window-sills, the pigeons fluttered up to the rafters, the sheep and cows lay down behind the pigs and began to chew the cud. The two cart-horses, Boxer and Clover, came in together, walking very slowly and setting down their vast hairy hoofs with great care lest there should be some small animal concealed in the straw. Clover was a stout motherly mare approaching middle life, who had never quite got her figure back after her fourth foal. Boxer was an enormous beast, nearly eighteen hands high, and as strong as any two ordinary horses put together. A white stripe down his nose gave him a somewhat stupid appearance, and in fact he was not of first-rate intelligence, but he was universally respected for his steadiness of character and tremendous powers of work. After the horses came Muriel, the white goat, and Benjamin, the donkey. Benjamin was the oldest animal on the farm, and the worst tempered. He seldom talked, and when he did, it was usually to make some cynical remark—for instance, he would say that God had given him a tail to keep the flies off, but that he would sooner have had no tail and no flies. Alone among the animals on the farm he never laughed. If asked why, he would say that he saw nothing to laugh at. Nevertheless, without openly admitting it, he was devoted to Boxer; the two of them usually spent their Sundays together in the small paddock beyond the orchard, grazing side by side and never speaking.

The two horses had just lain down when a brood of ducklings, which had lost their mother, filed into the barn, cheeping feebly and wandering from side to side to find some place where they would not be trodden on. Clover made a sort of wall round them with her great foreleg, and the ducklings nestled down inside it and promptly fell asleep. At the last moment Mollie, the foolish, pretty white mare who drew Mr. Jones's trap, came mincing daintily in, chewing at a lump of sugar. She took a place near the front and began flirting her white mane, hoping to draw attention to the red ribbons it was plaited with. Last of all came the cat, who looked round, as usual, for the warmest place, and finally squeezed herself in between Boxer and Clover; there she purred contentedly throughout Major's speech without listening to a word of what he was saying.

All the animals were now present except Moses,

the tame raven, who slept on a perch behind the back door. When Major saw that they had all made themselves comfortable and were waiting attentively, he cleared his throat and began:

"Comrades, you have heard already about the strange dream that I had last night. But I will come to the dream later. I have something else to say first. I do not think, comrades, that I shall be with you for many months longer, and before I die, I feel it my duty to pass on to you such wisdom as I have acquired. I have had a long life, I have had much time for thought as I lay alone in my stall, and I think I may say that I understand the nature of life on this earth as well as any animal now living. It is about this that I wish to speak to you.

"Now, comrades, what is the nature of this life of ours? Let us face it: our lives are miserable, laborious, and short. We are born, we are given just so much food as will keep the breath in our bodies, and those of us who are capable of it are forced to work to the last atom of our strength; and the very instant that our usefulness has come to an end we are slaughtered with hideous cruelty. No animal in England knows the meaning of happiness or leisure after he is a year old. No animal in England is free. The life of an animal is misery and slavery: that is the plain truth.

"But is this simply part of the order of nature? Is it because this land of ours is so poor that it cannot afford a decent life to those who dwell upon it? No, comrades, a thousand times no! The soil of

England is fertile, its climate is good, it is capable of affording food in abundance to an enormously greater number of animals than now inhabit it. This single farm of ours would support a dozen horses, twenty cows, hundreds of sheep—and all of them living in a comfort and a dignity that are now almost beyond our imagining. Why then do we continue in this miserable condition? Because nearly the whole of the produce of our labour is stolen from us by human beings. There, comrades, is the answer to all our problems. It is summed up in a single word—Man. Man is the only real enemy we have. Remove Man from the scene, and the root cause of hunger and overwork is abolished for ever.

"Man is the only creature that consumes without producing. He does not give milk, he does not lay eggs, he is too weak to pull the plough, he cannot run fast enough to catch rabbits. Yet he is lord of all the animals. He sets them to work, he gives back to them the bare minimum that will prevent them from starving, and the rest he keeps for himself. Our labour tills the soil, our dung fertilises it, and yet there is not one of us that owns more than his bare skin. You cows that I see before me, how many thousands of gallons of milk have you given during this last year? And what has happened to that milk which should have been breeding up sturdy calves? Every drop of it has gone down the throats of our enemies. And you hens, how many eggs have you laid in this last year, and how many of those eggs ever hatched into chickens? The rest have all gone to market to bring in money for Jones and his men. And you, Clover, where are those four foals you bore, who should have been the support and pleasure of your old age? Each was sold at a year old—you will never see one of them again. In return for your four confinements and all your labour in the fields, what have you ever had except your bare rations and a stall?

"And even the miserable lives we lead are not allowed to reach their natural span. For myself I do not grumble, for I am one of the lucky ones. I am twelve years old and have had over four hundred children. Such is the natural life of a pig. But no animal escapes the cruel knife in the end. You young porkers who are sitting in front of me, every one of you will scream your lives out at the block within a year. To that horror we all must come—cows, pigs, hens, sheep, everyone. Even the horses and the dogs have no better fate. You, Boxer, the very day that those great muscles of yours lose their power, Jones will sell you to the knacker, who will cut your throat and boil you down for the fox-hounds. As for the dogs, when they grow old and toothless, Jones ties a brick round their necks and drowns them in the nearest pond.

"Is it not crystal clear, then, comrades, that all the evils of this life of ours spring from the tyranny of human beings? Only get rid of Man, and the produce of our labour would be our own. Almost overnight we could become rich and free. What then must we do? Why, work night and day, body and soul, for the overthrow of the human race! That is my message to you, comrades: Rebellion! I do not know when that Rebellion will come, it might be in a week or in a hundred years, but I know, as surely as I see this straw beneath my feet, that sooner or later justice will be done. Fix your eyes on that, comrades, throughout the short remainder of your lives! And above all, pass on this message of mine to those who come after you, so that future generations shall carry on the struggle until it is victorious.

"And remember, comrades, your resolution must never falter. No argument must lead you astray. Never listen when they tell you that Man and the animals have a common interest, that the prosperity of the one is the prosperity of the others. It is all lies. Man serves the interests of no creature except himself. And among us animals let there be perfect unity, perfect comradeship in the struggle. All men are enemies. All animals are comrades."

At this moment there was a tremendous uproar. While Major was speaking four large rats had crept out of their holes and were sitting on their hind-quarters, listening to him. The dogs had suddenly caught sight of them, and it was only by a swift dash for their holes that the rats saved their lives. Major raised his trotter for silence.

"Comrades," he said, "here is a point that must be settled. The wild creatures, such as rats and rabbits—are they our friends or our enemies? Let us put it to the vote. I propose this question to the

7

meeting: Are rats comrades?"

The vote was taken at once, and it was agreed by an overwhelming majority that rats were comrades. There were only four dissentients, the three dogs and the cat, who was afterwards discovered to have voted on both sides. Major continued:

"I have little more to say. I merely repeat, remember always your duty of enmity towards Man and all his ways. Whatever goes upon two legs is an enemy. Whatever goes upon four legs, or has wings, is a friend. And remember also that in fighting against Man, we must not come to resemble him. Even when you have conquered him, do not adopt his vices. No animal must ever live in a house, or sleep in a bed, or wear clothes, or drink alcohol, or smoke tobacco, or touch money, or engage in trade. All the habits of Man are evil. And, above all, no animal must ever tyrannise over his own kind. Weak or strong, clever or simple, we are all brothers. No animal must ever kill any other animal. All animals are equal.

"And now, comrades, I will tell you about my dream of last night. I cannot describe that dream to you. It was a dream of the earth as it will be when Man has vanished. But it reminded me of something that I had long forgotten. Many years ago, when I was a little pig, my mother and the other sows used to sing an old song of which they knew only the tune and the first three words. I had known that tune in my infancy, but it had long since passed out of my mind. Last night, however, it came back to me in my dream. And what is more, the words of the song also came back—words, I am certain, which were sung by the animals of long ago and have been lost to memory for generations. I will sing you that song now, comrades. I am old and my voice is hoarse, but when I have taught you the tune, you can sing it better for yourselves. It is called 'Beasts of England'."

Old Major cleared his throat and began to sing. As he had said, his voice was hoarse, but he sang well enough, and it was a stirring tune, something between "Clementine" and "La Cucuracha". The words ran:

Beasts of England, beasts of Ireland,
Beasts of every land and clime,
Hearken to my joyful tidings
Of the golden future time.

Soon or late the day is coming,
Tyrant Man shall be o'erthrown,
And the fruitful fields of England
Shall be trod by beasts alone.

Rings shall vanish from our noses,
And the harness from our back,
Bit and spur shall rust forever,
Cruel whips no more shall crack.

Riches more than mind can picture,
Wheat and barley, oats and hay,
Clover, beans, and mangel-wurzels
Shall be ours upon that day.

Bright will shine the fields of England,
Purer shall its waters be,
Sweeter yet shall blow its breezes
On the day that sets us free.

For that day we all must labour,
Though we die before it break;
Cows and horses, geese and turkeys,
All must toil for freedom's sake.

Beasts of England, beasts of Ireland,
Beasts of every land and clime,
Hearken well and spread my tidings
Of the golden future time.

The singing of this song threw the animals into the wildest excitement. Almost before Major had reached the end, they had begun singing it for themselves. Even the stupidest of them had already picked up the tune and a few of the words, and as for the clever ones, such as the pigs and dogs, they had the entire song by heart within a few minutes. And then, after a few preliminary tries, the whole farm burst out into "Beasts of England" in tremendous unison. The cows lowed it, the dogs whined it, the sheep bleated it, the horses whinnied it, the ducks quacked it. They were so delighted with the song that they sang it right through five times in succession, and might have continued singing it all night if they had not been interrupted.

Unfortunately, the uproar awoke Mr. Jones,

who sprang out of bed, making sure that there was a fox in the yard. He seized the gun which always stood in a corner of his bedroom, and let fly a charge of number 6 shot into the darkness. The pellets buried themselves in the wall of the barn and the meeting broke up hurriedly. Everyone fled to his own sleeping-place. The birds jumped on to their perches, the animals settled down in the straw, and the whole farm was asleep in a moment.

2

THREE nights later old Major died peacefully in his sleep. His body was buried at the foot of the orchard.

This was early in March. During the next three months there was much secret activity. Major's speech had given to the more intelligent animals on the farm a completely new outlook on life. They did not know when the Rebellion predicted by Major would take place, they had no reason for thinking that it would be within their own lifetime, but they saw clearly that it was their duty to prepare for it. The work of teaching and organising the others fell naturally upon the pigs, who were generally recognised as being the cleverest of the animals. Pre-eminent among the pigs were two young boars named Snowball and Napoleon, whom Mr. Jones was breeding up for sale. Napoleon was a large, rather fierce-looking Berkshire boar, the only Berkshire on the farm, not much of a talker, but with a reputation for getting his own way. Snowball was a more vivacious pig than Napoleon, quicker in speech and more inventive, but was not considered to have the same depth of character. All the other male pigs on the farm were porkers. The best known among them was a small fat pig named Squealer, with very round cheeks, twinkling eyes, nimble movements, and a shrill voice. He was a brilliant talker, and when he was arguing some difficult point he had a way of skipping from side to side and whisking his tail which was somehow very persuasive. The others said of Squealer that he could turn black into white.

These three had elaborated old Major's teachings into a complete system of thought, to which they gave the name of Animalism. Several nights a week, after Mr. Jones was asleep, they held secret meetings in the barn and expounded the principles of Animalism to the others. At the beginning they met with much stupidity and apathy. Some of the animals talked of the duty of loyalty to Mr. Jones, whom they referred to as "Master", or made elementary remarks such as "Mr. Jones feeds us. If he were gone, we should starve to death." Others asked such questions as "Why should we care what happens after we are dead?" or "If this Rebellion is to happen anyway, what difference does it make whether we work for it or not?" and the pigs had great difficulty in making them see that this was contrary to the spirit of Animalism. The stupidest questions of all were asked by Mollie, the white mare. The very first question she asked Snowball was: "Will there still be sugar after the Rebellion?"

"No," said Snowball firmly. "We have no means of making sugar on this farm. Besides, you do not need sugar. You will have all the oats and hay you want."

"And shall I still be allowed to wear ribbons in my mane?" asked Mollie.

"Comrade," said Snowball, "those ribbons that you are so devoted to are the badge of slavery. Can you not understand that liberty is worth more than ribbons?"

Mollie agreed, but she did not sound very convinced.

The pigs had an even harder struggle to counteract the lies put about by Moses, the tame raven. Moses, who was Mr. Jones's especial pet, was a spy and a tale-bearer, but he was also a clever talker. He claimed to know of the existence of a mysterious country called Sugarcandy Mountain, to which all animals went when they died. It was situated somewhere up in the sky, a little distance beyond the clouds, Moses said. In Sugarcandy Mountain it was Sunday seven days a week, clover was in season all the year round, and lump sugar and linseed cake grew on the hedges. The animals hated Moses because he told tales and did no work, but some of them believed in Sugarcandy Mountain, and the pigs had to argue very hard to persuade them that there was no such place.

Their most faithful disciples were the two cart-horses, Boxer and Clover. These two had great difficulty in thinking anything out for themselves, but, having once accepted the pigs as their teachers, they absorbed everything that they were told, and passed it on to the other animals by simple arguments. They were unfailing in their attendance at the secret meetings in the barn, and led the singing of "Beasts of England", with which the meetings always ended.

Now, as it turned out, the Rebellion was achieved much earlier and more easily than anyone had expected. In past years Mr. Jones, although a hard master, had been a capable farmer, but of late he had fallen on evil days. He had become much disheartened after losing money in a lawsuit, and had taken to drinking more than was good for him. For whole days at a time he would lounge in his Windsor chair in the kitchen, reading the newspapers, drinking, and occasionally feeding Moses on crusts of bread soaked in beer. His men were idle and dishonest, the fields were full of weeds, the buildings wanted roofing, the hedges were neglected, and the animals were underfed.

June came and the hay was almost ready for cutting. On Midsummer's Eve, which was a Saturday, Mr. Jones went into Willingdon and got so drunk at the Red Lion that he did not come back till midday on Sunday. The men had milked the cows in the early morning and then had gone out rabbiting, without bothering to feed the animals. When Mr. Jones got back he immediately went to sleep on the drawing-room sofa with the *News of the World* over his face, so that, when evening came, the animals were still unfed. At last they could stand it no longer. One of the cows broke in the door of the store-shed with her horn and all the animals began to help themselves from the bins. It was just then that Mr. Jones woke up. The next moment he and his four men were in the store-shed with whips in their hands, lashing out in all directions. This was more than the hungry animals could bear. With one accord, though nothing of the kind had been planned beforehand, they flung themselves upon their tormentors. Jones and his men suddenly found themselves being butted and kicked from all sides. The situation was quite out of their control. They had never seen animals behave like this before, and this sudden uprising of creatures whom they were used to thrashing and maltreating just as they chose, frightened them almost out of their wits. After only a moment or two they gave up trying to defend themselves and took to their heels. A minute later all five of them were in full flight down the cart-track that led to the main road, with the animals pursuing them in triumph.

Mrs. Jones looked out of the bedroom window, saw what was happening, hurriedly flung a few possessions into a carpet bag, and slipped out of the farm by another way. Moses sprang off his perch and flapped after her, croaking loudly. Meanwhile the animals had chased Jones and his men out on to the road and slammed the five-barred gate behind them. And so, almost before they knew what was happening, the Rebellion had been successfully carried through: Jones was expelled, and the Manor Farm was theirs.

For the first few minutes the animals could hardly believe in their good fortune. Their first act was to gallop in a body right round the boundaries of the farm, as though to make quite sure that no human being was hiding anywhere upon it; then they raced back to the farm buildings to wipe out the last traces of Jones's hated reign. The harness-room at the end of the stables was broken open; the bits, the nose-rings, the dog-chains, the cruel knives with which Mr. Jones had been used to castrate the pigs and lambs, were all flung down the well. The reins, the halters, the blinkers, the degrading nosebags, were thrown on to the rubbish fire which was burning in the yard. So were the whips. All the animals capered with joy when they saw the whips going up in flames. Snowball also threw on to the fire the ribbons with which the horses' manes and tails had usually been decorated on market days.

"Ribbons," he said, "should be considered as clothes, which are the mark of a human being. All animals should go naked."

When Boxer heard this he fetched the small straw hat which he wore in summer to keep the flies out of his ears, and flung it on to the fire with the rest.

In a very little while the animals had destroyed

17

everything that reminded them of Mr. Jones. Napoleon then led them back to the store-shed and served out a double ration of corn to everybody, with two biscuits for each dog. Then they sang "Beasts of England" from end to end seven times running, and after that they settled down for the night and slept as they had never slept before.

But they awoke at dawn as usual, and suddenly remembering the glorious thing that had happened, they all raced out into the pasture together. A little way down the pasture there was a knoll that commanded a view of most of the farm. The animals rushed to the top of it and gazed round them in the clear morning light. Yes, it was theirs—everything that they could see was theirs! In the ecstasy of that thought they gambolled round and round, they hurled themselves into the air in great leaps of excitement. They rolled in the dew, they cropped mouthfuls of the sweet summer grass, they kicked up clods of the black earth and snuffed its rich scent. Then they made a tour of inspection of the whole farm and surveyed with speechless admiration the ploughland, the hayfield, the orchard, the pool, the spinney. It was as though they had never seen these things before, and even now they could hardly believe that it was all their own.

Then they filed back to the farm buildings and halted in silence outside the door of the farmhouse. That was theirs too, but they were frightened to go inside. After a moment, however, Snowball and Napoleon butted the door open with their shoulders and the animals entered in single file, walking with the utmost care for fear of disturbing anything. They tiptoed from room to room, afraid to speak above a whisper and gazing with a kind of awe at the unbelievable luxury, at the beds with their feather mattresses, the looking-glasses, the horsehair sofa, the Brussels carpet, the lithograph of Queen Victoria over the drawing-room mantelpiece. They were just coming down the stairs when Mollie was discovered to be missing. Going back, the others found that she had remained behind in the best bedroom. She had taken a piece of blue ribbon from Mrs. Jones's dressing-table, and was holding it against her shoulder and admiring herself in the glass in a very foolish manner. The others reproached her sharply, and they went outside. Some hams hanging in the kitchen were taken out for burial, and the barrel of beer in the scullery was stove in with a kick from Boxer's hoof, otherwise nothing in the house was touched. A unanimous resolution was passed on the spot that the farmhouse should be preserved as a museum. All were agreed that no animal must ever live there.

The animals had their breakfast, and then Snowball and Napoleon called them together again.

"Comrades," said Snowball, "it is half-past six and we have a long day before us. Today we begin the hay harvest. But there is another matter that must be attended to first."

The pigs now revealed that during the past three months they had taught themselves to read and write from an old spelling book which had belonged to Mr. Jones's children and which had been thrown on the rubbish heap. Napoleon sent for pots of black and white paint and led the way down to the five-barred gate that gave on to the main road. Then Snowball (for it was Snowball who was best at writing) took a brush between the two knuckles of his trotter, painted out MANOR FARM from the top bar of the gate and in its place painted ANIMAL FARM. This was to be the name of the farm from now onwards. After this they went back to the farm buildings, where Snowball and Napoleon sent for a ladder which they caused to be set against the end wall of the big barn. They explained that by their studies of the past three months the pigs had succeeded in reducing the principles of Animalism to Seven Commandments. These Seven Commandments would now be inscribed on the wall; they would form an unalterable law by which all the animals on Animal Farm must live for ever after. With some difficulty (for it is not easy for a pig to balance himself on a ladder) Snowball climbed up and set to work, with Squealer a few rungs below him holding the paint-pot. The Commandments were written on the tarred wall in great white letters that could be read thirty yards away. They ran thus:

1. Whatever goes upon two legs is an enemy.
2. Whatever goes upon four legs, or has wings, is a friend.
3. No animal shall wear clothes.
4. No animal shall sleep in a bed.
5. No animal shall drink alcohol.
6. No animal shall kill any other animal.
7. All animals are equal.

It was very neatly written, and except that "friend" was written "freind" and one of the "S's" was the wrong way round, the spelling was correct all the way through. Snowball read it aloud for the benefit of the others. All the animals nodded in complete agreement, and the cleverer ones at once began to learn the Commandments by heart.

"Now, comrades," cried Snowball, throwing down the paint-brush, "to the hayfield! Let us make it a point of honour to get in the harvest more quickly than Jones and his men could do."

But at this moment the three cows, who had seemed uneasy for some time past, set up a loud lowing. They had not been milked for twenty-four hours, and their udders were almost bursting. After a little thought, the pigs sent for buckets and milked the cows fairly successfully, their trotters being well adapted to this task. Soon there were five buckets of frothing creamy milk at which many of the animals looked with considerable interest.

"What is going to happen to all that milk?" said someone.

"Jones used sometimes to mix some of it in our mash," said one of the hens.

"Never mind the milk, comrades!" cried Napoleon, placing himself in front of the buckets. "That will be attended to. The harvest is more important. Comrade Snowball will lead the way. I shall follow in a few minutes. Forward, comrades! The hay is waiting."

So the animals trooped down to the hayfield to begin the harvest, and when they came back in the evening it was noticed that the milk had disappeared.

3

HOW they toiled and sweated to get the hay in! But their efforts were rewarded, for the harvest was an even bigger success than they had hoped.

Sometimes the work was hard; the implements had been designed for human beings and not for animals, and it was a great drawback that no animal was able to use any tool that involved standing on his hind legs. But the pigs were so clever that they could think of a way round every difficulty. As for the horses, they knew every inch of the field, and in fact understood the business of mowing and raking far better than Jones and his men had ever done. The pigs did not actually work, but directed and supervised the others. With their superior knowledge it was natural that they should assume the leadership. Boxer and Clover would harness themselves to the cutter or the horse-rake (no bits or reins were needed in these days, of course) and tramp steadily round and round the field with a pig walking behind and calling out "Gee up, comrade!" or "Whoa back, comrade!" as the case might be. And every animal down to the humblest worked at turning the hay and gathering it. Even the ducks and hens toiled to and fro all day in the sun, carrying tiny wisps of hay in their beaks. In the end they finished the harvest in two days' less time than it had usually taken Jones and his men. Moreover, it was the biggest harvest that the farm had ever seen. There was no wastage whatever; the hens and ducks with their sharp eyes had gathered up the very last stalk. And not an animal on the farm had stolen so much as a mouthful.

All through that summer the work of the farm went like clockwork. The animals were happy as they had never conceived it possible to be. Every mouthful of food was an acute positive pleasure, now that it was truly their own food, produced by themselves and for themselves, not doled out to them by a grudging master. With the worthless parasitical human beings gone, there was more for everyone to eat. There was more leisure too, inexperienced though the animals were. They met with many difficulties—for instance, later in the year, when they harvested the corn, they had to tread it out in the ancient style and blow away the chaff with their breath, since the farm possessed no threshing machine—but the pigs with their cleverness and Boxer with his tremendous muscles always pulled them through. Boxer was the admiration of everybody. He had been a hard worker even in Jones's time, but now he seemed more like three horses than one; there were days when the entire work of the farm seemed to rest upon his mighty shoulders. From morning to night he was pushing and pulling, always at the spot where the work was hardest. He had made an arrangement with one of the cockerels to call him in the mornings half an hour earlier than anyone else, and would put in some volunteer labour at whatever seemed to be most needed, before the regular day's work began. His answer to every problem, every set-back, was "I will work harder!"—which he had adopted as his personal motto.

But everyone worked according to his capacity. The hens and ducks, for instance, saved five bushels of corn at the harvest by gathering up the stray grains. Nobody stole, nobody grumbled over his rations, the quarrelling and biting and jealousy which had been normal features of life in the old days had almost disappeared. Nobody shirked—or almost nobody. Mollie, it was true, was not good at getting up in the mornings, and had a way of leaving work early on the ground that there was a stone in her hoof. And the behaviour of the cat was somewhat peculiar. It was soon noticed that when there was work to be done the cat could never be found. She would vanish for hours on end, and then reappear at meal-times, or in the evening after work was over, as though nothing had happened. But she always made such excellent excuses, and purred so affectionately, that it was impossible not to believe in her good intentions. Old Benjamin, the donkey, seemed quite unchanged since the

Rebellion. He did his work in the same slow obstinate way as he had done it in Jones's time, never shirking and never volunteering for extra work either. About the Rebellion and its results he would express no opinion. When asked whether he was not happier now that Jones was gone, he would say only "Donkeys live a long time. None of you has ever seen a dead donkey," and the others had to be content with this cryptic answer.

On Sundays there was no work. Breakfast was an hour later than usual, and after breakfast there was a ceremony which was observed every week without fail. First came the hoisting of the flag. Snowball had found in the harness-room an old green tablecloth of Mrs. Jones's and had painted on it a hoof and a horn in white. This was run up the flagstaff in the farmhouse garden every Sunday morning. The flag was green, Snowball explained, to represent the green fields of England, while the hoof and horn signified the future Republic of the Animals which would arise when the human race had been finally over-thrown. After the hoisting of the flag all the animals trooped into the big barn for a general assembly which was known as the Meeting. Here the work of the coming week was planned out and resolutions were put forward and debated. It was always the pigs who put forward the resolutions. The other animals understood how to vote, but could never think of any resolutions of their own. Snowball and Napoleon were by far the most active in the debates. But it was noticed that these two were never in agreement: whatever suggestion either of them made, the other could be counted on to oppose it. Even when it was resolved—a thing no one could object to in itself—to set aside the small paddock behind the orchard as a home of rest for the animals who were past work, there was a stormy debate over the correct retiring age for each class of animal. The Meeting always ended with the singing of "Beasts of England", and the afternoon was given up to recreation.

The pigs had set aside the harness-room as a headquarters for themselves. Here, in the evenings, they studied blacksmithing, carpentering, and other necessary arts from books which they had brought out of the farmhouse. Snowball also busied himself with organising the other animals into what he called Animal Committees. He was indefatigable at this. He formed the Egg Production Committee for the hens, the Clean Tails League for the cows, the Wild Comrades' Re-education Committee (the object of this was to tame the rats and rabbits), the Whiter Wool Movement for the sheep, and various others, besides instituting classes in reading and writing. On the whole, these projects were a failure. The attempt to tame the wild creatures, for instance, broke down almost immediately. They continued to behave very much as before, and when treated with generosity, simply took advantage of it. The cat joined the Re-education Committee and was very active in it for some days. She was seen one day sitting on a roof and talking to some sparrows who were just out of her reach. She was telling them that all animals were now comrades and that any sparrow who chose could come and perch on her paw; but the sparrows kept their distance.

The reading and writing classes, however, were a great success. By the autumn almost every animal on the farm was literate in some degree.

As for the pigs, they could already read and write perfectly. The dogs learned to read fairly well, but were not interested in reading anything except the Seven Commandments. Muriel, the goat, could read somewhat better than the dogs, and sometimes used to read to the others in the evenings from scraps of newspaper which she found on the rubbish heap. Benjamin could read as well as any pig, but never exercised his faculty. So far as he knew, he said, there was nothing worth reading. Clover learnt the whole alphabet, but could not put words together. Boxer could not get beyond the letter D. He would trace out A, B, C, D, in the dust with his great hoof, and then would stand staring at the letters with ears back, sometimes shaking his forelock, trying with all his might to remember what came next and never succeeding. On several occasions, indeed, he did learn E, F, G, H, but by the time he knew them, it was always discovered that he had forgotten A, B, C and D. Finally he decided to be content with the first four letters, and used to write them out once or twice every day to refresh his memory. Mollie refused to learn any but the six letters which spelt her own name. She would form these very neatly out of pieces of twig, and would then decorate them with a flower or two and walk round them admiring them.

None of the other animals on the farm could get further than the letter A. It was also found that the stupider animals, such as the sheep, hens, and ducks, were unable to learn the Seven Commandments by heart. After much thought Snowball declared that the Seven Commandments could in effect be reduced to a single maxim, namely: "Four legs good, two legs bad". This, he said, contained the essential principle of Animalism. Whoever had thoroughly grasped it would be safe from human influences. The birds at first objected, since it seemed to them that they also had two legs, but Snowball proved to them that this was not so.

"A bird's wing, comrades," he said, "is an organ of propulsion and not of manipulation. It should therefore be regarded as a leg. The distinguishing mark of Man is the *hand*, the instrument with which he does all his mischief."

The birds did not understand Snowball's long words, but they accepted his explanation, and all the humbler animals set to work to learn the new maxim by heart. FOUR LEGS GOOD, TWO LEGS BAD, was inscribed on the end wall of the barn, above the Seven Commandments and in bigger letters. When they had once got it by heart, the sheep developed a great liking for this maxim, and often as they lay in the field they would all start bleating "Four legs good, two legs bad! Four legs good, two legs bad!" and keep it up for hours on end, never growing tired of it.

Napoleon took no interest in Snowball's committees. He said that the education of the young was more important than anything that could be done for those who were already grown up. It happened that Jessie and Bluebell had both whelped soon after the hay harvest, giving birth between them to nine sturdy puppies. As soon as they were weaned, Napoleon took them away from their mothers, saying that he would make himself responsible for their education. He took them up into a loft which could only be reached by a ladder from the harness-room, and there kept them in such seclusion that the rest of the farm soon forgot their existence.

The mystery of where the milk went to was soon cleared up. It was mixed every day into the pigs' mash. The early apples were now ripening, and the grass of the orchard was littered with windfalls. The animals had assumed as a matter of course that these would be shared out equally; one day, however, the order went forth that all the windfalls were to be collected and brought to the harness-room for the use of the pigs. At this some of the other animals murmured, but it was no use. All the pigs were in full agreement on this point, even Snowball and Napoleon. Squealer was sent to make the necessary explanations to the others.

"Comrades!" he cried. "You do not imagine, I hope, that we pigs are doing this in a spirit of selfishness and privilege? Many of us actually dislike milk and apples. I dislike them myself. Our sole object in taking these things is to preserve our health. Milk and apples (this has been proved by Science, comrades) contain substances absolutely necessary to the well-being of a pig. We pigs are brain-workers. The whole management and organisation of this farm depend on us. Day and night we are watching over your welfare. It is for *your* sake that we drink that milk and eat those apples. Do you know what would happen if we pigs failed in our duty? Jones would come back! Yes, Jones would come back! Surely, comrades," cried Squealer almost pleadingly, skipping from side to side and whisking his tail, "surely there is no one among you who wants to see Jones come back?"

Now if there was one thing that the animals were completely certain of, it was that they did not want Jones back. When it was put to them in this light, they had no more to say. The importance of keeping the pigs in good health was all too obvious. So it was agreed without further argument that the milk and the windfall apples (and also the main crop of apples when they ripened) should be reserved for the pigs alone.

4

BY the late summer the news of what had happened on Animal Farm had spread across half the county. Every day Snowball and Napoleon sent out flights of pigeons whose instructions were to mingle with the animals on neighbouring farms, tell them the story of the Rebellion, and teach them the tune of "Beasts of England".

Most of this time Mr. Jones had spent sitting in the taproom of the Red Lion at Willingdon, complaining to anyone who would listen of the monstrous injustice he had suffered in being turned out of his property by a pack of good-for-nothing animals. The other farmers sympathised in principle, but they did not at first give him much help. At heart, each of them was secretly wondering whether he could not somehow turn Jones's misfortune to his own advantage. It was lucky that the owners of the two farms which adjoined Animal Farm were on permanently bad terms. One of them, which was named Foxwood, was a large, neglected, old-fashioned farm, much overgrown by woodland, with all its pastures worn out and its hedges in a disgraceful condition. Its owner, Mr. Pilkington, was an easy-going gentleman farmer who spent most of his time in fishing or hunting according to the season. The other farm, which was called Pinchfield, was smaller and better kept. Its owner was a Mr. Frederick, a tough shrewd man, perpetually involved in lawsuits and with a name for driving hard bargains. These two disliked each other so much that it was difficult for them to come to any agreement, even in defence of their own interests.

Nevertheless, they were both thoroughly frightened by the rebellion on Animal Farm, and very anxious to prevent their own animals from learning too much about it. At first they pretended to laugh to scorn the idea of animals managing a farm for themselves. The whole thing would be over in a fortnight, they said. They put it about that the animals on the Manor Farm (they insisted on calling it the Manor Farm; they would not tolerate the name "Animal Farm") were perpetually fighting among themselves and were also rapidly starving to death. When time passed and the animals had evidently not starved to death, Frederick and Pilkington changed their tune and began to talk of the terrible wickedness that now flourished on Animal Farm. It was given out that the animals there practised cannibalism, tortured one another with redhot horseshoes, and had their females in common. This was what came of rebelling against the laws of Nature, Frederick and Pilkington said.

However, these stories were never fully believed. Rumours of a wonderful farm, where the human beings had been turned out and the animals managed their own affairs, continued to circulate in vague and distorted forms, and throughout that year a wave of rebelliousness ran through the countryside. Bulls which had always been tractable suddenly turned savage, sheep broke down hedges and devoured the clover, cows kicked the pail over, hunters refused their fences and shot their riders on to the other side. Above all, the tune and even the words of "Beasts of England" were known everywhere. It had spread with astonishing speed. The human beings could not contain their rage when they heard this song, though they pretended to think it merely ridiculous. They could not understand, they said, how even animals could bring themselves to sing such contemptible rubbish. Any animal caught singing it was given a flogging on the spot. And yet the song was irrepressible. The blackbirds whistled it in the hedges, and pigeons cooed it in the elms, it got into the din of the smithies and the tune of the church bells. And when the human beings listened to it, they secretly trembled, hearing in it a prophecy of their future doom.

Early in October, when the corn was cut and stacked and some of it was already threshed, a flight of pigeons came whirling through the air and alighted in the yard of Animal Farm in the wildest excitement. Jones and all his men, with half a dozen others from Foxwood and Pinchfield, had entered the five-barred gate and were coming up the cart-track that led to the farm. They were all carrying sticks, except Jones, who was marching ahead with a gun in his hands. Obviously they were going to attempt the recapture of the farm.

This had long been expected, and all preparations had been made. Snowball, who had studied an old book of Julius Caesar's campaigns which he had found in the farmhouse, was in charge of the defensive operations. He gave his orders quickly, and in a couple of minutes every animal was at his post.

As the human beings approached the farm buildings, Snowball launched his first attack. All the pigeons, to the number of thirty-five flew to and fro over the men's heads and muted upon them from mid-air; and while the men were dealing with this, the geese, who had been hiding behind the hedge, rushed out and pecked viciously at the calves of their legs. However, this was only a light skirmishing manoeuvre, intended to create a little disorder, and the men easily drove the geese off with their sticks. Snowball now launched his second line of attack. Muriel, Benjamin, and all the sheep, with Snowball at the head of them, rushed forward and prodded and butted the men from every side, while Benjamin turned round and lashed at them with his small hoofs. But once again the men, with their sticks and their hobnailed boots, were too strong for them; and suddenly, at a squeal from Snowball, which was the signal for retreat, all the animals turned and fled through the gateway into the yard.

The men gave a shout of triumph. They saw, as they imagined, their enemies in flight, and they rushed after them in disorder. This was just what Snowball had intended. As soon as they were well inside the yard, the three horses, the three cows, and the rest of the pigs, who had been lying in ambush in the cowshed, suddenly emerged in their rear, cutting them off. Snowball now gave the signal for the charge. He himself dashed straight for Jones. Jones saw him coming, raised his gun and fired. The pellets scored bloody streaks along Snowball's back, and a sheep dropped dead. Without halting for an instant, Snowball flung his fifteen stone against Jones's legs. Jones was hurled into a pile of dung and his gun flew out of his hands. But the most terrifying spectacle of all was Boxer, rearing up on his hind legs and striking out with his great iron-shod hoofs like a stallion. His very first blow took a stable-lad from Foxwood on the skull and stretched him lifeless in the mud. At the sight, several men dropped their sticks and tried to run. Panic overtook them, and the next moment all the animals together were chasing them round and round the yard. They were gored, kicked, bitten, trampled on. There was not an animal on the farm that did not take vengeance on them after his own fashion. Even the cat suddenly leapt off a roof on to a cowman's shoulders and sank her claws in his neck, at which he yelled horribly. At a moment when the opening was clear, the men were glad enough to rush out of the yard and make a bolt for the main road. And so within five minutes of their invasion they were in ignominious retreat by the same way as they had come, with a flock of geese hissing after them and pecking at their calves all the way.

All the men were gone except one. Back in the yard Boxer was pawing with his hoof at the stable-lad who lay face down in the mud, trying to turn him over. The boy did not stir.

"He is dead," said Boxer sorrowfully. "I had no intention of doing that. I forgot that I was wearing iron shoes. Who will believe that I did not do this on purpose?"

"No sentimentality, comrade!" cried Snowball, from whose wounds the blood was still dripping. "War is war. The only good human being is a dead one."

"I have no wish to take life, not even human life," repeated Boxer, and his eyes were full of tears.

"Where is Mollie?" exclaimed somebody.

Mollie in fact was missing. For a moment there was great alarm; it was feared that the men might have harmed her in some way, or even carried her off with them. In the end, however, she was found hiding in her stall with her head buried among the hay in the manger. She had taken to flight as soon as the gun went off. And when the others came back from looking for her, it was to find that the stable-lad, who in fact was only stunned, had already recovered and made off.

The animals had now reassembled in the wildest excitement, each recounting his own exploits in the battle at the top of his voice. An impromptu celebration of the victory was held immediately. The flag was run up and "Beasts of England" was sung a number of times, then the sheep who had been killed was given a solemn funeral, a hawthorn bush being planted on her grave. At the graveside Snowball made a little speech, emphasising the need for all animals to be ready to die for Animal Farm if need be.

The animals decided unanimously to create a military decoration, "Animal Hero, First Class", which was conferred there and then on Snowball and Boxer. It consisted of a brass medal (they were really some old horse brasses which had been found in the harness-room), to be worn on Sundays and holidays. There was also "Animal Hero, Second Class", which was conferred posthumously on the dead sheep.

There was much discussion as to what the battle should be called. In the end, it was named the Battle of the Cowshed, since that was where the ambush had been sprung. Mr. Jones's gun had been found lying in the mud, and it was known that there was a supply of cartridges in the farmhouse. It was decided to set the gun up at the foot of the flagstaff, like a piece of artillery, and to fire it twice a year—once on October the twelfth, the anniversary of the Battle of the Cowshed, and once on Midsummer Day, the anniversary of the Rebellion.

5

AS winter drew on, Mollie became more and more troublesome. She was late for work every morning and excused herself by saying that she had overslept, and she complained of mysterious pains, although her appetite was excellent. On every kind of pretext she would run away from work and go to the drinking pool, where she would stand foolishly gazing at her own reflection in the water. But there were also rumours of something more serious. One day as Mollie strolled blithely into the yard, flirting her long tail and chewing at a stalk of hay, Clover took her aside.

"Mollie," she said, "I have something very serious to say to you. This morning I saw you looking over the hedge that divides Animal Farm from Foxwood. One of Mr. Pilkington's men was standing on the other side of the hedge. And—I was a long way away, but I am almost certain I saw this—he was talking to you and you were allowing him to stroke your nose. What does that mean Mollie?"

"He didn't! I wasn't! It isn't true!" cried Mollie, beginning to prance about and paw the ground.

"Mollie! Look me in the face. Do you give me your word of honour that that man was not stroking your nose?"

"It isn't true!" repeated Mollie, but she could not look Clover in the face, and the next moment she took to her heels and galloped away into the field.

A thought struck Clover. Without saying anything to the others, she went to Mollie's stall and turned over the straw with her hoof. Hidden under the straw was a little pile of lump sugar and several bunches of ribbon of different colours.

Three days later Mollie disappeared. For some weeks nothing was known of her whereabouts, then the pigeons reported that they had seen her on the other side of Willingdon. She was between the shafts of a smart dogcart painted red and black, which was standing outside a public-house. A fat red-faced man in check breeches and gaiters, who looked like a publican, was stroking her nose and feeding her with sugar. Her coat was newly clipped and she wore a scarlet ribbon round her forelock. She appeared to be enjoying herself, so the pigeons said. None of the animals ever mentioned Mollie again.

In January there came bitterly hard weather. The earth was like iron, and nothing could be done in the fields. Many meetings were held in the big barn, and the pigs occupied themselves with planning out the work of the coming season. It had come to be accepted that the pigs, who were manifestly cleverer than the other animals, should decide all questions of farm policy, though their decisions had to be ratified by a majority vote. This arrangement would have worked well enough if it had not been for the disputes between Snowball and Napoleon. These two disagreed at every point where disagreement was possible. If one of them suggested sowing a bigger acreage with barley, the other was certain to demand a bigger acreage of oats, and if one of them said that such and such a field was just right for cabbages, the other would declare that it was useless for anything except roots. Each had his own following, and there were some violent debates. At the Meetings Snowball often won over the majority by his brilliant speeches, but Napoleon was better at canvassing support for himself in between times. He was especially successful with the sheep. Of late the sheep had taken to bleating "Four legs good, two legs bad" both in and out of season, and they often interrupted the Meeting with this. It was noticed that they were especially liable to break into "Four legs good, two legs bad" at crucial moments in Snowball's speeches. Snowball had made a close study of some back numbers of the *Farmer and Stockbreeder* which he had found in the farmhouse, and was full of plans for innovations and improvements. He talked learnedly about field-drains, silage, and basic slag, and had worked out a complicated scheme for all animals to drop their dung directly in the fields, at a different spot every day, to save the labour of cartage. Napoleon produced no schemes of his own, but said quietly that Snowball's would come to nothing, and seemed to be biding his time. But of all their controversies, none was so bitter as the one that took place over the windmill.

In the long pasture, not far from the farm buildings, there was a small knoll which was the highest point on the farm. After surveying the ground, Snowball declared that this was just the place for a windmill, which could be made to operate a dynamo and supply the farm with electrical power. This would light the stalls and warm them in winter, and would also run a circular saw, a chaff-cutter, a mangel-slicer, and an electric milking machine. The animals had never heard of anything of this kind before (for the farm was an old-fashioned one and had only the most primitive machinery), and they listened in astonishment while Snowball conjured up pictures of fantastic machines which would do their work for them while they grazed at their ease in the fields or improved their minds with reading and conversation.

Within a few weeks Snowball's plans for the windmill were fully worked out. The mechanical details came mostly from three books which had belonged to Mr. Jones—*One Thousand Useful Things to Do About the House, Every Man His Own*

Bricklayer, and Electricity for Beginners. Snowball used as his study a shed which had once been used for incubators and had a smooth wooden floor, suitable for drawing on. He was closeted there for hours at a time. With his books held open by a stone, and with a piece of chalk gripped between the knuckles of his trotter, he would move rapidly to and fro, drawing in line after line and uttering little whimpers of excitement. Gradually the plans grew into a complicated mass of cranks and cogwheels, covering more than half the floor, which the other animals found completely unintelligible but very impressive. All of them came to look at Snowball's drawings at least once a day. Even the hens and ducks came, and were at pains not to tread on the chalk marks. Only Napoleon held aloof. He had declared himself against the windmill from the start. One day, however, he arrived unexpectedly to examine the plans. He walked heavily round the shed, looked closely at every detail of the plans and snuffed at them one or twice, then stood for a little while contemplating them out of the corner of his eye; then suddenly he lifted his leg, urinated over the plans, and walked out without uttering a word.

The whole farm was deeply divided on the subject of the windmill. Snowball did not deny that to build it would be a difficult business. Stone would have to be quarried and built up into walls, then the sails would have to be made and after that there would be need for dynamos and cables. (How these were to be procured, Snowball did not say.) But he maintained that it could all be done in a year. And thereafter, he declared, so much labour would be saved that the animals would only need to work three days a week. Napoleon, on the other hand, argued that the great need of the moment was to increase food production, and that if they wasted time on the windmill they would all starve to death. The animals formed themselves into two factions under the slogans, "Vote for Snowball and the three-day week" and "Vote for Napoleon and the full manger". Benjamin was the only animal who did not side with either faction. He refused to believe either that food would become more plentiful or that the windmill would save work. Windmills or no windmill, he said, life would go on as it had always gone on—that is, badly.

Apart from the disputes over the windmill, there was the question of the defence of the farm. It was fully realised that though the human beings had been defeated in the Battle of the Cowshed they might make another and more determined attempt to recapture the farm and reinstate Mr. Jones. They had all the more reason for doing so because the news of their defeat had spread across the countryside and made the animals on the neighbouring farms more restive than ever. As usual Snowball and Napoleon were in disagreement. According to Napoleon, what the animals must do was to procure firearms and train themselves in the use of them. According to Snowball, they must send out more and more pigeons and stir up rebellion among the animals on the other farms. The one argued that if they could not defend themselves they were bound to be conquered, the other argued that if rebellion happened everywhere they would have no need to defend themselves. The animals listened first to Napoleon, then to Snowball, and could not make up their minds which was right; indeed, they always found themselves in agreement with the one who was speaking at the moment.

At last the day came when Snowball's plans were completed. At the Meeting on the following Sunday the question of whether or not to begin work on the windmill was to be put to the vote. When the animals had assembled in the big barn, Snowball stood up and, though occasionally interrupted by bleating from the sheep, set forth his reasons for advocating the building of the windmill. Then Napoleon stood up to reply. He said very quietly that the windmill was nonsense and that he advised nobody to vote for it, and promptly sat down again; he had spoken for barely thirty seconds, and seemed almost indifferent as to the effect he produced. At this Snowball sprang to his feet, and shouting down the sheep, who had begun bleating again, broke into a passionate appeal in favour of the windmill. Until now the animals had been about equally divided in their sympathies, but in a moment Snowball's eloquence had carried them away. In glowing sentences he painted a picture of

Animal Farm as it might be when sordid labour was lifted from the animals' backs. His imagination had now run far beyond chaff-cutters and turnip-slicers. Electricity, he said, could operate threshing machines, ploughs, harrows, rollers, and reapers and binders, besides supplying every stall with its own electric light, hot and cold water, and an electric heater. By the time he had finished speaking, there was no doubt as to which way the vote would go. But just at this moment Napoleon stood up and, casting a peculiar sidelong look at Snowball, uttered a high-pitched whimper of a kind no one had ever heard him utter before.

At this there was a terrible baying sound outside, and nine enormous dogs wearing brass-studded collars came bounding into the barn. They dashed straight for Snowball, who only sprang from his place just in time to escape their snapping jaws. In a moment he was out of the door and they were after him. Too amazed and frightened to speak, all the animals crowded through the door to watch the chase. Snowball was racing across the long pasture that led to the road. He was running as only a pig can run, but the dogs were close on his heels. Suddenly he slipped and it seemed certain that they had him. Then he was up again, running faster than ever, then the dogs were gaining on him again. One of them all but closed his jaws on Snowball's tail, but Snowball whisked it free just in time. Then he put on an extra spurt and, with a few inches to spare, slipped through a hole in the hedge and was seen no more.

Silent and terrified, the animals crept back into the barn. In a moment the dogs came bounding back. At first no one had been able to imagine where these creatures came from, but the problem was soon solved: they were the puppies whom Napoleon had taken away from their mothers and reared privately. Though not yet full-grown, they were huge dogs, and as fierce-looking as wolves. They kept close to Napoleon. It was noticed that they wagged their tails to him in the same way as the other dogs had been used to do to Mr. Jones.

Napoleon, with the dogs following him, now mounted on to the raised portion of the floor where Major had previously stood to deliver his speech. He announced that from now on the Sunday-morning Meetings would come to an end. They were unnecessary, he said, and wasted time. In future all questions relating to the working of the farm would be settled by a special committee of pigs, presided over by himself. These would meet in private and afterwards communicate their decisions to the others. The animals would still assemble on Sunday mornings to salute the flag, sing "Beasts of England", and receive their orders for the week; but there would be no more debates.

In spite of the shock that Snowball's expulsion had given them, the animals were dismayed by this announcement. Several of them would have protested if they could have found the right arguments. Even Boxer was vaguely troubled. He set

48

his ears back, shook his forelock several times, and tried hard to marshal his thoughts; but in the end he could not think of anything to say. Some of the pigs themselves, however, were more articulate. Four young porkers in the front row uttered shrill squeals of disapproval, and all four of them sprang to their feet and began speaking at once. But suddenly the dogs sitting round Napoleon let out deep, menacing growls, and the pigs fell silent and sat down again. Then the sheep broke out into a tremendous bleating of "Four legs good, two legs bad!" which went on for nearly a quarter of an hour and put an end to any chance of discussion.

Afterwards Squealer was sent round the farm to explain the new arrangement to the others.

"Comrades," he said, "I trust that every animal here appreciates the sacrifice that Comrade Napoleon has made in taking this extra labour upon himself. Do not imagine, comrades, that leadership is a pleasure! On the contrary, it is a deep and heavy responsibility. No one believes more firmly than Comrade Napoleon that all animals are equal. He would be only too happy to let you make your decisions for yourselves. But sometimes you might make the wrong decisions, comrades, and then where should we be? Suppose you had decided to follow Snowball, with his moonshine of windmills—Snowball, who, as we now know, was no better than a criminal?"

"He fought bravely at the Battle of the Cowshed," said somebody.

"Bravery is not enough," said Squealer. "Loyalty and obedience are more important. And as to the Battle of the Cowshed, I believe the time will come when we shall find that Snowball's part in it was much exaggerated. Discipline, comrades, iron discipline! That is the watchword for today. One false step, and our enemies would be upon us. Surely, comrades, you do not want Jones back?"

Once again this argument was unanswerable. Certainly the animals did not want Jones back; if the holding of debates on Sunday mornings was liable to bring him back, then the debates must stop. Boxer, who had now had time to think things over, voiced the general feelings by saying: "If Comrade Napoleon says it, it must be right." And from then on he adopted the maxim, "Napoleon is always right", in addition to his private motto of "I will work harder".

By this time the weather had broken and the spring ploughing had begun. The shed where Snowball had drawn his plans of the windmill had been shut up and it was assumed that the plans had been rubbed off the floor. Every Sunday morning at ten o'clock the animals assembled in the big barn to receive their orders for the week. The skull of old Major, now clean of flesh, had been disinterred from the orchard and set up on a stump at the foot of the flagstaff, beside the gun. After the hoisting of the flag, the animals were required to file past the skull in a reverent manner before entering the barn. Nowadays they did not sit all together as they had done in the past. Napoleon, with Squealer and another pig named Minimus, who had a remarkable gift for composing songs and poems, sat on the front of the raised platform, with the nine young dogs forming a semicircle round them, and the other pigs sitting behind. The rest of the animals sat facing them in the main body of the barn. Napoleon read out the orders for the week in a gruff soldierly style, and after a single singing of "Beasts of England", all the animals dispersed.

On the third Sunday after Snowball's expulsion, the animals were somewhat surprised to hear Napoleon announce that the windmill was to be built after all. He did not give any reason for having changed his mind, but merely warned the animals that this extra task would mean very hard work; it might even be necessary to reduce their rations. The plans, however, had all been prepared, down to the last detail. A special committee of pigs had been at work upon them for the past three weeks. The building of the windmill, with various other improvements, was expected to take two years.

That evening Squealer explained privately to the other animals that Napoleon had never in reality been opposed to the windmill. On the contrary, it was he who had advocated it in the beginning, and the plan which Snowball had drawn on the floor of the incubator shed had actually been stolen from among Napoleon's papers. The windmill was, in fact, Napoleon's own creation. Why, then, asked somebody, had he spoken so strongly against it?

51

Here Squealer looked very sly. That, he said, was Comrade Napoleon's cunning. He had *seemed* to oppose the windmill, simply as a manoeuvre to get rid of Snowball, who was a dangerous character and a bad influence. Now that Snowball was out of the way, the plan could go forward without this interference. This, said Squealer, was something called tactics. He repeated a number of times, "Tactics, comrades, tactics!" skipping round and whisking his tail with a merry laugh. The animals were not certain what the word meant, but Squealer spoke so persuasively, and the three dogs who happened to be with him growled so threateningly, that they accepted his explanation without further questions.

6

ALL that year the animals worked like slaves. But they were happy in their work; they grudged no effort or sacrifice, well aware that everything that they did was for the benefit of themselves and those of their kind who would come after them, and not for a pack of idle, thieving human beings.

Throughout the spring and summer they worked a sixty-hour week, and in August Napoleon announced that there would be work on Sunday afternoons as well. This work was strictly voluntary, but any animal who absented himself from it would have his rations reduced by half. Even so, it was found necessary to leave certain tasks undone. The harvest was a little less successful than in the previous year, and two fields which should have been sown with roots in the early summer were not sown because the ploughing had not been completed early enough. It was possible to foresee that the coming winter would be a hard one.

The windmill presented unexpected difficulties.

There was a good quarry of limestone on the farm, and plenty of sand and cement had been found in one of the outhouses, so that all the materials for building were at hand. But the problem the animals could not at first solve was how to break up the stone into pieces of suitable size. There seemed no way of doing this except with picks and crowbars, which no animal could use, because no animal could stand on his hind legs. Only after weeks of vain effort did the right idea occur to somebody—namely, to utilise the force of gravity. Huge boulders, far too big to be used as they were, were lying all over the bed of the quarry. The animals lashed rope round these, and then all together, cows, horses, sheep, any animal that could lay hold of the rope—even the pigs sometimes joined in at critical moments—they dragged them with desperate slowness up the slope to the top of the quarry, where they were toppled over the edge, to shatter to pieces below. Transporting the stone when it was once broken was comparatively simple. The horses carried it off in cartloads, the sheep dragged single blocks, even Muriel and Benjamin yoked themselves into an old governess-cart and did their share. By late summer a sufficient store of stone had accumulated, and then the building began, under the superintendence of the pigs.

But it was a slow, laborious process. Frequently it took a whole day of exhausting effort to drag a single boulder to the top of the quarry, and sometimes when it was pushed over the edge it failed to break. Nothing could have been achieved without Boxer, whose strength seemed equal to that of all the rest of the animals put together. When the boulder began to slip and the animals cried out in despair at finding themselves dragged down the hill, it was always Boxer who strained himself against the rope and brought the boulder to a stop. To see him toiling up the slope inch by inch, his breath coming fast, the tips of his hoofs clawing at the ground, and his great sides matted with sweat, filled everyone with admiration. Clover warned him sometimes to be careful not to overstrain himself, but Boxer would never listen to her. His two slogans, "I will work harder" and "Napoleon is always right", seemed to him a sufficient answer to all problems. He had made arrangements with the cockerel to call him three-quarters of an hour earlier in the mornings instead of half an hour. And in his spare moments, of which there were not many nowadays, he would go alone to the quarry, collect a load of broken stone, and drag it down to the site of the windmill unassisted.

The animals were not badly off throughout that summer, in spite of the hardness of their work. If they had no more food than they had had in Jones's day, at least they did not have less. The advantage of only having to feed themselves, and not having to support five extravagant human beings as well, was so great that it would have taken a lot of failures to outweigh it. And in many ways the animal method of doing things was more efficient and saved labour. Such jobs as weeding, for instance, could be done with a thoroughness impossible to human beings. And again, since no animal now stole, it was unnecessary to fence off pasture from arable land, which saved a lot of labour on the upkeep of hedges and gates. Nevertheless, as the summer wore on, various unforeseen shortages began to make themselves felt. There was need of paraffin oil, nails, string, dog biscuits, and iron for the horses' shoes, none of which could be produced on the farm. Later there would also be need for seeds and artificial manures, besides various tools and, finally, the machinery for the windmill. How these were to be procured, no one was able to imagine.

One Sunday morning, when the animals assembled to receive their orders, Napoleon announced that he had decided upon a new policy. From now onwards Animal Farm would engage in trade with the neighbouring farms: not, of course, for any commercial purpose, but simply in order to obtain certain materials which were urgently necessary. The needs of the windmill must override everything else, he said. He was therefore making arrangements to sell a stack of hay and part of the current year's wheat crop, and later on, if more money were needed, it would have to be made up by the sale of eggs, for which there was always a market in Willingdon. The hens, said Napoleon, should welcome this sacrifice as their own special contribution towards the building of the windmill.

Once again the animals were conscious of a vague uneasiness. Never to have any dealings with human beings, never to engage in trade, never to make use of money—had not these been among the earliest resolutions passed at that first triumphant Meeting after Jones was expelled? All the animals remembered passing such resolutions: or at least they thought that they remembered it. The four young pigs who had protested when Napoleon abolished the Meetings raised their voices timidly, but they were promptly silenced by a tremendous growling from the dogs. Then, as usual, the sheep broke into "Four legs good, two legs bad!" and the momentary awkwardness was smoothed over. Finally Napoleon raised his trotter for silence and announced that he had already made all the arrangements. There would be no need for any of the animals to come in contact with human beings, which would clearly be most undesirable. He intended to take the whole burden upon his shoulders. A Mr. Whymper, a solicitor living in Willingdon, had agreed to act as intermediary between Animal Farm and the outside world, and would visit the farm every Monday morning to receive his instructions. Napoleon ended his speech with his usual cry of "Long live Animal Farm!", and after the singing of "Beasts of England" the animals were dismissed.

Afterwards Squealer made a round of the farm and set the animals' minds at rest. He assured them that the resolution against engaging in trade and using money had never been passed, or even suggested. It was pure imagination, probably traceable in the beginning to lies circulated by Snowball. A few animals still felt faintly doubtful, but Squealer asked them shrewdly, "Are you certain that this is not something that you have dreamed, comrades? Have you any record of such a resolution? Is it written down anywhere?" And since it was certainly true that nothing of the kind existed in writing, the animals were satisfied that they had been mistaken.

Every Monday Mr. Whymper visited the farm as had been arranged. He was a sly-looking little man with side whiskers, a solicitor in a very small way of business, but sharp enough to have realised earlier than anyone else that Animal Farm would need a broker and that the commissions would be worth having. The animals watched his coming and going with a kind of dread, and avoided him as much as possible. Nevertheless, the sight of Napoleon, on all fours, delivering orders to Whymper, who stood on two legs, roused their pride and partly reconciled them to the new arrangement. Their relations with the human race were now not quite the same as they had been before. The human beings did not hate Animal Farm any less now that it was prospering; indeed, they hated it more than ever. Every human being held it as an article of faith that the farm would go bankrupt sooner or later, and, above all, that the windmill would be a failure. They would meet in the public-houses and prove to one another by means of diagrams that the windmill was bound to fall down, or that if it did stand up, then that it would never work. And yet, against their will, they had developed a certain respect for the efficiency with which the animals were managing their own affairs. One symptom of this was that they had begun to call Animal Farm by its proper name and ceased to pretend that it was called the Manor Farm. They had also dropped their championship of Jones, who had given up hope of getting his farm back and gone to live in another part of the country. Except through Whymper, there was as yet no contact between Animal Farm and the outside world, but there were constant rumours that Napoleon was about to enter into a definite business agreement either with Mr. Pilkington of Foxwood or with Mr. Frederick of Pinchfield—but never, it was noticed, with both simultaneously.

It was about this time that the pigs suddenly moved into the farmhouse and took up their residence there. Again the animals seemed to remember that a resolution against this had been passed in the early days, and again Squealer was able to convince them that this was not the case. It was absolutely necessary, he said, that the pigs, who were the brains of the farm, should have a quiet place to work in. It was also more suited to the dignity of the Leader (for of late he had taken to speaking of Napoleon under the title of "Leader") to live in a house than in a mere sty. Nevertheless, some of the animals were disturbed when they heard that the pigs not only took their meals in the kitchen and used the drawing-room as a recreation room, but also slept in the beds. Boxer passed it off as usual with "Napoleon is always right!" but Clover, who thought she remembered a definite ruling against beds, went to the end of the barn and tried to puzzle out the Seven Commandments which were inscribed there. Finding herself unable to read more than individual letters, she fetched Muriel.

"Muriel," she said, "read me the Fourth Commandment. Does it not say something about never sleeping in a bed?"

With some difficulty Muriel spelt it out.

"It says, 'No animal shall sleep in a bed *with sheets*'," she announced finally.

Curiously enough, Clover had not remembered that the Fourth Commandment mentioned sheets; but as it was there on the wall, it must have done so. And Squealer, who happened to be passing at this moment, attended by two or three dogs, was able to put the whole matter in its proper perspective.

"You have heard, then, comrades," he said, "that we pigs now sleep in the beds of the farmhouse? And why not? You did not suppose, surely, that there was ever a ruling against *beds*? A bed merely means a place to sleep in. A pile of straw in a stall is a bed, properly regarded. The rule was against *sheets*, which are a human invention. We have removed the sheets from the farmhouse beds, and sleep between blankets. And very comfortable beds they are too! But not more comfortable than we need, I can tell you, comrades, with all the brainwork we have to do nowadays. You would not rob us of our repose, would you, comrades? You would not have us too tired to carry out our duties? Surely none of you wishes to see Jones back?"

The animals reassured him on this point immediately, and no more was said about the pigs sleeping in the farmhouse beds. And when, some days afterwards, it was announced that from now on the pigs would get up an hour later in the mornings than the other animals, no complaint was made about that either.

By the autumn the animals were tired but happy. They had had a hard year, and after the sale of part of the hay and corn, the stores of food for the winter were none too plentiful, but the windmill compensated for everything. It was almost half built now. After the harvest there was a stretch of clear dry weather, and the animals toiled harder than ever, thinking it well worth while to plod to and fro all day with blocks of stone if by doing so they could raise the walls another foot. Boxer would even come out at nights and work for an hour or two on his own by the light of the harvest moon. In their spare moments the animals would walk round and round the half-finished mill, admiring the strength and perpendicularity of its walls and marvelling that they should ever have been able to build anything so imposing. Only old Benjamin refused to grow enthusiastic about the windmill, though, as usual, he would utter nothing beyond the cryptic remark that donkeys live a long time.

November came, with raging south-west winds. Building had to stop because it was now too wet to mix the cement. Finally there came a night when the gale was so violent that the farm buildings rocked on their foundations and several tiles were blown off the roof of the barn. The hens woke up squawking with terror because they had all dreamed simultaneously of hearing a gun go off in the distance. In the morning the animals came out of their stalls to find that the flagstaff had been blown down and an elm tree at the foot of the orchard had been plucked up like a radish. They had just noticed this when a cry of despair broke from every animal's throat. A terrible sight had met their eyes. The windmill was in ruins.

With one accord they dashed down to the spot. Napoleon, who seldom moved out of a walk, raced ahead of them all. Yes, there it lay, the fruit of all their struggles, levelled to its foundations, the stones they had broken and carried so laboriously scattered all around. Unable at first to speak, they stood gazing mournfully at the litter of fallen stone. Napoleon paced to and fro in silence, occasionally snuffing at the ground. His tail had grown rigid and twitched sharply from side to side, a sign in him of intense mental activity. Suddenly he halted as though his mind were made up.

"Comrades," he said quietly, "do you know who is responsible for this? Do you know the enemy who has come in the night and overthrown our windmill? SNOWBALL!" he suddenly roared in a voice of thunder. "Snowball has done this thing! In sheer malignity, thinking to set back our plans and avenge himself for his ignominious expulsion, this traitor has crept here under cover of night and destroyed our work of nearly a year. Comrades, here and now I pronounce the death sentence upon Snowball. 'Animal Hero, Second Class', and half a bushel of apples to any animal who brings him to justice. A full bushel to anyone who captures him alive!"

The animals were shocked beyond measure to learn that even Snowball could be guilty of such an action. There was a cry of indignation, and everyone began thinking out ways of catching Snowball if he should ever come back. Almost immediately the footprints of a pig were discovered in the grass at a little distance from the knoll. They could only be traced for a few yards, but appeared to lead to a hole in the hedge. Napoleon snuffed deeply at them and pronounced them to be Snowball's. He gave it as his opinion that Snowball had probably come from the direction of Foxwood Farm.

"No more delays, comrades!" cried Napoleon when the footprints had been examined. "There is work to be done. This very morning we begin rebuilding the windmill, and we will build all through the winter, rain or shine. We will teach this miserable traitor that he cannot undo our work so easily. Remember, comrades, there must be no alteration in our plans: they shall be carried out to the day. Forward, comrades! Long live the windmill! Long live Animal Farm!"

7

I T was a bitter winter. The stormy weather was followed by sleet and snow, and then by a hard frost which did not break till well into February. The animals carried on as best they could with the rebuilding of the windmill, well knowing that the outside world was watching them and that the envious human beings would rejoice and triumph if the mill were not finished on time.

Out of spite, the human beings pretended not to believe that it was Snowball who had destroyed the windmill: they said that it had fallen down because the walls were too thin. The animals knew that this was not the case. Still, it had been decided to build the walls three feet thick this time instead of eighteen inches as before, which meant collecting much larger quantities of stone. For a long time the quarry was full of snowdrifts and nothing could be done. Some progress was made in the dry frosty weather that followed, but it was cruel work, and the animals could not feel so hopeful about it as they had felt before. They were always cold, and usually hungry as well. Only Boxer and Clover never lost heart. Squealer made excellent speeches on the joy of service and the dignity of labour, but the other animals found more inspiration in Boxer's strength and his never-failing cry of "I will work harder!"

In January food fell short. The corn ration was drastically reduced, and it was announced that an extra potato ration would be issued to make up for it. Then it was discovered that the greater part of the potato crop had been frosted in the clamps, which had not been covered thickly enough. The potatoes had become soft and discoloured, and only a few were edible. For days at a time the animals had nothing to eat but chaff and mangels. Starvation seemed to stare them in the face.

It was vitally necessary to conceal this fact from the outside world. Emboldened by the collapse of the windmill, the human beings were inventing fresh lies about Animal Farm. Once again it was being put about that all the animals were dying of famine and disease, and that they were continually fighting among themselves and had resorted to cannibalism and infanticide. Napoleon was well aware of the bad results that might follow if the real facts of the food situation were known, and he decided to make use of Mr. Whymper to spread a contrary impression. Hitherto the animals had had little or no contact with Whymper on his weekly visits: now, however, a few selected animals, mostly sheep, were instructed to remark casually in his hearing that rations had been increased. In addition, Napoleon ordered the almost empty bins in the store-shed to be filled nearly to the brim with sand, which was then covered up with what remained of the grain and meal. On some suitable pretext Whymper was led through the store-shed and allowed to catch a glimpse of the bins. He was deceived, and continued to report to the outside world that there was no food shortage on Animal Farm.

Nevertheless, towards the end of January it became obvious that it would be necessary to procure some more grain from somewhere. In these days Napoleon rarely appeared in public, but spent all his time in the farmhouse, which was guarded at each door by fierce-looking dogs. When he did emerge, it was in a ceremonial manner, with an escort of six dogs who closely surrounded him and growled if anyone came too near. Frequently he did not even appear on Sunday mornings, but issued his orders through one of the other pigs, usually Squealer.

One Sunday morning Squealer announced that the hens, who had just come in to lay again, must surrender their eggs. Napoleon had accepted, through Whymper, a contract for four hundred eggs a week. The price of these would pay for enough grain and meal to keep the farm going till summer came on and conditions were easier.

When the hens heard this, they raised a terrible outcry. They had been warned earlier that this sacrifice might be necessary, but had not believed that it would really happen. They were just getting their clutches ready for the spring sitting, and they protested that to take the eggs away now was murder. For the first time since the expulsion of Jones, there was something resembling a rebellion. Led by three young Black Minorca pullets, the hens made a determined effort to thwart Napoleon's wishes. Their method was to fly up to the rafters and there lay their eggs, which smashed to pieces on the floor. Napoleon acted swiftly and ruthlessly. He ordered the hens' rations to be stopped, and decreed that any animal giving so much as a grain of corn to a hen should be punished by death. The dogs saw to it that these orders were carried out. For five days the hens held out, then they capitulated and went back to their nesting boxes. Nine hens had died in the meantime. Their bodies were buried in the orchard, and it was given out that they had died of coccidiosis. Whymper heard nothing of this affair, and the eggs were duly delivered, a grocer's van driving up to the farm once a week to take them away.

All this while no more had been seen of Snowball. He was rumoured to be hiding on one of the neighbouring farms, either Foxwood or Pinchfield. Napoleon was by this time on slightly better terms with the other farmers than before. It happened that there was in the yard a pile of timber which had been stacked there ten years earlier when a beech spinney was cleared. It was well seasoned, and Whymper had advised Napoleon to sell it; both Mr. Pilkington and Mr. Frederick were anxious to buy it. Napoleon was hesitating between the two, unable to make up his mind. It was noticed that whenever he seemed on the point of coming to an agreement with Frederick, Snowball was declared to be in hiding at Foxwood, while, when he inclined towards Pilkington, Snowball was said to be at Pinchfield.

Suddenly, early in the spring, an alarming thing was discovered. Snowball was secretly frequenting the farm by night! The animals were so disturbed that they could hardly sleep in their stalls. Every night, it was said, he came creeping in under cover of darkness and performed all kinds of mischief. He stole the corn, he upset the milk-pails, he broke the eggs, he trampled the seed-beds, he gnawed the bark off the fruit trees. Whenever anything went wrong it became usual to attribute it to Snowball. If a window was broken or a drain was blocked up, someone was certain to say that Snowball had come in the night and done it, and when the key of the store-shed was lost, the whole farm was convinced that Snowball had thrown it down the well. Curiously enough, they went on believing this even after the mislaid key was found under a sack of meal. The cows declared unanimously that Snowball crept into their stalls and milked them in their sleep. The rats, which had been troublesome that winter, were also said to be in league with Snowball.

Napoleon decreed that there should be a full

investigation into Snowball's activities. With his dogs in attendance he set out and made a careful tour of inspection of the farm buildings, the other animals following at a respectful distance. At every few steps Napoleon stopped and snuffed the ground for traces of Snowball's footsteps, which, he said, he could detect by the smell. He snuffed in every corner, in the barn, in the cowshed, in the henhouses, in the vegetable garden, and found traces of Snowball almost everywhere. He would put his snout to the ground, give several deep sniffs, and exclaim in a terrible voice, "Snowball! He has been here! I can smell him distinctly!" and at the word "Snowball" all the dogs let out blood-curdling growls and showed their side teeth.

The animals were thoroughly frightened. It seemed to them as though Snowball were some kind of invisible influence, pervading the air about them and menacing them with all kinds of dangers. In the evening Squealer called them together, and with an alarmed expression on his face told them that he had some serious news to report.

"Comrades!" cried Squealer, making little nervous skips, "a most terrible thing has been discovered. Snowball has sold himself to Frederick of Pinchfield Farm, who is even now plotting to attack us and take our farm away from us! Snowball is to act as his guide when the attack begins. But there is worse than that. We had thought that Snowball's rebellion was caused simply by his vanity and ambition. But we were wrong, comrades. Do you know what the real reason was? Snowball was in league with Jones from the very start! He was Jones's secret agent all the time. It has all been proved by documents which he left behind him and which we have only just discovered. To my mind this explains a great deal, comrades. Did we not see for ourselves how he attempted—fortunately without success—to get us defeated and destroyed at the Battle of the Cowshed?"

The animals were stupefied. This was a wickedness far outdoing Snowball's destruction of the windmill. But it was some minutes before they could fully take it in. They all remembered, or thought they remembered, how they had seen Snowball charging ahead of them at the Battle of the Cowshed, how he had rallied and encouraged them at every turn, and how he had not paused for an instant even when the pellets from Jones's gun had wounded his back. At first it was a little difficult to see how this fitted in with his being on Jones's side. Even Boxer, who seldom asked questions, was puzzled. He lay down, tucked his fore hoofs beneath him, shut his eyes, and with a hard effort managed to formulate his thoughts.

"I do not believe that," he said. "Snowball fought bravely at the Battle of the Cowshed. I saw him myself. Did we not give him 'Animal Hero, First Class', immediately afterwards?"

"That was our mistake, comrade. For we know now—it is all written down in the secret documents that we have found—that in reality he was trying to lure us to our doom."

"But he was wounded," said Boxer. "We all saw him running with blood."

"That was part of the arrangement!" cried Squealer. "Jones's shot only grazed him. I could show you this in his own writing, if you were able to read it. The plot was for Snowball, at the critical moment, to give the signal for flight and leave the field to the enemy. And he very nearly succeeded—I will even say, comrades, he *would* have succeeded if it had not been for our heroic Leader, Comrade Napoleon. Do you not remember how, just at the moment when Jones and his men had got inside the yard, Snowball suddenly turned and fled, and many animals followed him? And do you not remember, too, that it was just at that moment, when panic was spreading and all seemed lost, that Comrade Napoleon sprang forward with a cry of 'Death to Humanity!' and sank his teeth in Jones's leg? Surely you remember *that*, comrades?" exclaimed Squealer, frisking from side to side.

Now when Squealer described the scene so graphically, it seemed to the animals that they did remember it. At any rate, they remembered that at the critical moment of the battle Snowball had turned to flee. But Boxer was still a little uneasy.

"I do not believe that Snowball was a traitor at the beginning," he said finally. "What he has done since is different. But I believe that at the Battle of the Cowshed he was a good comrade."

72

"Our Leader, Comrade Napoleon," announced Squealer, speaking very slowly and firmly, "has stated categorically—categorically, comrade—that Snowball was Jones's agent from the very beginning—yes, and from long before the Rebellion was ever thought of."

"Ah, that is different!" said Boxer. "If Comrade Napoleon says it, it must be right."

"That is the true spirit, comrade!" cried Squealer, but it was noticed he cast a very ugly look at Boxer with his little twinkling eyes. He turned to go, then paused and added impressively: "I warn every animal on this farm to keep his eyes very wide open. For we have reason to think that some of Snowball's secret agents are lurking among us at this moment!"

Four days later, in the late afternoon, Napoleon ordered all the animals to assemble in the yard. When they were all gathered together, Napoleon emerged from the farmhouse, wearing both his medals (for he had recently awarded himself "Animal Hero, First Class", and "Animal Hero, Second Class"), with his nine huge dogs frisking round him and uttering growls that sent shivers down all the animals' spines. They all cowered silently in their places, seeming to know in advance that some terrible thing was about to happen.

Napoleon stood sternly surveying his audience; then he uttered a high-pitched whimper. Immediately the dogs bounded forward, seized four of the pigs by the ear and dragged them, squealing with pain and terror, to Napoleon's feet. The pigs' ears were bleeding, the dogs had tasted blood, and for a few moments they appeared to go quite mad. To the amazement of everybody, three of them flung themselves upon Boxer. Boxer saw them coming and put out his great hoof, caught a dog in mid-air, and pinned him to the ground. The dog shrieked for mercy and the other two fled with their tails between their legs. Boxer looked at Napoleon to know whether he should crush the dog to death or let it go. Napoleon appeared to change countenance, and sharply ordered Boxer to let the dog go, whereat Boxer lifted his hoof, and the dog slunk away, bruised and howling.

Presently the tumult died down. The four pigs waited, trembling, with guilt written on every line of their countenances. Napoleon now called upon them to confess their crimes. They were the same four pigs as had protested when Napoleon abolished the Sunday Meetings. Without any further prompting they confessed that they had been secretly in touch with Snowball ever since his expulsion, that they had collaborated with him in destroying the windmill, and that they had entered into an agreement with him to hand over Animal Farm to Mr. Frederick. They added that Snowball had privately admitted to them that he had been Jones's secret agent for years past. When they had finished their confession, the dogs promptly tore their throats out, and in a terrible voice Napoleon demanded whether any other animal had anything to confess.

The three hens who had been the ringleaders in the attempted rebellion over the eggs now came forward and stated that Snowball had appeared to them in a dream and incited them to disobey Napoleon's orders. They, too, were slaughtered. Then a goose came forward and confessed to having secreted six ears of corn during the last year's harvest and eaten them in the night. Then a sheep confessed to having urinated in the drinking pool—urged to do this, so she said, by Snowball—and two other sheep confessed to having murdered an old ram, an especially devoted follower of Napoleon, by chasing him round and round a bonfire when he was suffering from a cough. They were all slain on the spot. And so the tale of confessions and executions went on, until there was a pile of corpses lying before Napoleon's feet and the air was heavy with the smell of blood, which had been unknown there since the expulsion of Jones.

When it was all over, the remaining animals, except for the pigs and dogs, crept away in a body. They were shaken and miserable. They did not know which was more shocking—the treachery of the animals who had leagued themselves with Snowball, or the cruel retribution they had just witnessed. In the old days there had often been scenes of bloodshed equally terrible, but it seemed to all of them that it was far worse now that it was happening among themselves. Since Jones had left the farm, until today, no animal had killed another animal. Not even a rat had been killed. They had made their way on to the little knoll where the half-finished windmill stood, and with one accord they all lay down as though huddling together for warmth—Clover, Muriel, Benjamin, the cows, the sheep, and a whole flock of geese and hens— everyone, indeed, except the cat, who had suddenly disappeared just before Napoleon ordered the animals to assemble. For some time nobody spoke. Only Boxer remained on his feet. He fidgeted to and fro, swishing his long black tail against his sides and occasionally uttering a little whinny of surprise. Finally he said:

"I do not understand it. I would not have believed that such things could happen on our farm. It must be due to some fault in ourselves. The solution, as I see it, is to work harder. From now onwards I shall get up a full hour earlier in the mornings."

And he moved off at his lumbering trot and made for the quarry. Having got there, he collected two successive loads of stone and dragged them down to the windmill before retiring for the night.

The animals huddled about Clover, not speaking. The knoll where they were lying gave them a wide prospect across the countryside. Most of Animal Farm was within their view—the long pasture stretching down to the main road, the hayfield, the spinney, the drinking pool, the ploughed fields where the young wheat was thick and green, and the red roofs of the farm buildings with the smoke curling from the chimneys. It was a clear spring evening. The grass and the bursting hedges were gilded by the level rays of the sun. Never had the farm—and with a kind of surprise they remembered that it was their own farm, every inch of it their own property—appeared to the animals so desirable a place. As Clover looked down the hillside her eyes filled with tears. If she could have spoken her thoughts, it would have been to say that this was not what they had aimed at when they had set themselves years ago to work for the overthrow of the human race. These scenes of terror and slaughter were not what they had looked forward to on that night when old Major first stirred them to rebellion. If she herself had had any picture of the future, it had been of a society of animals set free from hunger and the whip, all equal, each working according to his capacity, the strong protecting the weak, as she had protected the lost brood of ducklings with her foreleg on the night of Major's speech. Instead—she did not know why—they had come to a time when no one dared speak his mind, when fierce, growling dogs roamed everywhere, and when you had to watch your comrades torn to pieces after confessing to shocking crimes. There was no thought of rebellion or disobedience in her mind. She knew that, even as things were, they were far better off than they had been in the days of Jones, and that before all else it was needful to prevent the return of the human beings. Whatever happened she would remain faithful, work hard, carry out the orders that were given to her, and accept the leadership of Napoleon. But still, it was not for this that she and all the other animals had hoped and toiled. It was not for this that they had built the windmill and faced the bullets of Jones's gun. Such were her thoughts, though she lacked the words to express them.

At last feeling this to be in some way a substitute for the words she was unable to find, she began to sing "Beasts of England". The other animals sitting round her took it up, and they sang it three times over—very tunefully, but slowly and mournfully, in a way they had never sung it before.

They had just finished singing it for the third time when Squealer, attended by two dogs, approached them with the air of having something important to say. He announced that, by a special decree of Comrade Napoleon, "Beasts of England" had been abolished. From now onwards it was forbidden to sing it.

The animals were taken aback.

"Why?" cried Muriel.

"It is no longer needed, comrade," said Squealer stiffly.

" 'Beasts of England' was the song of the Rebellion. But the Rebellion is now completed. The execution of the traitors this afternoon was the final act. The enemy both external and internal has been defeated. In 'Beasts of England' we expressed our longing for a better society in days to come. But that society has now been established. Clearly this song has no longer any purpose."

Frightened though they were, some of the animals might possibly have protested, but at this moment the sheep set up their usual bleating of "Four legs good, two legs bad", which went on for several minutes and put an end to the discussion.

So "Beasts of England" was heard of no more. In its place Minimus, the poet, had composed another song which began:

Animal Farm, Animal Farm,
Never through me shalt thou come to harm!

and this was sung every Sunday morning after the hoisting of the flag. But somehow neither the words nor the tune ever seemed to the animals to come up to "Beasts of England".

8

A FEW days later, when the terror caused by the executions had died down, some of the animals remembered—or thought they remembered—that the Sixth Commandment decreed: "No animal shall kill any other animal". And though no one cared to mention it in the hearing of the pigs or the dogs, it was felt that the killings which had taken place did not square with this. Clover asked Benjamin to read her the Sixth Commandment, and when Benjamin, as usual, said that he refused to meddle in such matters, she fetched Muriel. Muriel read the Commandment for her. It ran: "No animal shall kill any other animal *without cause*". Somehow or other, the last two words had slipped out of the animals' memory. But they saw now that the Commandment had not been violated; for clearly there was good reason for killing the traitors who had leagued themselves with Snowball.

Throughout that year the animals worked even harder than they had worked in the previous year. To rebuild the windmill, with walls twice as thick as before, and to finish it by the appointed date, together with the regular work of the farm, was a tremendous labour. There were times when it seemed to the animals that they worked longer hours and fed no better than they had done in Jones's day. On Sunday mornings Squealer, holding down a long strip of paper with his trotter, would read out to them lists of figures proving that the production of every class of foodstuff had increased by two hundred per cent, three hundred per cent, or five hundred per cent, as the case might be. The animals saw no reason to disbelieve him, especially as they could no longer remember very clearly what conditions had been like before the Rebellion. All the same, there were days when they felt that they would sooner have had less figures and more food.

All orders were now issued through Squealer or one of the other pigs. Napoleon himself was not seen in public as often as once in a fortnight. When he did appear, he was attended not only by his retinue of dogs but by a black cockerel who marched in front of him and acted as a kind of trumpeter, letting out a loud "cock-a-doodle-doo" before Napoleon spoke. Even in the farmhouse, it was said, Napoleon inhabited separate apartments from the others. He took his meals alone, with two dogs to wait upon him, and always ate from the Crown Derby dinner service which had been in the glass cupboard in the drawing-room. It was also announced that the gun would be fired every year on Napoleon's birthday, as well as on the other two anniversaries.

Napoleon was now never spoken of simply as "Napoleon". He was always referred to in formal style as "our Leader, Comrade Napoleon", and the pigs liked to invent for him such titles as Father of All Animals, Terror of Mankind, Protector of the Sheep-fold, Ducklings' Friend, and the like. In his speeches, Squealer would talk with the tears rolling down his cheeks of Napoleon's wisdom, the goodness of his heart, and the deep love he bore to all animals everywhere, even and especially the unhappy animals who still lived in ignorance and slavery on other farms. It had become usual to give Napoleon the credit for every successful achievement and every stroke of good fortune. You would often hear one hen remark to another, "Under the guidance of our Leader, Comrade Napoleon, I have laid five eggs in six days"; or two cows, enjoying a drink at the pool, would exclaim, "Thanks to the leadership of Comrade Napoleon, how excellent this water tastes!" The general feeling on the farm was well expressed in a poem entitled "Comrade Napoleon", which was composed by Minimus and which ran as follows:

Friend of the fatherless
Fountain of happiness!
Lord of the swill-bucket! Oh, how my soul is on
Fire when I gaze at thy
Calm and commanding eye,

Like the sun in the sky,
Comrade Napoleon!

Thou art the giver of
All that thy creatures love,
Full belly twice a day, clean straw to roll upon;
Every beast great or small
Sleeps at peace in his stall,
Thou watchest over all,
Comrade Napoleon!

Had I a sucking-pig,
Ere he had grown as big
Even as a pint bottle or as a rolling-pin,
He should have learned to be
Faithful and true to thee,
Yes, his first squeak should be
"Comrade Napoleon!"

Napoleon approved of this poem and caused it to be inscribed on the wall of the big barn, at the opposite end from the Seven Commandments. It was surmounted by a portrait of Napoleon, in profile, executed by Squealer in white paint.

Meanwhile, through the agency of Whymper, Napoleon was engaged in complicated negotiations with Frederick and Pilkington. The pile of timber was still unsold. Of the two, Frederick was the more anxious to get hold of it, but he would not offer a reasonable price. At the same time there were renewed rumours that Frederick and his men were plotting to attack Animal Farm and to destroy the windmill, the building of which had aroused furious jealousy in him. Snowball was known to be still skulking on Pinchfield Farm. In the middle of the summer the animals were alarmed to hear that three hens had come forward and confessed that, inspired by Snowball, they had entered into a plot to murder Napoleon. They were executed immediately, and fresh precautions for Napoleon's safety were taken. Four dogs guarded his bed at night, one at each corner, and a young pig named Pinkeye was given the task of tasting all his food before he ate it, lest it should be poisoned.

At about the same time it was given out that Napoleon had arranged to sell the pile of timber to Mr. Pilkington; he was also going to enter into a regular agreement for the exchange of certain products between Animal Farm and Foxwood. The relations between Napoleon and Pilkington, though they were only conducted through Whymper, were now almost friendly. The animals distrusted Pilkington, as a human being, but greatly preferred him to Frederick, whom they both feared and hated. As summer wore on, and the windmill neared completion, the rumours of an impending treacherous attack grew stronger and stronger. Frederick, it was said, intended to bring against them twenty men all armed with guns, and he had already bribed the magistrates and police, so that if he could once get hold of the title-deeds of Animal Farm they would ask no questions. Moreover, terrible stories were leaking out from

Pinchfield about the cruelties that Frederick practised upon his animals. He had flogged an old horse to death, he starved his cows, he had killed a dog by throwing it into the furnace, he amused himself in the evenings by making cocks fight with splinters of razor-blade tied to their spurs. The animals' blood boiled with rage when they heard of these things being done to their comrades, and sometimes they clamoured to be allowed to go out in a body and attack Pinchfield Farm, drive out the humans, and set the animals free. But Squealer counselled them to avoid rash actions and trust in Comrade Napoleon's strategy.

Nevertheless, feeling against Frederick continued to run high. One Sunday morning Napoleon appeared in the barn and explained that he had never at any time contemplated selling the pile of timber to Frederick; he considered it beneath his dignity, he said, to have dealings with scoundrels of that description. The pigeons who were still sent out to spread tidings of the Rebellion were forbidden to set foot anywhere on Foxwood, and were also ordered to drop their former slogan of "Death to Humanity" in favour of "Death to Frederick". In the late summer yet another of Snowball's machinations was laid bare. The wheat crop was full of weeds, and it was discovered that on one of his nocturnal visits Snowball had mixed weed seeds with the seed corn. A gander who had been privy to the plot had confessed his guilt to Squealer and immediately committed suicide by swallowing deadly nightshade berries. The animals now also learned that Snowball had never—as many of them had believed hitherto—received the order of "Animal Hero, First Class". This was merely a legend which had been spread some time after the Battle of the Cowshed by Snowball himself. So far from being decorated, he had been censured for showing cowardice in the battle. Once again some of the animals heard this with a certain bewilderment, but Squealer was soon able to convince them that their memories had been at fault.

In the autumn, by a tremendous, exhausting effort—for the harvest had to be gathered at almost the same time—the windmill was finished. The machinery had still to be installed, and Whymper was negotiating the purchase of it, but the structure was completed. In the teeth of every difficulty, in spite of inexperience, of primitive implements, of bad luck and of Snowball's treachery, the work had been finished punctually to the very day! Tired out but proud, the animals walked round and round their masterpiece, which appeared even more beautiful in their eyes than when it had been built the first time. Moreover, the walls were twice as thick as before. Nothing short of explosives would lay them low this time! And when they thought of how they had laboured, what discouragements they had overcome, and the enormous difference that would be made in their lives when the sails were turning and the dynamos running—when they thought of all this, their tiredness forsook them and they gambolled round and round the windmill, uttering cries of triumph. Napoleon himself, attended by his dogs and his cockerel, came down to inspect the completed work; he personally congratulated the animals on their achievement, and announced that the mill would be named Napoleon Mill.

Two days later the animals were called together for a special meeting in the barn. They were struck dumb with surprise when Napoleon announced that he had sold the pile of timber to Frederick. Tomorrow Frederick's wagons would arrive and begin carting it away. Throughout the whole period of his seeming friendship with Pilkington, Napoleon had really been in secret agreement with Frederick.

All relations with Foxwood had been broken off; insulting messages had been sent to Pilkington. The pigeons had been told to avoid Pinchfield Farm and to alter their slogan from "Death to Frederick" to "Death to Pilkington". At the same time Napoleon assured the animals that the stories of an impending attack on Animal Farm were completely untrue, and that the tales about Frederick's cruelty to his own animals had been greatly exaggerated. All these rumours had probably originated with Snowball and his agents. It now appeared that Snowball was not, after all, hiding on Pinchfield Farm, and in fact had never been there in his life: he was living—in considerable luxury, so it was said—at Foxwood, and had in reality been a pensioner of Pilkington for years past.

The pigs were in ecstasies over Napoleon's cunning. By seeming to be friendly with Pilkington he had forced Frederick to raise his price by twelve pounds. But the superior quality of Napoleon's mind, said Squealer, was shown in the fact that he trusted nobody, not even Frederick. Frederick had wanted to pay for the timber with something called a cheque, which, it seemed, was a piece of paper with a promise to pay written upon it. But Napoleon was too clever for him. He had demanded payment in real five-pound notes, which were to be handed over before the timber was removed. Already Frederick had paid up; and the sum he had paid was just enough to buy the machinery for the windmill.

Meanwhile the timber was being carted away at high speed. When it was all gone, another special meeting was held in the barn for the animals to inspect Frederick's banknotes. Smiling beatifically, and wearing both his decorations, Napoleon reposed on a bed of straw on the platform, with the money at his side, neatly piled on a china dish from the farmhouse kitchen. The animals filed slowly past, and each gazed his fill. And Boxer put out his nose to sniff at the banknotes, and the flimsy white things stirred and rustled in his breath.

Three days later there was a terrible hullabaloo. Whymper, his face deadly pale, came racing up the path on his bicycle, flung it down in the yard and rushed straight into the farmhouse. The next moment a choking roar of rage sounded from Napoleon's apartments. The news of what had happened sped round the farm like wildfire. The banknotes were forgeries! Frederick had got the timber for nothing!

Napoleon called the animals together immediately and in a terrible voice pronounced the death sentence upon Frederick. When captured, he said, Frederick should be boiled alive. At the same time he warned them that after this treacherous deed the worst was to be expected. Frederick and his men might make their long-expected attack at any moment. Sentinels were placed at all the approaches to the farm. In addition, four pigeons were sent to Foxwood with a conciliatory message, which it was hoped might re-establish good relations with Pilkington.

The very next morning the attack came. The animals were at breakfast when the look-outs came racing in with the news that Frederick and his followers had already come through the five-barred gate. Boldly enough the animals sallied forth to meet them, but this time they did not have the easy victory that they had had in the Battle of the Cowshed. There were fifteen men, with half a dozen guns between them, and they opened fire as soon as they got within fifty yards. The animals could not face the terrible explosions and the stinging pellets, and in spite of the efforts of Napoleon and Boxer to rally them, they were soon driven back. A number of them were already wounded. They took refuge in the farm buildings and peeped cautiously out from chinks and knot-holes. The whole of the big pasture, including the windmill, was in the hands of the enemy. For the moment even Napoleon seemed at a loss. He paced up and down without a word, his tail rigid and twitching. Wistful glances were sent in the direction of Foxwood. If Pilkington and his men would help them, the day might be won. But at this moment the four pigeons, who had been sent out on the day before, returned, one of them bearing a scrap of paper from Pilkington. On it was pencilled the words: "Serves you right".

Meanwhile Frederick and his men had halted about the windmill. The animals watched them, and a murmur of dismay went round. Two of the men had produced a crowbar and a sledge hammer. They were going to knock the windmill down.

"Impossible!" cried Napoleon. "We have built the walls far too thick for that. They could not knock it down in a week. Courage, comrades!"

But Benjamin was watching the movements of the men intently. The two with the hammer and the crowbar were drilling a hole near the base of the windmill. Slowly, and with an air almost of amusement, Benjamin nodded his long muzzle.

"I thought so," he said. "Do you not see what they are doing? In another moment they are going to pack blasting powder into that hole."

Terrified, the animals waited. It was impossible now to venture out of the shelter of the buildings. After a few minutes the men were seen to be running in all directions. Then there was a deafening roar. The pigeons swirled into the air, and all the animals, except Napoleon, flung themselves flat on their bellies and hid their faces. When they got up again, a huge cloud of black smoke was hanging where the windmill had been. Slowly the breeze drifted it away. The windmill had ceased to exist!

At this sight the animals' courage returned to them. The fear and despair they had felt a moment earlier were drowned in their rage against this vile, contemptible act. A mighty cry for vengeance went up, and without waiting for further orders they charged forth in a body and made straight for the enemy. This time they did not heed the cruel pellets that swept over them like hail. It was a savage, bitter battle. The men fired again and again, and, when the animals got to close quarters, lashed out with their sticks and their heavy boots. A cow, three sheep, and two geese were killed, and nearly everyone was wounded. Even Napoleon, who was directing operations from the rear, had the tip of his tail chipped by a pellet. But the men did not go unscathed either. Three of them had their heads broken by blows from Boxer's hoofs; another was gored in the belly by a cow's horn; another had his trousers nearly torn off by Jessie and Bluebell. And when the nine dogs of

Napoleon's own bodyguard, whom he had instructed to make a detour under cover of the hedge, suddenly appeared on the men's flank, baying ferociously, panic overtook them. They saw that they were in danger of being surrounded. Frederick shouted to his men to get out while the going was good, and the next moment the cowardly enemy was running for dear life. The animals chased them right down to the bottom of the field, and got in some last kicks at them as they forced their way through the thorn hedge.

They had won, but they were weary and bleeding. Slowly they began to limp back towards the farm. The sight of their dead comrades stretched upon the grass moved some of them to tears. And for a little while they halted in sorrowful silence at the place where the windmill had once stood. Yes, it was gone; almost the last trace of their labour was gone! Even the foundations were partially destroyed. And in rebuilding it they could not this time, as before, make use of the fallen stones. This time the stones had vanished too. The force of the explosion had flung them to distances of hundreds of yards. It was as though the windmill had never been.

As they approached the farm Squealer, who had unaccountably been absent during the fighting, came skipping towards them, whisking his tail and beaming with satisfaction. And the animals heard, from the direction of the farm buildings, the solemn booming of a gun.

"What is that gun firing for?" said Boxer.

"To celebrate our victory!" cried Squealer.

"What victory?" said Boxer. His knees were bleeding, he had lost a shoe and split his hoof, and a dozen pellets had lodged themselves in his hind leg.

"What victory, comrade? Have we not driven the enemy off our soil—the sacred soil of Animal Farm?"

"But they have destroyed the windmill. And we had worked on it for two years!"

"What matter? We will build another windmill. We will build six windmills if we feel like it. You do not appreciate, comrade, the mighty thing that we have done. The enemy was in occupation of this very ground that we stand upon. And now— thanks to the leadership of Comrade Napoleon— we have won every inch of it back again?"

"Then we have won back what we had before," said Boxer.

"That is our victory," said Squealer.

They limped into the yard. The pellets under the skin of Boxer's leg smarted painfully. He saw ahead of him the heavy labour of rebuilding the windmill from the foundations, and already in imagination he braced himself for the task. But for the first time it occurred to him that he was eleven years old and that perhaps his great muscles were not quite what they had once been.

But when the animals saw the green flag flying, and heard the gun firing again—seven times it was fired in all—and heard the speech that Napoleon made, congratulating them on their conduct, it did seem to them after all that they had won a great victory. The animals slain in the battle were given a solemn funeral. Boxer and Clover pulled the wagon which served as a hearse, and Napoleon himself walked at the head of the procession. Two whole days were given over to celebrations. There were songs, speeches, and more firing of the gun, and a special gift of an apple was bestowed on every animal, with two ounces of corn for each bird and three biscuits for each dog. It was announced that the battle would be called the Battle of the Windmill, and that Napoleon had created a new decoration, the Order of the Green Banner, which he had conferred upon himself. In the general rejoicings the unfortunate affair of the banknotes was forgotten.

It was a few days later than this that the pigs came upon a case of whisky in the cellars of the farmhouse. It had been overlooked at the time when the house was first occupied. That night there came from the farmhouse the sound of loud singing, in which, to everyone's surprise, the strains of "Beasts of England" were mixed up. At about half-past nine Napoleon, wearing an old bowler hat of Mr. Jones's, was distinctly seen to emerge from the back door, gallop rapidly round the yard, and disappear indoors again. But in the morning a deep silence hung over the farmhouse. Not a pig appeared to be stirring. It was nearly nine o'clock when Squealer made his appearance, walking slowly and dejectedly, his eyes dull, his tail hanging limply behind him, and with every appearance of being seriously ill. He called the animals together and told them that he had a terrible piece of news to impart. Comrade Napoleon was dying!

A cry of lamentation went up. Straw was laid down outside the doors of the farmhouse, and the animals walked on tiptoe. With tears in their eyes they asked one another what they should do if their Leader were taken away from them. A rumour went round that Snowball had after all contrived to introduce poison into Napoleon's food. At eleven o'clock Squealer came out to make another announcement. As his last act upon earth, Comrade Napoleon had pronounced a solemn decree: the drinking of alcohol was to be punished by death.

By the evening, however, Napoleon appeared to be somewhat better, and the following morning Squealer was able to tell them that he was well on the way to recovery. By the evening of that day Napoleon was back at work, and on the next day it was learned that he had instructed Whymper to purchase in Willingdon some booklets on brewing and distilling. A week later Napoleon gave orders that the small paddock beyond the orchard, which it had previously been intended to set aside as a grazing-ground for animals who were past work, was to be ploughed up. It was given out that the pasture was exhausted and needed reseeding; but it soon became know that Napoleon intended to sow it with barley.

About this time there occurred a strange incident which hardly anyone was able to understand. One night at about twelve o'clock there was a loud crash in the yard, and the animals rushed out of their stalls. It was a moonlit night. At the foot of the end wall of the big barn, where the Seven Commandments were written, there lay a ladder broken in two pieces. Squealer, temporarily stunned, was sprawling beside it, and near at hand there lay a lantern, a paint-brush, and an overturned pot of white paint. The dogs immediately made a ring round Squealer, and escorted him back to the farmhouse as soon as he was able to walk. None of the animals could form any idea as to what this meant, except old Benjamin, who nodded his muzzle with a knowing air, and seemed to understand, but would say nothing.

But a few days later Muriel, reading over the Seven Commandments to herself, noticed that there was yet another of them which the animals had remembered wrong. They had thought that the Fifth Commandment was "No animal shall drink alcohol", but there were two words that they had forgotten. Actually the Commandment read: "No animal shall drink alcohol *to excess*".

9

BOXER'S split hoof was a long time in healing. They had started the rebuilding of the windmill the day after the victory celebrations were ended. Boxer refused to take even a day off work, and made it a point of honour not to let it be seen that he was in pain. In the evenings, he would admit privately to Clover that the hoof troubled him a great deal. Clover treated the hoof with poultices of herbs which she prepared by chewing them, and both she and Benjamin urged Boxer to work less hard. "A horse's lungs do not last for ever," she said to him. But Boxer would not listen. He had, he said, only one real ambition left—to see the windmill well under way before he reached the age for retirement.

At the beginning, when the laws of Animal Farm were first formulated, the retiring age had been fixed for horses and pigs at twelve, for cows at fourteen, for dogs at nine, for sheep at seven, and for hens and geese at five. Liberal old-age pensions had been agreed upon. As yet no animal had actually retired on pension, but of late the subject had been discussed more and more. Now that the small field beyond the orchard had been set aside for barley, it was rumoured that a corner of the large pasture was to be fenced off and turned into a grazing-ground for superannuated animals. For a horse, it was said, the pension would be five pounds of corn a day and, in winter, fifteen pounds of hay, with a carrot or possibly an apple on public holidays. Boxer's twelfth birthday was due in the late summer of the following year.

Meanwhile life was hard. The winter was as cold as the last one had been, and food was even shorter. Once again all rations were reduced, except those of the pigs and the dogs. A too rigid equality in rations, Squealer explained, would have been contrary to the principles of Animalism. In any case he had no difficulty in proving to the other animals that they were *not* in reality short of food, whatever the appearances might be. For the time being, certainly, it had been found necessary to make a readjustment of rations (Squealer always spoke of it as a "readjustment", never as a "reduction"), but in comparison with the days of Jones, the improvement was enormous. Reading out the figures in a shrill, rapid voice, he proved to them in detail that they had more oats, more hay, more turnips than they had had in Jones's day, that they worked shorter hours, that their drinking water was of better quality, that they lived longer, that a larger proportion of their young ones survived infancy, and that they had more straw in their stalls and suffered less from fleas. The animals believed every word of it. Truth to tell, Jones and all he stood for had almost faded out of their memories. They knew that life nowadays was harsh and bare, that they were often hungry and often cold, and that they were usually working when they were not asleep. But doubtless it had been worse in the old days. They were glad to believe so. Besides, in those days they had been slaves and now they were free, and that made all the difference, as Squealer did not fail to point out.

There were many more mouths to feed now. In the autumn the four sows had all littered about simultaneously, producing thirty-one young pigs between them. The young pigs were piebald, and as Napoleon was the only boar on the farm, it was possible to guess at their parentage. It was announced that later, when bricks and timber had been purchased, a schoolroom would be built in the farmhouse garden. For the time being, the young pigs were given their instruction by Napoleon himself in the farmhouse kitchen. They took their exercise in the garden, and were discouraged from playing with the other young animals. About this time, too, it was laid down as a rule that when a pig and any other animal met on the path, the other animal must stand aside: and also that all pigs, of whatever degree, were to have the privilege of wearing green ribbons on their tails on Sundays.

The farm had had a fairly successful year, but

was still short of money. There were the bricks, sand, and lime for the schoolroom to be purchased, and it would also be necessary to begin saving up again for the machinery for the windmill. Then there were lamp oil and candles for the house, sugar for Napoleon's own table (he forbade this to the other pigs, on the ground that it made them fat), and all the usual replacements such as tools, nails, string, coal, wire, scrap-iron, and dog biscuits. A stump of hay and part of the potato crop were sold off, and the contract for eggs was increased to six hundred a week, so that that year the hens barely hatched enough chicks to keep their numbers at the same level. Rations, reduced in December, were reduced again in February, and lanterns in the stalls were forbidden, to save oil. But the pigs seemed comfortable enough, and in fact were putting on weight if anything. One afternoon in late February a warm, rich, appetising scent, such as the animals had never smelt before, wafted itself across the yard from the little brew-house, which had been disused in Jones's time, and which stood beyond the kitchen. Someone said it was the smell of cooking barley. The animals sniffed the air hungrily and wondered whether a warm mash was being prepared for their supper. But no warm mash appeared, and on the following Sunday it was announced that from now onwards all barley would be reserved for the pigs. The field beyond the orchard had already been sown with barley. And the news soon leaked out that every pig was now receiving a ration of a pint of beer daily, with half a gallon for Napoleon himself, which was always served to him in the Crown Derby soup tureen.

But if there were hardships to be borne, they were partly offset by the fact that life nowadays had a greater dignity than it had had before. There were more songs, more speeches, more processions. Napoleon had commanded that once a week there should be held something called a Spontaneous Demonstration, the object of which was to celebrate the struggles and triumphs of Animal Farm. At the appointed time the animals would leave their work and march round the precincts of the farm in military formation, with the pigs leading, then the horses, then the cows, then the sheep, and then the poultry. The dogs flanked the procession and at the head of all marched Napoleon's black cockerel. Boxer and Clover always carried between them a green banner marked with the hoof and the horn and the caption, "Long live Comrade Napoleon!" Afterwards there were recitations of poems composed in Napoleon's honour, and a speech by Squealer giving particulars of the latest increases in the production of foodstuffs, and on occasion a shot was fired from the gun. The sheep were the greatest devotees of the Spontaneous Demonstration, and if anyone complained (as a few animals sometimes did, when no pigs or dogs were near) that they wasted time and meant a lot of standing about in the cold, the sheep were sure to silence him with a tremendous bleating of "Four legs good, two legs bad!" But by and large the animals enjoyed these celebrations. They found it comforting to be reminded that, after all, they were truly their own masters and that the work they did was for their own benefit. So that, what with the songs, the processions, Squealer's lists of figures, the thunder of the gun, the crowing of the cockerel, and the fluttering of the flag, they were able to forget that their bellies were empty, at least part of the time.

In April, Animal Farm was proclaimed a Republic, and it became necessary to elect a President. There was only one candidate, Napoleon, who was elected unanimously. On the same day it was given out that fresh documents had been discovered which revealed further details about Snowball's complicity with Jones. It now appeared that Snowball had not, as the animals had previously imagined, merely attempted to lose the Battle of the Cowshed by means of a stratagem, but had been openly fighting on Jones's side. In fact, it was he who had actually been the leader of the human forces, and had charged into battle with the words "Long live Humanity!" on his lips. The wounds on Snowball's back, which a few of the animals still remembered to have seen, had been inflicted by Napoleon's teeth.

In the middle of the summer Moses the raven suddenly reappeared on the farm, after an absence of several years. He was quite unchanged, still did no work, and talked in the same strain as ever about Sugarcandy Mountain. He would perch on a stump, flap his black wings, and talk by the hour to anyone who would listen. "Up there, comrades," he would say solemnly, pointing to the sky with his large beak—"up there, just on the other side of that dark cloud that you can see—there it lies, Sugarcandy Mountain, that happy country where we poor animals shall rest for ever from our labours!" He even claimed to have been there on one of his higher flights, and to have seen the everlasting fields of clover and the linseed cake and lump sugar growing on the hedges. Many of the animals believed him. Their lives now, they reasoned, were hungry and laborious; was it not right and just that a better world should exist somewhere else? A thing that was difficult to determine was the attitude of the pigs towards Moses. They all declared contemptuously that his stories about Sugarcandy Mountain were lies, and yet they allowed him to remain on the farm, not working, with an allowance of a gill of beer a day.

After his hoof had healed up, Boxer worked harder than ever. Indeed, all the animals worked like slaves that year. Apart from the regular work of the farm, and the rebuilding of the windmill, there was the schoolhouse for the young pigs, which was started in March. Sometimes the long hours on insufficient food were hard to bear, but Boxer never faltered. In nothing that he said or did was there any sign that his strength was not what it had been. It was only his appearance that was a little altered; his hide was less shiny than it had used to be, and his great haunches seemed to have shrunken. The others said, "Boxer will pick up when the spring grass comes on"; but the spring came and Boxer grew no fatter. Sometimes on the slope leading to the top of the quarry, when he braced his muscles against the weight of some vast boulder, it seemed that nothing kept him on his feet except the will to continue. At such times his lips were seen to form the words, "I will work harder"; he had no voice left. Once again Clover and Benjamin warned him to take care of his health, but Boxer paid no attention. His twelfth birthday was approaching. He did not care what happened so long as a good store of stone was accumulated before he went on pension.

Late one evening in the summer, a sudden rumour ran round the farm that something had happened to Boxer. He had gone out alone to drag a load of stone down to the windmill. And sure enough, the rumour was true. A few minutes later two pigeons came racing in with the news: "Boxer has fallen! He is lying on his side and can't get up!"

About half the animals on the farm rushed to the knoll where the windmill stood. There lay Boxer, between the shafts of the cart, his neck stretched out, unable even to raise his head. His eyes were glazed, his sides matted with sweat. A thin stream of blood had trickled out of his mouth. Clover dropped to her knees at his side.

"Boxer!" she cried, "how are you?"

"It is my lung," said Boxer in a weak voice. "It does not matter. I think you will be able to finish the windmill without me. There is a pretty good store of stone accumulated. I had only another month to go in any case. To tell you the truth, I had been looking forward to my retirement. And perhaps, as Benjamin is growing old too, they will let him retire at the same time and be a companion to me."

"We must get help at once," said Clover. "Run, somebody, and tell Squealer what has happened."

All the other animals immediately raced back to the farmhouse to give Squealer the news. Only Clover remained, and Benjamin, who lay down at Boxer's side, and, without speaking, kept the flies off him with his long tail. After about a quarter of an hour Squealer appeared, full of sympathy and concern. He said that Comrade Napoleon had learned with the very deepest distress of this misfortune to one of the most loyal workers on the farm, and was already making arrangements to send Boxer to be treated in the hospital at Willingdon. The animals felt a little uneasy at this. Except for Mollie and Snowball, no other animal had ever left the farm, and they did not like to think of their sick comrade in the hands of human beings. However, Squealer easily convinced them that the veterinary surgeon in Willingdon could treat Boxer's case more satisfactorily than could be done on the farm. And about half an hour later, when Boxer had somewhat recovered, he was with difficulty got on to his feet, and managed to limp back to his stall, where Clover and Benjamin had prepared a good bed of straw for him.

For the next two days Boxer remained in his stall. The pigs had sent out a large bottle of pink medicine which they had found in the medicine chest in the bathroom, and Clover administered it to Boxer twice a day after meals. In the evenings she lay in his stall and talked to him, while Benjamin kept the flies off him. Boxer professed not to be sorry for what had happened. If he made a good recovery, he might expect to live another three years, and he looked forward to the peaceful days that he would spend in the corner of the big pasture. It would be the first time that he had leisure to study and improve his mind. He intended, he said, to devote the rest of his life to learning the remaining twenty-two letters of the alphabet.

However, Benjamin and Clover could only be with Boxer after working hours, and it was in the middle of the day when the van came to take him away. The animals were all at work weeding turnips under the supervision of a pig, when they were astonished to see Benjamin come galloping from the direction of the farm buildings, braying at the top of his voice. It was the first time that they had ever seen Benjamin excited—indeed, it was the first time that anyone had seen him gallop. "Quick, quick!" he shouted. "Come at once!

They're taking Boxer away!" Without waiting for orders from the pig, the animals broke off work and raced back to the farm buildings. Sure enough, there in the yard was a large closed van, drawn by two horses, with lettering on its side and a sly-looking man in a low-crowned bowler hat sitting on the driver's seat. And Boxer's stall was empty.

The animals crowded round the van. "Good-bye, Boxer!" they chorused, "good-bye!"

"Fools! Fools!" shouted Benjamin, prancing round them and stamping the earth with his small hoofs. "Fools! Do you not see what is written on the side of that van?"

That gave the animals pause and there was a hush. Muriel began to spell out the words. But Benjamin pushed her aside and in the midst of a deadly silence he read:

"'Alfred Simmonds, Horse Slaughterer and Glue Boiler, Willingdon. Dealer in Hides and Bone-Meal. Kennels Supplied.' Do you not understand what that means? They are taking Boxer to the knacker's!"

A cry of horror burst from all the animals. At this moment the man on the box whipped up his horses and the van moved out of the yard at a smart trot. All the animals followed, crying out at the tops of their voices. Clover forced her way to the front. The van began to gather speed. Clover tried to stir her stout limbs to a gallop, and achieved a canter. "Boxer!" she cried. "Boxer! Boxer!

Boxer!" And just at this moment, as though he had heard the uproar outside, Boxer's face, with the white stripe down his nose, appeared at the small window at the back of the van.

"Boxer!" cried Clover in a terrible voice. "Boxer! Get out! Get out quickly! They are taking you to your death!"

All the animals took up the cry of "Get out, Boxer, get out!" But the van was already gathering speed and drawing away from them. It was uncertain whether Boxer had understood what Clover had said. But a moment later his face disappeared from the window and there was the sound of a tremendous drumming of hoofs inside the van. He was trying to kick his way out. The time had been when a few kicks from Boxer's hoofs would have smashed the van to matchwood. But alas! his strength had left him; and in a few moments the sound of drumming hoofs grew fainter and died away. In desperation the animals began appealing to the two horses which drew the van to stop. "Comrades, comrades!" they shouted. "Don't take your own brother to his death!" But the stupid brutes, too ignorant to realise what was happening, merely set back their ears and quickened their pace. Boxer's face did not reappear at the window. Too late, someone thought of racing ahead and shutting the five-barred gate; but in another moment the van was through it and rapidly disappearing down the road. Boxer was never seen again.

Three days later it was announced that he had

died in the hospital at Willingdon, in spite of receiving every attention a horse could have. Squealer came to announce the news to the others. He had, he said, been present during Boxer's last hours.

"It was the most affecting sight I have ever seen!" said Squealer, lifting his trotter and wiping away a tear. "I was at his bedside at the very last. And at the end, almost too weak to speak, he whispered in my ear that his sole sorrow was to have passed on before the windmill was finished. 'Forward, comrades!' he whispered. 'Forward in the name of the Rebellion. Long live Animal Farm! Long live Comrade Napoleon! Napoleon is always right.' Those were his very last words, comrades."

Here Squealer's demeanour suddenly changed. He fell silent for a moment, and his little eyes darted suspicious glances from side to side before he proceeded.

It had come to his knowledge, he said, that a foolish and wicked rumour had been circulated at the time of Boxer's removal. Some of the animals had noticed that the van which took Boxer away was marked "Horse Slaughterer", and had actually jumped to the conclusion that Boxer was being sent to the knacker's. It was almost unbelievable, said Squealer, that any animal could be so stupid. Surely, he cried indignantly, whisking his tail and skipping from side to side, surely they knew their beloved Leader, Comrade Napoleon, better than that? But the explanation was really very simple. The van had previously been the property of the knacker, and had been bought by the veterinary surgeon, who had not yet painted the old name out. That was how the mistake had arisen.

The animals were enormously relieved to hear this. And when Squealer went on to give further graphic details of Boxer's death-bed, the admirable care he had received, and the expensive medicines for which Napoleon had paid without a thought as to the cost, their last doubts disappeared and the sorrow that they felt for their comrade's death was tempered by the thought that at least he had died happy.

Napoleon himself appeared at the meeting on the following Sunday morning and pronounced a short oration in Boxer's honour. It had not been possible, he said, to bring back their lamented comrade's remains for interment on the farm, but he had ordered a large wreath to be made from the laurels in the farmhouse garden and sent down to be placed on Boxer's grave. And in a few days' time the pigs intended to hold a memorial banquet in Boxer's honour. Napoleon ended his speech with a reminder of Boxer's two favourite maxims, "I will work harder" and "Comrade Napoleon is always right"—maxims, he said, which every animal would do well to adopt as his own.

On the day appointed for the banquet, a grocer's van drove up from Willingdon and delivered a large wooden crate at the farmhouse. That night there was the sound of uproarious singing, which was followed by what sounded like a violent quarrel and ended at about eleven o'clock with a tremendous crash of glass. No one stirred in the farmhouse before noon on the following day, and the word went round that from somewhere or other the pigs had acquired the money to buy themselves another case of whisky.

10

YEARS passed. The seasons came and went, the short animal lives fled by. A time came when there was no one who remembered the old days before the Rebellion, except Clover, Benjamin, Moses the raven, and a number of the pigs.

Muriel was dead; Bluebell, Jessie, and Pincher were dead. Jones too was dead—he had died in an inebriates' home in another part of the county. Snowball was forgotten. Boxer was forgotten, except by the few who had known him. Clover was an old stout mare now, stiff in the joints and with a tendency to rheumy eyes. She was two years past the retiring age, but in fact no animal had ever actually retired. The talk of setting aside a corner of the pasture for superannuated animals had long since been dropped. Napoleon was now a mature boar of twenty-four stone. Squealer was so fat that he could with difficulty see out of his eyes. Only old Benjamin was much the same as ever, except for being a little greyer about the muzzle, and, since Boxer's death, more morose and taciturn than ever.

There were many more creatures on the farm now, though the increase was not so great as had been expected in earlier years. Many animals had been born to whom the Rebellion was only a dim tradition, passed on by word of mouth, and others had been bought who had never heard mention of such a thing before their arrival. The farm possessed three horses now besides Clover. They were fine upstanding beasts, willing workers and good comrades, but very stupid. None of them proved able to learn the alphabet beyond the letter B. They accepted everything that they were told about the Rebellion and the principles of Animalism, especially from Clover, for whom they had an almost filial respect; but it was doubtful whether they understood very much of it.

The farm was more prosperous now, and better organised; it had even been enlarged by two fields which had been bought from Mr. Pilkington. The windmill had been successfully completed at last, and the farm possessed a threshing machine and a hay elevator of its own, and various new buildings had been added to it. Whymper had bought himself a dogcart. The windmill, however, had not after all been used for generating electrical power. It was used for milling corn, and brought in a handsome money profit. The animals were hard at work building yet another windmill; when that one was finished, so it was said, the dynamos would be installed. But the luxuries of which Snowball had once taught the animals to dream, the stalls with electric light and hot and cold water, and the three-day week, were no longer talked about. Napoleon had denounced such ideas as contrary to the spirit of Animalism. The truest happiness, he said, lay in working hard and living frugally.

Somehow it seemed as though the farm had grown richer without making the animals themselves any richer—except, of course, for the pigs and the dogs. Perhaps this was partly because there were so many pigs and so many dogs. It was not that these creatures did not work, after their fashion. There was, as Squealer was never tired of explaining, endless work in the supervision and organisation of the farm. Much of this work was of a kind that the other animals were too ignorant to understand. For example, Squealer told them that the pigs had to expend enormous labours every day upon mysterious things called "files", "reports", "minutes", and "memoranda". These were large sheets of paper which had to be closely covered with writing, and as soon as they were so covered, they were burnt in the furnace. This was of the highest importance for the welfare of the farm, Squealer said. But still, neither pigs nor dogs produced any food by their own labour; and there were very many of them, and their appetites were always good.

As for the others, their life, so far as they knew, was as it had always been. They were generally hungry, they slept on straw, they drank from the pool, they laboured in the fields; in winter they were troubled by the cold, and in summer by the flies. Sometimes the older ones among them racked their dim memories and tried to determine whether in the early days of the Rebellion, when Jones's expulsion was still recent, things had been better or worse than now. They could not remember. There was nothing with which they could compare their present lives: they had nothing to go upon except Squealer's lists of figures, which invariably demonstrated that everything was getting better and better. The animals found the problem insoluble; in any case, they had little time for speculating on such things now. Only old Benjamin professed to remember every detail of his long life and to know that things never had been, nor ever could be much better or much worse—hunger, hardship, and disappointment being, so he said, the unalterable law of life.

And yet the animals never gave up hope. More, they never lost, even for an instant, their sense of honour and privilege in being members of Animal Farm. They were still the only farm in the whole county—in all England!—owned and operated by animals. Not one of them, not even the youngest, not even the newcomers who had been brought from farms ten or twenty miles away, ever ceased to marvel at that. And when they heard the gun booming and saw the green flag fluttering at the masthead, their hearts swelled with imperishable pride, and the talk turned always towards the old heroic days, the expulsion of Jones, the writing of the Seven Commandments, the great battles in which the human invaders had been defeated. None of the old dreams had been abandoned. The Republic of the Animals which Major had foretold, when the green fields of England should be untrodden by human feet, was still believed in. Some day it was coming: it might not be soon, it might not be within the lifetime of any animal now living, but still it was coming. Even the tune of "Beasts of England" was perhaps hummed secretly here and there: at any rate, it was a fact that every animal on the farm knew it, though no one would have dared to sing it aloud. It might be that their lives were hard and that not all of their hopes had been fulfilled; but they were conscious that they were not as other animals. If they went hungry, it was not from feeding tyrannical human beings; if they worked hard, at least they worked for themselves. No creature among them went upon two legs. No creature called any other creature "Master". All animals were equal.

One day in early summer Squealer ordered the sheep to follow him, and led them out to a piece of waste ground at the other end of the farm, which had become overgrown with birch saplings. The sheep spent the whole day there browsing at the leaves under Squealer's supervision. In the evening he returned to the farmhouse himself, but, as it was warm weather, told the sheep to stay where they were. It ended by their remaining there for a whole week, during which time the other animals saw nothing of them. Squealer was with them for the greater part of every day. He was, he said, teaching them to sing a new song, for which privacy was needed.

It was just after the sheep had returned, on a pleasant evening when the animals had finished work and were making their way back to the farm buildings, that the terrified neighing of a horse sounded from the yard. Startled, the animals stopped in their tracks. It was Clover's voice. She neighed again, and all the animals broke into a gallop and rushed into the yard. Then they saw what Clover had seen.

It was a pig walking on his hind legs.

Yes, it was Squealer. A little awkwardly, as though not quite used to supporting his considerable bulk in that position, but with perfect balance, he was strolling across the yard. And, a moment later, out from the door of the farmhouse came a long file of pigs, all walking on their hind legs. Some did it better than others, one or two were even a trifle unsteady and looked as though they would have liked the support of a stick, but every one of them made his way right round the yard successfully. And finally there was a tremendous baying of dogs and a shrill crowing from the black cockerel, and out came Napoleon himself, majestically upright, casting haughty glances from side to side, and with his dogs gambolling round him.

He carried a whip in his trotter.

There was a deadly silence. Amazed, terrified, huddling together, the animals watched the long line of pigs march slowly round the yard. It was as though the world had turned upside-down. Then there came a moment when the first shock had worn off and when, in spite of everything—in spite of their terror of the dogs, and of the habit, developed through long years, of never complaining, never criticising, no matter what happened—they might have uttered some word of protest. But just at that moment, as though at a signal, all the sheep burst out into a tremendous bleating of—

"Four legs good, two legs *better*! Four legs good, two legs *better*! Four legs good, two legs *better*!"

It went on five minutes without stopping. And by the time the sheep had quieted down, the chance to utter any protest had passed, for the pigs had marched back into the farmhouse.

Benjamin felt a nose nuzzling at his shoulder. He looked round. It was Clover. Her old eyes looked dimmer than ever. Without saying anything, she tugged gently at his mane and led him round to the end of the big barn, where the Seven Commandments were written. For a minute or two they stood gazing at the tarred wall with its white lettering.

"My sight is failing," she said finally. "Even when I was young I could not have read what was written there. But it appears to me that that wall looks different. Are the Seven Commandments the same as they used to be, Benjamin?"

For once Benjamin consented to break his rule,

and he read out to her what was written on the wall. There was nothing there now except a single Commandment. It ran:

> ALL ANIMALS ARE EQUAL
> BUT SOME ANIMALS ARE MORE EQUAL THAN OTHERS.

After that it did not seem strange when next day the pigs who were supervising the work of the farm all carried whips in their trotters. It did not seem strange to learn that the pigs had bought themselves a wireless set, were arranging to install a telephone, and had taken out subscriptions to *John Bull*, *Tit-Bits*, and the *Daily Mirror*. It did not seem strange when Napoleon was seen strolling in the farmhouse garden with a pipe in his mouth—no, not even when the pigs took Mr. Jones's clothes out of the wardrobes and put them on, Napoleon himself appearing in a black coat, ratcatcher breeches, and leather leggings, while his favourite sow appeared in the watered silk dress which Mrs. Jones had been used to wear on Sundays.

A week later, in the afternoon, a number of dog-carts drove up to the farm. A deputation of neighbouring farmers had been invited to make a tour of inspection. They were shown all over the farm, and expressed great admiration for everything they saw, especially the windmill. The animals were weeding the turnip field. They worked diligently, hardly raising their faces from the ground, and not knowing whether to be more frightened of the pigs or of the human visitors.

That evening loud laughter and bursts of singing came from the farmhouse. And suddenly, at the sound of the mingled voices, the animals were stricken with curiosity. What could be happening in there, now that for the first time animals and human beings were meeting on terms of equality? With one accord they began to creep as quietly as possible into the farmhouse garden.

At the gate they paused, half frightened to go on, but Clover led the way in. They tiptoed up to the house, and such animals as were tall enough peered in at the dining-room window. There, round the long table, sat half a dozen farmers and half a dozen of the more eminent pigs, Napoleon himself occupying the seat of honour at the head of the table. The pigs appeared completely at ease in their chairs. The company had been enjoying a game of cards, but had broken off for the moment, evidently in order to drink a toast. A large jug was circulating, and the mugs were being refilled with beer. No one noticed the wondering faces of the animals that gazed in at the window.

Mr. Pilkington, of Foxwood, had stood up, his mug in his hand. In a moment, he said, he would ask the present company to drink a toast. But before doing so, there were a few words that he felt it incumbent upon him to say.

It was a source of great satisfaction to him, he said—and, he was sure, to all others present—to feel that a long period of mistrust and misunderstanding had now come to an end. There had been a time—not that he, or any of the present company, had shared such sentiments—but there had been a time when the respected proprietors of Animal Farm had been regarded, he would not say with hostility, but perhaps with a certain measure of misgiving, by their human neighbours. Unfortunate incidents had occurred, mistaken ideas had been current. It had been felt that the existence of a farm owned and operated by pigs was somehow abnormal and was liable to have an unsettling effect in the neighbourhood. Too many farmers had assumed, without due enquiry, that on such a farm a spirit of licence and indiscipline would prevail. They had been nervous about the effects upon their own animals, or even upon their human employees. But all such doubts were now dispelled. Today he and his friends had visited Animal Farm and inspected every inch of it with their own eyes, and what did they find? Not only the most up-to-date methods, but a discipline and an orderliness which should be an example to all farmers everywhere. He believed that he was right in saying that the lower animals on Animal Farm did more work and received less food than any animals in the county. Indeed, he and his fellow-visitors today had observed many features which they intended to introduce on their own farms immediately.

He would end his remarks, he said, by emphasising once again the friendly feelings that subsisted, and ought to subsist, between Animal Farm and its neighbours. Between pigs and human beings there was not, and there need not be, any clash of interests whatever. Their struggles and their difficulties were one. Was not the labour problem the same everywhere? Here it became apparent that Mr. Pilkington was about to spring some carefully prepared witticism on the company, but for a moment he was too overcome by amusement to be able to utter it. After much choking, during which his various chins turned purple, he managed to get it out: "If you have your lower animals to contend with," he said, "we have our lower classes!" This *bon mot* set the table in a roar; and Mr. Pilkington once again congratulated the pigs on the low rations, the long working hours, and the general absence of pampering which he had observed on Animal Farm.

And now, he said finally, he would ask the company to rise to their feet and make certain that their glasses were full. "Gentlemen," concluded Mr. Pilkington, "gentlemen, I give you a toast: To the prosperity of Animal Farm!"

There was enthusiastic cheering and stamping of feet. Napoleon was so gratified that he left his place and came round the table to clink his mug against Mr. Pilkington's before emptying it. When the cheering had died down, Napoleon, who had remained on his feet, intimated that he too had a few words to say.

Like all of Napoleon's speeches, it was short and to the point. He too, he said, was happy that the period of misunderstanding was at an end. For a long time there had been rumours—circulated, he had reason to think, by some malignant enemy—that there was something subversive and even revolutionary in the outlook of himself and his colleagues. They had been credited with attempting to stir up rebellion among the animals on neighbouring farms. Nothing could be further from the truth! Their sole wish, now and in the past, was to live at peace and in normal business relations with their neighbours. This farm which he had the honour to control, he added, was a co-operative enterprise. The title-deeds, which were in his own possession, were owned by the pigs jointly.

He did not believe, he said, that any of the old suspicions still lingered, but certain changes had been made recently in the routine of the farm which should have the effect of promoting confidence still further. Hitherto the animals on the farm had had a rather foolish custom of addressing one another as "Comrade". This was to be suppressed. There had also been a very strange custom, whose origin was unknown, of marching every Sunday morning past a boar's skull which was nailed to a post in the garden. This, too, would be suppressed, and the skull had already been buried. His visitors might have observed, too, the green flag which flew from the masthead. If so, they would perhaps have noted that the white hoof and horn with which it had previously been marked had now been removed. It would be a plain green flag from now onwards.

He had only one critcism, he said, to make of Mr. Pilkington's excellent and neighbourly speech. Mr. Pilkington had referred throughout to "Animal Farm". He could not of course know—for he, Napoleon, was only now for the first time announcing it—that the name "Animal Farm" had been abolished. Henceforward the farm was to be known as "The Manor Farm"—which, he believed, was its correct and original name.

"Gentlemen," concluded Napoleon, "I will give you the same toast as before, but in a different form. Fill your glasses to the brim. Gentlemen, here is my toast: To the prosperity of the Manor Farm!"

There was the same hearty cheering as before, and the mugs were emptied to the dregs. But as the animals outside gazed at the scene, it seemed to them that some strange thing was happening. What was it that had altered in the faces of the pigs? Clover's old dim eyes flitted from one face to another. Some of them had five chins, some had four, some had three. But what was it that seemed to be melting and changing? Then, the applause having come to an end, the company took up their cards and continued the game that had been interrupted, and the animals crept silently away.

But they had not gone twenty yards when they

stopped short. An uproar of voices was coming from the farmhouse. They rushed back and looked through the window again. Yes, a violent quarrel was in progress. There were shoutings, bangings on the table, sharp suspicious glances, furious denials. The source of the trouble appeared to be that Napoleon and Mr. Pilkington had each played an ace of spades simultaneously.

Twelve voices were shouting in anger, and they were all alike. No question, now, what had happened to the faces of the pigs. The creatures outside looked from pig to man, and from man to pig, and from pig to man again; but already it was impossible to say which was which.

November 1943—February 1944.

THE END

PAY ANY PRICE
by Ted Allbeury
After the Kennedy killings the heat was on—on the Mafia, the KGB, the Cubans, and the FBI. . .

MY SWEET AUDRINA
by Virginia Andrews
She wanted to be loved as much as the first Audrina, the sister who was perfect and beautiful—and dead.

PRIDE AND PREJUDICE
by Jane Austen
Mr. Bennet's five eligible daughters will never inherit their father's money. The family fortunes are destined to pass to a cousin. Should one of the daughters marry him?

CHINESE ALICE
by Pat Barr
The story of Alice Greenwood gives a complete picture of late 19th century China.

UNCUT JADE
by Pat Barr
In this sequel to CHINESE ALICE, Alice Greenwood finds herself widowed and alone in a turbulent China.

THE GRAND BABYLON HOTEL
by Arnold Bennett
A romantic thriller set in an exclusive London Hotel at the turn of the century.

A HERITAGE OF SHADOWS
by Madeleine Brent
This romantic novel, set in the 1890's, follows the fortunes of eighteen-year-old Hannah McLeod.

BARRINGTON'S WOMEN
by Steven Cade
In order to prevent Norway's gold reserves falling into German hands in 1940, Charles Barrington was forced to hide them in Borgas, a remote mountain village.

THE PLAGUE
by Albert Camus
The plague in question afflicted Oran in the 1940's.

THE RIDDLE OF THE SANDS
by Erskine Childers
First published in 1903 this thriller, deals with the discovery of a threatened invasion of England by a Continental power.

WHERE ARE THE CHILDREN?
by Mary Higgins Clark
A novel of suspense set in peaceful Cape Cod.

KING RAT
by James Clavell
Set in Changi, the most notorious Japanese POW camp in Asia.

THE BLACK VELVET GOWN
by Catherine Cookson
There would be times when Riah Millican would regret that her late miner husband had learned to read and then shared his knowledge with his family.

THE WHIP
by Catherine Cookson
Emma Molinero's dying father, a circus performer, sends her to live with an unknown English grandmother on a farm in Victorian Durham and to a life of misery.

SHANNON'S WAY
by A. J. Cronin
Robert Shannon, a devoted scientist had no time for anything outside his laboratory. But Jean Law had other plans for him.

THE JADE ALLIANCE
by Elizabeth Darrell

The story opens in 1905 in St. Petersburg with the Brusilov family swept up in the chaos of revolution.

BERLIN GAME
by Len Deighton

Bernard Samson had been behind a desk in Whitehall for five years when his bosses decided that he was the right man to slip into East Berlin.

HARD TIMES
by Charles Dickens

Conveys with realism the repulsive aspect of a Lancashire manufacturing town during the 1850s.

THE RICE DRAGON
by Emma Drummond

The story of Rupert Torrington and his bride Harriet, against a background of Hong Kong and Canton during the 1850s.

THE GLASS BLOWERS
by Daphne Du Maurier

A novel about the author's forebears, the Bussons, which gives an unusual glimpse of the events that led up to the French Revolution, and of the Revolution itself.

THE DOGS OF WAR
by Frederic Forsyth
The discovery of the existence of a mountain of platinum in a remote African republic causes Sir James Manson to hire an army of trained mercenaries to topple the government of Zangaro.

THE DAYS OF WINTER
by Cynthia Freeman
The story of a family caught between two world wars—a saga of pride and regret, of tears and joy.

REGENESIS
by Alexander Fullerton
It's 1990. The crew of the US submarine ARKANSAS appear to be the only survivors of a nuclear holocaust.

THE TORCHBEARERS
by Alexander Fullerton
1942: Captain Nicholas Everard has to escort a big, slow convoy . . . a sacrificial convoy. . .

DAUGHTER OF THE HOUSE
by Catherine Gaskin
An account of the destroying impact of love which is set among the tidal creeks and scattered cottages of the Essex Marshes.

FAMILY AFFAIRS
by Catherine Gaskin
Born in Ireland in the Great Depression, the illegitimate daughter of a servant, Kelly Anderson's birthright was poverty and shame.

THE SUMMER OF THE SPANISH WOMAN
by Catherine Gaskin
Clonmara—the wild, beautiful Irish estate in County Wicklow is a fitting home for the handsome, reckless Blodmore family.

THE TILSIT INHERITANCE
by Catherine Gaskin
Ginny Tilsit had been raised on an island paradise in the Caribbean. She knew nothing of her family's bitter inheritance half the world away.

THE FINAL DIAGNOSIS
by Arthur Hailey
Set in a busy American hospital, the story of a young pathologist and his efforts to restore the standards of a hospital controlled by an ageing, once brilliant doctor.

IN HIGH PLACES
by Arthur Hailey
The theme of this novel is a projected Act of Union between Canada and the United States in order that both should survive the effect of a possible nuclear war.

RED DRAGON
by Thomas Harris
A ritual murderer is on the loose. Only one man can get inside that twisted mind— forensic expert, Will Graham.

CATCH–22
by Joseph Heller
Anti-war novels are legion; this is a war novel that is anti-death, a comic savage tribute to those who aren't interested in dying.

THE SURVIVOR
by James Herbert
David is the only survivor from an accident whose aftermath leaves a lingering sense of evil and menace in the quiet countryside.

LOST HORIZON
by James Hilton
A small plane carrying four passengers crash-lands in the unexplored Tibetan wilderness.

THE TIME OF THE HUNTER'S MOON
by Victoria Holt

When Cordelia Grant accepts an appointment to a girls' school in Devon, she does not anticipate anyone from her past re-emerging in her new life.

THE FOUNDER OF THE HOUSE
by Naomi Jacob

The first volume of a family saga which begins in Vienna, and introduces Emmanuel Gollantz.

"THAT WILD LIE . . ."
by Naomi Jacob

The second volume in the Gollantz saga begun with THE FOUNDER OF THE HOUSE.

IN A FAR COUNTRY
by Adam Kennedy

Christine Wheatley knows she is going to marry Fred Deets, that is until she meets Roy Lavidge.

AUTUMN ALLEY
by Lena Kennedy

Against the background of London's East End from the turn of the Century to the 1830's a saga of three generations of ordinary, yet extraordinary people.

LADY PENELOPE
by Lena Kennedy

Lady Penelope Devereux, forced to make a marriage of convenience, pours all the affection of her generous nature into her children . . . and her lovers.

LIZZIE
by Lena Kennedy

Tiny, warm-hearted but cruelly scarred for life, Lizzie seems to live only for, and through, her burly, wayward husband Bobby.

ACT OF DARKNESS
by Francis King

What happens inside a family when an act of brutal violence suddenly erupts without warning or explanation?

THE LITTLE DRUMMER GIRL
by John Le Carré

The secret pursuit by Israeli intelligence agents of a lethally dangerous and elusive Palestinian terrorist leader.

THE SHAPIRO DIAMOND
by Michael Legat

Set in the late 19th century, the story of a man struggling against fate to prove himself worthy of his family's name.

THE SILVER FOUNTAIN
by Michael Legat
Jean-Paul Fontaine came to London in 1870 with a burning ambition to be the proprietor of an exclusive restaurant.

THE CRUEL SEA
by Nicholas Monsarrat
A classic record of the heroic struggle to keep the Atlantic sea lanes open against the German U-boat menace.

BETWEEN TWO WORLDS
by Maisie Mosco
Alison Plantaine was born to the theatre. As a child she knew only the backstage world of provincial theatres. Then as a young girl she discovers with the shock of the unexpected, her Jewish heritage.

ANIMAL FARM
by George Orwell
The world famous satire upon dictatorship. The history of a revolution that went wrong.

THE FAMILY OF WOMEN
by Richard Peck
A panoramic story of women whose indomitable spirit brings them through the turbulent, events of the 1850's Gold Rush to the Europe of 1939.

SNAP SHOT
by A.J. Quinnell

On Sunday, 7th June 1981 an Israeli F.16 jet aircraft bombed and destroyed the Iraqi nuclear installation at Tammuz. This is the subject of this thriller.

THE BETSY
by Harold Robbins

Loren Hardeman rose to become the driving force behind Bethlehem Motors. At 91, still dynamic but confined to a wheelchair, he makes a last desperate gamble to head the entire industry.

SPELLBINDER
by Harold Robbins

Takes the reader into the world of the newest and most disturbing phenomenon in contemporary American life—the rise of religious leaders.

THE SEA CAVE
by Alan Scholefield

The naked body of a woman is found washed up on a wild stretch of African coastline. A young immigrant is drawn inexorably into the resulting murder enquiry.

MY SOUL TWIN

MY SOUL TWIN

NINO HARATISCHVILI

Translated by Charlotte Collins

SCRIBE
Melbourne • London

Scribe Publications
2 John St, Clerkenwell, London, WC1N 2ES, United Kingdom
18–20 Edward St, Brunswick, Victoria 3056, Australia
3754 Pleasant Ave, Suite 100, Minneapolis, Minnesota 55409, USA

Originally published as *Mein sanfter Zwilling* in German by Frankfurter Verlagsanstalt
GmbH in 2011
Published in English by Scribe 2022

Text copyright © Frankfurter Verlagsanstalt GmbH, Frankfurt am Main 2011
English translation © Charlotte Collins 2022

The translation of this work was supported by a grant from the Goethe-Institut which is
funded by the German Ministry of Foreign Affairs.

Typeset in Fournier by the publishers

Printed and bound in the UK by CPI Group (UK) Ltd, Croydon CR0 4YY

Scribe is committed to the sustainable use of natural resources and the use of paper products
made responsibly from those resources.

978 1 913348 42 7 (UK edition)
978 1 922310 33 0 (Australian edition)
978 1 957363 10 3 (US edition)
978 1 922586 56 8 (ebook)

Catalogue records for this book are available from the National Library of Australia and the
British Library.

scribepublications.co.uk
scribepublications.com.au
scribepublications.com

The body of another person is a wall; it prevents me from seeing his soul. Oh, how I hate this wall!

MARINA TSVETAEVA

PART I
THERE

I look at your face, so pale, so peaceful, and still feel the old, familiar feeling, and mistrust it even as I feel it. I wonder how it can be that I still feel this closeness. Even now …

I will never be able to explain this feeling to anyone. I am not supposed to feel it, given what happened. But this is how it is, and I am slowly accepting it, this emotion that seems to outlast everything else.

For the first time I stand alone, in every way: mentally, physically, emotionally. But even now it seems that my feeling, your feeling, what I am feeling here, now, looking at your face — it overcomes all fear, blocks it out. All that remains is this tremendous closeness, this gentleness.

I don't know how it can be that you were able to give me this gentle closeness, because no feeling can be gentle, because it is in the very nature of gentleness that it doesn't last — it is a phenomenon that appears like a pinprick and vanishes into nothingness. Yet my gentleness endures. It is of a different order; it is more enduring than anything else in my life. And I have long since ceased to question it.

So here I sit, a few days before my departure, on the beach, our beach, from which we would always swim out into the cold water; on the sand, which is cool and damp, because it's been raining for two days. In a moment I will cut off my hair and meet the new thoughts and the cool wind with a shorn head. Strand for strand, I will grow lighter, more weightless, perhaps freer, too. I'm sitting in our bay, where no one but us ever came, because this place seems so cold and bleak; here, where I first tried to offer you my love and you could not yet accept it, where we spent so many mornings and evenings after you learned to speak again, where so often we whispered our secrets, promises, desires, and plans to the sea.

I sit here. I look at you, and I feel the exhilaration of closeness: I dance this exhilaration on the grave of loneliness, because for me it is a denial of loneliness, a victory of elemental, Dionysian greed.

I am gentle; I am soft as wool, and my inside is silky smooth, as if I were a baby, a foetus, secure, wanted, untouched by the world.

You told me so often that I had forgotten who I was, and perhaps it is actually true. And perhaps, with you, I never knew it. Perhaps I only realised it when I stopped fighting this gentleness in me. But I know that I am not you, not anymore.

And just as I am not afraid of the solitude, the silence, the questions that will come after all of this, that perhaps are encapsulated in the word *future*, I am not afraid of this realisation. I will have to weep. All that I cannot process I must push out of me, and there will be no one to hold my brow — I am aware of that as well. But what does it matter?

I look at your face. You are beautiful. You are as beautiful as ever, and I find myself smiling. I look at your face and think that I am grateful to you, for this gentle closeness and this terrible alienation. That even though this closeness is a feeling I can never share with anyone again — I let it go.

I look at you.

1

It all really started with the end.

That morning, Tulia called and told me he was here. She woke me. Mark had taken Theo to school and I had stayed in bed, feeling bad because I hadn't got up, hadn't made breakfast, hadn't played a part in my family's morning. Overcoming my guilty conscience proved easier than I feared, though, and my lie-in was worth every missed second of the grey Hamburg morning.

The door barely seemed to have closed behind them when the phone started ringing. When it didn't stop, I forced myself out of bed and, cursing the squandering of those precious minutes of sleep, crawled over to my mobile, which was on top of the chest of drawers. Apparently, it was a law of nature for it always to be left in the most inconvenient places.

'Wake up; I know you're there. He's back.'

'Tulia, my God, do you know what you're doing to me right now? I've just managed to get a bit of sleep for the first time in a hundred years, and now you come along and wake me up. Please, can't you call later ...'

'No, I can't. Didn't you hear me? He's back! I can't believe it. He walked in just like that, our young Adonis; you can't imagine how well he looks. Seven in the morning he calls me, says he's here, he wants to stay here for a while, he wants —'

'Tulia, who? Who are you talking about? Who do you mean, for heaven's sake?'

'Ivo, Ivo, our Ivo!'

★

I almost dropped the phone. Maybe I did actually drop it and I don't remember. I was so shaken that I staggered backwards and sat down on the edge of the bed. Or rather, I fell.

I couldn't consciously recall a single day when I hadn't thought of him, hadn't wondered what he might be doing, where he was, how he was. Over the last eight years, though, these thoughts had become routine, quiet, calm, self-evident — so much so that I was quite convinced they had nothing to do with reality. I had my Ivo, who lived inside my head, and whom I worried about, but the actual, real Ivo, of flesh and blood — this Ivo I hadn't seen for eight years. He had vanished from my life and followed his own path, which was so removed from mine that every step he took distanced him still further from me.

'What's he doing here?' was the best I could manage.

'How should I know! He's only been at my place an hour; he's just gone out to buy cigarettes. So I had to call you …'

'But he must have said something, surely?'

'Who cares! He's back, that's the main thing. He's said he wants to stay here for a while, and I'm not going to try and talk him out of it.'

'Did he ask after me?'

'I was smothering him with kisses for the first hour; he could hardly speak, poor boy. I think I practically strangled him.'

I could hear an excitement in Tulia's voice that I had almost forgotten, which always gripped her whenever he was talked about. A mixture of maternal pride in a child who had drawn the short straw in life and so had to be loved all the more conspicuously and explicitly, and a certain pride in herself, because Ivo embodied all the things she felt were worth striving for, and she presumably saw the influence of her child-rearing most strongly reflected in him.

★

'What am I supposed to do? Jump for joy? And why are you calling *me*, particularly? I mean, what do you want from me?' I said helplessly — and was immediately annoyed at myself for asking this silly question, because within seconds I had manoeuvred myself back into the role of the little girl, Tulia's ward.

There was a brief silence on the line. I knew perfectly well that Tulia was inconsistent, governed entirely by her emotions, that she didn't always think before she said or did something. Perhaps she had rung me without considering the implications. But when it came to Ivo, I didn't trust her, because in all those years I had never quite figured out what she really thought about it, about Ivo and me.

'Oh, there's the doorbell — he's back. I have to go — I'll call again in a few hours. Or he'll call you himself. I'll expect you here soon, anyway.'

*

I wanted to reply, but Tulia had already hung up. My need for sleep had suddenly evaporated. I was wide awake. I tried to put my thoughts in order, went into the kitchen, made coffee, and sat at the breakfast bar for which Mark had fought for so long, which I had never liked. I was shaking from head to toe, and my eyes were burning. Clutching the coffee cup, I stared out of the window at the grey drizzle. A customary picture to which I would never grow accustomed. My eyes fell on my wedding ring — narrow, understated, it had taken me such a long time to decide whether it really was the one I wanted to accompany me for the rest of my life.

I knew that everything was going to change. I knew it would be best to defend myself against this — to call Mark and ask him to take me with him on his next business trip, to drop our little boy at his grandparents' and disappear somewhere until the clouds had passed.

Ivo had been bound to come back some day. I had expected it; had often pictured this moment, run through every conceivable scenario in my head. I had armed myself, lulled myself into a sense of security. But until today it had only played out in my head. Until now, I had been the puppeteer. Had held the strings in my hand.

Despite all that had happened between us, I had never tried to erase Ivo from my life. Ignoring everyone's advice, I had put our childhood photos up in our apartment, told Mark a modified version of our story, sent parcels on Ivo's birthday with no message — for as long as I still had his address — and proposed toasts to him at parties, which not infrequently led to heated arguments and even shouting at the table.

But I had embalmed him in a sealed past, deprived him of space in which to grow — I was well aware of this, too. I had preserved him in my head as the child, the boy, the man who had shared his life with me, who existed in me, in my universe. But he was absent — absent from my life, and absent from his true life, which for so long I had also considered mine.

I wrenched myself out of my reverie, went to the bathroom, took a shower, drank another coffee, and put on some black trousers. I stood in front of the wardrobe trying to decide on a top, went blank, and just stared at the shelves stuffed with jerseys, T-shirts, and blouses. I stared and stared, as if hidden in there was the solution, the clarification, the quiet I so desperately needed. In my mind's eye I saw his face, the last time I'd seen him, and I instinctively covered my mouth to stop myself from screaming.

Yes, it all really started with the end. But my life had always been that way: the family structure I grew up in, we grew up in, was always upside down. Eventually, I no longer trusted myself to use possessive pronouns when talking about my relatives. Because if I said *my* father or *my* mother, *my* brother or *my* grandmother, I always had to add a *kind of*.

'Your father? And why don't you live with him?'

'Because my parents are divorced.'

'And why don't you live with your mother?'

'Because she lives in America.'

'But why didn't she take you with her?'

'Because that's what we decided.'

'And does she sometimes come over?'

'No, we always go to her.'

'And why do you live with Tulia?'

'She's my father's aunt; she's like my grandmother.'

'And why don't you live with your real grandmother?'

'She is my real grandmother; we don't have another grandmother.'

'And why does your sister have the same name as you, and your brother doesn't?'

'Because my brother's adopted, and he kept his parents' name.'

Later, to avoid all this, I said: This is Leni. This is Tulia. This is Ivo. This is …

★

I awoke from my comatose state holding a dark-blue T-shirt, and put it on. It reminded me of my husband, my child; that I was in the here, the now, and that everything my brain was clutching at was in the past. I took a deep breath and forced myself to smile: I needed to feel the ground beneath my feet again.

I looked for the phone, which had ducked under the duvet this time, and called my editor.

'Hey, Leo. I'd like to take a few days out of the office; I have to do some research for the biennale and won't be back in till Wednesday. Is that okay with you?'

'Oh … sure. What about tomorrow, though? Nadia's surprise party, remember?'

I'd completely forgotten. 'Remind me again tomorrow; I'll try and show up for a little while at least, okay?'

'Is everything all right?'

'Yes. Why?'

'You sound tense.'

'Just the usual family stress. You know how it is.'

'Fine, I'll give you a ring tomorrow. Try to come. It would mean a lot to her. Yeah?'

'I'll do my best. Take care.'

I hung up, ashamed that I had accused my little family of stressing me out. This old pattern was also familiar: me lying, me lying for Ivo. I hadn't had to do it for so long, and although this lie was really quite harmless, I was ashamed, and wished I hadn't answered the phone earlier, wished Tulia had never called me, the old bat. But again I was resisting facts — I couldn't control Tulia, and I had to accept that Ivo had been leading his own life beyond the bounds of my imagination.

I went into my office and turned on the laptop. An hour later, I gave up. I sat at my desk, sobbing, clutching a photo of my son — a last anchor, a last point of reference. Eyes screwed shut, I pressed my face into the desk, and only just managed to stop myself from screaming as loud as I could for help.

2

Ivo's arrival in our family was also an end that started everything.

His mother, with whom my father had had an affair, was dead; his father in prison, where he died a few years later; Ivo himself mute, refusing to say a word to anybody. And I the only one who could understand his language and speak for him. Which was also the reason they left Ivo with us.

I was seven, my sister eleven.

Our parents had split up, and my mother had moved to the United States to work for a big pharmaceutical company, where she mixed various harmful chemicals together in the hope that the harm would be vindicated by a brighter and healthier future. And she had moved there because of James: yes, James, whom she later married. She made us choose, and although, looking back, it's absolutely inconceivable, my sister and I decided, for very different reasons, to stay with our father, even though he was actually the main reason our family and our life had fallen apart. But that's how it was.

My mother had to renounce her custody rights; although she was entitled to them, she was tired, very tired. We were all tired. If she had gone to court, we would never have stayed with Papa — they would never have allowed it — but she decided not to.

Similarly, they should never have allowed Papa to adopt Ivo; but strangely enough, we all ended up staying with him.

My sister had turned her back on our mother; she couldn't understand why she would want to leave a man whom women would literally die for. Leni staying with Papa was an act of defiance, because up until then they hadn't had much to do with each other. Unlike me, she hadn't been particularly close to him when she was small; she stayed to hurt Mama, whom she couldn't forgive for leaving, for loving another man, for fighting for her happiness — without us, if necessary.

I stayed with him because I was afraid they wouldn't give Ivo to Mama, and we would be separated.

Our mother argued with our father, hysterical and screeching like a Fury. In the end she just sat down in front of my sister and me and asked us where we would like to live. Today, I think that was the most honest, honourable thing she could have done for us: to give us our freedom. Not to make us move against our will to the oppressive foreignness of another country. Nonetheless, my sister never forgave her, and I always had an emptiness inside me, precisely because she had asked us to make this decision to which we could never have been equal.

She handed us over to our father, who was drinking and screwing around more than ever, and who then took in his dead lover's son. My father, who lost his job and started living at the expense of his children, who were supported by their mother, thanks to the pharmaceutical industry and James. Soon, Papa couldn't cope at all, and this was the point when Tulia stepped in.

Tulia was my father's aunt. Several times divorced, middle-aged, with no children, she lived in a converted barn, drove an old truck, and, contrary to expectation, did not have any cats. She loved poems and all dead poets, listened to Italian opera arias, and earned her living from an old boat-hire company she had inherited from her second or third husband. Curiously, she hardly ever talked about her husbands. Her life consisted of a multitude of stories, both true and invented, and she herself eventually believed in them so strongly that they merged into one big life story, and it became impossible to separate reality from fiction. Reality always seemed like fiction with Tulia. She believed in astrology, mysticism, and nature. She had Persian blood in her veins, she said, and a face like a Babylonian queen — you could see it! — with very distinctive features that my father, too, had inherited, and which were thought to be one of the reasons why he was so attractive to women.

★

We went to live with her when I was eight, beside the sea, in a sleepy coastal village called Niendorf. My sister Leni, Ivo, and me. My father had us at weekends, and the month of July was spent in Newark, New Jersey, with Mama and James. During those summers we always pretended our life with Papa was fabulous, and Tulia just a nice little bonus, because our barn, our alcoholic father with his ever-changing women, the dangerous boat trips we undertook by ourselves, Tulia's revolting quince jam — it all seemed to us much nicer than Newark and Mama's desperate efforts to bond with us.

The strange thing was that, of the three of us, Ivo was ultimately the only one who gave her the feeling of still being our mother, who conveyed a certainty that we could never replace her, and would never want to. It was always that way; he created for our mother an illusion of closeness.

Our attempted family was a source of suffering for us all. At first, Ivo was silent; I tried to be as inconspicuous as possible — ideally, to become invisible and concentrate solely on serving as a kind of mouthpiece for Ivo; and Leni increasingly shut herself off. She started apportioning blame for everything, especially to our mother and Ivo, and forgot how to smile.

Mama suffered, too. She argued with James, and showered us with innumerable pointless presents, or took us on fraught outings to various wildlife or national parks. She continued to perch on the edge of our beds when we were long past the age of bedtime stories.

I missed her terribly, but I was too proud to let her know, and always acted as if our life were the quintessence of normality. I feigned the uncomplicated daughter, and Ivo — who already had a remarkable instinct for people — conformed, became soft, affectionate, eventually chatty, brimming with eagerness for the tedious hiking tours and excursions, full of genuine enthusiasm for everything my mother organised for us.

We reconciled ourselves to the situation and, once Leni finally stopped punishing Ivo for being the embodiment of our family's misfortune, accepted that our life was as it was. So it was an almost happy childhood: a little crazy, a little eccentric, a little neglected, and practically overflowing with love bestowed on us by these troubled adults, which could never really be healthy, or was at least administered in an unhealthy form.

This was the version of my childhood I later confided to my husband, friends, and a few close acquaintances. I went to great lengths to ensure people acknowledged our right to call ourselves a family. The rest I worked out for myself. The rest I worked out with Ivo.

He called after I had washed my puffy, tear-stained face, poured myself another cup of coffee, and abandoned all hope of imposing some sort of order on the day.

He didn't explain anything, just said he was going to come round, was I there, did I have any objection? I didn't answer, just nodded mutely. He promised he would be with me in forty minutes; he was already on the way.

I spent the time wrapped in a blanket on my balcony, gazing down at the street. Ships sounded their horns in the distance, lulling me into a dreamlike trance. My brain finally stopped seething and groaning. I didn't bother to put on make-up, to paint on a face that might conceal my fear.

He was punctual. I stood by the door for a long time, trying to control my breathing, before I opened it. He was wearing a black leather jacket, his hair, as ever, very close-cropped. He seemed taller than I remembered; I wondered whether grown-ups continue to grow, or whether it's an effect of the passage of time. He was smiling at me, a tiny flower in his hand, a snowdrop from Tulia's garden — I laughed, despite myself.

We didn't speak. He started slinking around my apartment like a hyena, surveying the rooms, stopping in front of the photos displayed on a shelf. He stared at a picture of Theo for a long time, then set it back down abruptly. Eventually he sat at our breakfast bar and said:

'This breakfast bar is so not bourgeois!'

This was the first thing I heard from Ivo after almost eight years. Then he asked if he could have a drink.

'Gin and tonic or something would be great. You're bound to have gin and tonic in an apartment like this, right?'

'Mark and I occasionally drink gin, so we probably do have some, but not because I think we should have some *in an apartment like this.* And there's nothing wrong with the breakfast bar!'

'Hey — are you offended, or what?'

'Stop it.'

Having said this, I felt a bit surer of myself. And, in an instant, the malicious lightness I remembered from before was back.

I gave in, gave up, and mixed him a gin and tonic. I didn't have to think long before pouring myself one as well. It was one o'clock in the afternoon.

He smiled and pressed his glass to his lips.

'You've got older. But I like the little laughter lines. And your hair is darker somehow. I think your apartment's perfectly fine, by the way. It's just weird that you live like this now ... Tulia seems very taken with your husband, anyway, so that's a good sign.'

Tulia must have lied through her teeth, because she thought Mark was a crashing bore; at first she'd even threatened to ban me from her house when I'd announced that I was going to marry him.

'Is she now,' I sighed, sipping my drink. The warming, slightly befuddling effect of alcohol in the daytime liberated me from myself.

'It's good to see you. You're very beautiful. Just as I always imagined you'd look in your mid-thirties. You're definitely a late bloomer — your best years are yet to come!'

'Ivo, what the hell is all this? You've got a nerve, just showing up here all of a sudden! Where've you been all this time? Why did you never get in touch?'

'That was what you wanted.'

'Fuck that. I was worried about you. I —'

'Frank always knew where I was living. So Tulia would have known as well. And I bet Gesi gave you news of me every week.'

'You know what I mean. You don't seriously think I would ask anyone else about you — where you're living, what continent you happen to be on?!'

'That's how you wanted it, Stella. So don't reproach me. It was your decision.'

'So if it was my decision that we wouldn't see each other anymore, what are you doing here?'

'Because I never stick to agreements, on principle.'

I looked at him, and had to suppress a laugh. He was as beautiful as ever — the sad, almost alarming beauty of a lonely man. A man who despaired of himself. His almond-shaped eyes — dark grey, watery, with long lashes — were still full of secrets I had tried for so long to decode, and the slight, impish grin around the corners of his mouth hadn't changed, either. My love for him was like a wound that had never really healed.

'Long story short: I still live in New York. If you can call it a life.'

He took his cigarettes out of his pocket. I tried to remember when I had last smoked.

'I travel a lot; I've gone freelance. The contracts are pretty good; I take everything the others won't do. I've been in Kabul the past three months. It got a bit uncomfortable sometimes. But my friend War and I still get along brilliantly. I'm not married: I would definitely have invited the family to my wedding. I see Gesi quite often. James hasn't been too well lately, but Gesi comes and visits when I'm in New York. We still argue about toxins and experiments on animals, but it doesn't matter. The world hasn't changed; astonishingly, I still haven't managed to save it. You see, Stella, I'm doing fine. I missed you sometimes. That's all, really. And my love life works out pretty well for the two or three months I spend in any one place.'

He had stood up, and was looking out of the window.

'I'd like to see your son,' he said suddenly, and I noticed that speaking mostly English had softened his German, and that it suited his voice.

'You can meet him.'

'Will I meet your husband, too?'

'Yes, you can meet my husband, too.'

We both looked out of the window for a while. Finally, I mustered the courage to ask: 'Why did you come back?'

'I suddenly felt I didn't know who I was anymore. I don't think you can put your life on fast-forward. I did, though, and it worked for quite a while. But now I have to rewind. I have to rewind, and I can't do that without Frank, and Tulia — maybe I even need Leni — but most of all I need you, Stella. I have to be here again; I have to do this for a while. You mix an excellent G&T. You didn't use to. A skill acquired in recent years, I suspect.'

'We closed that chapter, Ivo. And I don't think it would be a good idea now to —'

'We didn't close anything. Don't kid yourself.'

His voice suddenly became cold, distant, slightly scornful: that incredible coldness he emanated whenever he was afraid of being rejected. How he hurt me with that, even though I knew it was put on, that he was only acting; but he acted so convincingly that it was impossible, in the moment, not to be affected by it.

'It's closed, Ivo. I have a new life. I have other priorities now. Above all, I have a child, whose happiness is more important to me than feeling a certain way. I've found my peace.'

'You've found your peace, have you? Wow, that's great. Listen, Stella. You have to help me, and maybe I can help you.'

'Help? You, help me? I've already been helped. I don't need any more help. And you — how am I supposed to help you? How do you see that working? You went your own way. You're a different person to who you were *back then*. You've had different experiences, you have different feelings, different thoughts. I can't act as if no time's gone by. It unsettles me, still — I'm confused; it's all a bit much, because you're here, and I'm happy that you are, maybe even relieved. But I don't know what I can do. If you want to talk, we can talk, but that's all, Ivo.'

'I just need to try to remember. And you can help me with that, can't you?'

I wouldn't answer him, so for a while we both stared into our glasses in silence. The telephone rang, and I jumped up to look for it. The hated phone offered me a reprieve, the possibility of escape. I wondered why I felt so hopelessly exposed again — to Ivo, our past, to whatever was going to happen next — but I was relieved when I heard a woman's voice on the line.

'Who's speaking?' I didn't recognise the name.

'I'm calling from Theo's school. He hasn't been picked up, and I just wanted to —'

Immediately, I hated the phone again.

'Oh my God! I'll be there in twenty minutes. Could you look after him until then … ?'

'Yes, of course.'

'My husband and I got things mixed up.' I was lying again.

Ivo had got up and had gone back to looking at the family photos on the shelf.

'I have to go. I have to pick up Theo.'

'We can do that together.'

'I think it's better if I go alone.'

'No, come on. That way I can meet him, can't I?'

'This really isn't the best time, Ivo!'

But he had already emptied his glass and picked up his leather jacket. I could feel the effects of the alcohol, which I wasn't at all used to during the day. My ears were buzzing as if I'd developed a weird form of tinnitus, and I was sweating.

We hurried down the stairs, me throwing on my coat as I ran. Ivo seemed relaxed and mildly amused, as ever.

When I tried to unlock the car and the key slipped out of my hand, he grinned, and indicated that I should take the passenger seat.

'Let me,' he said, and I acquiesced with relief. For the second time that day, I felt I was about to burst into tears.

He drove fast and with confidence, aware that he was exuding that characteristic complacency that so annoyed me. I wondered whether he came across as this confident and laid-back in all his damned conflict zones, where he had to go to research his oh-so-truthful and revealing reports. Whether he strolled around this casually, this amused, in bombed-out cities, streets littered with corpses. Sure of himself, always a little superior, a little more self-aware than the others, always a little freer, more assured, more inscrutable.

I knew — I remembered precisely — when he had started to be like this. How he began to smoke cigarettes right down to the filter, bite his fingernails, and eye up women hungrily; I remembered his sad gaze, which others always thought was a challenge, and the notebooks that he would fill right to the edges, like casting a little anchor into the ocean.

'Left here.' A few brief directions were all I could manage on the way to Theo's school.

He smoked, although it was Mark's car and he would notice the stink and be cross about it, but I didn't dare point this out to Ivo; I couldn't stop thinking about the 'not bourgeois' breakfast bar and didn't want him to go on judging me.

He had rolled down the window and was looking around, as curious as a schoolboy. He seemed to be recognising the city again, or not recognising it and marvelling at it for the first time; I couldn't tell.

I made him wait in the car. Theo was sitting in a ground-floor classroom, chewing a carrot. He made a sulky face, but apparently wasn't sulky enough not to leap to his feet immediately and run to me. I thanked the teacher and tried to look relaxed and confident, as if it had all just been a misunderstanding.

For a long time, I didn't want to have children; in fact, I had never really wanted to have children, precisely because I didn't feel equal to the task of being a mother, and long before I became pregnant with Theo I sensed that, no matter what I did, I would never be good enough. Not for myself, and not for my child, either.

'Where's Papa?' asked Theo, sticking the remains of the carrot in his jacket pocket. The other children, who were mostly older, sat quietly drawing or doing their homework, ignoring Theo. He didn't say goodbye to anyone, either, except the teacher.

'It's me this afternoon. You know that.'

'So why did you forget to pick me up?'

'I didn't forget you. I'm here, aren't I? I'm just a bit late.'

'Were you working?'

'No, I'm late because we have a visitor.'

'A visitor?'

His dark-brown eyes lit up, and his anger at my lateness seemed forgotten.

'Someone very important to me. A member of the family. I've already told you about him, if you remember.'

'Your family or Papa's family?'

'My family.'

I hadn't said *brother* for years to describe Ivo. No one in our family referred to him as my brother. But I was surprised that I didn't say it now to Theo. I tried to deal with him seriously and respectfully, to be as honest as Tulia had been with us. Perhaps it had taken the lightheartedness out of our relationship, but it had made all three of us independent people.

We approached the car park where the car was waiting. Ivo was looking out of the window, smoking another cigarette. He was watching us, I knew, although I couldn't see his face at that distance.

'That's Papa's car,' said Theo. And at that moment, I could have shaken him for demonstrating this possessive mentality, this capitalistic childhood disease, as Tulia would call it, so openly. There wasn't much about my childhood that I was proud of. Our freedom, perhaps; Ivo; the fact that we could always swim better than others, and that we always shared everything. Possessions were frowned on in our house. Mark's childhood didn't resemble mine in the slightest. He didn't see anything wrong with his son learning early on what he was entitled to; he even encouraged it.

'Mine's at the garage, darling,' I said, clutching Theo's small hand a little tighter. He tried to loosen my grip but I wouldn't let him, and in the throes of our little power struggle we found we were already standing by the car. Ivo got out and offered my son his hand. Theo looked up at him, wrested his hand from mine, and shook it.

'This is Ivo, Theo,' I said, watching them expectantly. Seeing the two of them together was disconcerting; it augured a huge change for which I was absolutely not ready.

'You've got a funny name,' said my six-year-old son, climbing into the car. 'We've got a photo of you at home.'

'Really?'

'Yes. But you look different in it. Your hair's different.'

'That's true. I think it wasn't just my hair that was different.'

'What else was?'

It occurred to me that perhaps I should have warned Ivo not to get drawn into answering Theo's questions, because they would never end. As a rule, Theo hardly showed any interest in other people or anything around him, but once his curiosity was awakened, it was apparently limitless. I sometimes wished it were possible to direct this curiosity, because not everything he was interested in interested me — and vice versa.

'Well, everything, I reckon.'

Theo seemed to consider this.

Ivo gave me an enquiring look. 'Where to, ladies and gentlemen?' he cried, acting jolly.

'Home first — I have to change quickly. Then on to football. I can't be late, okay?' said Theo, dictating from the back seat. I didn't reply, just accepted his imperious tone and nodded.

On the way there, Theo wouldn't stop asking questions. Where had Ivo been, why hadn't he visited us more often, and why did he smoke, because Papa didn't actually want smokers in his car; he told him about his football practice and his best friend, whose father bred rabbits; about the really big building where his father worked, where he was sometimes allowed to go; he told him he had beaten Tulia once in arm-wrestling, and that he thought Leni's eldest son was silly because he liked girls and had got really stuck-up ever since he had been given an electric bike.

When we got home, I made Theo a sandwich; I didn't have the time or imagination to prepare something hot. I was also completely preoccupied with Ivo's presence and the question of what his being there would mean for me.

Theo took the remains of his carrot out of his pocket and demonstratively placed it in the fruit bowl. When I suggested that we throw the carrot away because it didn't look very appetising, he got angry, insisting that it was his carrot and he could do what he liked with it. Ivo seemed amused by this glimpse into our everyday life, glancing curiously first at me, then at Theo.

I felt an irrepressible desire to barricade myself in the bedroom until very late that night and just be left alone. I gave in, yet again. The half-eaten carrot sat on top of the fruit, a symbol of Tulia's capitalistic childhood disease, a token of my impotence.

The three of us drove to my son's football pitch in my husband's car. Seen from outside, the picture looked fine, with one small exception: the husband was wrong. The husband who actually belonged in this picture was probably in the studio right now, editing one of his documentaries: my husband, who had not the faintest idea that, this morning, the entire life we had fought to build together — our daily routine, our habits, our promises, our similarities and differences, our nights, our holiday plans, our parties that we so enjoyed planning and hosting together — was all being called into question. And that I was doing nothing to stop it. On the contrary: I was driving to the football pitch with a borrowed life, in a borrowed car, with a borrowed husband, and wondering how it was possible for it to happen so quickly — for everything, absolutely everything around me to feel so wrong. How much was I risking for a relationship that had finished long ago, that had never promised any kind of happiness, that, in all the thirty-six years I had been on this earth, I had never been able to name.

3

I have only a vague recollection of the rest of the day.

At some point, after driving me home and parking my husband's car in the garage, Ivo disappeared. He just said he had something else he had to do. I was in a daze and didn't ask any more questions.

Later, Mark came home with Theo, having picked him up from football in my car, which he had collected from the repair shop.

We ate supper, and Mark pestered me with questions about Ivo and what his sudden reappearance might signify. I think he was jealous. Then he wanted to sleep with me to reassure himself that nothing had changed. He wanted confirmation, and I gave it to him. I slept with him, and tried to appear fully present.

When he fell asleep, I sat up and contemplated my naked body for some time. I don't know why. I don't know what kind of confirmation I was looking for.

The craziness began the next day. Suddenly the whole family seemed to be restored. Even Mama called, wanting to know if Ivo had arrived safely and how we had all reacted to his return. To my surprise, though, my life continued without interruption. I sat at my laptop, drove Theo to school, made phone calls, made an effort with Mark.

Then, later that afternoon, my sister showed up at our apartment. Leni's hair shimmered an artificial, hennaed red, and her bag was brimming with her youngest child's toys.

All her life Leni had been trying to make up for the childhood that, as she put it, she had missed out on. She had studied sociology, then started writing children's books. Success had eluded her until she met her husband, who ran a children's book publishing company, after which she was able to make a living from her writing. She started to turn her back on Tulia, and seemed increasingly ashamed of her. She had three children, and moved to a posh area where there were lots of big houses. She played her new part perfectly: at every get-together she held forth to family members and anyone else present about how to raise children, how to reconfigure the world in a child-orientated way, how to write children's books. As if the real purpose of our lives was having children, raising children, and writing children's books.

The only reason I had never really distanced myself from Leni was that I needed her. For me, she was confirmation of everything that had happened but was never talked about; what everyone knew and no one in our family wanted to remember, but that she, too, had experienced, albeit — unlike Ivo and me — indirectly. That had damaged her, too. That she, too, was trying to put behind her. And she was confirmation of the only clear-cut statement in my life: Leni was my sister, and with her I didn't have to add *kind of*.

However, after she had had her third son, and given up hope of a girl for whom she could buy pink frilly clothes and braid cute blonde plaits, I found the staid conventionality she radiated almost intolerable: her increasingly provincial beauty, which resulted in her putting on weight and hennaing her hair, and the fact that she drove a Golf because she was afraid it might come across as a provocation in her suburban idyll if she were to own a bigger car.

'Tulia's invited us on Saturday. We're all supposed to go. Celebrate the return of the prodigal son. What do we say to that?' she announced pointedly, sitting down on the sofa, only to jump up again a moment later and rummage through my kitchen cupboards in search of herbal tea. One of the characteristics I had found increasingly annoying in recent years was Leni's permanent frustrated sarcasm.

'He's already been round.'

'What? You've already seen him? The Phantom of the Opera showed up on your doorstep again? How marvellous. And what did the gentleman have to say? Is his stock high or low?'

'He's looking good. He's in need of a bit of a break.'

'I'm surprised — no, really. And that Gesi let him come and see us, just like that!'

Leni liked to play the abandoned daughter, forgetting that it was she who, at the age of eleven, had protested vehemently against moving to Newark. She cast our mother as the guilty party, and was glad to be able to make her the scapegoat for anything that ever went wrong. She had almost no contact with her, and had refused right from the beginning to take her children there on holiday.

'So Gesi sees him occasionally — is that a crime?'

'And there you go again.'

'What do you mean?'

'Well, you're defending him again.'

'I'm not defending him. That's just how it is.'

She gave me a suspicious look and continued to root through my cupboards. I realised that this was actually a very unusual sight: Leni alone, without children. I tried to remember when the last time had been, and couldn't. Right from the start, Leni had ostentatiously embraced her maternal role, thereby making clear to all the world that a woman who had been abandoned by her mother did not necessarily go on to be a bad mother herself. Leni managed her family life to perfection — and wanted to make sure everyone knew it.

She found a tea that met her high organic standards and, without asking, made a cup for me as well. This was also typical Leni: she always knew what was good or bad for everyone else.

'I'm glad he's back.' I tried, as I had a thousand times, to speak frankly with her.

'I doubt you know what's good for you and what isn't. You know what he's like — or you should. So you should draw the necessary conclusions about his visit.'

'What's that supposed to mean?'

'It was the best thing for us all, him going to America. It was the best thing for all of us that he went away. And stayed away. It was only then that you got your life together. It was only after he'd gone that

Papa calmed down. Even Tulia was more stable. It was just better that way. He wasn't good for us!'

Leni had never stopped seeing Ivo as the root of all evil, just as she had never stopped blaming Mama for something for which she was the least to blame. But Leni was stubborn, and once she had made up her mind about something, nothing could convince her otherwise.

I looked at her face. Her face that had once been very pretty, with pale-brown eyes and full lips that so many had been tempted to kiss, a tanned complexion, and prominent cheekbones. If you looked only at her face and not at her heavy body, her clothes, her manner, she was a very beautiful woman who had inherited all the family's best features: our mother's honey-coloured eyes, our father's full mouth. But the moment she opened this mouth, the moment you paid attention to her body language, something almost awful was revealed: self-conscious gestures, a ramrod-straight back, the beginnings of a double chin, neglected hands, the matronly softness of her body. The awareness of this made my heart ache, and once again I had the indescribable sense of standing outside my own life — I was like an actress in one of my husband's docudramas.

'I don't want a fennel tea right now.'

'Oh, stop it; you have to do something good for yourself now and then.'

'But it isn't good for me. I don't even like fennel tea; it gives me stomach cramps.'

'No one gets stomach cramps from fennel tea.'

'I hate fennel.'

Leni gave me a reproachful look that said I was completely wrong, that I ate all the wrong things, that I drank all the wrong teas.

She drank her healthy tea and looked around. As if she could infer the state of my life from the state of my apartment.

'So, are you going to go?' I asked, to break the uncomfortable silence.

'What do you mean? Go where?'

'On Saturday, to Tulia's?'

'Well, I have to, don't I? Or I'll be excommunicated. Tulia, in particular, is absolutely beside herself. She's got her beloved boy back. When you think about it, Ivo was always the better grandchild, the better son, the better child — better than we ever were, anyway. Unbelievable.'

Leni, always jealous. Being the eldest child, she was forced to confront the realities, the disasters of our past more directly than we were. Perhaps that was why she had never got over the feeling of not being enough. Perhaps her obsession with children was all just an escape, a yearning for an unblemished childhood.

'Have you already spoken to Papa?' I asked casually, glancing at the clock. As if Theo, whom Mark must soon be bringing home, could save me from this torture. The steaming cups with the strong fennelly smell sat on the breakfast bar like symbols of our failure as sisters, next to the fruit bowl where the remnants of Theo's carrot were still enthroned.

'Papa will be there, with his floozy. My God! Did you take a proper look at her last time, on his birthday? It's unbelievable; she looks like a toad.'

'They're the right age for each other, at least.'

'Oh, bollocks. There's nothing right about her. You can see from a mile off that she's got no class — and that terrible accent! Makes me want to puke.'

'Calm down. She's been with him over two years now. That's an achievement in itself.'

'Papa's still a good-looking guy; he could do better. I sometimes think he just feels sorry for her. She's not going to find another decent man, is she — at her age, in her position?'

Leni loved our father. After our mother left, she came to absolutely idolise him, and always regarded him as the victim of our terrible fate. The world had not been fair to Frank; his wife, his children, had not helped him; he, the knight in shining armour, had adopted a boy, a wretched, neglected child whom everyone had abandoned, and *he* hadn't shown him any gratitude, either. Leni contrived to twist and rearrange every fact, every scrap of memory, to create the image of Papa that she wanted to see and, above all, to preserve.

'Don't be so bitchy all the time. She's good for him.'

'What do you mean, 'bitchy'? She's a common whore, that's all. With her peroxide hair and all that make-up, thinks she's in a Hollywood film …'

Leni would have gone on, but just then her mobile rang. Her husband seemed annoyed: had she forgotten that their second child's karate class was cancelled, could she please go and pick him up? Leni, overcome with panic at marring her maternal image with this small failure, leaped to her feet, accidentally knocking over her bag as she did so. A rubber duck, a plastic car minus one wheel, a Kinder Surprise egg covered in biro scribbles, and a bottle of lube rolled across the flagstones of my kitchen.

The bottle of lube was thin, pink, and adorned with glittery stars; it blended well with the toy world in her bag. When Leni saw I'd noticed the glittery object, she acted as if it were the most normal thing in the world, casually gathering everything up — demonstratively leaving the lube till last — and putting it all back in the bag. Since reaching adulthood, we had had a silent understanding that we would maintain this silence on matters that might reveal something about us. And so, I refrained from comment.

But then, as she was standing in the hall, about to leave, it slipped out.

'You two are having pretty hot sex, then?' I grinned, and it felt good to be fifteen again and allowed to take such an open interest in your sister's sex life.

'Stella! What a stupid question!' Leni blushed; I knew she had tensed and was secretly balling her fists.

'Why? I'm just interested!'

'What are you interested in? Whether and how I sleep with my husband?'

'Yes, why not? I mean, you're my sister; I used to be able to ask you things like that before.'

'Before isn't now,' she said, and ran out. I heard her call up the stairs: 'See you on Saturday!'

I closed the door behind her, leaned against it, and started laughing. The situation was so absurd, but at the same time I was shocked by my own laughter. I was shocked because I knew that breaking established patterns had everything to do with *before*, and the name of this *before* was Ivo.

★

Tulia announced that she was preparing the party of the century and anyone who didn't accept her invitation was no longer her family. I called Papa; Papa called Leni; Leni called me; Tulia called Papa; Papa grumbled about Tulia's ingratiating, maternal manner; I soothed Papa; Leni called me and complained about Papa, that he wasn't looking after himself. Tulia discussed things with Mama; Mama called me again, complained about Leni's tactlessness, and said she was afraid she would spoil Ivo's homecoming. And so it went on, for the whole of that stressful week.

Ivo had installed himself in the beach house in Niendorf, where he was enjoying Tulia's care and attention. He didn't actually call any of us himself, just went along with Tulia's plans for a welcome-home party that would double as a family reunion.

Mark had just signed a contract to make a new documentary and was busy arranging his trip to check out shooting locations in Cyprus. Most of the time, Theo and I were alone.

I had missed the party for my colleague, of course; everyone at the office seemed pissed off with me about it. Leo, our editor-in-chief, was particularly annoyed because he was keen on Nadia, whose party it was, and had been counting on me both for moral support and to set him up with her. I was working on an article about an art biennale that was supposedly 'modern, ground-breaking and trailblazing', but was, in fact, just old-fashioned, conventional, and utterly conservative. I asked for a deadline extension, which didn't do much to improve the general atmosphere.

There were times in my job when I was required to lie — to present things that were totally meaningless as 'modern, ground-breaking, and trailblazing', and extol works of art, artist interviews, film premieres, and book launches as important, when in reality they were utterly decadent, sheer vanity, and entirely devoid of ideas. Now, though, this professional lying felt completely impossible.

Theo was ratty; something was bothering him, and he grizzled and whinged. The carrot remained in the bowl; he made Mark and me swear an oath that we would neither eat it nor throw it away. Trying to figure out his issue with the carrot was too much for my aching brain, and I set it aside as something to deal with later, once Saturday was over.

'I'm flying to Nicosia on Friday,' said Mark, unzipping his jeans, as I emerged from the bathroom wrapped in his dressing gown; I refused to buy one of my own.

'What about Tulia's party?' I asked.

'I can't postpone my flight.'

'I have to go.'

'I didn't say you shouldn't.'

'I'll take Theo with me and stay the night. We'll come back on Sunday.'

'He's got football practice on Sunday.'

'Oh — yes. I'll try and get away early on Sunday, then.'

'Are you sure you want to go?'

'Mark ...'

'It's fine, I was just asking.'

'I wish you were coming.'

'It's your family; they won't eat you.'

I had the feeling that when he said *your family*, what he actually meant was *Ivo*. That he was afraid to say aloud what was weighing on his mind.

'I'm not used to it anymore. Those parties! And I'm not used to *him* anymore.'

'Hey, come here. What's wrong? Why does he bother you so much? I thought the business between you had been resolved?'

'I'm nervous, that's all. I'm not in the mood for Leni's comments, Frank's binge-drinking, Tulia's stories about the olden days. I think, more than anything, I'm just tired.'

'You know, this Easter, we could actually go away together for once. One of those boring package holidays with childcare and embarrassing tourists. It would be good for us, something like that.'

He began to massage my neck, and I believed him again, I believed in our idea of happiness. I'd always wondered how it was possible that Mark, the only child in a family of academics too liberal even to force him to attend violin lessons, had married me. How this man, who got everything right in life, and didn't seem to know the word *problems*, who had studied history and English in Heidelberg and London and now produced first-rate documentaries, wanted me to be his wife. Mark, who was good-looking, who liked books — including the kind of literature I enjoyed reading — who was the best driver in the world, who worshipped his son, and who was a better father than I was a mother; how did he manage to live with me? Unlike me, Mark had no earlier, or other, life, no *before*; his life had been straightforward, and the only possible blemish you could point to in his biography was the depressive ex with whom he had occasionally got stoned. Or perhaps his pursuit of perfection at all costs, his weakness for fast cars, and fastidiousness where his own body was concerned; but then, you could reach for a banal pop-psychology explanation and blame all that on his upbringing. Mark was a match for the challenges of life, and the few times he had yelled at me and left the house in a fury, I had been the one who provoked him.

★

I first met him just a few weeks after Ivo left, at the screening of a television programme he had produced. Some people from our editorial department were invited. The programme was about a drug scandal a colleague and I had reported on, involving people in public administration. I'd researched it for a left-wing newspaper; an informant had slipped me explosive details about the case. At the after-party, Mark was very open and charming, entertaining the guests with amusing anecdotes and topping up our glasses. He was not a man who belonged in my life. He flirted with one of his colleagues, looking at me the whole time. I remember he shook my hand as we were leaving the building, and held on for a little too long. He had already offered to drive me home. I had declined. He had expressed admiration for my courage, and asked for my phone number.

At the time, I was having an affair with a man who played the drums and had a pretty serious alcohol problem. I didn't think I was suited to anyone better.

'You can do it. I'll call you, okay?' said Mark. He started nibbling my earlobe.

'Yes,' I whispered, and kissed his wrist.

4

It was raining, and Theo was complaining, because he was tired and would rather have been playing computer games with his football friends. I clutched the steering wheel and focused on the autobahn.

The phone had been ringing non-stop since the early morning. Leni — what should she wear; Mama — had Frank said he was coming; Tulia — could I please bring cheese from the delicatessen? Eventually, I turned the phone off.

'Why are we celebrating, Mama?' asked Theo in a bored voice, drawing monsters on the fogged-up car window.

'Because he's part of our family and because he hasn't been here with us for a long time.'

'Is he going to stay here with us for ever now?'

'We don't know; he's only just arrived.'

'I don't feel like seeing Andres. He'll just go on about his electric bike again.'

'You don't have to play with him if you don't want to. Anyway, Alex will be there too; you can build something with him, with the blocks. That's always fun, isn't it?'

Alex was my sister's middle son and the most bearable member of her family. The first-born, Andres, was a spotty, pubescent creature who tyrannised everyone around him. Two-year-old Anton was still treated like a baby and not allowed to play with the other boys. It was no accident that all three children had names beginning with A; they were supposed to signal that the bearers of these names took precedence.

'Can we go out in the boat?' Theo persisted.

'It's too cold, and anyway, the sea will be rough.'

'You don't know that! We're not even there yet!'

'I grew up there, Theo. Your mama knows all about water.'

We always used to spend a few weeks in summer working for the old boat-hire business before we went to New Jersey, Leni on the early shift, Ivo and me on late. Other village kids would work there, too. I found myself thinking of Harry, the Dutch boy who spent two summers with us as a mechanic, and to whom I sacrificed my virginity. Harry, who had such pale skin because he sat in the darkness of the workshop the whole time, and who smelled so agreeably of oil. Freckles, and a filthy pair of jeans with a rip in the seat. Ivo liked him a lot, and the summer I was fifteen I decided, out of pure jealousy, to like him too, and to like him differently to Ivo. And after a few weeks I did in fact succeed in getting the eighteen-year-old Harry, who listened to heavy metal and wanted to go to sea, to grab my bum and push me up against the cold concrete wall. I knew Ivo was around; I knew he could walk into the workshop at any moment. That was the only reason I tolerated Harry's oily hands on my backside.

Harry had only just started when Ivo walked in. Within seconds, he was on the ground with Ivo's boot at his throat. Just as quickly, I found myself out in the back yard with Ivo leaning over me, yelling in my face. I don't remember exactly what he said, but I do remember he had tears in his eyes.

Two nights later, I snuck out of the house and made my way to Harry, who was staying in a little attic apartment. I climbed the tree outside, and when he opened the window and looked at me in shock, his face still covered in bruises, I undid my coat and showed him my naked body.

We made love in his squeaky, far-too-narrow bed. He put his hand over my mouth the whole time, while making weird noises himself. I felt nothing but a dull pain and a total lack of interest in his body; I just allowed it to happen, clinging to the idea that my doing so constituted a profound hurt and humiliation for Ivo: my coldness, my stiffness, the purely mechanical performance of something he could have had, that I would have given quite differently — tenderly, lovingly, passionately — to him.

★

'Careful!'

I automatically slammed on the brakes. I'd come within a whisker of driving straight into a lorry, quickly wrenching the steering wheel to avoid it. Fortunately, there was no one behind us.

'Sorry, my love!' I said. I took a deep breath. The shock brought me to my senses. Everything had skidded out of control since Ivo had reappeared, and I needed to bring things to a halt; I couldn't mess up Mark's or Theo's life. For the rest of the drive to Niendorf and Tulia's isolated barn beside the sea, I tried to impress upon myself that now, in my mid-thirties, I had a very orderly life, that I was a mother, a wife, and that this life was one in which I felt happy.

I was the last to arrive: I'd got stuck in a traffic jam on the way into the village. Leni and Papa's cars were parked outside the house. We could hear the racket Leni's boys were making as soon as we entered the front garden. Theo clung to me and hid his face in my coat.

'Do we have to stay the night?'

I knew why he was asking. Like his father, he loved comfort and hated even the smallest change in his warm, secure world. He loved Tulia, he loved her little eccentricities, and he loved his grandfather with his pompous monologues, but he hated the narrow wooden bed he had to sleep in, hated the chilly corridor to the shower. I felt anger rising up in me; I felt helpless, let down.

Just then my father appeared in the doorway and waved to us.

'It's just one night, Theo. And it's important to me to have you with me. Okay?' I whispered, as we walked towards my father, who stood in the entrance, very upright, with a conspicuous paunch, but as elegant and self-satisfied as ever, smiling at me triumphantly, as he always did, as if he and I shared a secret, as if we knew each other inside out because we were essentially alike. I never knew whether to be happy or sad about the phoney way he acted around me. On seeing his grandfather, Theo quickly forgot his reservations about the night ahead and scrambled up him like a little koala. My father patted him, kissed his head, then put him down, because Leni's two eldest had already come roaring around the corner to lay claim to him.

There was a smell of roasting meat, and for a moment it felt as if it were Christmas, that perhaps this was just an ordinary Christmas dinner. But already Tulia was swooping down on me, laughing or crying, I wasn't sure which, hugging me so tightly I could hardly breathe. Tulia's scent was unmistakable: an old-fashioned perfume, the name of which she would never divulge to me. Despite her age, her hair was jet-black, like her grandmother's and great-grandmother's, the latter supposedly a Persian queen: not a single grey hair had mingled with the rest since the last time I had seen her. Her glasses dangled from a gold chain in front of her chest, and her lips, painted dark red and looking slightly surreal, opened wide. 'Now we're all together again, at last!'

Tulia's kitchen was very large, with a long wooden table and two equally long wooden benches. There were flowers everywhere, in big earthenware vases; the whole kitchen was full of bowls, plates, bags of flour, salt cellars, and little vials of the spices Tulia grew, dried, and bottled herself, as she did the quinces for her jam. We all had these little vials with Tulia's dried spices in our kitchen cupboards. I even remembered seeing some in my mother's kitchen in Newark.

Papa had disappeared, and Ivo hadn't come to greet me. Leni was helping in the kitchen, baking diligently; Anton was sitting in our ancient high chair, which I had once sat in — he was too big for it, really — drawing coloured stripes on a chalkboard.

Hanna, my father's girlfriend, had installed herself in the furthest corner of the kitchen. She wasn't at all the tart my sister saw her as, but a feeble, affectionate woman who came across as not particularly bright. Papa had met her in hospital, where she was working as a nurse when he was treated for pneumonia. She was childless, selfless, admired Papa, started a relationship with him, and right from the beginning accepted all his constantly changing women without protest. She looked lost over in her corner; presumably Tulia had allocated her this spot, put an ashtray in front of her, and left her there to do nothing.

I looked out into the wildly overgrown garden. In front of the kitchen was a big patio with a hammock; toys were scattered everywhere; children squealed in the distance. Papa and Ivo were standing under an apple tree at the far end of the garden, smoking, deep in what looked like serious conversation.

'As you can see, the gentlemen want to be by themselves. Jan will be along later; he had to go back to the office,' Leni announced, mixing her dough.

'Have you brought the Gouda? Ivo says you can't get any decent cheese in the States,' Tulia cried euphorically.

'Oh, poor thing, one does feel sorry for him,' said Leni derisively. Tulia looked at her, affronted, and Leni immediately fell silent.

'He's a good-looking man,' Hanna piped up suddenly, from her smoker's corner. Everyone turned to look at her. She was gazing thoughtfully out into the garden, at the men under the tree.

Nobody said anything else. Tulia was planning the various courses, Leni was preoccupied with her cake; I took over the childcare and disappeared into the garden, carrying Anton. The boys had holed up in the treehouse Papa had built for us all those years ago, which continued to withstand the harsh coastal weather. Theo quickly shooed me away. I checked Leni wasn't looking in our direction, then set Anton carefully down on the ground. Immediately, he crawled away, tried to stand, fell over, and valiantly picked himself up again. Papa and Ivo were still standing under the apple tree. Papa beckoned to me to join them. I took Anton by the hand and went over. Ivo kissed me on the cheek and took my right hand in his.

'We've had a bit of a chat,' said Papa, smiling at me in that peculiar phoney way again. I knew this territory; all three of us knew it. But we acted as if we didn't. That look always contained the knowledge of something that was better forgotten. But perhaps I was just imagining it, because as soon as Ivo, Papa and I were alone together, I couldn't help but think of the past, of what had happened, of what I so wanted to forget.

'It's beautiful here, as always,' said Ivo, looking at me.

Papa walked off. Ivo and I stood there in silence. We gazed into the distance, listening to the sea.

'You look good, Stella.'

'Thanks.'

We fell silent again. I picked up the thread.

'Good old happy families, eh. You must have missed it.'

'Don't be unfair.'

'I'm not.'

'Yes, you are. It's nice to be here, to see everyone again. Frank, Leni, Tulia. The children I hadn't met. You.'

'You could always have visited us, you know that.'

'No. I couldn't.'

I stopped talking. I felt miserable, forced back into the same old part, the same old family pattern; here, beneath the tree, surrounded by the sounds of the children, which could have been our own voices, as if, in the space of seconds, time had been turned back decades.

The wind picked up, and I caught Ivo's smell. It rushed into my nose with an absurd intensity, and I had to drop Anton's hand for a moment because I began to reel. Ivo's smell had not changed: flowery and pungent in an idiosyncratic way, almost not human, as if from a long-lost plant, an unknown spice — a smell whose toxicity was precisely what made it so seductive. I grabbed Anton's hand again and stepped backwards. It was impossible for Ivo to feel unfamiliar, however hard I tried.

I looked at him, and the grief I felt for him, for us, made me small and vulnerable.

Someone was calling me. Tulia couldn't find the shopping bag with the cheese, and I staggered back to the house, dragging a wailing Anton behind me.

From what I remember, it was a very pleasant evening. We ate

Tulia's roast and Leni's apple cake; the children squabbled surprisingly little — even when they had to go to bed they didn't protest too much. Anton fell asleep without his usual tyrannical bawling, and Papa went easy on the alcohol. Unpleasant topics were avoided.

Today, I believe it was because of Ivo: his presence, the entertaining tales of his travels around the world, his good humour, the charm with which he wrapped us round his little finger. Everyone had to laugh; even Hanna was not made to feel an outsider in our family, at this, our table, this place from our past that we had hijacked into the present for a few hours. Tulia conjured up increasingly obscure and unusual after-dinner drinks: plum brandy, liquorice liqueur, which Leni and I sampled with our eyes closed, holding our noses and giggling.

For this short time, it was true: we were a family, and being a family felt good.

Papa's usual pompous after-dinner speech was tolerably succinct. He even proposed a toast to Mama, whom he described, quite unironically, as his *dear ex-wife* — Mama, normally a taboo subject with him. No one made any snide comments about it later, either. Seated between Tulia and Leni, Ivo kept hugging and kissing them; he called the boys over and joked and whispered with them, and, just as in the old days, drank a huge quantity of wine and didn't seem to get drunk. From time to time I would glance at him and look away immediately if he noticed. It was painful to be so very aware of his presence, to have him so obviously there in front of me. His presence, which for me, equated to an even more intense absence than in the years when he was actually away. Even Leni and her husband, Jan, who joined us later, were being really nice. When Mark rang, late, and I went out to take the call, I felt profoundly at peace.

★

'So — what are your plans?' asked Leni suddenly. She narrowed one eye, waved her schnapps glass coquettishly in Ivo's face, and swallowed his cigarette smoke, coughing. Papa had also lit a cigarette, and that legitimised everything.

'How do you mean?' asked Ivo, sipping at his glass with a disarming smile.

'Well, are you going to stay here, or will you be moving on again?'

Everyone looked at each other, and Tulia put a protective arm around Ivo's shoulders to emphasise, again, that he was the guest of honour.

'I don't know. I think that depends entirely on Stella.'

I choked on my drink. I wanted to pretend I hadn't heard, but everyone else had, and they turned to look at me, confused. I gave him an enquiring look.

'On Stella?' said Leni archly, her mouth stretching into a broad grin. I could have throttled her.

'Well, I think there are a few things she and I need to clear up.'

I tried to work out from the tone of his voice whether it was the alcohol or his sheer love of provocation that was making him say this now.

'Please, not *that*, not now,' Tulia implored. I stared at my plate.

'Is this really necessary?' Papa gave a loud groan and knocked back his wine in one gulp. 'I don't feel this is appropriate, Ivo. The two of you should discuss it between yourselves, if at all.'

'Why? If it was everyone's business before, I'm not going to keep it from everyone now. I mean, before, it was discussed openly — now we're suddenly supposed to be discreet?'

'Ivo, stop it!' Having finally managed to formulate a sentence, I looked at him. His eyes held a strange mixture of amusement, contempt, and ignorance.

'It's over,' said Papa. 'Finished, done with! If ever anything was discussed, it was only because you were not exactly good for each other. As long as things were okay, I didn't interfere. But they weren't okay. You practically tore each other apart. That's why. The family has always supported you, both of you. Ivo, you know that.'

Papa's honesty tugged the last of the ground from under my feet, and I wished I'd never come. I needed to say something, but I was so angry I couldn't speak.

'You think so?' Ivo continued, pouring himself more wine, remembering to check Tulia's glass and putting the bottle down with an amused smile when he saw that it was still full. 'I disagree. But to clear that up we'd have to start much further back, which would ruin our evening. I don't want to be misunderstood. I would like at this point to express my heartfelt thanks to all of you. I thank you all for my borrowed life. And I thank you in particular, Stella. For the life I got to borrow *from you*. Thank you, thank you very much.'

He stood up, downed his glass of wine, excused himself, made an ostentatious bow, and left the long table. Tulia rushed after him in consternation, and Leni shook her head, outraged. Papa sighed, and I just sat there, frozen. Although I knew I was expected to smooth things over and save the evening. And suddenly I didn't mind that once again I was the focus of attention, of the impending calamity; suddenly I didn't mind that everyone was staring at me, inspecting me. I was calm, my anger had dissipated, and all I thought about was Theo, who was sleeping peacefully next to Alex and Anton in the old children's room, who lacked nothing, absolutely nothing in this world. No matter how much the uproar around the table might upset me, I was reassured by this thought. And so I sat there, motionless, as if none of it had anything to do with me. It was only Hanna's fearful glances that occasionally reminded me of the absurdity of my situation.

'It isn't easy. I'm incredibly happy that he's here, and I want us all to be happy. We all stick together, that's the main thing. And, Stella … Stella, are you actually listening?' My father was leaning towards me; I could see his proud, imperious reflection in Leni's eyes. 'I don't want anything kicking off again. You hear me? He has every right to be back.'

Papa went on for a while about our family and how we all stuck together, but his efforts to create the illusion of harmony — one that,

for him, had required so many women, so many years, so many bottles
— aroused in me nothing but pity. He was doing all he could to stop
his world falling apart, and everyone — including Tulia, who had
returned to the table — seemed to be encouraging him, but I knew I
would do nothing to hold back this past that had so quickly, so easily,
eaten its way into the present. I secretly felt something almost like
schadenfreude: at the unpleasantness, at Ivo's provocative manner, at
the questions that would come and that no one would want to answer.
I felt an urge to rip apart the veil that had settled so heavily over us all,
to finally breathe fresh air.

Ivo had not reappeared, and none of us made a move to persuade
him to return to the table. Papa was left to entertain us on his own,
until eventually Tulia fetched her guitar and sang songs in a forgotten
or unidentifiable language that she claimed was Persian Romani, the
language of her forefathers.

We went on drinking, and the cloud that had briefly darkened the
evening seemed forgotten. I enjoyed seeing their faces; I enjoyed Tulia's
scratchy singing, Papa's increasingly loud, imperious voice, Hanna's
forlorn smile, my sister with her silent, always slightly aggrieved
husband. I ate the rest of the apple cake; I thought contentedly of
sleeping Theo; I heard the old wooden boards creak in the corridor,
the shriek of the March wind.

At about two in the morning, Leni and her husband retired to
the guest room in the attic. Papa sat on the patio with Tulia a while
longer, and, as always, they duelled with words, affectionately teasing,
rebuking and criticising, and never, on principle, reaching a consensus
on anything. Around three o'clock, Tulia offered us espressos, but
Papa was already nodding off and went upstairs to sleep in the first-
floor living room. I'd said I didn't mind sleeping in the children's
room with my son and nephews.

I was about to switch off the light on the patio when I caught
sight of Ivo's silhouette in the garden. He was standing, motionless,
smoking a cigarette; his outline seemed to dissolve with the smoke. I

paused, then wrapped a blanket Papa had left on the chair around my shoulders and went over to him.

'What do you want from me?' I asked, straight out.

'You owe me something,' he replied, as if he had been waiting all evening for my question. He moved towards me. The wind had died down; the night was now so quiet we could hear the sound of the sea, and I inhaled the heavy, salty air like a remedy.

'I owe you absolutely nothing. I've paid all my debts, if you insist on using that metaphor. And I'm not interested in these games. I forbid you to interfere in my life again.'

'In your life? Your life, Stella? Have you ever asked yourself whether it really is your life — whether you really are living your life, oh-so-independent and self-determined? The life that is yours, and yours alone?'

'What are you talking about? Who do you think you are?'

'I want the truth. You owe it to yourself, Stella, and to me.'

In that moment I realised what this was all about. I started to feel sick. I hoped it was just because I had drunk too much. I hoped in vain. It wasn't about what everybody knew. It was about what nobody knew.

'What do you want from me?'

'Don't you remember? Shall I jog your memory, Stella?'

'You're drunk. Let's go in.'

'No, tell me that you remember. I'm here because I want to know whether I owe you the life I've been living as mine. Whether maybe the life that you're living belongs to me. Whether maybe one day we'll find our way back to each other — to us, to what we should have been.'

'Ivo, please, stop.'

'I can't …'

For the first time since his arrival, I heard a wounded quality in his voice that silenced me. I watched him stub out his cigarette on the damp earth; I felt him move closer, felt him brush almost imperceptibly against my shoulder. I felt within me the long-forgotten, carnal impulse from the time when I had idolised him, the impulse that for years had defined my days and nights: I wanted to touch him. I recoiled. It frightened me that, once again, my desire was so strong. For a while we stood quietly, side by side, listening to the night, to the sound of the sea, with the sleeping house and the stories of its sleeping occupants behind us.

'What are you planning?' I asked.

'I'd like you to help me.'

'How am I meant to help you, Ivo?'

We were honest. For the first time since seeing each other again, we spoke honestly with each other.

'That scene at dinner was completely out of order.'

'They all know anyway, Stella. Don't kid yourself.'

'What do they know? What? You're driving me crazy!'

'For example, they know that I'm only here because of you, that I only went away because of you. And they know that you're not where you should be, and they know that I'm not where I should be. They know, because none of them are where they should be, either. So we're all affected.'

'You're wrong, Ivo. Each of us has our own life. Each of us is doing our own thing. You can't claim to know what's better for us; we're all adults.'

'Exactly: we're adults, and what's missing is the beginning. Our childhood.'

'Please don't start psychologising.'

'Fuck psychology or esotericism or whatever. It's all bullshit, just pathetic excuses. The fact is that it's the same fucking story that binds us all together.'

'Ivo, enough!'

'We are all going round in circles. Look at Frank; look at Leni, always fretting and uptight; Tulia, living in constant fear that her safe little house will be blown away by the storm. Look at you!'

'Oh, what about me? Tell me: what exactly is wrong with my life? You show up here after eight years, you've not even been here a week, and already you know best about everything, already you know what my life is like. You have no idea about my life. I have a family I love, when are you going to understand that? And I have a job, and I—'

'What job? Reporting on little exhibitions in the foyers of provincial banks?'

'You're vile! Why don't you take a look at yourself? Maybe there's something wrong with *your* life.'

'Correct. There's a lot wrong with my life, and for the past few years I haven't been able to shake the feeling that I'm acting in the wrong play.'

'You always dodge everything, don't you? You just put on your skates and glide away.'

'When you're alone — I mean, really alone, without your shiny husband, free of maternal cares — do you sometimes think about that afternoon?'

'Stop it!'

'Do you?'

'You are *not* going to destroy it — I will not allow you to destroy me again. Do you hear?' I'd raised my voice, and it was shaking.

'I'm trying to put things back together again, Stella. That's all,' he whispered, and touched my hand. I tried to pull away, but his cold fingers encircled my wrist, and I relented. And so we stood there like two awkward teenagers, staring away from each other into the night.

'I love them,' I said, repeating the thought out loud. I kept telling myself: that I loved them, my two men — my husband, my child — and my home, my life. *I love them*: as if the sentence were an anchor I was throwing out.

'I believe you. I don't want to take your love away from you. I just want my love back.'

'Let's go inside,' I repeated, wresting my hand from his.

'I want my life back,' he insisted stubbornly.

He had planted himself in front of me, blocking my path. I saw his body and his smooth, chiselled features — striking, and different. Nothing that could have come from our family, nothing that resembled us.

Fighting back tears, I suddenly realised that I was freezing — with cold, with fear, with too much Ivo.

'Why did you come back?' I asked.

He stepped towards me and reached for my shoulder. 'To remind you. To remind myself.'

I wriggled free and ran into the house.

Lying beside Theo's warm little body, between two sleeping children, I came to myself again, and put my arm around Theo's waist. I hoped a little of his peacefulness might transfer itself to me.

5

My love for him was like a rare, exquisite wine that you're reluctant to open and instead guard, save, and secretly look forward to drinking; but always you postpone the savouring of it, setting it aside for a special occasion that never comes, because for this wine no occasion ever seems good enough. And you save and save it, until one day, for some stupid reason, the bottle breaks and the wine spills onto the ground. Is irretrievably gone. What remains is a mixture of regret, grief, the unspecified longing for something lost, and the hope of finding precisely this wine again somewhere, someday, and drinking it all at once, in a single gulp.

The day I was first introduced to Ivo, I was about the same age Theo was when he first met him. I had just started at our pseudo-liberal primary school, a quick-witted, precocious little thing who worshipped her good-looking father above all else.

We lived in Hamburg, in Eimsbüttel, a part of town where people didn't flaunt their money and drove dark-blue Volkswagens, despite secretly dreaming of owning scarlet convertibles, which they could easily have afforded. The house belonged to my mother; it still belonged to her after she and my father divorced, but she let him have it — even though to buy her out he would have had to pay her in instalments for the rest of his life, which of course he didn't, because he didn't have any money, and because our mother had moved to another country and would in any case no longer be living in the house herself.

A beautiful, old house that had survived the Second World War undamaged, with romantic, curlicued ornamentation on the façade.

My sister, four years older and already at secondary school, was very different to me. She was a mummy's girl, very conscientious and disciplined, a bit snooty and spoiled, who took riding, organ, and ballet lessons: driving her around between these was one of Mama's duties. At the time, our mother was freelancing for a fairly innocuous chemical company, but she would sometimes go on demonstrations against animal testing and capitalism for the sake of my father and his left-wing ideals. Later, she was embarrassed by this, because Mama came from a respected, well-to-do family of doctors who hosted private concerts at the weekends and spent their summer holidays on the fashionable island of Sylt.

In a bid to emancipate herself from her parental home, she had fallen in love with our free-spirited father, a political science and sociology student who wrote radical pamphlets and considered himself a communist, but who in reality was nothing like as wildly radical and communist as he would have liked to have been.

In short: devoted to my father, I was a socialist child who went around in the rubber boots he had brought back for me from East Germany, and Leni was the child of the bourgeoisie to whom Mama gave a pony called Willow. Our parents' illusions eventually bit the dust: my mother's attempts to shake off her family's middle-class attitudes failed, while Papa sacrificed his socialist calling to that of his cock, and we didn't even stay in a squat anymore on our summer holidays in Italy. Mama stopped going on demos just out of politeness, and acquired a taste for money instead. She climbed the career ladder and became head of department at the chemical company, justifying herself by saying that you couldn't escape your origins, especially as hers had definite advantages — unlike those of her husband, who had grown up fatherless, with a failed actress for a mother, whose blood was a hotchpotch of Europe and the Middle East, and who had an aunt so bizarre, with such a dubious reputation, that she was practically a tourist attraction in the village where she lived.

Sometimes I wonder whether things would have happened as they did if it had been Leni in my place. Was it sheer chance that, when Mama and Papa tried to split the child-rearing equally between them

— though absolutely not with the intention of rearing those children completely differently — I became a rebellious, socialist daddy's girl? If I had happened to be the child with the extra-curricular activities and tailor-made dresses, would I have accompanied my father to the house near the port, would I have met Ivo?

★

Papa worked for a publishing house that specialised in left-wing, underground literature but made very little money. He edited copy, networked, travelled around, and wrote. I idolised him, and he took me with him everywhere. As he worked nearby, he would pick me up after school on his bike; then we would cycle back to his office and stay together till late in the evening, sitting in pubs while his friends had heated political discussions over cool, apolitical beer. It brought us even closer, as it entailed lying to Mama: I knew she mustn't find out that at the age of six I had already ridden a moped, drunk beer, and sung grown-up songs about carnal love.

I lived in Papa's world, and I loved it, but even then cracks had begun to appear. More and more often Mama would come to Leni's and my room after an argument, red-faced, eyes swollen, and spend the night there. Our world had begun to separate into two camps. Fearing the prospect of Willow and ballet, I allied myself with Papa's smoky pubs, back-room publishers, and noisy cronies.

It was then that I first discovered that it was possible for a person to shatter like a porcelain cup. After the summer holidays, when we spent a few weeks in Italy fighting to preserve what was left of our domestic happiness, it began.

★

One autumn day, the weather still warm, Papa took me with him to visit his friend for the first time. She lived in a little house with a small garden just up from Hamburg port, near the jetties where the museum ships lay at anchor at the start of a long promenade that was always windy, full of fish stalls, lost tourists and entwined couples, permanently cloaked in the salty smell of the sea and the noisy hooting of freighters. In the middle of the narrow rise, with the edge of the red-light district and a host of little snack bars and cafés on the other side, was the house and its garden, surrounded by a fence, guarded by a huge black dog, with overgrown raspberry bushes and brightly coloured swings that creaked and groaned in every gust of wind.

He introduced her: a colleague of mine, he said, and she offered me a boiled sweet, I remember that clearly, a lemon-flavoured boiled sweet.

They left me on my own for a while with the dog, and I explored the garden with him. It was a sunny afternoon that smelled of water, of the sea. After a while, Papa and the woman came back out of the house. They were laughing, and had wine glasses in their hands. I hadn't seen my father so relaxed for a long time, and I laughed along with them.

From then on, we no longer went from the office to meet his friends in the pub; we cycled to Emma's instead. That was the woman's name: Emma. Not Auntie Emma, or Mrs So-and-So: just Emma.

She was small and slight; she always had bright-red lips and seemed pale and rather sickly, perhaps because she wore her dark-brown hair pulled back in a tight bun, and her round, hazelnut eyes were always somehow veiled, unreadable. Her manner, her bearing, gave nothing away. She wasn't beautiful; she wasn't not beautiful. There was nothing special about her. When I think back, it's as if someone has wiped a sponge across her face and erased her features, her eyes, like the traces of the previous lesson from a school blackboard. But she was nice to me; she gave me plenty of sweets and let me do what I liked: wander freely around the garden, play with the dog, even watch television, which Mama didn't allow.

While I occupied myself like this, Papa and Emma would be in the house, in one of the dark, musty rooms at the end of the corridor, and when they came out, they would be grinning like Cheshire cats.

Even as a six-year-old I realised that we were spending more time with Emma than at home, and that there must be something wrong with this, because I wasn't to tell Mama about it. But I was a child; I was happy, Papa was happy, and before that we used to sit around in pubs for hours. It had to be all right.

★

One damp, drizzly October day we cycled up the little hill to Emma's house as usual, and saw her standing at the door, waving to us. Beside her stood a lanky boy with sticky-out ears and a guarded expression.

'Ivo, my son.' This was how Emma introduced him to me. 'And this is Stella, Frank's daughter. I know you're going to be friends. Come on, Ivo, don't be shy; shake hands, say hello.'

Ivo just gave a brief nod and vanished into the house. The dog barked and followed him, wagging its tail.

Panic welled up inside me. I sensed that all the sweets, the garden, the television, even the dog's attention, the grown-ups giving me loving looks because I was so well behaved — all these were in jeopardy. From now on, I would have to compete for everything. Also, I didn't like boys, certainly not ones who scowled and had sticky-out ears.

At first he didn't say a word to me. Unsure of myself, I retreated, hiding in the garden when he was in the house or wandering aimlessly around the gloomy living room while he played outside with the dog. I was bored; he monopolised the television, and the dog just stuck to his heels. There were still boiled sweets and other little treats, but that did not console me. I was overcome with sorrow, and my father's distant laughter seemed to mock me. Like a balloon, I swelled with disappointment and anger over my lost throne. When winter came, the cold was the last straw: retreating to the garden was no longer an option.

'So where were you before, when I was here and you weren't?' I asked him one day, when, obliged to watch television together, we were sitting staring at it in boredom.

'With Papa.'

'Where's your papa?'

'In Switzerland. He works a lot.'

We fell silent again, and I carefully stole a glance at him. He was a bit taller than me, and the sullen expression seemed to be imprinted on his face. His eyes immediately reminded me of his mother's: they were more open, but never completely so, and, as with hers, a veil of mist seemed to hang in front of them. He had a long nose, and crooked teeth. There was something very adult and decisive about him; I didn't dare contradict him, or fight him for this territory that for weeks I had considered mine.

Suddenly he got up and offered to show me his room. I'd never dared go to the end of the corridor, because that was where my father and Emma were shut away. Encouraged by Ivo's boldness, I followed him down the narrow corridor, and we went into the room next to where Emma and Papa were. It was smaller and a bit brighter than the others I'd seen in the house. The only things in it were a small bed and a green writing desk. Some cars sat neatly lined up on a shelf; there were no other toys. Perhaps I looked a little disappointed, because he asked me if I had lots of toys.

'My sister has loads. I have lots, too, but not as many as her,' I said, sitting down on his bed.

There was a squeaking noise on the other side of the wall, followed by a growl. I jumped; Ivo spun around and listened. For the first time I noticed something that made me clearly aware of the danger, though I still didn't understand what it was: the danger in the afternoon, something dark, forbidden, terrible — the danger that stalked the house, made the floorboards creak, that burst through the open windows like a storm. I looked at Ivo and sensed that danger in his movements, in his small, balled fists, in his serious face.

'Mama?' he blurted out. He immediately seemed embarrassed by his fear, and fell silent. There was no reply; instead we heard a stifled giggle from the other room.

'How do they know each other?' I asked quietly. I got up off the bed, went over to him, and we stood there, side by side. I'd never been so close to him before.

'I don't know.'

'Papa told me they were colleagues.'

'That's rubbish!'

'What do you think they're doing?' I asked the question, hoping Ivo would answer with a lie.

'What grown-ups do when they're together.'

'But they're not together.'

'Of course they are.'

'But … they're not going out together.'

'They're not going out, they're lying down.'

I could see how angry he was. His pupils were dilated, and he was breathing heavily, trying to be strong.

★

Later, as we cycled home along the waterfront, I asked Papa how he knew Emma. He answered that they were colleagues and friends. I persisted: she wasn't at the publisher's, so how were they colleagues? Because she worked for another publisher. And where was Ivo's father, I wanted to know. He was abroad. So why weren't Emma and Ivo with him? Because he worked there and Emma here, and Ivo was going to school in Hamburg.

For a moment we cycled through the gathering dusk without speaking as I tried to make sense of his answers. Then I asked if he was planning to marry Emma. At this he stopped abruptly and lifted me down. He put his arms around me and pressed my head against his face. He stroked me and kissed my cheeks. He comforted me, told me I mustn't worry, that everything was fine, I was his girl and I always would be, always. He loved Leni, too, and Mama, very, very much, and everything was fine. I mustn't worry. It was just that he and Emma got along very well, Mama was so busy with her new job, he needed friends so he wasn't all on his own — and so on.

I knew he was lying, but I let him do it. I wanted to be lied to; the danger I had smelled in the air that afternoon had not gone away. I could feel it lying in wait for me, like a spectre; it had claws, and it was shouting my name.

★

'Stella? Stella? Didn't you hear us?'

Mark stood in front of me in his boxer shorts with foam in his hair, looking puzzled.

'Oh, sorry. Were you calling me?'

'Yes, Theo's been shouting for you.'

'I must have been miles away.'

I was sitting at my laptop, trying to make the final corrections to my article. Tomorrow was the last possible deadline, and I knew I wouldn't get another reprieve, but I also knew that the article was no good.

Theo was in the bath. Mark sat beside him on the stool and told him stories — he always made up stories at bath time — while Theo laughed and slapped the water with his hands.

'Mama, look,' he shouted excitedly the moment he saw me. Holding his nose and scrunching up his eyes, he ducked below the surface of the water. Seconds later he shot up again, puffing dramatically and gasping for breath.

'Wow, that's really brave,' I said encouragingly, fetching his towel. After a few attempts to persuade us to let him stay in the water a bit longer, he admitted defeat and came to my arms, where the dry towel was outspread, waiting for him.

When we had put Theo to bed, I sat at my laptop again and stared reluctantly at the rows of type. Half an hour later, Mark came into my study with a bottle of wine and perched on the edge of my desk. I couldn't not look at him.

'What's wrong?' He uncorked the wine and poured it into the crystal glasses Tulia had given us for our wedding; she had said they were valuable pieces from the estate of her Persian ancestors, who for some peculiar reason had lived in Hungary. Mark always fetched these glasses with a view to us having special sex later on, or if he wanted to have a particular conversation with me.

'Not now. You can see I'm working. And I'm not making any progress. The deadline's tomorrow.'

'That's not what's bothering you.'

'I just feel overwhelmed right now. I need this time to myself. I'll be all right again soon. First there was Tulia's, then this article, and Theo, and —'

'Ivo? You've been acting oddly ever since he showed up.'

'Yes, of course, I'm sure it has something to do with that as well. And last weekend was really weird. All of us sitting there together, just like in the old days, except it's not like the old days, and this or that inevitably comes up again. I'll get over it soon.'

'Maybe we should go away for a few days? We could leave Theo with my parents.'

'How would that work? I'm hopelessly behind as it is. There's still so much I need to —'

He took my face in his hands and pressed his lips to mine. He tasted of wine, and for a moment I was reminded of our first kiss. We had both tasted of wine then, too, but back then the wine in our mouths had been joyful and sweet; now, the taste was bitter.

Adulthood is the point when you stop just living, just feeling — when everything, absolutely everything, has to have a reason in order for you to feel or live it, I thought. I looked at him.

'Don't be like this, please ...' he murmured. He sat on the old, creaky chair opposite me, legs crossed, confident, unruffled. He looked good: I often caught myself noticing this, again. And he was good: good to me, good for Theo, good for our life, our future. A sensitive man, forbearing, one who was always there when you needed him; in the first months of our marriage, I couldn't believe that from then on he really would wake up beside me every morning. And so I always woke up a little before him, and observed him, his face, his sleep, which was so healthy, so free of care, the way chronic insomniacs imagine sleep to be, and in those moments I experienced unmerited happiness.

'*What* am I being like?'

I stood up, closed the laptop and went over to him, took his hand in mine and looked him straight in the eye.

'Distant. As if you can't even conceive that I might be able to share your worries with you.'

'Oh, Mark.'

'Tell me about him. You never talk about it. I know it's not easy, but come on, Stella — I'd like to know everything, I'd like to understand why something from so long ago still bothers you so much. I promise you I'm not jealous; I'll really try. I know it's unusual, and I'm sure it's not easy; I mean, you were kind of like brother and sister, and —'

'There's really not much else to say about it.'

'You see, you're —'

'What? I am how I am. Mark, it's just a shitty period right now; please don't make it any harder for me; bloody hell!'

I grabbed his glass, finished off his wine, and went over to the window seat. I looked down onto the street, the cars driving past, the playground where I had spent so much time with Theo. I'd always felt observed whenever I was there: Stella the disorganised mother, beside all the beautiful, perfect mothers who were completely committed to the role, always knew what was best for their child, were always ready with a word of advice, always on hand with new children's clothes or children's toys or children's health foods, bragging about them.

I could tell that by now Mark was finding it impossible to suppress his mounting irritation; he started massaging his fingers in an effort to keep his composure. I felt so sorry for him: sorry that I couldn't embrace him and his offers of help, that I was just abandoning him to his worry about me.

I sat on his lap and started to kiss him frantically: his face with its light stubble and full lips, the candid, bright-blue eyes that had still never experienced defeat and only ever reflected the positive in life, the small, snub nose Theo had inherited from him.

Confused, he put his arms around my waist and hugged me tight. He pulled up my jersey; I smelled traces of bubble bath on him, I smelled our son on him, I tried to transform my sorrow into passion. I clung to him.

And as I tugged at his hair and he unbuttoned my trousers and wondered if he should carry me into the bedroom, because Theo was asleep in the next room, I remembered how, over the past few years, he had managed to introduce me to his tender, gentle love, his painless love, and how he had cured me of mine — my scarred, tormenting, tormented, sutured love. And at that moment I hated him for it. I hated him for his careful sex, his clear moral principles, his warm hands, his sympathetic manner, his strong sense of responsibility, his blamelessness. Even more than this, I hated myself, because I also felt a yearning for pain, for the possibility of having my guilt confirmed once more, of being allowed to go on hurting myself.

'Wait, Stella, no,' he murmured, glancing at the half-open door to Theo's room.

'Stay,' I groaned, pulling down his trousers. I ran my hands over his body, searching for scars, flaws, deformities, a piece of him that might remind me of me, and found nothing.

He sat there, unmoving, and surrendered himself. Inching my way, I laid claim to his body; little by little I took possession of him, began to move faster, clutched harder and harder at his back.

When he came, it felt as if I had made love to myself. And that consequently nothing, not a trace, had been left in me.

Then he got up and closed the door.

6

'It's a bad exhibition, that's all there is to say. How am I supposed to write anything good about it? A vanity project by a bunch of self-important guys patting themselves on the back — how do you put together a report of any substance about such an embarrassing event?' I exclaimed, when Leo, looking serious, told me I had screwed up and needed to rewrite the article as soon as possible.

Leo was an old hand at print journalism, always in the right place at the right time. This had helped him make it to editor-in-chief of a medium-sized, mediocre newspaper. I'd been there for six years, and each year he'd promised he would put me in charge of the entire culture section. This had been run since the dawn of time by a totally overrated editor whose feature pages were enough to make you weep. Sales were good, and the company was looking at ways of targeting its audience more directly, which would increase both circulation and Leo's salary. As a result, he had recently started to pay scrupulous attention to our articles, and to criticise them.

When I first arrived, he made some very unsubtle advances to me, which I repeatedly rebuffed, until after a while I took on only pretty female interns, who distracted him. It proved an effective strategy. Since then, we had got along well; he let me get on with things, and from time to time I was even permitted to be more critical than the paper's official line, which was decreed from on high.

'I hope you realise that the sponsors of this exhibition are also our biggest advertisers this season? You can't write what you've written here, Stella.'

Leo had raised his voice. He flicked through my pages noisily, skim-reading them one after another and shaking his head, then set them aside, only to pick them up again.

'I stand by what I said. The art is atrocious, the curator's a disaster, the group is no good — it's a cabal of conceited bastards who've been marinating in their own juices for years.'

'What's it to you? I didn't ask you to put them forward for a major national award, I just asked for a neutral review.'

'But that's not possible. Nothing about this exhibition is neutral!'

'Stella, what's wrong with you?' He shook the pages at me and slapped the table with them. 'You know how things are right now. I can't allow myself even the tiniest slip. Are you under stress at home?'

'But you're asking me to write a load of nonsense, a total fabrication — I can't write such a shameless pack of lies.'

'Stella, I have a meeting now, and I cannot and will not argue with you about this. We go to press tomorrow, and I want you to rewrite the article and report on the exhibition in a neutral, impartial way. I don't mind if you keep it short and snappy. You're not being asked for your opinion here. It has to toe the line. You can do an interview or profile next month, if you like; find yourself some talented, unconceited individual who's going to change the world, but right now, let's just get on with our work.'

He led me to the door of his office. I stood in the corridor outside, shaking with fury. I knew it wasn't fair of me to be angry with Leo; I'd been allowed to get away with stuff for years, and now he expected me to hold my tongue and back him up, but for some reason I found it impossible. Even though I knew that what I was really angry with was myself; this job, which I usually did without protest; my life, where suddenly I no longer seemed to fit.

*

I went into my little office at the end of the corridor, the walls covered in notes, photos, cuttings — six years of memories. I called over my new intern, a tall, doll-like girl who seemed so unbelievably organised, down-to-earth, and ambitious that at times it was almost spooky.

'I'd like you to write this article. Nothing critical. Find a positive angle. Imply that this was an important exhibition, then write your name under it and hand it to Leo tomorrow just before eight in the morning. You can take all the information from my draft. Don't look at me like that; it's fine, you won't get into trouble. Come on, this is your chance to finally get Leo to appreciate your work — what more do you want?' I lied, and saw her initial mistrust turn to enthusiasm.

In the foyer, I stopped and took out my phone.

'I have to speak to him,' I shouted. Tulia seemed out of breath; she must have just run downstairs, or in from the garden.

'He's not here anymore; he's in town, been there a couple of days now. He's writing. I gather he's taken a room in a hotel somewhere.'

'Which one?'

'No idea. It'll be some cheap dive, you know him. I always tell him he should treat himself to something better, and he —'

'Come on, Tulia, he must have told you. It's important.'

'You've seen each other already. There's really no need for more than that.'

'So — where?'

'The Pacific. In St Pauli, if I remember rightly.'

Tulia had a phenomenal memory.

'Thank you.'

'Don't do anything stupid, you hear me!'

I hung up and ran to the car. Empty paper cups and Theo's toys were scattered across the interior. I drove off. A Led Zeppelin song was playing on the radio; I remembered my father closing his eyes whenever he heard it.

It took me a while to find the hotel; I parked badly and ran down several side streets before I finally arrived at a small, greyish building that, despite the grand-sounding name, was indeed a dive. I asked for Ivo. The porter called him, and soon Ivo was standing before me in the dilapidated lobby. He smiled and spread his arms.

'You're the last person I expected to see.'

'What are you doing in a hotel like this? Can't you afford anything better?'

'I like it here. You don't feel so important in rooms like these.'

We took the lift to his room on the second floor, where we emptied the minibar. I needed the alcohol; this was the second time since his return that I was drinking in broad daylight.

I sat on his bed. He was wearing black jeans and a T-shirt full of holes — such apparently casual clothes, so thoughtlessly put together, but they always looked amazing on him. He looked at me, his grin widening until it became almost insufferable. He seems to know me so well, I thought. I reached for the cheap wine and put the bottle to my lips.

A laptop lay open on the shabby desk; beside it was an expensive Nikon. A few copies of *The Times*, open notebooks, and, scattered about the room, lots of pieces of paper covered in writing. I picked up some of the papers, leafed through the newspaper cuttings, looked at the photos, while Ivo watched me with amusement. It all related to Georgia, a country I knew nothing about, that meant nothing to me.

Finally, I turned to him. I saw his short, clipped fingernails, his unpolished boots with the trodden-down heels. Apart from the chaotic paperwork, the room was so painstakingly tidy that it made me sad; it was as if I could see his loneliness.

'Please go away again, Ivo. I don't want this. I have a child: please, think of Theo, if nothing else. It's starting again. I can't work anymore. It's all starting again; I don't have the strength for this.'

'If a child's mother doesn't know who she is anymore, do you think that child will be happy?'

'Don't be a smart-arse, okay? You know nothing about him.'

'You're saying I know nothing about what it's like to be six, seven, eight years old and have an unhappy mother?'

'I am not unhappy!'

I had shouted, and jumped up, but dropped back onto the bed

straight away. He stepped closer and leaned over me. His skin was raw, and his eyes were shining; veiled, grey eyes. Eyes that could hide so much.

He knelt in front of me and took my hand. I shrank back, and the small, half-empty bottle of wine toppled over onto the carpet. Neither of us took any notice; neither of us glanced at the door to see whether it was open or closed. In the world of long-dead dreams there are no doors, no children, there is no daily routine and no normality. Just like those afternoons when I would sneak around the garden with him and peer into the grown-ups' world. Ivo held my hand firmly in his cool, damp one. I rested my face against his forehead and sat there stiffly.

'I want you to come with me.'

'I can't.'

'Did you miss me? Did you think about me?'

'I thought about you.'

'Often?'

'Often.'

We looked at each other, and suddenly his eyes no longer seemed so veiled, and I was touched by the soft midday light, the softness in his face, the softness in me. I closed my eyes, let go, and he kissed me. I felt a peculiar jolt, a kind of cold shudder. Then everything fell silent. The sounds of the city, of honking cars, of life outside our room were absorbed into the curtains, into the distance, until they disappeared completely.

When I'd thought I was standing on the edge of the abyss, I'd been fooling myself. I was already falling.

He bent towards me, and I turned my face away. There — there it was again: my love, my painful, scarred, sutured love.

'Please don't turn away.' Suddenly Ivo put his hands over his face and began to sob; he wept, as he had wept back then, when I told him I could never be with him, that I wouldn't be able to live with him. I put my arms around him; I could smell the sour stench of the wine we had spilled. I held him tight and rocked him, the way I rocked Theo when he had a stomach ache and couldn't sleep.

He kissed me again, and his tears made the kiss taste of salt, of all that had gone before, rather than the future. He pulled me to him, pressed me against the side of the bed; I felt the wood dig into my spine, and there it was again, the love I was most used to: love with sharp edges you cut yourself on.

He licked my neck, and I gripped his shoulders.

'Stop!' I cried, rolling away. He sat there, motionless, looking at me. His eyes were red, the corners of his mouth turned down. I sat up and stroked my hair out of my face.

'I have to go now.'

'Forget it!'

He gave me a piercing stare, and it was then, in that moment, that I decided to give up. Perhaps if I'd held on for another two or three seconds, it wouldn't have happened; but it was always a matter of seconds with us, brief moments, any one of which might have changed everything — unpredictable, fragile, which is what we became when we were together.

I took off my coat and hung it carefully over the chair. I unbuttoned my jeans, unlaced my shoes; I placed the black jersey carefully over the coat, unhooked my bra and pulled down my knickers. I stood before him, naked.

Then I lay down on the bed and held out my left hand. He stood for a long time without moving, then slowly came towards me, taking off his clothes, and lay down beside me.

This closeness was a thin rope, and we were two tightrope walkers dancing along it.

I turned, stretched, twisted, as if trying to disappear into a tiny hiding place, far away from the rest of the world.

And when I looked for my prints on him, I found them everywhere: in the small mark under his nipple, beside the scratch on his navel, in the little scar on his chin.

Ivo and I had soon become friends. We got to know each other during our parents' long afternoons of love. The fact that we had a joint secret to keep quickly created a very strong bond. Because we were both aware of the danger: we saw it constantly, lying in wait for us around the house, and in our childish naïveté we decided we would protect the grown-ups from it; we would make sure — as best we could — that they didn't sense this danger.

Ivo was shy, but headstrong; I was stubborn and demanding. We accepted each other as we were. In our small, isolated world near the water, we created our own little island, a paradise shaped by the imprints of the adults, our own little footprints in the sand, and the distant sounds that drifted in from the port.

When we went to our island, there was no school, there were no other people, no memories. The more my father and his mother cut themselves off from the outside world, the more energetically we defended them, and us, and the secret.

At home, Papa and Mama argued, while Leni grew cranky and contracted one childhood illness after another. The thing I can't forget from this period is Leni's constant crying. How, when she woke suddenly in the night and screamed for Mama, she started to call for Papa as well, even though during the day she defied him more and more and would hardly let him near her.

Today, looking back, I have to assume that Mama had known for some time about Papa and Emma's affair; I don't know, even now, why she pretended she didn't for so long. I can only assume that she was afraid, that she herself wasn't sure what she still felt for her husband. Perhaps she believed her marriage could be saved, that it really was possible for a doctor's daughter to love a failed revolutionary. Perhaps. And because they never named the reason why the marriage was falling apart, they argued over little things instead.

She reproached him for his dissolute lifestyle, his indifference to all aspects of housekeeping, his consumption of alcohol; for the unmown lawn, the unrepaired bicycle, the dirty shoes. And so on and so forth.

Sometimes I wonder how, as a six- or seven-year-old, I managed to keep our secret for more than a year, to say nothing for so long. And today, I am even more amazed by how little Papa worried — about me, and what he was asking of me when he made me swear not to tell.

But as the months went by and as, little by little, my family became increasingly distant; as I did worse and worse at school, stopped getting on with my sister, and could no longer look my mother in the eye, I discovered the great fixed reference point of my life: Ivo.

★

Then Ivo's father, who worked as a manager for an electronics company in Bern, came to Hamburg for a week. Papa and I stayed at home. Suddenly, in an accelerated catch-up programme, my homework was subjected to careful scrutiny and close attention paid to the regularity of my meals. The longer he was unable to see Emma, the more his guilty conscience came to the fore.

Mama began to feel her maternal status was being undermined; there were days when she would actually get quite bad-tempered if I said anything good about Papa.

I think that without her doctor's-daughter complex she would have filed for divorce much earlier. Instead, she tried so hard to please everyone while gradually losing control of herself, her life, her husband, and her daughters.

Sometimes I want to call Mama to tell her that I forgave her long ago, if there was actually anything for me to forgive. I think she has spent most of her life reproaching herself, and still does, even now. I would like to tell her that I understand, after everything that happened, after everything she had to endure; that I totally understand her running away, back then, like a deer that's been hit by a car and flees into the forest, trailing blood. She made it; she pulled through.

For years all she heard was reproaches; for years Leni held up a mirror to her mistakes, and I said nothing.

Now, looking back, I feel sorry for her, and I haven't given up hope of telling her this one day, of giving her a modicum of peace. Today I know that, however hard you try to be a good mother, it will never be enough; that it will never be enough to patch all the holes life makes; that you'll never succeed in protecting your own child from life. I'd like to tell her that I know, I've come to understand; that I can see all her genuine grief in her decision to start again in a new country, with a new husband, and not to have any more children.

★

'What's the time?'

I sat up abruptly and glanced over at Ivo, who was sitting at the desk, fully dressed and freshly shaved, looking at me and smiling.

'Half past three. You fell asleep.'

'Shit. Shit! I have to pick Theo up from football.'

'Do you want a coffee?'

'I have to go! Are you deaf?'

I jumped up, exasperated; this was all too much, and it took me twice as long as usual to get my body into my clothes.

'You don't have to beat yourself up just because you've slept with me.'

'Shut up, will you? The last thing I need right now is your advice.'

'I'll give you all the time you need. I know now that it's still there. And that means a lot to me. At least it's a start.'

'It's the end, Ivo — the end. This is absolutely the end.'

'Have you never been unfaithful to him before?'

'None of your business. Where are my shoes, for God's sake? I'm going to be late again!'

Ivo bent down and pulled them out from under the bed. Then he knelt in front of me and put them on my feet. I stared down at his hair and couldn't move or speak.

He looked at me, his hand encircling my ankle; then it wandered up my calf, my inner thigh, and stopped between my legs. And again I felt myself go ice-cold, felt that jolt pass through my body, felt that, for this, I would leave my son standing on the football pitch in the rain, and stay here. I would be capable of doing it, and for that I hated myself. It was this hatred that made me grab his hand and push him away.

'You're a bastard, do you know that? An egotistical bastard.'

'I need you,' he called after me, as I wrenched open the door and ran to the lift.

7

I sat on the patio at Tulia's, watching the blustery spring wind whirling dust and grains of sand high into the air. I knew it would die down, that when it did it would mark the start of the sailing season, and that Tulia's mood would improve considerably; I knew that, after this, quiet days on the beach would be blown in with the clouds. I had spent the second part of my childhood here, in the sleepy village of Niendorf, and it seemed to have nothing — absolutely nothing — in common with the first.

Tulia came outside with coffee and cake; she patted my knee as she sat down beside me on the swing seat and lit one of her rollies.

'I'm worried about you,' she said, taking a drag.

There was something almost surreal about her: her face, her outfit seemed not of this world, or, more specifically, looked out of place in this small village on the northern German coast. Perhaps somewhere else Tulia would have appeared quite at home: with a nomadic tribe somewhere in the desert, or in a different era, as a queen in the Persian Gulf. I looked at her, then rested my head on her shoulder, took her left hand in mine, and sat without moving. She was the only person in our family with whom I could always feel like a child. I could access the feeling immediately: I only had to touch her and close my eyes for a moment, and instantly I was her little girl whom she protected, spoiled, chastised.

'He wants to clarify something; I don't really understand what, and it's driving me crazy. He's harassing me; he keeps saying he needs my help.'

There was a smell of salt, a smell of the old days, and I wondered what exactly it was that always made me look back, compulsively; why my present seemed so flimsy, so incorporeal to me, while my past was very much flesh and blood.

'I've no idea what it is he's trying to clarify, but I'm certain that you absolutely should not engage with it. You have other responsibilities now; you need to be sensible.'

I said nothing. I didn't know where to begin, or whether I even had a clear thought in my head beyond a naked, wordless fear for myself, my son, my husband, for the happiness I had laboriously cobbled together.

I took a slice of cake and gulped down the strong coffee. I would have liked to have crawled away somewhere and waited until the storm outside blew over. Until the start of the bathing season. Until …

Tulia turned to me and gave me a searching look, as she always did when she wanted to ascertain whether I was lying to her. I tried to return her gaze.

'Oh no,' she groaned. She turned away, stood up, paced, smoking, and sat back down beside me with a sigh. I was pretty sure I knew what she was getting at, so I looked at her and tried not to guard myself anymore; unlike Ivo's, my eyes have never been capable of veiling anything. They have often betrayed me, because I have my mother's eyes — eyes both Leni and I inherited, a doctor's daughter's eyes: always a little too fearful for this world, always a little uncertain.

'What?' I asked, just to be sure.

'You went to see him, at the hotel?'

'Yes.'

'Stella, you can't be serious. Why are you doing this? Let him live his life and you get on with yours. He says he has to leave again soon; he's researching something, following up some story, he says. And I'm not sure he's planning to come back ever again. I don't think he even intends to go back to New York. I saw some papers on his desk: he's given up his apartment there and taken his things to Gesi's, apparently.'

'What am I supposed to do?' I said, gazing up at the turbulent sky, heavy dark grey alternating with blue.

'Let's start with you asking yourself what you want.'

'I don't know!' I replied, defiantly.

'Stella, look at me. Look at me and answer my question. Do you want him? Do you want him back again? Do you want to put your husband, your family, on the line — for him? Do you want the old life that's no good for you? Do you want all that? Do you?'

I got up and walked away. She hurried after me; she wasn't going to leave me alone now, grabbing my elbow and pulling me round to face her. I could see that she was afraid.

Suddenly, I felt irritated. I realised that Tulia, too, refused to look back: that Ivo's quest might be troubling for her, too; that she gave us her love with an open heart, but on her own terms; that she still tacitly expected both Ivo and me not to do anything to disturb the hard-won peace.

'I wish I didn't want it, Tulia. But what can I say? Sometimes I think that perhaps it made sense for him to come and get answers to his questions. That perhaps it's just the logical thing for him to be here, and for me to give him what he's asking of me.'

'Are you out of your mind? What exactly are you trying to achieve? What is it you should, and want to, give him? You're not children anymore. Grow up, Stella! Look around; look at your life, look at him.'

'Yes, that's exactly what I'm doing. That's exactly what I mean. No one — no one — has conceded to him, not in all these years, that he has an absolute right to speak, to remember. Not Papa, not me …'

'You were little children. There's nothing he can do about it. Why are you going on about this?'

'We can all do something about it; we all bear the consequences. Did Papa ever talk about it? Did I? Did Leni? And now we want everything to carry on just as before; we don't want to be troubled. But that's not normal!'

'What's not normal is an adult woman who doesn't want to take responsibility for her life, because she and a child she happened to play with years ago messed something up.'

'That's not true. That's bullshit — it wasn't like that. You weren't there; no one was there. How would you know anything about it? Why doesn't anyone ask us; why did no one ever ask us what happened back then, what it was like for us?!'

'For God's sake, Stella, he spent long enough having all kinds of therapy; we all did our best — what do you think we were trying to do? And we gave him everything we could. We gave all of you the best we could. And look at him — he's a successful, independent man; he's not the problem here.'

'Oh, so I'm the problem? Right — I'm the problem in this family, okay, okay ...'

'Nobody's saying that!'

'Maybe it's not about what you gave us, but what you didn't take from us?'

'What this is about is the fact that you were not good for each other. You damaged each other and you ripped each other apart, and none of us want to have to go on worrying about you both.'

'Sometimes it's not enough — sometimes it's not enough to be there for someone, to love them; it's not enough for them to forget, no matter how hard people try,' I said, and started crying. It was ages since I'd cried as often as I had in the past few days. I leaned against a tree, my whole body racked with sobs; our treehouse gazed down at me from above, disconsolate and lonely. Tulia put her arm around my shoulders, looked at me, and shook her head; she shook her head at me over and over again, at herself, and at all that was to come.

★

Tulia and I had sat down again and were staring into space. I had gobbled the cake. It was drizzling lightly. She stroked my hand. I wished I could climb up into the treehouse and hide.

'There's no point — there's really no point in going back. You have to go forward, progress; you have to keep doing that, believe me,' she said, turning her wonderful blue eyes on me.

I admired her; I've always admired her, even back when I lived in Eimsbüttel and was torn between the insubstantial Emma and my down-to-earth mother. All her life Tulia had been 'different', and she had always known how to turn this difference to her advantage. I admired her pride and her strength, her love of the sea, her penchant for the theatrical, her wild roses, her unshakable love, and her stamina. She had stepped into the role of surrogate mother, not only for us, but for our father, too, whose own mother had suffered from depression and alcohol addiction; she would often leave her son at home alone while she chased her grand dreams of an acting career in some seedy post-war cabaret club, until she died of protracted pneumonia when Papa was fourteen. After that, Tulia became his mother. I hated Tulia's silence more than my own, more than Mama's silence, Papa's, Leni's. Perhaps because, to me, she had always been a sort of role model, and I hoped that she, of all people, would be honest with me. Perhaps what I wanted most from her was for her to ask me questions. Strangely, I could accept the forgetting more easily in my parents than in her. The older I got, the more I distrusted her peaceful life, the idyll she had created for herself in this sleepy village; the more I distrusted her dream world, and the more I wondered whether the life she lived wasn't just as much of an escape as the lives of everyone in my family.

'I don't know, Tulia. My mind's a blank. Where do I start? I mean, what is he hoping to find?'

And the moment I said it out loud, I already knew the answer. The moment I said it, I knew it was wrong to keep repeating this question. And I also realised, quite without self-pity, that the answer would ruin my life. That he had come to hear my confession.

He had often told me he felt he was leading a borrowed life: it was a feeling that had haunted him since childhood. And that afternoon, sitting there with Tulia, I suddenly understood what he meant.

★

I first fell in love with Ivo when I was six. Back then, my love was lonely, distressing, and steadfast. Our parents' secret had made us tight-lipped and precocious.

The second time I fell in love with him was after he had stopped speaking and had moved in with us; when he would wake up in the night crying and screaming and no one could calm him down, this boy with the pointy teeth and big ears. When I learned to fill in his words as we developed a silent vocabulary of our own. When I accompanied him to all his appointments with therapists and social workers, because I was the only one who could translate his gestures and expressions, until they became more my therapy sessions than his; though I always tried to convey his world as I saw it, I could only do so through my eyes.

I fell in love for the third time after we had moved to Tulia's in Niendorf because it was all too much for my father; after Ivo had been silent for over a year; when he had started to go rowing, was getting good at swimming, and was going to school again; the morning he knocked on Leni's and my door, woke me up, and said: 'Come on, it's warm, let's go to the beach.' Those were the first words of his new life with us, and they belonged to me.

The fourth and last time, it was the love of a hot summer that clung to my ankles and temples like the salty sweat I could never wash away: when I was fifteen and saw him bathe for the first time, saw him get undressed and enter the water. I'd seen him walk into the water hundreds and thousands of times before, but this time it was different: something in my gaze had shifted.

I watched him from a distance; some strange instinct made me stay put, although I longed for nothing more than to throw off my clothes and run into the water. To Ivo. Into the sea.

Yes, I think that was the feeling I so loved about him that summer, in those afternoons at the beach, the hours we spent in the boathouse, between the freshly painted boats of Tulia's rental company: a sense of the present moment that he distributed like a king, scattering it imperiously like glitter at a carnival parade. He existed in the present like no one else. Sometimes his apparent lack of a future or a past drove everyone around him crazy, even me. He never knew what day it was tomorrow, where he needed to go, what classes we had at school in two days' time, when people's birthdays were; but the fascinating thing was that, as soon as the day actually dawned, as soon as tomorrow became today, he would remember everything and be present, alert and curious.

The absence of a yesterday or a tomorrow made it possible for us, that summer and for many summers afterwards, to have a today stronger and more alive than any dream I'd cherished until then. His reality was so anchored in the moment, in life itself, that it put all dreams in the shade. He lived, I dreamed, and, little by little, with him, I learned to see my dreams as part of my present, or else to let them go. It's difficult to explain to strangers; it was impossible to explain to my family.

Perhaps, in his period of silence, mourning his parents' tragedy, locked in his closed world as if self-punishment were necessary — perhaps he erased everything that wasn't happening in the moment; perhaps it was to rule out any possibility of loss, disappointment, or another farewell. I don't know, but I do know that he clung to the now. Until the day he decided, after eight years, to return.

To me, and, in doing so, to yesterday.

Perhaps that was what I found alarming about the situation, the thing I couldn't handle: the fact that I was seeing a different Ivo, one who was suddenly looking for his past, who had abandoned his today and made his tomorrow conditional on yesterday.

That summer, at the beach, I saw him in the distance, far out at sea, and all the yesterdays, todays, and tomorrows collapsed into the now. Into the tiny dot in the sea, moving further and further away.

When he swam back, I was waiting for him, sitting on his towel, holding two apples I'd plucked from our apple tree as I'd hurried past. He was freezing, and I dried his back as the sun retreated into the sea. He smelled of salt, and grains of sand were caught in his wet hair. He was very tall, a head taller than when the summer began, and he looked down on me with a friendly smile. He had strong bones, unlike his mother, who had seemed so thin and frail; there was always something incredibly tough about him.

His ribs stood out beneath his smooth skin, and drops of water shimmered on his stomach like little stars. I sat there, not daring to look at him, rubbing and rubbing until he seized my hand, looked at me, and asked what had got into me all of a sudden.

We were alone; the little bay was our secret. Tourists hardly ever strayed this far; the area was deemed unsuitable for bathing because fishing boats were moored here, and the wooden jetty stretched endlessly into the water, and people found the waves too cold. But we had made the place our own and adapted to the rough, cool sea.

He put his T-shirt on and his teeth stopped chattering. He was beautiful, drenched in sun, with his sombre gaze, the sharp teeth that were just a little too pointy, full lips, and the dark stubble he had proudly sported, cultivated, and trimmed for a year now. That was the day I first desired him, and the desire was simultaneously painful, exciting, and shameful.

I kept my head down, hugging my knees. Back then I had a pageboy haircut, and I bit my fingernails; my toenails were painted with Tulia's bright-red varnish, and I was wearing a linen summer dress with a red bow at the waist that my mother, in a fit of sentimentality, had bought in a posh shop in New York. I called it my fancy-schmancy New York dress, and was secretly proud it had been given to me and not Leni.

He raised my chin and forced me to look at him.

'Have you got a crush on someone, or what?' he said, in his typical, rather indifferent tone. I didn't reply. Then he laughed, and just at that moment the last ray of sunshine touched his forehead; illuminated by the gentle summer light, he had the aspect of a saint. His eyes were veiled, as usual, and I felt like crying. The grief I felt was so profound that I aged several years in a second. Perhaps I was so sad because I suddenly realised that the love we felt could never be categorised, so it will always remain a secret from everyone else. But I hated secrets; I'd hated them ever since the day Ivo's father came home …

Perhaps I realised all this as I sat in front of Ivo and, for the first time ever, couldn't tell him what was going on in my head. Perhaps it was intuitive grief for all the simple, fundamental things we were giving up when we sat in front of each other like that and I started to look at his body. Perhaps.

Noticing my sorrow, he stroked my shoulders. He had stopped grinning and was waiting for me to face him again.

'Who is it? Come on, tell me,' he joked, and took a bite of his apple.

'You,' I said quietly. I looked at him. He choked, or pretended to, to buy himself a few seconds, then put the apple down on the towel.

'Stella.' Searching for words, he instinctively backed away a little. I felt a kind of relief, and gazed up at the darkening sky. Along the jetty, the fishing boats could be heard pitching and tossing in synchronised rhythm.

'Yes,' I confirmed, and felt the word giving me unexpected strength. I rolled onto my side and stretched. He stared at the water, playing with his fingers.

'It wouldn't work,' he said, glancing at me. His eyes were dark; the irises had practically disappeared.

'Why not?' I asked, and sat up again. It was strange, him looking down on me like that.

'Because it wouldn't. You're not stupid.'

'It wouldn't work because you … because … well, because of the family, or it wouldn't work because you don't feel the same?'

'Both.'

I flinched, my new-found strength instantly transformed into a fear that took my breath away. I started to bite my fingernails. But I wasn't ready to give up; I didn't believe him, and I didn't want to surrender my strength without testing it.

I took off my clothes. I undid the bow on my dress, and although Ivo had often watched me getting dressed and undressed, although we had often run naked into the water, I knew that my simple declaration of love had turned it all into something else entirely.

I pulled the dress over my head, set it aside. Ivo watched me, perplexed, still not sure how to behave, but he watched me, he looked at me, he looked at my body — which had now, suddenly, from one moment to the next, become a body.

'What are you doing?' he asked uncertainly. He shifted to a crouch, as if bracing himself for what was to follow.

I undid my bra in a gesture that was still unpractised, not yet casual or sexy. But I did my best, and managed not to get in a tangle; before I knew it I was sitting in front of him, topless, taking off my knickers. He grabbed my wrist and twisted my hand. He looked at me. And then I leaned forward and kissed him. He tasted just as I had imagined: of salt, of apples, of life. Whenever I wanted to kiss Ivo, this taste would heighten my anticipation.

He kissed me back, then ran the hand that had grabbed my wrist over my elbow and up to my collarbone, where he paused, his fingers at my neck. I kissed him again; he pushed me onto the sand and threw himself on top of me. I don't know whether Ivo had had many girls before me; he never told me. Back then, he was very popular with the girls at school, but too strange for them seriously to want to get close to him. He was mature, though, more so than me; mature in his desire, in the claim he was making on my body. He lay on me, and I opened my legs; and then he leaped up, turned, and ran away. He ran into the water, and I lay there, alone, with a fire between my legs and a vast emptiness in the pit of my stomach. I felt as if I were burning up inside; I doubled over and started screaming. I screamed so loudly that the echo of my voice hurt my ears. I screamed, pounding my stomach over and over again; I wanted the burning to stop.

When he came back, I was sitting fully clothed, hugging my knees and munching an apple. Those minutes when he had disappeared into the sea had changed me. I had grown up, suddenly, quickly, without warning.

'It wouldn't work,' he said. He was naked, and his penis hung down between his legs, limp from the cold water. He wrapped himself in the towel and sat beside me.

'Okay, then, it wouldn't,' I said, and stood. 'I'm going.'

'Hey, wait, Stella. Wait!'

I marched off. He called my name, but I didn't turn around.

Two weeks later, I went to Harry and pressed my groin against his buttocks as he stood bent over a motorboat, mending something. And satisfied my need for retaliation when I climbed in through his bedroom window.

Ivo only found out a few days later. I'd told one of the village girls, whom I hated because she had been throwing herself at Ivo, and who hated me because I robbed her of Ivo's attention. I knew, of course, that she would tell him; and he, of course, knew why I had done it.

Tulia always used to say that when we love we don't love just the man, the woman, the child, the mother or father, the brother. That we always want to love everything and everyone all at once, in one and the same person. That the categorisation of love is a decadent obsession of our age, the insistence on giving emotions a structure. She said that we always need to get everything from the one person whom we love. That we're always longing to unite all these people in one, and that, ultimately, the longing overshadows the love. Because we can never be all things, not all at once. But love, by its nature, seeks plurality, and the unification within us of all that is already inside us. Tulia said a love like this would be possible if we hadn't created systems and societies, if we had preserved the fundamental part of us, but … Tulia said a lot of things.

Perhaps love really is comparable to anarchy?

Perhaps I've never lived the life I should have lived?

Perhaps Ivo had to borrow his life from us all?

Perhaps I really don't know who I am?

Perhaps it's only now that I will find the answers — now, light years away from what I called my life for so long.

I look to the present, which is empty and promises nothing. But I know that only the present can provide me with answers for the past, and perhaps also for what is to come.

★

There are three days in my life that have made me what I am today. The first day was the wintry afternoon when Ivo's father came home unexpectedly. The second was that day on the beach with Ivo. The third was the birth of my son, and although the third day has nothing to do with Ivo, when I roused myself from my exhaustion and saw my blood-streaked son, the nurse who put Theo to my breast asked me who Ivo was. I must have called out his name in my agony. She assumed he was the father of my child. I didn't disabuse her.

8

We had sat down to lunch and I was trying, as best I could, to stay out of the conversation. Theo was sitting on his grandmother's lap, nibbling at the fish fingers that had been cooked especially for him. Mark and his father were deep in conversation about the political issues of the week. The self-conscious effort one always had to make to raise and discuss supposedly important topics at their table got on my nerves. Mark's father was a retired professor of history and politics, his mother a respected psychologist with her own practice. They described themselves as free thinkers: typical educated upper-middle-class, house in the posh suburb of Blankenese, a couple of sponsored children in Nigeria and Guatemala; they liked to cook Indian food.

Mark's mother was still busily looking for faults in me that might have rubbed off on her son. I regarded it as a kind of *déformation professionelle*, her occupational disease, and was resigned to it. Mark was the only child, Theo the only grandchild, and both were so idolised and pampered that it was almost unbearable.

Suddenly I had an uncontrollable urge to smoke a cigarette. I could remember precisely when I'd last had a smoke. When I was pregnant, the craving was so strong that I had to walk to the petrol station at night and furtively light up on a street corner, like a teenager afraid of getting caught.

What a fucking dictatorship of happiness life is, I thought. I decided I would buy myself some cigarettes as soon as I got out of there.

Dessert was fruit salad with mango lassi. I waited impatiently for the martini, which Mark's parents never served until after the meal. Having exhausted political topics, Mark began to talk about his new project. His current series was getting top ratings, and he was now preparing for the documentary about Cyprus.

His parents hung on his every word. I looked around the table. We were all so self-satisfied: the grandparental couple enjoying their prosperity, with a straightforward, successful, exemplary life behind them. My husband, who in equally exemplary fashion had taken the best from his background and made it his own. My son, whose prospects of an exemplary upbringing and a correspondingly exemplary life seemed assured. And me in the middle, the odd one out amid all this exemplariness. Because my past was certainly not a straightforward path to this oh-so-tastefully decorated minimalist living room with its designer furniture. I, who had recently had painful sex in a seedy hotel room with a man who could be described as my brother; who had let the intern rewrite my newspaper article because I was too obstinate to do it myself; who suddenly felt an infinite longing for the sea, while something dark was growing inside me, spreading into every fibre of my body. It got darker and darker, while everything around me seemed so bright, so white, so clean. With me a blot in the middle. A dark blot.

★

It was painful, very painful; I was suddenly in such pain that I excused myself, left the table, and went to the bathroom. I held my face under the stream of cold water for a long time, then stared into the mirror: a Villeroy & Boch mirror, presumably hideously expensive, hideously upmarket.

Who was I, if I didn't want to remember? Trapped between countless squandered possibilities. I stared at myself and wanted to scream. I put my fingers to the mirrored glass and studied my fingerprints.

Things had gone well for me. I'd been lucky. In fact, things were still going well for me. The people out there waiting for me, chatting so amiably among themselves, loved each other. They loved my son, they loved my husband, they accepted me. For the sake of their grandchild, at least — my son. Whom I could not have had without Mark, not because there wouldn't have been other men, but because he had made me believe I could be — was allowed to be — a mother. And now an empty face was staring back at me, the face of a stranger.

Dilated pupils, the corners of my mouth turned down. A few laughter wrinkles around the eyes; a pointed nose, still too small for my face. Smudged lipstick, the remains of the red just an unhealthy shimmer, futile, imprecise.

As a child I would often stand in front of the mirror to see if I looked like anyone. I wanted to belong; I wanted to be sure that I belonged to my family. Were my eyes like Leni's? They were narrower, more like Mama's. All of us had honey-coloured eyes, soft, pale brown, inclined to tears, a little too tired, too wistful for life. But whereas my gaze had sharpened with the years, Leni's had lost clarity.

I'd got my cheekbones from Tulia, that was obvious: high, angular cheekbones I'd been proud of since I was a child, not least because Tulia was so beautiful and I wanted to be beautiful like her. My forehead was like my father's: wide, and a little too high; my lips were full and small. *You and your kissy mouth*, my mother would always say, when she kissed these lips. I'd got them from Papa, too.

But no one else had my nose. It wasn't Mama's upturned, European nose, nor was it Papa's. Papa's nose was long and a bit bumpy, but proud and handsome. I was always trying to touch his nose when I was little. Leni's nose? She had Mama's. But mine was mine alone, which was why it had made me so sad, in the evening sometimes, in Tulia's old, run-down house, when I would lock myself in the bathroom in search of myself. My unfamiliar nose. And then — then — Ivo had told me my nose was the most beautiful nose in the world.

And now I looked at my face and wondered where these eyes were looking, towards what future; why my lips were pressed together, so stiff and lifeless; why I was so pale, paler than usual. Why my hair — thick, dark, shoulder-length — hung down so limply on my neck.

I looked at myself, and didn't know who it was I saw.

Theo was allowed to stay with his grandparents for the weekend. Mark and I drove back along the Elbe in his SUV. On the way, he suggested we take advantage of the child-free evening and go out for a drink. I was lost, and gratefully agreed.

We went to the bar of the Atlantic; they did good cocktails there. I stuck with a martini. The genteel atmosphere of the place, so well suited to Mark's casual, yet elegant clothes, made me feel depressed. It wasn't the first time we'd gone to this bar. Mark and I had always enjoyed evenings there listening to jazz. But now it no longer felt right, though I knew perfectly well that I was what was wrong.

Mark was talking at me. I stared into my glass and tried to listen.

'Stella?'

'Mm?'

'Are you actually listening to me? What's the matter? Come here, come on.'

He was a little drunk, which always made him tactile. He put his arm around my shoulder and pressed my head against his neck. I stiffened.

'Why aren't you saying anything?'

'I'm just thinking.'

He ordered another whiskey. I sensed his disappointment: in me, in my detachment. He was always strangely euphoric after visiting his parents; by rebuffing him, making myself unavailable, I was threatening to spoil his good mood. Mark kept drinking, and the drink made him brave, convinced him that he was completely in the moment and there was no need to think about anything disagreeable, even if only the question of how we were going to get home.

I finished my drink and avoided looking at him.

'I don't think this is right,' I said, astonished by the sudden decisiveness in my voice. I hadn't made a decision to speak; I'd simply felt a powerful impulse and stopped trying to fight it.

'What's not right?' Mark put down his glass and stared at me.

'Everything. How I'm living. How I am right now.'

'What are you talking about?'

'I'm trying to explain. Give me time. It's not easy; a lot of it is just how I feel, not a rational argument; a lot of it isn't even clear to me.'

'Okay, okay, I'm listening.'

He was impatient; he obviously didn't like the turn the conversation seemed to be taking. Perhaps he was bracing himself for a monologue about my mood swings, fortifying himself in advance by drinking faster. My internal resistance intensified; I could feel my anger rising. I tried again.

'I thought I could learn it — I mean, the kind of life we have now. I thought it was right. I mean, I still think that, but I feel the problem lies elsewhere, beyond right and wrong. Beyond criteria like that. The only measure of life is life itself. A lot of things are coming apart. Time is running through my fingers, and I don't know what to do.'

Mark looked at me, and I could see him trying to suppress his irritation; he glanced away, sipped his drink, lowered his head. Eventually he touched my wrist, a small indication of how hard he was trying at that moment to find a way back to me and our conversation.

'It's as if nothing is real anymore, as if I were standing outside myself the whole time, watching myself and laughing at myself, because —'

'Hey, hey — it's all fine, it'll all be fine. I understand; it's not always easy to see someone you used to be with again. I mean, the situation with the two of you is a tricky one, maybe a bit extreme, because you … But what's past is past. It was a mistake, your weird involvement, but it wasn't incest or anything.'

I looked at him, and realised that he hadn't understood a word of what I'd said. Not because he wasn't capable of it, but because that was what he had decided: at some point he had made the decision not to want to understand certain things. Just as I had made the decision to banish from my memory things that pulled the ground from under my feet.

There was a rift between us, a deep chasm opening up, and in saying what I'd just said, I had burned the bridge to the other side.

'The problem is not that I had an affair with a man I grew up with. It's something else — it's more than that.'

Making an effort to adopt a patient, rather paternal tone, which annoyed me even more, Mark asked what exactly *was* the problem.

'I slept with him,' I said, and looked him in the eye.

His lips parted, as if to come out with a well-prepared, politically correct sentence that would persuade me, quietly, meekly, to follow him home. Then all his composure collapsed; I regretted my stupidity, and lowered my gaze. He stared at me without speaking, went on looking at me, not saying a word. Then suddenly he stood up, grabbed the car keys, and left.

I stayed at the bar. I glanced around; I was the last customer. I ordered another drink, and the wearier and more sluggish I became, the more my mind cleared.

From time to time the barkeeper gave me an encouraging look, but he didn't dare throw me out; people are considerate about marital quarrels, especially when the husband is a regular. And I stayed and stayed. Eventually I stumbled into the lobby and asked the porter to call the Pacific. Ivo was there, and promised to come and get me.

I was now in freefall. I stood in the street, looking for him in the cars that drove past. He arrived in a taxi and came running towards me. I laughed. He asked no questions. The first thing I asked for was a cigarette. He gave me one he'd just lit for himself.

'You're drunk,' he observed in amusement as, wheezing and coughing, I took my first drag.

'I'm clearer than I've ever been,' I replied, and followed him. He stopped another taxi, and we drove to a bar in St Pauli — I can't remember which; I know that it was packed and loud and we sat in the window seat in a corner and I drank more martinis. He didn't say much; he watched me, and at one point he touched my knee. I looked down at his hand as it strayed upwards, and I pressed my legs together. I felt dizzy.

'Shall I take you home?' he asked, and I shook my head. We went to his hotel. He undressed me and carried me into the bathroom. He ran me a bath and put me in. The water wasn't warm enough, and I whimpered. He massaged shampoo into my hair and rinsed off the foam. It stung, and I wailed. I asked for more alcohol; he wouldn't give me any. At some point I pulled him down to me and kissed him. He let me do it, and got wet. I was aroused, and indifferent; something in me was crying out to forget all the rules. Even though I was so drunk, I realised that tomorrow would be terrible; I knew that then I would come crashing down. Now I was still falling — it was a wonderful feeling, as if I were flying, as if there were no gravity — but sooner or later I would hit the ground and shatter into a thousand pieces; perhaps there would be nothing left at all.

Every night I had ever spent with Ivo had been like a fight. I don't know how, in my drunken and exhausted state, I was able to muster such strength, such an appetite for this fight. In his seedy hotel bed.

I took him, I took his body; I conquered his brusqueness, his feigned nonchalance; layer by layer I stripped them away.

I gripped his hands, and my lips roamed across his groin, his chest, his navel. He denied himself, refused, as he always had, to accept gifts. But he had no choice. I brought him off with my hand, watching him as I did it, watching his tired face, his half-closed eyes, and his slightly parted lips, saw him battle with himself, and how alone he was in this battle, and how he finally succumbed and found a brief, painful release in my hand.

We lay next to each other for a long time without speaking. Then he sat up and looked at me. I lay there, naked, still dazed, trying to collect my thoughts.

'What will you do?' he asked, and put his forefinger between my legs.

'I'll tell you what it is you want to hear. But I won't go with you.'

'I just want us to remember. That's all I want.'

'What for?'

'To stop this, to put an end to these battles. I like the way you're looking at me now: as if you know more than I do, as if you know all the things I can never know, just because you're you.'

I spread my legs and waited for him to lie on top of me.

'But I don't like the fact that you've forgotten so much: things it's impossible to forget. Or you act as if you have.'

He lay on top of me.

'The fact that you cling to this guilt, that you won't let go, that you stand in your own way. There are still some things we have to find out together. Because no one else can, or wants to. You know that.'

I took him inside me, and it hurt.

'You do, don't you? I often think about that afternoon, Stella. I've been thinking about my mother a lot lately, and that maybe it was wrong not to ask any questions back then.'

He moved faster, and I raised myself up slightly so he had to look at me, look at me again and again each time he hurt me. I shifted towards him, putting my fist under my back to prop myself up.

'I've fucking tried to make my peace with it, but somehow I just can't seem to do it. And do you know what I ask myself, Stella, shall I tell you?'

His voice shook; he began to breathe faster.

'I ask myself what the fuck it is with the two of us. You're so bloody clever, why the hell didn't you see it — that we should have found a way to end it early on, we should have fought it out, talked it out, fucked it out.'

He wrapped his arm tight around my neck and pressed me to him. I freed myself from his grasp and pushed him away.

'Why did we break off in the middle — of life, of the fucking — why did we break it off? Maybe we could have found some peace; we'd have had the climax of our lives, wouldn't we? I mean, maybe then we'd have this crappy normality that's apparently so important to you! We could have had it ourselves, this fucking normality!'

Then he pushed me up against the head of the bed and screamed in my face, screamed that I'd had no right to ruin his life, first to take everything, demand everything, and then to walk away, disappear into my fucking normality; that I'd destroyed his peace of mind and made him homeless; he couldn't stand himself anymore, and it was my fault, my fault. Me with my affectations and my propriety, my fear of what had happened. That there was no substitute for a childhood, that there was no substitute for love, no substitute for life, your own life.

And he kept pushing me against the headboard; my back was hurting again, just as it had the first time we slept together. His anger made him rougher, and my body groaned, gasped and thrashed as if in a fever; and yet, and yet, I didn't give in, I even felt a perverse relief, a moment of absolute emptiness and truth.

9

Maybe there never really was a beginning for Ivo and me. Maybe that was precisely what was so disastrous about that cold afternoon when his father came home unannounced. That this stole our beginning; that our beginning happened at the end.

Back at my apartment, I took a long shower and went to bed. It had not been made, and there were empty beer bottles lying around the kitchen. I don't know why I didn't panic, or feel overcome with guilt. Mark wasn't there. Theo wasn't home yet; Mark was picking him up that evening. Then we would read him a bedtime story.

I fell asleep immediately. Perhaps I had long since passed the point when I abandoned control, when I turned my back on my life.

The emptiness inside me was beguiling, and I slept, oblivious, all through the grey April Sunday, which was unusually cool and quiet.

I was woken by the sound of the key in the lock and the creak of floorboards in the hall. A moment later Mark stood before me, unshaven, hands in his trouser pockets, looking shocked. I can't imagine what he was expecting, whether he thought I would already have moved out, or that I would be sitting at the table, red-faced and crying; he certainly hadn't expected to find me sleeping peacefully in our marital bed.

'Where were you?' he asked, staring at me with tired eyes. He would certainly have got drunk the previous night.

'I was at Leni's.'

'You're lying.'

I don't know why I lied to him: out of pride, out of fear, a last instinct of self-preservation, perhaps. But I was sure he would never have called Leni.

'No. I'm not. Why would I still be lying to you *now*?'

Yes: why? I wondered.

No substitute for love, no substitute for your own life … The words echoed inside me.

I got out of bed, fetched some clean clothes from the wardrobe, and began to get dressed.

Mark stood there a while longer, as if rooted to the spot, and watched me silently, then left the room. I gave a sigh of relief and sat down on the edge of the bed to collect my thoughts. It was starting again: the lies that would lead to many more, one after another, until no one would know what the truth was.

Just as it had been in the last two years I was with Ivo. Before the anguish consumed me, ripped me to shreds.

I jumped. It couldn't happen again. I had Theo now. I was seized with a sudden, terrible longing for him, and something in my body contracted painfully. I glanced at the clock. I had to pick him up from his grandparents' right now, then everything would be okay. If he were with me, if I could just hug him close enough, I would know where I belonged. At the same time, I knew perfectly well that this was a lie, but all that was left for me to do was to cling to this lie. No substitute, I thought again, and noticed my hands were shaking.

'It's perverse, you know that?' said Mark suddenly, from the kitchen. I leaped to my feet. His voice was cold, full of contempt. I wondered whether to go into the kitchen or wait for him to come to me. The kitchen was a neutral space.

My hair was still wet from the shower and stuck to my neck. I pinned it up and glanced quickly in the mirror to check whether my face still bore any traces of the previous night, but all I saw was a pale woman with wide eyes, quivering eyelids, and slightly swollen lips.

He was sitting at the breakfast bar, drinking beer. Desperate for a cigarette, I remembered that I had kept Ivo's packet. I fetched it, and lit one. Mark stared at me, aghast. Had he expected remorse and tears, that I would beg for forgiveness, fall to my knees, and promise never to do something so monstrous ever again? But I felt no remorse, only infinite emptiness. Not even the beginnings of an explanation or answer that could have justified or excused the previous night. Nor did I want his understanding; I was the one who needed to understand myself, to understand that I had ripped open the guilt again, the deep hurt, the wound inside me that had been plastered and whitewashed over.

★

I had tried to make clear to Mark from the beginning that my life had been fundamentally different to his. Little by little, I had told him about my past. He was the kind of man who, when he said *relationship*, meant exactly that, who had clear moral values and lived by them. And I knew I would have to be honest with him.

And I was tired, just plain tired, of all the rows, the attempts at clarification, the desperate longing and hide-and-seek of the preceding years. I met Mark, and I could see in his clear, resolute eyes that he would love me if I let him. I recognised that he was attracted to what he described as my *otherness*, the eccentric imprint of my family on me, and that he was trying, through me, to buy his way into a freedom he had never had in his youth, and had never allowed himself as an adult. And I was prepared to provide him with this little portion of otherness and freedom.

I realised that it would mean turning my own life back to front; that in order to do all the things I had never done before, I would have to learn to live according to Mark's system of right and wrong. When I decided that I wanted a life with Mark, I knew what I was doing. I had been yearning for this kind of normality, straightforwardness, and predictability; I longed to be healed, and knew that I needed to change my life if I were to avoid being completely overwhelmed by my own instability.

Mark was the fateful encounter I had secretly been hoping for; he was the lighthouse, the signpost pointing me towards my proper life.

Mark accepted as truth everything that, at the start of our relationship, I told him about me and my family, hesitantly at first, filtered, always slightly modified. Ivo also came into my stories; I allowed him to feature from time to time, but was careful not to speak of him too often.

It was only later I broke it to Mark that he was living with a woman who had shared her past with a man she had grown up with like a brother, a man with whom she had had a relationship that in every aspect was akin to a transgression. I told him I wanted to forget all this, that I accepted and was grateful for his help. He nodded, and kissed my wrist. Sympathetic. Understanding.

When he eventually asked me why I had left Ivo, I answered evasively: we weren't a very healthy combination, as it turned out, we hadn't always been good for one another. I also said that, as time went on, it became impossible to defy our family and all the others who didn't necessarily approve of our liaison. He nodded at this, too. Finally, in a moment of weakness, by which time we already had Theo, I blurted out the reason why Ivo had become part of our family, and Mark actually had tears in his eyes when, in bed one windy night, he heard the story of Ivo's parents for the first time.

He only ever asked me once whether my addiction to Ivo might also have been because of the sex. I looked him in the eye and gently kissed his lips. I was touched by his attempt to comprehend the abyss that was Ivo and me. I said the reasons had definitely also been physical in nature. Yes, I said, that too. It wasn't what he thought, I said.

'What do I think?' he asked, giving me a wary look.

'I think you're thinking he was better than you.'

'Was he?'

'That's not it. That's what I meant. That's not it.'

'So, was he?'

'No, he wasn't. It was just different with him, and I was different, too.'

'Different how?'

For Mark, sex was a way of talking about Ivo and me that he found accessible, comprehensible, and thus something that could be changed.

'Just ... different.'

'How exactly?'

I was surprised that he was so persistent in his interest. We were in the car, driving to a party some friends of his were giving; it was a late Saturday afternoon, the atmosphere relaxed.

'He was rougher, more urgent, much less romantic. It wasn't pleasant, if you must know. We hurt each other. We hurt each other very often, very much.'

He said nothing for a while; he seemed to be chewing on the thought. Then, concentrating hard on the road, he asked: 'So I'm soft, romantic, and my desire is less *urgent*?'

'Oh, Mark, come on, stop this nonsense. You're my husband. We don't have any problems in bed, do we, as far as I'm aware?'

'I didn't think we did either, until now.'

'Well, there you go.'

We didn't continue the conversation, but I remember we spent the night at his friends' place, a house in the country, and we drank a lot and then had sex in a tiny attic room, because Mark pushed me to, and I was terribly embarrassed because he was particularly loud and so was the provocatively squeaky bed. But that seemed to be exactly what Mark wanted; he seemed to want to prove to everyone, and especially to me, that he was totally capable of being wild, inconsiderate, and *urgent*.

★

In our eight years together, I was only unfaithful to Mark once. And I'd told him. Two months later.

It was on a research trip to London, when it turned out that the freelance photographer accompanying me was a man who reminded me of something I had lost. A good-looking, dark-haired man in dirty cowboy boots, who was always scratching his arms, smelled strongly of aftershave and nicotine, and whose fingernails, like mine, were bitten down to the quick. He was very professional and fulfilled the work brief precisely. We finished earlier than expected, went out for a drink, and ended up hanging around in a pub until two in the morning, telling each other about our jobs, then about our relationships.

Eventually we walked across snowy London back to our hotel. In the lobby he asked if he could come up to my room for a drink.

For the next few days, I could hardly believe I had slept with this man, but he didn't refer to it, and when we landed back in Hamburg we just gave each other a quick hug goodbye. It was only then that it dawned on me that I had betrayed my husband, according to his system of right and wrong, and that I had to tell him. When I confessed to Mark, he yelled at me, pacing furiously up and down in our bedroom. It was a shock for him; he would never have thought me capable of such a thing.

He stayed with friends for a week, refused to speak to me at first, impressed my guilt upon me any way he could; he punished me. Months later he would still regularly remind me of my transgression and his superiority, the superiority of the one who forgives. For weeks I had to acquiesce when he decided which restaurant we would go to, for weeks he decided which films we would watch, for weeks I no longer had the right to disagree. And I acquiesced, because I knew I had given him the right to punish me the moment I abandoned his system. At the time, I wanted to believe it was a system that would deliver me from my mistakes, my waywardness, my misguided search.

★

This time, though, was different, and I could see in his eyes that he felt the same. I was smoking, which provoked him, because he was a militant non-smoker and considered smoking a weakness that characterised people with no willpower.

'What are you doing, Stella?' he hissed, propping himself on the breakfast bar.

'I just feel like having a cigarette.'

'Aha. Another novelty. What else have you got up your sleeve? Go on, spit it out; I'm listening. I'm devoting today entirely to you, my wife, who doesn't come home at night and fucks around behind my back. With a man who's her brother, no less. I mean, it's worth making time for that. Theo will stay at my parents' tonight. I can't expect him to deal with a father who drinks and a mother who smokes.'

The sarcasm in his voice was unmistakable. It was a tone Mark borrowed from his father whenever he was at his wits' end, when he was stressed out and exhausted. All his conciliatory gestures and sympathetic looks seemed to have been exchanged for contempt. He kept shifting on the bar stool, and when he looked at me, it was with disgust.

'I can't explain it to you, Mark, and I cannot and will not behave the way you probably expect me to right now. I know what I've jeopardised; I may not have grasped the full extent of it yet, but I have an inkling, and believe me, it scares me to death. We need to find a solution.'

He stared at me, wide-eyed. He had anticipated a full-on fight, that we would shout at each other, say hurtful things, perhaps that we would both cry afterwards. But he was expecting an admission, an admission that I had behaved badly. He hadn't taken in anything I'd said to him at the bar the previous night; all that mattered was my egregious mistake.

'Can you hear what you're saying? Have you gone completely mad? What are you talking about, for God's sake?' he yelled. He stood and walked towards me, and when I tried to turn away, he grabbed my elbow and forced me to face him. We stared at each other, and again I doubted my strength, my will, to bear what was to come. But something inside me was throbbing, screaming, whirling. Something inside me was crying out to be lived. Something inside me yearned for chaos, the sensation of falling, the clarity that would come if I survived the storm. Fear tugged at me, plucked at my skin and stopped my breath. I was on the brink of throwing my arms around Mark's neck and begging him for forgiveness.

And I might have done it, if at that very moment he hadn't raised his hand and slapped me. It was the first time he had ever hit me. It was so unexpected that I staggered back, lost my balance, and banged into the corner of the table. The sharp edge dug into my back, but I felt no pain.

Shocked by his own behaviour, he stepped away and hid his face in his hands. I turned and propped myself up on the table; my left cheek was burning, and I felt numb.

I saw the fruit bowl, with the carrot on top, wizened and crooked, starting to go brown. It was perched on other, fresh pieces of fruit, which Mark always bought at the Turkish shop around the corner. There it sat, quite out of place next to all those lovely, plump fruits, its mere presence seeming to drain them of their colour, taste, and sheen.

Something about the image fascinated me. Why had Theo kept this carrot, and why had it sat there for so long? Why there, of all places? What was its significance?

'Why didn't we throw away the carrot?' I asked Mark. I looked at him. He stood before me, pale and ashamed, barely taking in what I was saying.

'I'm sorry,' he whispered, instead of answering my question.

'No need to be sorry. I'm not angry with you.' I poured myself a glass of water and drank thirstily. The burn on my cheek was subsiding.

How do you live without scars? How do you live without constantly cutting yourself on your own desires, your own sharp edges?

★

'What are you going to do now, Stella?'

It was the first meaningful sentence Mark had said to me that day. He was back on the bar stool again, his head propped on his hands, and he, too, was staring at the carrot.

'I don't know. I'll have to see. Everything feels so empty.'

'What about Theo? What's going to happen to us? Can't you see where all this is heading?'

I heard the despair in his voice, and I wished I could put my arms around him and reassure him that it would all be okay, that he just needed to give me some time. But that would be yet another lie, another promise I wouldn't be able to keep. I sat down on the stool beside him.

'How can I love, how can I be a wife to you, a mother to Theo, if I don't know who I am, Mark?'

'So all it takes is for him to turn up again after eight years, and you just throw everything overboard? Everything, Stella! You fuck him, then tell me some crap about finding yourself?'

'It's not about sex.'

'So why are you sleeping with him?'

'Perhaps because I thought it would help me remember something.'

'This all just sounds sick. Do you realise that?'

I suddenly wondered whether Mark had ever been unfaithful to me.

'Mark, I'm not asking you to understand. I'm well aware that I can't undo what's happened.'

'What has he done to you? The guy is sick. He's so sick even your family threw him out. Then he just disappears, and you — you have a good life, you have a bloody good life! And suddenly you're standing there telling me, in all seriousness, that you're screwing him in order to remember. What is it you want to remember, for fuck's sake?'

'Why it was the way it was with Ivo, why he is the way he is, why he took this path in life — it's all my fault. I was the reason he took the decisions he did. He's a very unhappy person.'

'Unhappy? Stella, I'm really trying here, but my imagination won't stretch to this. Unhappy! What about our son? Will *he* be happy if you're fucking Ivo?'

'I told you, it's not about that!' I shouted back. The room around us quivered. He opened his mouth as if to reply, then shook his head.

'It's not about that. But how can I explain it to you? Mark, please. I know it sounds terrible, but: I feel guilty. It's not humanitarian aid I'm offering. It's not a penance, either. There are many things I've denied for a very long time, and when you deny things, little by little you start to forget them. It's about me, it's all about me, please understand that. It's just … Ivo is the one who knows me, who knows everything about me, even things I've forgotten, and vice versa. I don't think we're able to love each other. I don't want that. It's just that we need each other. We tried —'

At the word *love*, Mark had stood up; he shook his head again and disappeared into the bedroom.

I followed him and kept talking; it was my last chance to try to clarify things. He had started to get his clothes and pack his sports bag; he went on throwing things in randomly, ignoring me. When I went over to him, he rammed me with his elbows, and when I stood between him and the wardrobe, he pushed me aside. It wasn't until he was in the hall that he stopped in front of me and looked at me sternly.

'I don't want to listen to this sick nonsense. I'll give you a few days, Stella. I've run out of patience. Think it over carefully. I won't give you a second or third chance. I'm going to leave Theo at my parents', and you're going to promise me you won't show your face there. I'll tell him you're ill and you need to be alone for a while. Is that clear, Stella? Are you listening to me? Please don't call me until you've decided. And I hope you realise that, if you don't manage to sort this shit out, you won't get to keep Theo without a fight.'

I wanted to respond, but he had already opened the door and gone down the stairs. His footsteps echoed in the stairwell. I stood in the doorway, heard the sound of the engine and the car driving away.

10

Leo had shouted at me down the phone, asked me what I was playing at, getting an intern to write my article, said it was disrespectful to him and to our sponsors, and as he hauled me over the coals at the top of his voice, it occurred to me that shouting had become a regular feature of my communications over the past few days, and would probably remain so for the foreseeable future.

'Leo, I'm really sorry if you have to deal with any unpleasantness on my account.' I tried to placate him.

'Unpleasantness? What are you talking about, Stella? I'll see you in my office on Wednesday, ten o'clock sharp!' he barked, and hung up.

It was happening again: doors were being slammed, I was being sidelined, phones hung up before conversations were over. 'The untouchability of the extreme,' Ivo had once said. I didn't mean to, but I couldn't help smiling.

I spent the whole morning in bed, weeping. It was Monday. Theo's grandparents had taken him to school; Mark would be in the studio. I had black circles around my eyes and a snotty nose.

On the floor was a half-drunk bottle of gin, beside me a packet of cigarettes. My mobile rang. I stared at the ceiling. In the living room the stereo was playing *La traviata*, an ancient CD Tulia had given me. I didn't know the first thing about opera, but my pain seemed to require exactly this degree of pomposity. The ringing didn't stop. The number was withheld.

'Stella?'

I pressed the cold, silvery object to my ear and said nothing. It was my father.

'What's the matter?'

'Nothing.'

'Yes, there is. I'd like to see you. I'm in the neighbourhood; will you be home a while longer?'

'No.'

'Yes, you will. Stay there, okay? I'll be with you in ten minutes.'

I sat up abruptly. Why wouldn't they leave me in peace?

I had only just washed my face and put on some moisturiser when the doorbell rang. I hid the gin bottle, took a deep breath, and pressed the entry button.

The front door opened downstairs. I heard my father's heavy steps, his heavy breathing.

I went into the kitchen and put on some coffee. He came in, threw his raincoat on the floor, and sat on the sofa, the only seat still able to accommodate him.

'Theo not here?'

'School.'

'Has Mark gone away?'

'Dad, why are you asking? He's at the studio.'

'Has he moved out?'

'What? What gave you that idea?'

'There aren't any trainers in the hall.'

Mark went jogging almost every evening.

'Why are you here?'

'I saw Ivo yesterday.'

'And that's why you're here?'

'Stella, I'm your father; I'd like to support you in whatever you're going through right now, but you need to know what you're doing. Make me an espresso. Have you been smoking again?'

He had spotted the half-full ashtray on the dishwasher.

Taking refuge in activity, I put two plates on the kitchen table. The carrot was still there; I didn't have the heart to throw it out. I'd taken it out of the bowl, and now it sat on the table all by itself, looking even more pitiful. Papa's deep-set eyes were fixed on me, and it was making me uncomfortable.

I handed him the little cup and put a piece of cheesecake on his plate. The cake Mark had bought for Theo — for his son, who deserved something sweet after his football practice. Things it never occurred to me to do.

Every object in the apartment seemed to remind me of things I had forgotten: fresh fruit, fresh vegetables. It all seemed so peaceful, so alarmingly perfect. The polished floor tiles, the neat pile of newspapers by the sofa, the freshly ironed shirts on the stool, the washed-up cups. And me in the middle. I, who was destroying all this, who wanted to throw it all away, who didn't seem to notice all the effort that went into these details; I, the bad mother; I, the woman who, after a conversation with her husband, had driven drunk to another man in a sleazy hotel and slept with him; I, the journalist who didn't do her job, who talked about things no one understood or was interested in.

How easy it must be to condemn me.

Papa blew on the hot, dark liquid in his cup. There he sat, the aged pasha, the man who, in all those years, had never said a single word about that afternoon; who had bought his way out of his guilt, had wiped his conscience clean by taking the boy in, only to pass him on to his aunt. Who drowned his guilt in whiskey, and sought to forget it in women's laps. The man who had robbed us of our childhood.

A pigeon settled on the balcony, cooing. The world outside was alive and reaching towards the sun, while I hid from it.

'Papa?'

I looked at him and paused for a moment; I wondered whether I should say what I wanted to say. Eventually I began again.

'Do you actually realise what's going on? What's been going on this whole time? What went on with Ivo and with me? What do you think it is? I'd like to know what it is you've thought all this time.'

'Is that what this is about? Is it about me?'

'You? You? No — it's about all of us: like it or not, we're chained together like a team of bloody huskies.'

'Stella, come here — come and sit with me. You don't look good. At all. And it's not good that you've started all this again, either. Of course it was bound to kick off when he came back. He can't help himself. I actually understand him. He'll survive it either way. But you — you're not made like that. You won't be able to cope; in the end you'll pick yourself up off the floor, look around, and realise everything's ruined. Just like before. But then Mark came along and set you back on your feet. He won't be there this time.'

I stared at him in dismay, wondering how he could sit there talking so calmly, as if he had nothing to do with it. He patted the sofa impatiently, still waiting for me to come and sit beside him. The idea was unbearable. I sat down facing him, on the stool.

'Stella, you are a grown woman, you have a family, you're a mother — pull yourself together!'

He had raised his voice, and I couldn't help the fact that when his voice got so loud, it still filled me with fear.

'You mustn't repeat your mother's mistakes!'

At this I jumped up and went over to him. I stood looking down at him. Suddenly, my fear completely disappeared.

'My mother? My mother's mistakes? Tell me, who was it who took away everything she had? Why don't we talk about that, for a change? She was so devastated she couldn't bear to come back to Germany, not until her parents died — and you're talking about *her mistakes?*'

My voice shook, and I struggled to keep my composure; I didn't want to cry in front of him, not now. My throat was dry and raw. I gulped down the hot coffee and felt it burn.

'Why do you say that?' He was almost whispering.

'Oh, please. As if you didn't know.' I looked at him, and held his gaze. He had grey eyes with heavy lids, like a tortoise, eyes that had learned from and grown tired of life, that had already seen everything, that had no expectations anymore. I wanted to pity him but wouldn't let myself; I couldn't afford pity right now.

'I needed Ivo; I needed him for my own sake. Do you want to know why? To have any idea of who I was. After what happened — after what happened to us. What we did. I needed him, because he seemed to have left all that shit behind. At least, so I thought.'

'But that's not true, Stella, that's what I was trying to explain to you all those years. It's his way of protecting himself, and it's also his Achilles heel. Why can't you see that?'

'I do see it. I do now. But still I was able to be happy with him. Somehow.'

'All the drugs, all the to-ing and fro-ing, the aggression, two lost and deeply unhappy people — what exactly was it that made you happy?'

'The feeling he gave me.'

'What did he ever give you? What, Stella, for God's sake? What is it that's worth you destroying everything, absolutely everything around you?'

'I can't go on like this.'

I turned on my heel and went out onto the balcony to stop myself from bursting into tears. He stayed on the sofa for a while, then followed me out. The pigeon had flown away, and the spring sun warmed my face, my shoulders. In the sunshine I could see how pale my skin was. Bells were ringing in the distance. A ship hooted in the port. Papa stood beside me, leaned on the railing, touched his elbow to mine.

I felt a pang of longing for Theo, for his soft, sweaty skin when he came home from football practice, for his sticky fingers, for his damp lips, for his thick, tousled hair it was so nice to run your fingers through.

'Ivo will be leaving soon. He's doing a big investigation. He has to go to Eastern Europe.'

I jumped. In all the chaos, I'd forgotten the simple facts: that Ivo had a life of his own, that he had things to do, that he continued to operate within his own world. I was the one who had stopped living my normal life. He had remained in his world and was inviting me in — he had absolutely no intention of stepping out of it. The sudden realisation made me furious. He wasn't straying from his path in the slightest, just making a little detour: to me, to this city, to his family. Soon he would leave me, us, the city, again.

I would have to be the one to step out. I would have to leave everything, absolutely everything behind, and go. Thoughts would become reality, words would shape new places.

Ivo had always lived a nomadic life; he worked as a freelance reporter for major newspapers and broadcasters all over the world. In places that sounded magical to me, but lay beyond the power of my imagination.

Now I felt a strange lightness, a relief. I would see Theo again, and soon I would forget all this and go back to my old life. Anything else was inconceivable: I was capable of talking endlessly with Ivo, night after night, of sleeping with him, but only in my imagination was I capable of going away. In reality, I couldn't bring myself to leave Hamburg, my son, my husband.

All the necessary arguments quickly presented themselves. Where would I get the money? I could work as a freelancer, but I would never make enough to live on, let alone maintain the style of living to which I was accustomed. All the luxury I enjoyed was made possible by Mark. If I left Hamburg for an indefinite period, I would have to give up my job. I would be making myself doubly dependent on Ivo, a thought that killed my yearning stone dead.

'What sort of investigation?' I asked my father. I almost felt like laughing; everything seemed to be resolving itself, no more questions crying out for an answer. When I thought about it logically and rationally, every possibility of following Ivo immediately ruled itself out, and I had the urge to fling my arms around my father's neck and thank him for saving me from my own madness.

'In the Caucasus. He's doing a story about a musician, a political refugee. He's all fired up about it, says he's on to something big.'

'What else did he tell you?'

'Oh, all sorts of things. About America. About your mother.'

'And what did he say?'

'Ask him yourself. I'm sure you see him more than I do.'

'What's that supposed to mean?'

'I don't know. Look at yourself. You've lost the plot. You think you can just give everything up and go back to how things were. And you don't seem to see what a colossal mistake you're making.'

His voice was calm and confident. Just as it had been the day he stopped the bike and assured me he would always love us and would never go away. So that I would go on lying for him — so everything could carry on as it was. So nothing would rock the boat. I didn't reply. I listened to the sound of the church bells carried on the wind, as if it were trying to hold on to the echo.

Papa stopped talking. He lit a cigarette and stared into the distance. We stood silently, lost in thought. Silence, it seemed, was what always worked; it kept us away from sharp corners that dug into our spines.

'Did you love her?' I asked. I put my hand on his wrist.

'Who?'

'Gesi.'

'What sort of question is that? She's your mother.'

'Just: whether you loved her. And when you stopped loving her. I mean, whether or not she's our mother has nothing to do with the question.'

'Of course I loved her — why else would I have wanted to have children with her?'

'But you left her. I mean, you'd already left her long before it all happened.'

'We both changed. We had nothing in common anymore.'

'Did you and Emma have a lot in common?'

It felt as if the name had lain forgotten for centuries. It was never spoken, the way heathen tribes never speak the name of the god of war. Immediately I saw the small, haggard woman before me, in nylon tights, with ribbons in her hair.

'No,' said Papa, his voice hardening.

'So why did you stay with her for so long?'

'Why all these questions, Stella? You're being childish! We're talking about you doing things you shouldn't be doing. My past is irrelevant.'

'For heaven's sake — it's my past as well!'

He shook his head, and for a moment was blinded by the sun.

I couldn't take my eyes off him. My father usually drank his first whiskey or wine around midday. It was now a little after twelve. He was hanging in there. For me. For my future, which was to be as sensible and normal as possible. Sensible … As if any Tissmar had ever led a sensible life.

'So — why?' I insisted, knowing that he might turn around, turn his back on me, and walk out, as Mark had done. But he persevered. He didn't look at me, but I could feel that he was present, fully present, with his thoughts, with his urging.

'She was a wonderful woman,' he whispered, and his tone was gentle, the roughness in his voice had disappeared.

'What did she give you?'

'What did she give me? A sense of being irreplaceable?'

'Couldn't Mama give you that?'

'Oh, Stella. These questions. It isn't that simple. She tried. We both tried. We were together for many years, but at some point it just wasn't working anymore.'

'And Emma. What was she like?'

'Well, you remember her, don't you.'

'Yes, I remember what she looked like, her voice, and the clothes she wore. But I didn't know her. She was always so abstracted, as if there were nothing in this world that could worry her.'

'That was how you saw her?'

'Kind of, yes.'

'She was very passionate, you might say, even if it wasn't immediately obvious. You had to give her time, look deep inside her. She wasn't easy to read. She never talked much. But when she did say something, it was usually very considered. Clever, in a very original way.'

'You said back then that things between us — you and Mama and Leni and me — would always stay the same. Do you remember that evening when we stopped on the way home from Emma's and I asked you if you were going to go away, and you said you'd never leave Mama and you'd never go away?'

'Let's stop this. I came here to tell you that if you get involved with Ivo again, you'll be making a mistake.'

'I get that! *You* don't need to tell me! *You're* the one who pushed things to the point where she got shot.'

I'd gone too far. When he turned to look at me, his lower lip was trembling. He walked past me into the kitchen and picked up his coat. I followed.

'I'm sorry.' I went up behind him, clasped my arms around him to make him stay. I closed my eyes and hid my face in his broad back. It felt so strong; there were so many parts of it where I could have hidden, safe and warm and secure. Like in the old days, when he would buckle me into the child seat on his bike and whizz off — fast, familiar with the route, so sure of himself.

In those days, there were no doubts.

'I didn't mean it,' I whispered into his back. He turned and hugged me close. I loved it when he took me in his arms; everything else seemed to disappear. He looked down at me, stroking the little hairs at the edge of my forehead.

He loved me. He had always loved me, yet the love had never been enough. It never seemed to be enough. It was always too much or too little.

'You are important to me. Possibly more important than anything else in the world, and right now I'm really afraid for you,' he said.

'When you were little, very little, we were always partners, you and me, a team. I was proud of it. Your mother was a bit jealous, and Leni still holds it against me, says you were my favourite. But it's not that — that's not what it was. It wasn't about favouritism. It was because you were so intent on living. Because you wanted so much. I loved that about you; but sometimes it's not such a good thing. Ivo's different. And I'm done with all that. I want to spend the rest of my days in peace and quiet. Anything else is just a waste of time.'

Papa patted me on the back and kissed my temple. Then he let go of me and left. I stood there, rooted to the spot, and all my thoughts turned to mush.

★

For a long time after my declaration of love at the beach, Ivo more or less ignored me. The following year, he finished school and went to stay with Mama in the States, whereas I went on helping out in Tulia's boathouse. Leni had already moved out and gone to Berlin to study. Ivo didn't get in touch, didn't write, didn't call. Mama said he had got himself an internship with a local newspaper.

I mourned, and, out of sheer pig-headedness, decided that I wouldn't fly to Newark that year. The summer was hot and enervating. Flies buzzed in the garden; I was tired and lazy, moving sluggishly as I helped Tulia water the flowers, go shopping, hire out boats. I sat barefoot on jetties, looking out to sea and hoping, in my romantic fervour, that Ivo, thousands of kilometres away, would sense how I was suffering on his account and feel remorse. Secretly, though, I hoped he would come back and apologise, declare his love, and court me.

I lay in the bay for hours, salt in my hair, chewing gum, watching the ships in the distance or reading depressing books. Tulia sensed what was wrong with me and sent me to stay with Papa in Hamburg. Back then he was still living alone in our old house, and we sat in the garden, not talking. I was rude, barely answering when he asked me anything; I just shrugged my shoulders. Papa bought me a moped, and my only diversion that summer was riding as fast as possible and breaking all the rules of the road. Until I rammed into an expensive car on our street, and they sent me to Berlin to stay with Leni, who had moved to a room in a student hostel and was belatedly catching up on her adolescence. When Mama called and asked me to come to Newark, I blurted out that I didn't feel like seeing Ivo. This rang alarm bells. A telephone network was established, secret conferences were held. They questioned Ivo, they questioned me, but they couldn't figure us out.

What was going on with us, had we argued, was that why I was acting so oddly? There was no end to the questions. My behaviour was put down to childish jealousy. They knew what chains bound Ivo and me together. And they accepted it.

At the end of September, he returned. Tall, lanky, suntanned, in cowboy boots. He was carrying a black rucksack and looked so free, so contented, so enviable, whereas I seemed to be wasting away in my misery, in one of Leni's old shirts, Tulia's rubber boots, cut-off jeans, my hair still in a childish bob. I felt terrible, and retreated to the boathouse, as if I had something to do in there.

That evening Papa stayed for dinner, and we all ate on the patio. Papa drank and told anecdotes, and suddenly Ivo, too, was offered a glass of wine. He accepted as if it were the most natural thing in the world. After dinner I excused myself and snuck out of the house. I heard Papa drive away in his old car, and Tulia complain that he shouldn't be driving in that state. I heard the cats yowl and music start up in Ivo's room. Strange music I couldn't relate to, that he had brought back from America. I went down to the jetty; I ran like a lunatic, threw myself onto the cool sand and sobbed convulsively. I screamed and ranted and raged at the world for being so cruel to me.

I lay there smoking a cigarette I'd nicked from Papa. I had started smoking out of sheer boredom. I knew Tulia wouldn't come looking for me, and so I stayed, toughing it out, braving the cold night air and hoping I would catch pneumonia as a punishment to Ivo.

'So this is where you are.'

He was standing behind me. I hadn't heard him approach. He sat down beside me and I moved away, both happy and disconcerted that he had come.

'What do you want?' I snarled, demonstratively blowing smoke in his face.

'Nothing. I just came to you.'

'Why?'

'Because I want to see you. We haven't seen each other in so long.'

'Aha.'

'Don't you believe me?'

'No.'

'Tough.'

'Bet it was nice at Mama's.'

'You could have come too. She's *your* mother, after all.'

'I didn't want to spoil your summer.'

'Spoil it? Why? What are you talking about? They've all been asking what's the matter with you.'

'Nothing. What would be the matter?'

'That's what I'm asking.'

'Leave me alone.'

'Why are you being like this with me, Stella?'

'I'm not being *like* anything.'

'Yes, you are.'

We sat in silence for a while, and for a moment everything felt like before, when we would spend our evenings by the sea and had endless space for our dreams.

'Stella,' he began, looking at me properly for the first time since he had arrived. 'It was all wrong, what happened. I want you to stop being so distant, and for us to be friends again.'

I wished for the uncertainty of the previous summer again, the silence. Anything seemed better than what he was saying to me.

'I'm not your girlfriend, and I'm not your sister, either.'

'Fine.' He got to his feet, offended.

'Ivo.' I jumped up, mustering all my courage. I stood in front of him; he was a head taller than me. I felt small and miserable. 'Don't go away again.' I chewed my thumb and looked at him, pleading. His expression gave nothing away.

Then he took me in his arms and kissed me on the temple, and the kiss felt so cold, so humiliating, that I stepped back and pulled his arms from my waist.

A gull shrieked in the darkness.

The following year, we avoided each other. Tulia became accustomed to our surliness and didn't ask any more questions; she put it down to growing up, to my stubbornness and Ivo's pride.

More and more often, Ivo stayed out all night. He would come home at dawn, and I can barely remember a single morning when I wasn't still lying awake, waiting for him. I was waiting for him to bring a girl back, but that never happened. He drank, listened to music, and sometimes got stoned with his friends, who were all coarse, unkempt, and utterly uncivilised, at least compared to Ivo with his innate charm.

I wasted away. I started to do badly at school, and I hardly ate. Sometimes Tulia would send me to Papa in Hamburg, or he would spend the weekend in the village. The two of them tried, in their liberal way, to get me back on track, with talk of good grades and job prospects.

I pottered about in the boathouse, or spent the evenings alone on the beach.

Even Leni got involved, telling me about amazing Berlin and her amazing university course to get me to concentrate on my schoolwork again.

★

After Ivo had finished school, no one had pestered him with questions about what future he had in mind; he had confidence in himself, and the family left him alone. As if he could never make mistakes, could never fail. He was always awarded the bonus of otherness.

He went to Kiel, where instead of his military service he did community service in a hospital and lived in a filthy dive with a guy called Arne who was permanently stoned. I could hardly bear the emptiness that radiated from his room; I kept entering it, secretly, as if it were a sacred temple, looking around, searching for traces of him, for what drove him, what was driving him further and further away from me. I was jealous of every photo of him without me, of every place he saw without me, every person to whom he paid attention who was not me.

He phoned Tulia from time to time; sometimes, rarely, we saw each other at family gatherings, or at Christmas. He always seemed to grow more handsome, taller, more mature, while I, in my ailing, drought-stricken loneliness, seemed to get more and more withered and sad.

My hair grew down to my waist, my fingernails were no longer bitten to the quick, my skin no longer seemed so pale, my breasts no longer so alien to my body, but none of that made any difference to the fact that, whatever I did and however I acted, he seemed better, more beautiful, more sophisticated. Everyone liked him, his wit, his apparent lightness, his cheerfulness and mischievous manner, whereas I was increasingly becoming the family's problem child, trailing broken fragments that my family tried to pick up after me. I only just passed my school-leaving exam. I was sent to Newark, to Mama. The idea was for me to reorientate myself and find my bearings, but my mother, worried and alarmed, made one mistake after another, preaching at me every day and pushing me further and further away.

I hung out, got hold of some weed, did my hair in little braids, and painted my fingernails black.

I got to know a whole load of Davids, Pauls, and Joes, as I was packed off every day to some course or other on campus because my mother had got it into her head that she was going to get me into university in New Jersey. I was bored, went to brainless parties with the boys, and didn't come home till dawn. Occasionally, I would spend the night with David, Paul, or Joe. I discovered that my heartache could be assuaged for a while with sex. But the nights left an even bigger emptiness in me, and on days like these I would ignore the whole world. I looked into its fish eyes and felt nothing but contempt.

Mama, James, and me in Florida. I remember that, too. Some sort of desperate entertainment arranged for us by my mother. It was hot and humid, which made me lethargic; all those months I felt as if the life were being sucked out of me.

So I came back to Europe and holed up in the old rooms of Tulia's house. She made me herbal teas and put damp handkerchiefs on my forehead, as if trying to drive out all the demons and fill me with new, strong, magnificent life. So that my blood would start to flow; so I would have colour in my cheeks again.

I longed for Ivo, and I hated him for it. For what I had not become, because he had not stayed with me.

★

That autumn I met Abi. Abi was from Iran, and had grown up in Hamburg. We met in a café in St Pauli where I was sitting with a book, ignoring the world. At first he got on my nerves, but he was impressively persistent, and attractive. I relented, and we went on together somewhere else, drinking, talking and laughing.

Abi was studying classical languages, and was a keen photographer. There are countless photos of me: in the bedroom, in various cafés, at ridiculous events we went to together. These photos are the nicest, most carefree scraps of my youth.

He fell in love with me, and I enjoyed the feeling. Being needed breathed a little life back into me, and, encouraged by my worried family, I marched right into Abi's life.

His skin was dark and shimmered like a cat's pelt in the moonlight. He was a man of great gentleness and unusual, elaborate words.

We ended up living together in his little apartment in the Karolinen district, which was just being discovered and taken over by artists, and where everything positively screamed otherness.

It was a new world for me, and I let myself slip into it, gently feeling my way, stroking, caressing. It was an autumn full of promises, an autumn of eyelids raised again.

Abi bought me fresh croissants and fed me little pickled artichokes. He quoted the Song of Songs to me, told me that my breasts looked like two pregnant trout and my neck smelled of cypresses, that my arms were as beautiful as an Egyptian paramour's and my knees were innocent. And I laughed and laughed. From anyone else such sentences would have been unthinkable, but the way he said them touched me.

Through Abi, I got to know a lot of people: students, artists, hedonists and crazies. We partied into the small hours, and every now and then we drove out to Tulia's and spent the weekend there. Tulia accepted him immediately, without Papa's forced friendliness or Leni's scepticism. When it was warm enough we went swimming, and we slept together in my little bed that creaked and groaned and complained about our lovemaking.

I think that, during this time, I was at peace. Abi gave me back some of my confidence. I started to think about my future, and enrolled at the university to study English, comparative literature, and art history. I discovered how to have fun. To enjoy life. For no reason. Leaving the bad memories behind.

I put my hair up in an old-fashioned bun and wore black eyeliner. I bought berets in several different colours. I swapped my trousers for knee-length pencil skirts I picked up at flea markets, and started wearing Tulia's pearl necklaces. I read everything I could get my hands on: Baudelaire, Kafka, Plath.

Abi had a fat cat called Xerxes. I would settle him beside me on the old sofa, wrap myself in a thick blanket when the heating conked out again, and immerse myself in a celebration of reading, Luckies, and my youth. I loved the hours I spent like this. They were so full of hope and promise for the future, which tasted, in those hours, of candyfloss, baked apples, carousels.

There's a picture of me, taken by Abi: I am curled up on the sofa, smoking, reading a book, and Xerxes is hiding his face in my lap. I am far away, yet still present. I like this picture. In this picture everything still seems so open. As if there are thousands and thousands of versions of my life, my self, and I only need to stretch out my hand and I will be someone.

★

In this period I took to visiting Papa more often. He had started bringing home younger and younger women. At the time he was working half-days as an editor with a non-fiction publisher, and I asked him to fix me up with a job. He introduced me to the director, and soon I was spending three days a week at the publisher's, laying out texts, correcting them, or typing up minutes.

Not long afterwards, I started to write myself. Abi had a friend, Michel, who wrote for a student newspaper and was into politics. I liked him, and we often met up and discussed politics and art.

I wrote essays and short notes. I had no ambitions for them at first. Later, I showed them to Michel. He seemed impressed, and a few weeks later he printed one of my essays in his newspaper.

Papa encouraged my desire to write. He had always wanted to write books and had always put it off, until one day the desire was completely gone, so he had spent his whole life writing reviews criticising or praising others, and, above all, correcting, editing, suggesting improvements. He always seemed unfulfilled; a sense of yearning always shone through. He was moved by the idea that Ivo and I would continue to plough his furrow, and Leni too, later, in her own way, because he liked to think that he'd had a hand in this; perhaps he'd even convinced himself of it. And perhaps he was actually right, I don't know.

★

Ivo went to London for a year and got a job at the *Evening Standard*.
Everyone at home raved about him. Tulia was constantly praising his
courage, his readiness to go to extremes. I didn't understand what was
supposed to be so extreme about London, and I was furious that Ivo's
successes completely overshadowed Leni and me.

It was the year when I tried to scrape him out of my life like old
wallpaper off a wall.

11

'Are you all right now?'

Theo sat in his filthy shirt on the bench beside the football pitch, eyeing me suspiciously. My mind was racing: I tried to guess from his looks and gestures what he had been told and how frightened or angry he was.

His face betrayed nothing. His face was like his father's. His slightly almond-shaped eyes reminded me of his grandfather, who drove an Audi TT and was forever telling the story of how he had once been arrested for participating in a demo against the Vietnam War.

I searched for myself in vain in the face of my son.

I searched for myself in vain in the face of my father.

I searched for myself in vain in the face of my husband.

'I'm feeling better. I miss you. How is it with Grandpa and Granny?'

I hadn't been able to bear it; I'd gone to Theo's football practice. It had been pouring with rain since morning, and I'd noticed for the first time that spring had arrived: a seamless transition from a rainy winter to a rainy spring.

'It's good. I might get a dog for my birthday.'

When he said this, I knew I was already one-nil down in the game with Mark, with his parents. And that the game had already begun. I suddenly realised that in two weeks' time Theo would be seven. And again I felt sick with fear, and again I had to take deep breaths, looking up at the grey sky and wondering why this child drove me so crazy with his precocious reserve and exaggerated politeness, and at the same time awakened such a longing in me for the little person inside and the warmth that emanated from him.

'We agreed that we couldn't have a dog just yet, didn't we, darling?' I replied. And even as I spoke, I thought: why not? When the mother goes away, abandons the family, the child is given a comfort dog. Perhaps that was why I had insisted on keeping my family name: I didn't want to belong to this 'la-di-da family', as Tulia called the Simons. Or perhaps it had been an irreparable mistake; perhaps I shouldn't have emphasised my otherness right from the start, because somehow, in making this decision, I'd made clear to Mark that I would never be part of him and his family.

'You know, Theo — you remember, don't you — we talked about how a dog isn't really possible right now, because of Mama's work and Papa's work and you being at school. We talked about it and about how a dog is an awful lot of work, and that you can only have a pet when you're able to take responsibility for it yourself.'

'Yes, but Grandpa said the dog will live with them and I'll only have to take care of it at weekends. Papa thinks it's a good idea, too,' Theo added.

I looked at him and started dabbing his sweaty head with his towel.

'I don't want that, Theo,' I said, and immediately knew what an incredible disappointment it must be for him, that in a moment he would protest, pull his head out of my hands. But he only lowered his eyes.

'What's the matter with you?' he asked. He didn't add *Mama*.

'I'm a bit overtired right now, Theo. I'll be all right again soon. I just need to think a bit, and be alone for a bit. And sleep a lot.'

I gave him an encouraging smile, and sensed that this time he believed me even less than before. My throat constricted, and I felt that I couldn't go on speaking. Not another word.

It had started raining heavily again. The other children ran across the pitch towards the changing rooms; mothers hurried after them with miniature sports bags. Until a few weeks ago I had been one of this species, and now I was creeping around the playing field like a thief so I could watch my son from afar.

'Why can't we go home?' he asked, and this time his voice was less controlled, and I could hear his fear: the fear that his normal life, his future, his home would be taken from him.

Had I become a threat to him? Would he loathe me for it? I would become like my own mother, when she went to a congress in New York just before the divorce and left us alone for the first time. For four weeks. When she got back, she took us to a café, ordered ice-cream sundaes, and started to cry. Then she told us that things weren't working out with our father.

Mama had never broken down like that: not at Ivo's mother's funeral, and not once during the terrible weeks after Emma was shot, the unbearable questioning by the police and other authorities. Now she sat before us like a shadow of her former self: weak, miserable, lonely, and filled with a deep anger that she didn't dare turn on her husband, who was the cause of all the suffering.

I was seven when my mother — or, for me, what was left of her — sat with us in that café, watching us uncertainly.

Theo would be seven, too, in two weeks.

'Listen to me carefully, look at me — Leni, Stella, please, stop prodding at your ice cream, listen to me — Stella! — I've been offered a job. I'm going to America. I'll be working for a big pharmaceutical company. I'll have a bigger salary, and they've guaranteed me lots of benefits. But it's in America. That means we have to move away, from here, from home — that we won't come back for a while. And it means we'll live without Papa,' she said. In retrospect I admired her for her consistency in continuing to refer to her husband as *Papa*.

'Of course we could go home now, my darling. Of course. But Papa thinks it's better if you go to your grandparents', you see, so that I can get completely well. It was Papa's idea.'

I saw that my answer comforted Theo a little; if Papa had a hand in it, it couldn't be that bad. He smiled again, and his face lit up.

'Look, I've got a huge lump on my elbow!' Proudly, he showed me his swollen limb.

I hugged him tight and ruffled his hair. He smelled of sweat and childhood. Of innumerable sweet promises.

I saw Mark walking towards us; he didn't look happy to see me there, but I knew he would control himself and not say anything inappropriate in front of Theo. He even gave me a hug, which surprised me, until I realised why: I saw that Theo was watching us, scrutinising us. And Mark was acting perfectly.

Theo chattered away as Mark and I stood outside the changing room, looking at each other. Mark shook his head and put his finger to his lips. I nodded.

'I have to talk to you,' I whispered, leaning towards him. I could smell his aftershave, and just then I felt strangely close to him; we were like two allies in the fight to save ourselves.

'Not now,' he said.

'We have to!'

'I'll come round to yours this evening; we can talk then.'

I nodded, and had to stop myself laughing out loud. We were turning into a pair of thieves, creeping into our own lives. The way he had said *I'll come round to yours*, as if it weren't his home, as if I weren't his wife, as if it weren't our life.

★

Mama told us it was a new beginning. Completely new. The New World. The hardest thing for her was telling us about a man she'd met at that congress: a man called James, in whom she saw the best chance of a new beginning. Finally she said it. Leni pouted, then stood up abruptly and ran to the toilet. I stayed where I was, opposite our mother, who swallowed the last of her tears and looked at me with a smile. Amid all that wreckage, there was suddenly a smile.

'I'm sorry, Stella,' she whispered. As if she'd been waiting for her elder daughter to leave the table so she could tell the younger that she'd known everything, and had hesitated for too long — far too long.

'I shouldn't have let him take you *there*.'

There. She had mentioned *the place* for the first time, and, for the first time, the place, and its people, took shape. Became real. I stared at my empty bowl and scratched it with my fork.

'I should have stopped it.'

'It's not your fault,' I said, putting the fork down. 'It's not Papa's fault, either. It's my fault.'

Mama recoiled, then placed her cool hand on mine in agitation. I pulled it away. She tried to meet my eyes. I looked away.

'No, sweetheart — no, no, it's not. You must never think such a thing, do you hear me, because it's not true, not at all!'

It's my fault.

It's my fault.

'I hate you,' my sister told our mother at the time. And I think that, at the time, Leni said *no* out of defiance; out of pure, incoherent anger she said *no* to the new life, even though her old life lay in ruins.

And perhaps, now, it was out of defiance that I was saying *no* to the present I was living.

★

'One night, towards the end of my pregnancy, I dreamed Theo was going to fall into a hole and I would lose him, that I wouldn't be able to bring him into the world. I woke up drenched in sweat; you were lying beside me, fast asleep, and I pressed up against you and listened to my heart pounding. I always felt as if I had a hole inside me. As if everything I felt would always fall into this hole in the end, as if I couldn't keep anything inside me for ever. I always hoped that over the years I would find a way of closing this hole, of filling it with life, or something, but I can't do it. Not long-term, anyway. I hoped you would be the way — you, Theo, my family, my work. But ...'

I sat in our living room saying this to Mark. Unshaven, with dark circles around his eyes, he watched while I drank gin and tonic and smoked, which visibly disgusted him and made me even less reliable in his eyes. He had come over that evening as he'd said he would, after I'd seen him on the football pitch, supposedly to pick up a few clothes to wear.

'How can you say such a thing? I mean, you're a mother now, above all else. That's where all your responsibility lies. I don't understand you, Stella. This whole thing is becoming seriously insane. I can't deal with it at all anymore. How can you say there's nothing in your life that matters to you?'

'I didn't say that, Mark. I just said that there's an emptiness inside me.'

'Look at you, Stella, look at you — you've cheated on me, you're jeopardising our relationship. Wake up. I don't know how long I can keep on forgiving you. I just don't know.'

The gulf between us was widening. Perhaps, at the very last minute, I would learn how to fly across it after all.

'I have to go to Cyprus by Saturday at the latest. They've already started filming. I have to be there for the shoot. It would be good if by then you were there for Theo again.'

His phoney generosity disgusted me; his studied understanding repelled me. I wiped the tears from my cheeks and blew my nose.

'I'm always there for Theo. You know that.'

'You're not, Stella. Not like this,' he said, and stood up.

'Wait.'

I don't know why I turned and tried to stop him. He looked at me in surprise. He didn't know what to say. I walked up to him.

'I'm sorry, I wish —'

He didn't let me finish; he held up his hand and avoided my gaze as if it were infectious.

'Please, let me go,' he said, and walked past. I hurried after him; I felt I wanted to explain everything to him, that I had to explain it, even though I knew it was impossible. I hung on to his sleeve. We were standing in the hall; it was dark, I hadn't switched on the light. I clung to him and tried to hug him. I tried to kiss him, as if it were the last remnant of an illusion of closeness, of being understood, of home.

'What are you doing?' he screamed at me — a suppressed scream; Mark was too much himself, I knew, to permit himself a *proper* scream.

'Listen to me!'

'It's not important, none of that is important. The only thing that matters is what you *do*,' he whispered, leaning back in the dark against the cool wall.

'Help me, Mark,' I said. I tried to take his hand; he pulled it away.

'Help you do what? Leave me? If that's what you want, you'll have to manage by yourself. I'll bring Theo home on Thursday,' he said, and left. I knew he was trying to blackmail me, that, like his parents with the dog, he was using our child to bring me back to my senses.

★

Ivo and I continued to avoid each other. He returned from London to Niendorf as the family's successful, celebrated son. He only stuck it out there for a week before moving to Hamburg to stay with Papa, and then with a succession of friends. Papa tried not to show how relieved he was that Ivo's professional career was on track. Then Leni wrote to me that Ivo had turned up at her place in Berlin; they had gone bar-hopping all night, and he had been very sweet and interested in everything. She said how much he'd changed for the better, and couldn't resist commenting that he hadn't mentioned me. Papa told me Ivo's good portfolio had won him a scholarship to Munich University, where he had been offered a place on the journalism course.

Around this time, I only saw Ivo once.

That day, I was going to visit Papa. I was on my bike, just turning into the street I had lived on when my mother was still there and Ivo's mother was still alive. I heard someone honk their horn, and when I turned, I saw Ivo on an old moped, dressed like a rebel in a white T-shirt and sunglasses, grinning at me as if we'd last seen each other just a couple of days ago.

I braked, stopped at the side of the road, and waited for him to dismount. He looked like a person who was sure of himself, who was following his path in life. I was definitely not on the same path.

He looked at me, took off the sunglasses, and opened his arms. I let him stand there, ignored the outspread arms, and didn't smile at him, either.

'You seem to be doing well,' I said.

'Won't you give me a kiss, Stella?'

'Better not.'

'Your boyfriend would be jealous, would he?'

His tone was sharp, cynical, and the grin that twitched at the corners of his mouth was a sheer provocation.

'No, he wouldn't, you can be assured of that.'

'So you haven't missed me, then?' he asked, lighting a cigarette.

'What's the point of all this, Ivo? Are you going to see Papa?'

'Depends where you're going.'

'What is this? Are we playing a game again?'

'I don't know yet. I've been wondering that for a long time.'

'Oh, come on, we're not kids anymore. Let's forget it. Everything's fine, isn't it?'

'Is it?' His tone had changed again; now he was serious and quiet, almost threatening.

'I hope so.'

We were silent for a while.

'Let's go for a drink instead, what do you say? Since chance has so kindly brought us together like this,' he said.

'Why would we do that?'

'Why not? We've got plenty to tell each other, about anything and everything.'

He was making fun of me. I turned away, furious, and was about to get back on my bike when he grabbed me by the arm, pulled me around, and looked at me. For the first time since we had been together on the beach, he really looked at me. And just then I would very much have liked to press his eyelids shut. Hard. Harder.

'Come with me. Please.'

I hesitated a little longer, as his smile grew milder and he repeated that *please* a few more times; his expression changed, he seemed more open, not as pointedly lascivious, and I allowed myself to relent.

I locked my bike and got on the back of his moped. We sped off. I'd stopped asking questions; I was intoxicated by the smell of him, the contact with his back, the joy at his *please*. Nothing seemed to matter, and instantly the old familiarity was back.

We ended up in a bar I didn't know, between the port and St Pauli. He ordered beers for us, and in the darkness of that room, somewhere beyond the sun, other people, my life, I allowed myself to fall. Suddenly it seemed the hatchet was buried; suddenly talking to him was so easy, so familiar; he listened patiently to my life, and told me about his. But we avoided anything that might have sparked fresh conflict.

He was charming, with a carefree lightness, dancing expertly around words and ideas, and it was only when he went to the bathroom that I had time to wonder how life had been possible without him for so long, why I had endured that long interval without him, why I hadn't just gone to him.

He was going to move to Munich; he was used to travelling and moving home; it made no difference to him which city he lived in; all cities were essentially the same. He was looking forward to studying journalism; he knew it would suit him. He asked about my plans.

It had got dark; empty beer glasses had collected on the table in front of us. Eventually, we staggered out of the pub, and he asked me if I wanted to go back with him; he had the use of a friend's place for a few days, did we want to go back there and have a smoke.

The apartment was a dump, not far from the bar. It overlooked a dark rear courtyard and stank of mildew and hamsters. Why hamsters, I don't know; I didn't see any.

We smoked a joint. Everything slowed down. Music emanated from an ancient radio, and everything felt nice, felt right. Everything was forgotten — the meeting with my father, the books waiting for me at home, the bed I shared with Abi, Xerxes with his white fur. I danced, slowly, moving languidly in the cramped kitchen of the unfamiliar apartment. Ivo watched me, laughing. Then suddenly he came and stood right in front of me and looked at me. I was confused by the expression in his eyes, but I held his gaze.

'It's not good that we're so distant,' he whispered, stroking a wisp of hair back from my sweaty face. It was summer; the heat of the day still stuck to our skin. I was ready. Ready for life to turn over like a card in a game; all I had to do was take a step towards him.

And so I stood on tiptoe, wobbled a little, but managed to keep my balance well enough to kiss him. I expected a rebuff, hesitation, a shout, but not reciprocation, and when he returned my kiss, I staggered back and closed my lips. He looked at me the way I had wished he would look at me that day on the beach, when I had undressed in front of him because I couldn't express my feelings in words. An eternity ago. But this eternity, it seemed, was made of wax; it was burning, dripping, melting together, creating the present.

We turned: he pressed me against the sink, and that was when, for the first time, I felt the sharp jab of an edge digging into my spine that has haunted me ever since. It was the first time I slept with Ivo.

We couldn't let each other go; we kept on and on, on and on, until it got light. Pressed up against the wall; in the corridor, where the skirting boards were missing; finally on an old mattress in the empty bedroom.

As dawn was breaking he suddenly got up, left me lying there naked, and went to shower. I listened to him turn on the water. After a while, I went to the bathroom and stepped into the shower stall with him.

'Aren't you tired? Shall we go to sleep?' I asked him, and he laughed. Loudly, amused. Then he turned me round and held my hands behind my back, gripping them firmly. He pressed himself against me, bent me forwards. I cried out and tried to turn, but I couldn't; I slipped, and banged my head against the glass of the shower stall. He took no notice; he kept going, like a wild thing.

I slid to the floor. Water streamed over me, and I began to cry.

'Why are you crying?'

'You hurt me.'

'I've always tried to tell you.'

'What? What, for fuck's sake? You know perfectly well —'

'I don't know anything, not anything, Stella! So stop it. You wanted it, and now you're crying. I tried to tell you: it isn't possible for it not to hurt.'

He calmly went back to washing himself, while I clutched my head and the pain crawled from the bump and lodged itself everywhere in my body. And yet I saw that he was beautiful. His ankles, his calves were beautiful — hairy, a little bony; his backside, too, a little too small; and his arms, suntanned up to where the sleeves of his T-shirt began.

'I won't regret it, Ivo. Even if you hurt me.'

He held out his hand. I stood up, and he massaged shampoo into my hair, running his hands carefully through it, the way my mother did when I was little and afraid shampoo would make me go blind, and would squeeze my eyes tight shut, tight, tight shut.

12

Leo assigned me to write an article about an architect I didn't know, who didn't interest me, with whom I had no connection. We argued. It was an exhausting day. I was like a sleepwalker. If I carried on like this, he would fire me. I carried on, with a childish stubbornness, turning my pointless ambition against myself, the ambition of someone who steps out of their own life and starts to sneer at everything from the outside.

I barely slept anymore.

Theo called, still at his grandparents', wanting to know where his birthday party was going to be held and what was happening; his grandparents, of course, had offered to have it at their house, which was bigger and lighter and more propitious than our apartment. I didn't argue with him; I just listened, feeling my anger grow, feeling the urge to kidnap him, right now, on the spot, to tear him away from the harmonious grandparental dictatorship he was imprisoned in, that he was being lulled into accepting. I said nothing.

Ivo didn't call.

Tulia invited me to come and see her: it had been such a long time since she'd cooked for me, she said. I turned off my phone. At home I stared out of the window and smoked. Smoking calmed me, made me listless, tired, docile. Papa called, checking my voice to see if my life could still be bent back into shape, the shape it was meant to be.

The following evening I got up and, as if in a dream, walked to the Pacific Hotel. I marched straight past reception to the lift.

I stopped outside his room, and this time I didn't think about the consequences. I was already living them. I knocked. Instantly the door flew open. He stood in front of me, fresh from the shower, a towel around his waist.

'Almost as if I knew you were coming,' he said, and I realised he had been drinking. The room was a chaos of papers, books, and newspaper articles, and the bedclothes were tangled. I immediately noticed the impressions of two bodies, two hollowed pillows. My stomach clenched.

'Was someone here?' I asked. The thought felt unbearable, more unbearable than the emptiness of my shell.

'No, why?'

I looked at the bed. He grinned, closed the door behind me, and pushed me into the room with one hand.

'Don't tell me you're jealous. *I'm* not the one who's married!'

'You stupid bastard!' I gasped, sinking onto the edge of the bed.

'All right, all right. Hey, you don't expect me to justify myself, do you?'

'You're ruining everything.'

'I just made your house of cards wobble a little. That's what happens with card houses!'

I jumped up, went over, and slapped his face. For the first slap he stood his ground; the second time I raised my hand, he caught my wrist and threw me onto the bed. He smelled of alcohol. The little hairs on his ears glistened in the artificial light of the bedside lamp.

'Listen to me, Stella. Listen to me, please. I have to go. I have to go in three or four days. I'll leave some papers for you so you can see what it's about. I'm flying to Tbilisi, to Georgia. It's important. I'm begging you to come and join me. This is the last thing I'll ask of you.'

'You're drunk. Let go of me.'

'No, for fuck's sake, look at me!'

He took my face in his hands and pressed his against it, so close that we both had to squint to see each other clearly.

'Please, just read the material. I'll stop, I promise; after that, I'll stop. You just have to be with me for a few weeks. A few weeks, and after that, all of it will stop. I promise. Then I'll be gone, if that's what you want. You can go back to wherever you want, or not. Stella, please.

I'm serious. Read this folder, read it all — promise me. Possibly the most important story I've ever done in my life, but it's more than that. It's more than a story.'

'Why? Why should I?'

'Because it has to do with you. Us.'

'You're writing about me?'

He didn't reply; he had loosened his grip and turned away, and I was able to sit up again. I stared at his back. I sat next to him, and we said nothing for a while. He reached for the vodka bottle beside the bed and drank as if it were water.

'Ivo, I'm frightened.'

'It's not a punishment, Stella. If that's what you're thinking.'

I wondered how he always managed to think so clearly, despite drinking as much as he did.

'I don't think anything anymore.'

'Yes, you do. Finally you're thinking about things again.'

'I would come, if it weren't for Theo ...'

'A mother who's away for a while is better than one who's never really there, whom you never really know. Don't you think?' He stood up abruptly.

'What's with Georgia? What are you actually talking about?'

'Promise me.'

'I can't promise you anything.'

'Just look at me. Only one more time, and then I'll do anything you want. I swear to you. I swear to you on the days we spent together in the sunshine at the bay. I swear to you by all that's sacred to me. By the afternoons in the boathouse. I swear to you by all the games of pirates in the garden.'

He went to the balcony door, pushed aside the yellowing curtain, and looked out. Noises drifted up from the street: people streamed past in search of pleasure and passion.

'Sometimes I think I'm a little tick,' I said. 'That I always was. One that's embedded itself, I mean. It's tenacious; it waits. Waits for blood, because that's its only chance of survival. Because it has nothing, because it's a tick. It waits, clinging to a twig, and then — you pass by, and it smells the blood, the good, healthy, successful, promising blood, and it lets go, drops down onto you, lodges between your ribs and feeds on you. As long as it can. As long as you have blood you can manage without. And then it starts to become too much for you. Then you get sick, and you remove it; you pluck it off with tweezers and throw it on the ground. And at first the tick thinks this is the end; it's gorged and sated and happy and it can't move, it just lies there, helpless, fat and useless, and it's afraid it'll get trampled to death, because nobody sees it. And so it lies there on the ground, waiting to die, and eventually it manages to crawl back up into the tree.'

By now I was speaking incredibly fast.

Ivo had turned to me, and I saw horror, absolute horror, in his face. He kept his distance, not moving from the balcony door. He had balled one of his hands into a fist, and looked strange in this unnatural posture.

'You're not a tick. That's disgusting and terrible, what you're saying.'

'Terrible? It's not terrible. That's what it feels like.'

'You're not the tick. And even if you were: we both fed on each other.'

'Oh, no. You went away. You lived. You. Alone.'

After a while I asked, almost in a whisper, 'Who was here?' and lay down on the bed. It smelled of him, of cigarettes, of paper, and of a peculiar, almost overpowering, feminine perfume.

'Just a fuck.'

'Did you need one?'

'Sometimes people do.'

'Why didn't you call me?'

He looked at me in amazement, shook his head, and started groping for his almost-empty vodka bottle again, which he had put down somewhere by the bed.

'Maybe I might have needed one, too.'

'You're not a fuck to me.'

'Sometimes I'd like to be. No more than that. Perhaps it would be easier.'

'No. You can be that for other people, as far as I'm concerned.'

He located the bottle, drained what was left, and lay down beside me.

And so we lay there: I in my clothes, he in his towel. In the white hotel bed, he on his side, I on the shadow of another woman who had no name, who had left behind only an overpowering scent.

I ran a hand over his face and breathed in his smell. He didn't move. He had often done this, before: just looked at me. In all the beds we had shared together. I let my hand wander over his body — it felt like a miracle to me, just being able to touch him — and it kept wandering, my hand, my palm, cool and damp, searching for his soul, wrapped in the hard, icy carapace of his body. My hands — one was not enough after a while — frisked him, searching for the essence of him. When they roamed like this, my hands became my eyes, supplanted all my senses.

'*This* is what's revolting; I find *this* disgusting, I find *this* repulsive: that you're willing to disappear, to go into hiding, for a fuck. What are you trying to prove?' I asked him.

'I'm not your husband,' he said, knowing that, with this, he rendered me powerless.

I got up, straightened my clothes, and left.

'I'll leave everything you need here, so you can decide,' he called after me. I shook my head, and ran down the stairs without waiting for the lift.

13

Three in the morning. I sat on my bed, wrapped in a woollen blanket, freezing. I was sick; I had a fever. I'd dreamed I was locked in a kennel. Strangers had walked past, staring, pointing at me. I wanted to scream, to say something, explain that it was a misunderstanding, but no sound came out.

I took an aspirin and put on a pair of thick woollen socks, then looked at the clock again, at the digits glowing on the bedside table, and thought of Theo. Of him quietly sleeping, his heavy eyelids in the morning, his smell. Of how he would sneak into bed with us at night, drunk with sleep, confused, a little frightened by a bad dream, or just because he wanted to be near us.

Slowly the night crawled past.

I picked up the phone and stared at the hard, meaningless little buttons, which quickly acquired importance and significance as soon as you dialled a particular number, as soon as you were dependent on this particular combination to connect you with another person.

I closed my eyes and blindly dialled the endless string of numbers. It rang. How late was it over there? Was it daytime, dark? Raining, dry? What was she doing right now? What was she dreaming of, if she was dreaming?

'Helloooo? Jeanie, is that you?' she said, in a broad, East Coast accent.

'Mama?'

A pause. A long pause. It was nobody's birthday, nobody was organising a family get-together, it was nobody's anniversary. This was a call of a different kind; we both knew it before I said a word. Mama groaned, then I heard an almost pleading '*Stella?*'

Unlike Ivo's, her German was precise and oddly timeless. A literary

German. Her words always acquired the aspect of a prayer when she spoke in her native language, the language of her past, the language in which she had been someone else. Into which she had sealed the memory of this other woman.

'Stella, is everything okay? It's the middle of the night for you, isn't it?'

'Yes ... no. It's just ... I've got a bit of a cold, I can't sleep, and I'd like to talk to you.'

'Sure. Hold on, let me sit down ... there we go ... right, here I am.'

I hadn't seen her in almost three years. Back then, Mark, Theo and I had visited, she had bought Theo an enormous plastic digger powered by a little engine, and Theo had dug up the whole of her garden.

I pictured her, sitting in her living room. The walls were covered in photos of us as children. Photos of two little girls who had a good life, a good childhood. When Leni still went to ballet and I still had short hair. And then there was a gap on the wall. The gallery continued with the addition of a tall, lanky boy with a pointed chin and sombre eyes. Then there were two more pictures of Leni and me, both taken in Tulia's front yard. Leni outside the barn, shovel in one hand, waving Papa away with the other. And me on one of the Niendorf horses. Small breasts outlined beneath my stripy shirt, my hair coarse, my face too serious and mistrustful for my age. The only happy thing in the photo was the horse.

'Has he really given up his Greenwich Village apartment? What did he say he was planning to do?'

'Have a bit of a holiday, then work. Stella, what's the matter?'

'I miss you.'

Pause. A pause that tasted of nothing.

'I miss you, too. Both of you, so much.'

'Then come and see us again. Come.'

She had only been back to Hamburg three times since moving to the States. Once when her mother died, then when her father died, and finally after my suicide attempt. The first two times she had stayed only as long as was absolutely necessary, flying back immediately after the funerals. On her last visit she had stayed longer, redecorating my little apartment with me and cooking me healthy food for several weeks.

'What's happened?'

'Nothing. Just that he turned up here and within seconds he managed to make me hate my life and make everything, absolutely everything, feel empty.'

'He can't help it, Stella. It's not his fault.'

'Is it my fault? Is it, Mama?'

'No — my God, no, it's not your fault. No one's saying that.'

'Yes! I'm saying it. Why won't anyone believe me? Why doesn't anyone want to hear it?'

'Stella, listen to me, listen to me. That's not what I mean! Do you remember that first summer you all came to stay with us in Newark? You and Leni, and Ivo, who wasn't speaking. And you were running back and forth translating for him. You spoke for him. He only seemed able to communicate with you. Do you remember?'

'Of course I remember.'

'And it didn't seem to bother you that he didn't speak. As if you could hear and understand him, anyway. One time it was raining, and the two of you were playing outside, you and Ivo, and he fell over and grazed his knee quite badly. Do you remember? And I came out of the house, and you were sitting on the steps crying. Ivo had already gone indoors, and I asked you why you were crying, and why you were sitting there on your own, and do you know what you said?'

'No.'

'You looked at me in amazement, as if my question was completely superfluous, because the reason was so obvious. And you said that Ivo had grazed his knee, and he couldn't cry because he didn't have a voice, and you were doing it for him so the graze would heal quicker. I'll never forget it.'

I had forgotten Ivo's grazed knee, but as Mama told me the story

I felt a dull, distant pain. I closed my eyes. The night wasn't so loud anymore; I no longer felt so hot.

'That answer explained so much for me. I liked Ivo, but I was scared of him, because he reminded me of … And you gave me this answer, and it seemed to me that there was still something so beautiful, a feeling like that, amid all the dirt.'

Her voice began to tremble, but I knew she wouldn't cry.

'And I thought that perhaps it wouldn't necessarily be so bad; that it would pass. If you — if at least one of us — was capable of feeling such a thing.'

It wasn't altogether clear to me what she meant by this, but I liked it. I surrendered to her soft voice, and eventually she managed to rock me into exhausted, fevered sleep.

★

Theo was grumpy and whiny. Mark had brought him by car and dropped him off at the door without coming upstairs. He let Theo pass on the message that he wouldn't be back in Germany before Wednesday, but could be reached on his mobile in an emergency. I picked Theo up and teased him a little, but he wriggled away and seemed cross with me. Apparently my opposition to the dog idea had caused ructions in the Simon household, too. This, at least, gave me a modicum of comfort, a sense that I still belonged.

That evening I took another aspirin, did a jigsaw of a knight with Theo, then sat with him and listened to an audio book. He didn't ask any questions, and the small illusion of a return to normality, the time alone with my son, the calm, all did me good.

The following day I went in to the office and apologised to Leo. I promised to hand the article in by Tuesday, and took the architect's contact details. Later, I even called my friend Lina; I'd seen far too little of her lately. We left her daughter and Theo with her husband and went to the cinema, then drank wine at an Italian restaurant in town.

I listened to her and drank the expensive wine. Everything seemed just like before.

★

Back at home, I put Theo to bed, waited until he fell asleep, and kissed his arms, as soft as June peaches. Then I tiptoed into my study, tapped unenthusiastically at my article, and resolved to cook for Mark again when he came home.

Around one in the morning there was a knock at the door. Not a ring, a knock. I thought I was imagining it at first. Cautiously I crept to the door and listened, still not believing my ears. The knock came again, and I knew it was Ivo.

I flung open the door. It had been raining, and he stood before me with dripping hair.

'Are you mad? What are you doing here? Theo might wake up.'

'That's why I knocked.'

'But if Mark —'

'Oh, come on. I know he's not there.'

'You can't just come round whenever you feel like it!'

'Here. I copied it for you. I wanted to be sure you got it.'

He shoved a paper bag into my hands.

'Where are you going?' I called after him in despair, abandoning the whisper. He turned, and called up from the dark stairwell.

'My flight leaves tomorrow.'

'Your flight?'

'I'll be waiting for you. You'll find it all in the envelope. Call me; I'll pick you up at the airport. I'll book your ticket, too.'

I heard him run down the stairs, heard the echo of his heels. I stood in the doorway as if turned to stone, listening for the sound of a car driving away, but none came. How long had he stood outside, watching the windows, knowing that I was alone? The thought made me shudder. I slammed the door and double-locked it.

In the kitchen I found a bottle of red wine, pulled the cork, poured myself a glass, and flopped on to the sofa. And all of a sudden I realised that he meant it, that tomorrow he really wouldn't be here; he would have vanished from my life. And this thought was so preposterous that it formed a tight, hard ball inside me. I ran to the balcony and looked down. It was dark and drizzly. I wanted to call his name, but realised how pointless this was and went back indoors. My body felt heavy; it seemed to have stopped functioning. I sat there listening to my breathing, as if that were my sole remaining purpose.

Then I saw the bag beside me, sodden with rain. I put it on my lap and pressed my chest against it. His smell, intensified by the rain, danced around my nostrils and made me dizzy. I reached inside and pulled out a thick, olive-green folder bound by an elastic band. On it was written *Lado*. A photo of a rather taciturn-looking middle-aged man fell out. I drained my glass of wine and fought back the impulse to run out into the street to look for Ivo, to tell him he shouldn't go, that he couldn't simply disappear again. That he couldn't just come and go as he pleased and leave me only the tiny space between these two extremes, these moments, in which to live.

I crept into Theo's bedroom and lay down beside him. He was sleeping peacefully, as if he'd never had a worry in his life. I curled around his back, drew up my legs and made myself small, fitting my body to his. I tried not to cry. I tried not to say goodbye to him.

★

In the days before Mark's return, I remained quiet and calm. Wrote my article, went shopping, took Theo to school, to football, to a birthday party he initially hadn't wanted to go to at all, but eventually did, after much persuasion, wearing a white shirt and clutching a gift voucher for the zoo. One afternoon I even met my sister for lunch. She talked about her children, and some more about her children, handed out advice concerning my child, and complained about

Papa and Hanna, whom for some reason she absolutely refused to accept, like almost all our father's women; she never thought them worthy of him. She drank her espresso with stiff little movements, examining her short, clean fingernails. Her voice disappeared into the background noise of Café Paris, and her words started dissolving like chemicals in a test tube.

'Stella?'

I had touched her wrist with my forefinger to remind myself of what she used to be like, a long time ago. For some strange reason it made me sentimental. I felt old, and the future seemed paralysed, pointless, cruelly predictable.

'Stella, what are you doing?' She brusquely pulled her cool hand away.

'I was remembering.'

'What?'

'You, when you were still *you*.'

'What's that supposed to mean?'

'At Tulia's, by the sea. You were beautiful. And you weren't this stern. You were just an angry girl who was waiting for life finally to begin. Who had nice clothes, and was good at arguing and always a little bit sad. There was a time when you listened obsessively to Bach. This heavy music was always coming from your room, and sometimes I would listen at the door. And you could swim better than me. And before that, much earlier — you were a spoiled little princess, and you used to get on my nerves, but you were still you, Leni. Not the Leni of today.'

She looked at me as if I were speaking a foreign language. Her expression darkened, and she pressed her lips into a thin line.

'What's brought on this tirade? I suggest we order some cake instead; they do excellent apple cake here.' She beckoned to the waiter.

I wasn't prepared to back down. I went on the offensive.

'You've become a stranger to me. And I to you. And maybe both of us are strangers to ourselves.'

'Don't get all philosophical on me!'

'It's not philosophical, it's a fact!'

'It's nonsense. And I do not want to discuss this nonsense now! You're better off just accepting that he's gone. And learning to draw a line under certain things. Otherwise you'll end up like Mama.'

'Mama *ended* something. She didn't *end up*. She did what you're telling me to do: she drew a line under it. And what good did it do her?'

'Just take a look at yourself and you'll see what he's gone and done! I said it would be like this, I said it to Tulia, I said it to Papa: all Ivo has to do is come, and Stella will crash again. Same old story. You're too unstable where Ivo is concerned. I mean, I understand, I really do. The cake is excellent — don't you want to try some? Or the rhubarb ...'

'I'm not unstable. Stop treating me like someone who needs to be helped.'

'After all that happened. I mean, Stella. Please. It's starting to get embarrassing. And what will happen, what will you achieve, if you keep going on about it, about the old days and what we were like, all of us oh-so-happy and free and whatnot? And our childhood. That was not a childhood! When are you going to realise that? Close the chapter, or go and get some therapy. I know a very good therapist in town, incidentally, I could —'

'Fuck your therapist!'

Leni stared at me with undisguised pity.

'Okay, okay ... What's wrong? What's happened? What does he want from you?'

'I don't want your pity, Leni, I don't want you condescending to me as if I were prostrate at your feet, deigning to listen to me out of the goodness of your heart.'

'My God, you're so ungrateful, do you know that?'

'I'm going now. You can pay for me.'

I got up and left, giving her no time to object.

★

Several months passed after that first night with Ivo, the traces of which I tried furiously to wipe from my memory. Not because I felt guilty about it: it was as if that night had been inevitable, as if it were predetermined and I had never had any option but to accept my fate.

Only afterwards, little by little, did doubt begin to creep in. I'd not expected much of Ivo, just a bit more complicity, some small acknowledgement of the secret we shared. But he disappeared again, and it was just as it had been in the preceding years: he headed off into the big wide world that simply couldn't wait to be conquered by him. And perhaps this was how it had been ever since he had started to speak again, depriving me of my indispensability; ever since he had no longer needed my voice to survive.

His disappearance was callous; he didn't think of me for one second. His disappearance was cruel and total.

Strangely enough, even in my befuddled state it was completely clear to me that I must on no account allow myself to succumb to the same apathy as before, after his last grand disappearance. This time, my longing was transformed into rage, and it spurred me on, banishing all thoughts of idleness. My mourning acquired furious overtones, and I threw myself into my studies, went on short trips with Abi to European cities, read a lot, studied, and celebrated life as best I could. I remember I didn't sleep much during this period, because even sleep felt to me like a waste of time. Suddenly people noticed me, they valued my opinion, and I strutted about like a proud revolutionary in my beret and pencil skirt.

Above all, I started writing a lot. I wrote essays, and scribbled down all my half-formed ideas, turning them into articles a few days later; I designed and revamped the student newspaper. Abi no longer seemed able to keep up with me, and I increasingly saw him as sad, dull, lacklustre.

★

That morning, I was standing in front of the mirror, getting dressed to go to university for the newspaper's editorial meeting. I had taken over as editor around the time Ivo moved to Munich. Abi came and stood behind me and touched my left breast. Xerxes was on the window ledge, stretching luxuriously in the morning sun. I looked at Abi in the mirror, his hand on my breast. For a brief moment I imagined that my skin had disappeared and his hand was inside my body, its bloody innards, palpating my heart.

After that first night, Ivo had coolly driven me back the next morning, dropping me off beside my bike as if nothing had happened, and I had picked up exactly where we'd met. He had said goodbye with a gentle kiss on the cheek, and I'd heard no more from him.

Abi held my breast hard, squeezed harder and harder. I gave a cry and wriggled out of his arms.

'That hurt, Abi.'

'I wanted to give you at least some idea of how it feels.'

'How *what* feels?'

It was only then that I noticed his face was sombre, his voice subdued. He sat on the edge of the bed and held out a crumpled scrap of paper. I had absolutely no idea what this was about. There wasn't the same closeness between us as before, but we didn't argue, and Abi had never been aggressive towards me; he would rather say nothing than discuss things openly. This was why I didn't understand at first what it was he was reading out loud to me.

I think of your body and hate you for it, for the fact that it belongs to you. You say I'm cruel to you. Perhaps it's true; perhaps I am. Perhaps I don't want another bond, because there is already enough that binds us. Perhaps you're right: one shouldn't want to be somebody else. I have no answers, yet you expect them of me, and that makes me furious. You're lazy, because you're afraid. And I expect more of you, in consideration of the day you became the person you are, and I became the person I am. I can't stand your apathy. More than anything, though, I want to tell you that you are incredibly beautiful. And having to think of that makes me weak. I can't afford to be weak.

Come and visit me — or rather, no — no euphemisms: come and sleep with me.

Ivo.

I made no attempt to interrupt. I listened carefully to every word, and I forgot that it was Abi reading it to me; I forgot that these words did not belong to him.

'Where did you get that letter?'

'Is that the only thing you have to say about it?'

'Why have you got that letter?'

'Do you not actually realise what's written here, or do you have so little conscience that you just don't care? The point is not when the letter was written, or why I've got it, the point is that it's your brother writing this to you!'

'Stop it, Abi!'

Abi had tears in his eyes. He stared at me, uncomprehending, appalled, contemptuous. I knew it was impossible to explain anything to him. He slammed the door as he left. I picked up the torn piece of paper and read the words in Ivo's small, angular handwriting over and over again. There was no envelope, and although I turned the apartment upside down, I couldn't find it; I didn't know when the letter had been written, or from where it had been sent. I called Tulia and, hoping Ivo and I would finally bury the hatchet, she immediately gave me his address.

Abi expected me to move out of the apartment. Little by little, fear of loss began to filter through to me: the loss of his friendship, his company, his understanding, his calm. Abi wanted explanations, apologies. Even if I had made all the sacrifices he demanded of me, I don't know that he would ever have forgiven me. The longer I made no attempt to do what he asked, the more his contempt grew. I knew that anything I could have said would only have made me seem even stranger to him. Every word would make him hate me. And I hated the thought of him hating me.

Xerxes was still with me, and I still couldn't clearly see the signs of

Abi's desertion; they hadn't yet come into focus.

I looked out onto the street, full of happy pedestrians. Their happiness filled me with loathing; I spat out of the window on two passers-by and ducked down like a guilty, but triumphant child.

I went into the bedroom, hastily packed a sports bag, put Xerxes in his little carrier, and took the bus to the station. After a seemingly endless journey, with a wild and furious cat, I arrived in Munich. It was dusty and windy. The city was unfamiliar, and I instantly felt miserable. Clutching my evidence, the letter and the address Tulia had given me, I took a taxi to Ivo's apartment. Tulia had told me the name on the buzzer. A flatshare, maybe, I thought. It was a dull, post-war block. Grey and ordinary. Nothing that looked like Ivo.

I rang. A female voice answered right away.

'Hello?'

'I'm Stella. I'm looking for Ivo.'

'Who?'

'Stella.'

'Oh. He's not here, but come up.'

Fighting back my impulse to flee, I trudged up the stairs like a whipped dog, hugging the heavy carrier with Xerxes inside.

A tall, dark-haired girl opened the door. She smiled at me politely and invited me in, introducing herself as Lily. A fairly ordinary apartment, sparsely furnished with absolutely no care and attention, almost devoid of any trace of life. I couldn't believe Ivo was living here; everywhere he went he left traces, visible, deep. We sat in the kitchen and resorted to talking about Xerxes, who was finally allowed out of his carrier and given something to eat.

'Are you a friend of Ivo's from Hamburg?'

'I'm his sister.'

There was nothing I hated more than using this appellation to describe myself, and as if to soften the categorisation, liberate myself from it a little, I added, 'His adoptive sister.'

'Oh, why didn't you say so before! I thought I was going to have to be jealous,' cried Lily, visibly relieved. 'He'll be home soon, you can wait for him here.'

She had narrow hips and full lips. She took me in her arms. Me, her boyfriend's sister. I blushed and bowed my head. For two whole hours I had to listen to Lily rave about Ivo. How happy she was to see me, because he talked so little about himself and his family. That this was actually her apartment, and that Ivo never stayed long in one place and was here with her at the moment because he'd been chucked out of the student hostel a few months ago and finding something of your own in Munich was really expensive, but he was getting along just fine and writing fantastic pieces and people were predicting he would have a great journalistic career, he was so brave and so radical. This paean made me feel increasingly nauseous and I had to nip to the bathroom to dunk my head under cold water.

It wasn't until just before midnight that a key turned in the lock, the door opened, and I heard noisy footsteps in the hall. Before the delightful Lily could announce the happy news of my arrival, he was already in the kitchen, staring in bewilderment at me, and at Xerxes cowering fearfully on my lap. Ivo stepped back and smiled, looking slightly embarrassed, then gave a loud laugh. He had filled out a bit; he seemed healthy, and light, as if he were not walking through life but dancing along a thin silken thread, like a virtuoso acrobat. Expert, full of grace. And yet again I felt robbed of my *raison d'être*; yet again I was unprepossessing, unimportant; and at the same time I was angry with myself for coming here, and already hated him for it. My confidence, hard-won and so recently acquired, melted away in seconds.

There was an awkward silence; even Lily noticed it, as she immediately started prattling, a stream of banalities, and kept assuring Ivo how happy she was to meet his sister.

After another excruciating hour, Ivo managed to explain to the girl that it would be better if he took me to a friend's as there was more space there, and he would like to spend tomorrow with me alone,

but we could all hang out together in the coming days. Lily seemed
disappointed, but eventually let us go.

Out on the street, in the dark of the summer night, I gripped
Xerxes' carrier, leaned against the cold wall of the building, and took
a deep breath. I felt as if I were about to keel over.

'Why are you here? Where did you get this address?' he asked,
roughly.

I barely had the strength to speak. I took out the letter and held it
towards him.

'But I sent that ages ago, with a different return address.'

'Abi opened it.'

He didn't reply; he came close and stared at me. For long time,
without blinking, fixed and expressionless.

'Okay, okay. Let's get out of here.'

He went to a phone booth and called someone, then we got on his
moped, Xerxes' carrier on my lap as I hung on to Ivo with my other
hand, and off we went.

It was in a small room in an apartment in an old building
somewhere on the outskirts of the city that I found traces of Ivo:
countless books, notepads, clothes scattered everywhere, dirty coffee
cups, cassettes, and a photo I hadn't seen before, of Tulia as a young
woman.

'The apartment belongs to a friend; I rent a room here. But it's a
long way out, and sometimes I don't make it back for the night …' he
said, apologetically, and it was the first friendly thing he had said to me
that day. Xerxes, exhausted from excitement and fear, immediately fell
asleep in a corner.

He fixed me some bread and cheese and fetched beers from the
kitchen. I took a swig, and the alcohol hit me like a bomb. I fell back
on the mattress and ran my arm along the bare wall. He sat beside me,
looking down at me. I could still see the indecision in his eyes, the
vacillation between desire and fear that, with him, so closely resembled
contempt. Then he lay down next to me and took me in his arms. For a

while I just lay there, motionless, rigid with tension, nausea, and lust. Then I clung to him tightly and pressed my mouth to his.

'You think I'm lazy and apathetic. You think I want answers from you,' I whispered, undressing him. He kissed me, and still it didn't seem possible that his body wasn't pulling away from mine. He put his hand over my mouth and bit my neck; it hurt, but the pain excited me, and I squeezed myself underneath him, pressed myself against him, transformed myself into a filament able to bend at will.

I saw Xerxes' eyes fixed on me in the dark, and shuddered: for a moment, it felt as if Abi were watching me. I sat up and contemplated Ivo's body, bathed in sweat.

'Is she your girlfriend?' I asked him. He didn't open his eyes.

'No, she's just a friend.'

'Whom you sleep with?'

'Yes, sometimes.'

'Do you love her?'

'Are you making fun of me?'

'Why? Are you not permitted to love?'

'Of course I'm permitted to, but I don't.'

'Don't you love anyone?'

'Don't ask me such stupid things.'

'I want to be with you.'

'That's not possible, you know that.'

'What are you so afraid of? Papa? Tulia?'

'I'm not afraid. Or if I am, then only of myself.'

'Why yourself?'

He sat up abruptly. Wiped the beads of sweat from his forehead with the sheet and pressed himself against me. Then he embraced my back, buried his face in my neck, and whispered in my ear.

'Stella, listen to me. I'll try to explain it to you, okay? And you have to understand, because you're you and you have to. You don't have a choice, you just have to want it.'

He spoke to me as if I were a child, and as if he were stifling his irritation and making an effort to explain something to me as patiently and simply as possible.

'What happened happened. And as chance would have it, we were there together, at that place, at that time. *You* were there. And from one moment to the next we became adults. Meaning that in those moments, on that day, we had to make a decision. Without knowing it at the time, of course: we had to make the decision to survive. Like a coin that can only fall on one side. I mean, the coin is made up of two sides, but they can never both be on the same side, they can never be there at the same time. And something similar happened with you and me — you turned right and I turned left, or vice versa, it doesn't matter. The paths ultimately lead to exactly the same point, but they can't run in parallel; they have to take different directions in order for that point, the endpoint, to come into existence. Do you understand? That was what happened back then. Exactly that. And it was right. I don't understand how you can think you're unimportant to me in any way. *You saved my life that day, and at the same time, you destroyed it.* That's it, Stella. That's what happened. Without you, I would never have been forced to decide; without you, I would have stayed silent. But perhaps, without you, I wouldn't have been ... It's as if we got mixed up. As if there was a massive explosion. All our future chances, all our possibilities, eventualities, aberrations, the whole of the future — all of it was whirled together and came hailing down again. And now we're busy trying to find out which of the qualities, which of the possibilities, which blueprints for the future belong to you, and which to me. Sssh, don't interrupt me, don't say anything yet; I have to finish thinking this through, finish speaking, because I don't know if I'll ever be able to repeat it, all of it. This is how it is, Stella, whether you admit it or not. I refuse to live a life that isn't mine. It's incredibly important to me to know that the life I'm living belongs to me, that it's mine and mine alone. Because there are a lot of things in my life that feel borrowed. It's important to me to know that I still exist beyond that afternoon, that not every cell in my body is shaped by it. When you're with me, I can't tell the difference anymore. It all gets mixed up again. The whirlwind exchanged our insides, as well. That's what it feels like to me. When you're with me, I can always see the explosion; and sometimes I yearn for it; sometimes I have to be able to see it in order to remember, in order to know who I am. But I'm not always able to bear it. Not always, Stella.'

I said nothing. I stayed silent all through his long monologue. Then I extricated myself from his arms. He didn't resist. I had never wanted to hear all that.

'And what do we do with everything that's got mixed up, in our insides?' I asked, coldly.

'I don't know. Take it out again, and implant it back in the other. A kind of mutual operation.'

'No. That would be horrendous.'

'I don't think we'd survive.'

'So?'

'So it'll go on hurting.'

And he laid his hand on my stomach, stroked his palm over my waist, my ribs, fondled my breast, pressed the tips of his fingers into my thighs, into my groin.

'Because my liver is too big for you and your spleen is too small for me; because your muscles are too tough for me and mine are too hard for you; because my blood flows too fast in you and yours too slowly in me. Because your earlobes are too beautiful for me.'

I couldn't help laughing. My heart hurt. It was physically painful. I knew he was right. But the knowledge didn't change the fact that there was nothing I wished for more fervently than that he were someone else. That our futures were free and open, and we could meet like two strangers.

I ran his hand over my stomach, up to my neck, and laid his forefinger on my pulse.

'What if neither of us ever had any other future apart from a future together, and the explosion only happened in order to make us see it?'

'That explosion cost my mother her life. My father, too, in a different way. And it gave me a strange new family that, by rights, I should have hated. What do you think — is that a desirable future? I don't want it, Stella. So let's try and satisfy it only occasionally, this wretched craving; a little ritual that we need, our secret ritual, to touch each other. And then let's go quietly back to our lives. Until we meet again somewhere, quietly and secretly, to touch each other again.'

14

Mark was back. We didn't talk to each other. I was present, fulfilled my duties, didn't complain, went on being Theo's mother, his scandalous mother.

We celebrated Theo's seventh birthday and had the party at his grandparents' in Blankenese, where the children could listen to loud music and romp undisturbed, eat cake, brandish water pistols and flood the garden.

I sat in the corner of the garden at a long table laden with sweet drinks and cakes. Mark was chatting to some of the other fathers and attending to the barbecue. I didn't make a particular effort to talk to anyone. The sun was shining. The day had turned warm, and I let the individual sunbeams dance along my arms, like a juggler. I observed my fingers, which looked so pale, bony, bare and ineffectual. I looked at my wedding ring and started twisting it; I pulled it up slightly, tried to take it off, then pushed it down again. With or without a ring, I had failed.

★

Abi had slapped me, then started to sob as I packed my things. Xerxes, frightened, had crept into a corner and watched with bewildered eyes as his world was split in two. I hadn't found another apartment; it was a hot summer, and the university vacation had just begun, so I'd decided to spend the next few weeks with Tulia until I had something lined up.

I spent the days in Niendorf in a hammock Tulia and I had strung up, staring at the sky. In the evening I went to the beach or wrote articles for the university magazine. I smoked, and listened to old records in the basement. Sometimes I helped Tulia with the boat hire business; we spent the days alongside each other in silence, asking no questions. From time to time she would make her famous apple cake and invite some cackling old ladies over, and I would get to serve them brandy and chauffeur them home. I hadn't told anyone where I was, and I hardly left the house or garden.

My mourning was not excessive, not bloody. It was tender, almost meek, patient even, and wonderfully assuaged by Tulia's liqueurs.

One Sunday evening — I had been at the beach, reading and making notes — I got back to the house and realised that something was different. At first I thought Papa had come to visit, but there was no sign of his car. The gate was open, and the old children's swing under the treehouse was swaying back and forth as if someone had brought it back to life.

I stood still and listened. Tulia was chattering excitedly, with a happy rasp in her voice, and I knew that he had come.

I ran inside and saw Ivo sitting at the table, his cheeks flushed, eating Tulia's soup. His big rucksack and his shoes stood in the hall.

I wasn't prepared for his visit, and it made me rather uncomfortable, because I didn't know what Tulia had written to him, whether he knew that I had left Hamburg. However, I shook off my confusion and rushed over to him. In this place it seemed so easy to sit beside him, with none of the tension, none of the hurt of recent years.

He was back from a trip, and wanted to hide away here at Tulia's for a week, he said. I had to laugh. Would it always be like this? Would we always be seeking refuge in the past and the places that belonged to it, always hiding away in order to remember?

'That sounds good. Eat, eat! Our girl is here with me too, hiding away from the world and its sorrows,' said Tulia, putting an arm around my shoulders as if to check I was still there. 'Come on, Stella, you must eat something as well. It's not good for you, spending all day down by the water and not eating properly!'

And she warmed the soup for me.

At night we sat on the swing, which creaked and groaned, humming songs to ourselves. I tried not to ask any questions; he had said in his letter that he didn't have any answers.

★

Those were good days. I remember that week very clearly. It was as if, in that one week, I was able to catch up on my lost childhood with Ivo. We took the boat out, even though the sea was rough and Tulia had forbidden it; we lay on the beach, played four-handed accordion, ate goulash, and sat on the patio in the evening listening to the night. He asked nothing, and I said nothing. This calm, this closeness was only possible because, in that week, we were brother and sister again, a brother and sister who had consciously chosen each other.

★

We were helping Tulia in the garden; the heavy coastal rains had destroyed the flowerbeds. I was wearing old rubber boots, and Ivo had taken off his shirt. I was helping dig over the earth and staking the plants that could still be saved. By chance, my elbow touched his spine: he was bent over slightly, hands dirty from the damp soil. Suddenly I was gripped by furious lust; I felt the urge to scream. I screamed. Ivo turned, lost his balance, landed in the dirt; I knelt down and kissed him. Mumbling, he pushed me away. He was looking around, looking for Tulia.

My throat constricted. I jumped up and ran from the garden as fast as I could. This time I didn't run to the beach, but into the house, under the shower. I hoped the hot water would wash off this new defeat. I pressed myself against the steamed-up wall of the shower stall.

The door handle turned, and he entered the bathroom. I opened the shower door.

'Go away!' I screamed, wrapping my arms around my body. I didn't want him to see me naked.

He stood there, not moving, only his nostrils quivering slightly. He was afraid, I could see it, and that made my defeat even more crushing. I turned my back on him, rubbed myself with Tulia's rose soap, and hid my face in my wet hair. Then I felt his hand on my behind. He stepped towards me and started to take off his clothes. The shower stall smelled of earth; he stepped inside and put his hand over my mouth.

We made love covertly, because he didn't want our love to leave any traces in the room. He took me that afternoon, took me as you take on a burden; he took me like an addict, without question; he surrendered to his lust, but he did not surrender to me.

I saw it, I saw it in his eyes as they evaded mine, I saw it in his hands that perceived my flesh as an impediment, and I ought to have screamed, to have freed myself, but instead I stretched, adjusted, made it easier for him to abuse my body and humiliate me.

★

He dried himself off while I stayed under the shower; my body ached and burned, and I let the water wash it clean. He looked at himself in the mirror; he seemed calm, himself again, in control of the situation. I crouched down and pressed my legs tightly together, hoping the pain would subside if I just pinched it off.

'It wouldn't be good if Tulia and the others ...' he whispered suddenly, and hastily started to get dressed. 'I'll go out and carry on in the garden. You wait for a bit.'

He said this very calmly, methodically, gazing at his face and running his hand over his cheeks, checking that the prints of his lust had faded. I think it was this calmness, the confidence in his voice, that made me explode, that gave me strength, even though I was crouching mutely under the shower. I don't know how else to explain why I reacted as I did. Why I suddenly felt filled with such strength that I leaped out of the cubicle in a single bound.

I stood before him, wet and naked, and looked him dead in the eye. Something in my expression made him step back; he froze, and stood stock-still.

'I'm not going to wait so much as a second, and I don't give a shit whether it'll be bad, worse, or worst for the others. I can't take this anymore. What do I care about the others? I've spent long enough thinking about the others. You hear me, Ivo? A man who loved me, who I loved and could have been happy with, has just left me — do you know why? Do you want to guess? Do you? I reckon you know the reason — yes, I think you do, although you always act surprised by it, this fucking reason! I'm not going to wait a single second, and you can't hold my mouth shut for ever. I've tried for years, ever since that shitty day on the beach, I've tried to do everything right, the way you think is right, and I realise now that this right is only right for you. For me, it's totally, utterly wrong. So I won't keep my mouth shut. If it's going to hurt, let's have it all at once. That I can cope with, but this — not like this.'

I stared into his eyes the whole time. His pupils were dilated, and for the first time I had a sense of myself as the person I wanted to be, the person I would be, were it not for this man who only had to blink an eye to thwart all my self-determination and all my plans. Day after day, year after year. And despite my pitiful situation, I sensed I had the strength to hold my ground.

'I want you, Ivo. I want you beside me. Yes — hear this. Look at me,' I continued.

'Please, stop it ...'

'No, you are not going to shut me up! No!' This time I shouted, and he instinctively placed a finger on his lips. His fear in this bathroom, in this confined space, liberated me at last. 'No, you're not! Stop telling me how to behave. We weren't like that — our relationship wasn't like that, it was always reciprocal, until you started to be ashamed of what I feel, of what you might feel, too, if you ... I don't want this anymore, Ivo. Do you really not understand me? Is it so hard to understand?'

'How do you see this working? I mean, should we get married and make cute little babies and let Frank and Leni be godparents?'

'You're not hurting me; I can't fall any further. My God, Ivo — is it just this?' I put my hand between my legs. 'Is it? It can't be, it can't just be that? It's not worth all this trouble just for that? I love you, Ivo.'

He lowered his eyes and stared at his bare feet. I couldn't help smiling; in that moment, just as so much seemed to be falling apart, I felt something start to heal. I smiled; I smiled at him.

'I love you — Ivo in the past, Ivo in the present, and Ivo in the future. I love you, perhaps because we were so lonely, so small and weak, and we still made it; because you needed my voice, because in spite of everything you appointed me to speak for you when you were silent, to look out at the world for you with my eyes. Because you expected it of me, and in doing that you gave me a mission, a purpose. Because I need that from you. I love the little birthmark on your right thigh, I love the way you smoke, I love your fear of my body, I love your anger at the world because it's so unfair to you; I love your kisses and your political discussions, I love the way you write, I love the way you peel a cucumber and bite into it with such relish; I love all your attempts to protect our family from everyone else, to defend it; and I want you to listen to me, to allow me to ask your forgiveness.'

There was a knock at the door. The water was still running, the abandoned shower head spraying the entire floor.

'Are you in there, you two?' asked Tulia, and in her voice I heard concern, the insecurity she usually hid so well, as if she were the most fearless person on earth, as if fear were one of the deadly sins.

Staring at me, aghast, he called, 'Everything's fine, Tulia. Stella cut her finger in the garden; we're just patching up her hand.' His voice sounded so cheerful, completely carefree, and again I did something I might not have done if he had been a little more sincere, less exultant.

Before he could grab me by the arm and hold me back, I ran to the door, opened it, and strolled past Tulia naked, leaving the battlefield exposed behind me. I no longer recall what I felt. All I remember is Tulia backing away in shock, Ivo shouting something and falling silent. I walked down the corridor, leaving a trail of damp footprints, and I walked with pride. With every step I was regaining the dignity he had taken away by making love to me while holding my mouth and eyes shut.

15

In the car we listened to Benjamin the Elephant, a CD Theo already knew off by heart. He wanted to hear it over and over again, which Mark thought was great, because his son should not be the kind of boy who goes crazy about computer games, he should remain a perfectly normal child who wants fairy tales read to him and worships football stars. His son would not turn out to be gay, would definitely not be aggressive, would definitely not experiment with drugs, and would definitely not disappoint his parents.

Theo, gorged on sweets and laden with presents after his birthday party, was dozing on the back seat, content with himself and the world. We stared at the road without speaking. I'd drunk a few martinis and felt heavy and lethargic.

Mark carried the sleeping Theo up to the apartment. He laid him on the bed, undressed him, pulled up the covers, kissed him, closed the Ninja Turtle curtains, and came into the living room, where I had sat down and started leafing through the newspapers he had picked up on the plane. He uncorked a bottle of wine and sat down with me. For a while he too leafed through magazines, drinking his wine in silence. I poured some for myself; he hadn't even put out a glass for me, as he usually did.

'Don't you think you've drunk enough? Even my mother noticed.'

'I don't care who in your family notices what, Mark. I've got a headache, and no appetite for an argument.'

'I'm not arguing. I just wanted to tell you I think it's okay if Theo gets a dog and my parents look after it. They don't mind, they'd be happy to do it.'

'No!'

'Theo would like a pet, and if my parents —'

'I don't give a shit what your parents want. I've said no, and that's that. I've already made it very clear to Theo. When he's old enough, he can have a pet and look after it himself. But not now. A dog is not a toy, and it's irresponsible of you.'

'Irresponsible of me? Me? You neglect him, you haven't been around for weeks, you don't say a word at his birthday party, you don't even say hello.'

'I told you, I don't want to argue.'

'Look, it seems as though you've decided to stay, and from what your sister told me, he's gone again. So we need to see where we begin — I mean, where we begin to sort this out, though I'm not even sure I can, or want to, or whether I'll survive it.'

'You talked to my sister about me?'

'I didn't need to tell her anything. Everyone can see what's going on. Yesterday your father called and asked if everything was all right again now that he's gone. And, I mean, just look at you!'

'I can't say anything that'll reassure you. So I'm not going to defend myself, or justify myself.'

'Stop drinking, for fuck's sake. You could at least start with that.'

'That's got nothing to do with it. We've always drunk wine together; it never bothered you before.'

'That was then! Besides, you never used to drink just to get shit-faced before!'

I stood, picked up my glass, poured the wine down the sink, and went into the bedroom. My head felt as if it were about to explode. I fell on the bed and hugged my knees; everything hurt, all the way to my temples. I hid my face in the pillow and was about to start sobbing when Mark grabbed my shoulders, turned me over, and lunged at me. I tried to stop him, to calm him down; I talked to him, apologised, but he wouldn't listen. I knew that if I defended myself, it would only provoke him further in his desire to hurt me, to assert his official claim as my husband, that it would only make everything worse, so I tried to persuade him quietly, gently, bring him to his senses. I even said

Theo's name, pointed out that the door was ajar, that our son could hear us, but not even that made any difference.

He had taken off his clothes, undone his trousers; tears glittered in his eyes. He kept saying that I belonged to him, that I was the mother of his son and had no right to do what I had done. He was trying to undress me at the same time, but his anger, perhaps also his fear of what he might be about to do, held him back. Or perhaps it was just the look in my eyes: empty, no reaction at all.

From begging and pleading he moved on to torrents of abuse. He called me a whore and a terrible mother, a liar, a woman without dignity. Then he clutched me in his arms and frantically kissed my face, hid his face in my neck and started crying, before jumping up again a moment later, grabbing his duvet and dashing into the study, where he spent the night, dragging the duvet behind him like an abdicated king his train.

★

Tulia sat in the kitchen staring out of the window, deep in thought. Ivo was nowhere to be seen. I'd come in to get a glass of water, thinking she would have gone to sleep long ago. She looked up, told me to come and sit down, and passed me the cherry liqueur.

'How long has this been going on?' she asked, and there was a metallic edge to her voice.

'I don't know what you mean.'

'Answer the question, please!'

She emptied her glass in a single gulp and slammed it down on the table. Her troubled eyes remained fixed on me throughout.

'If you want to blame someone, blame me. I'm the guilty one.'

'Don't you dare lie to me. He doesn't need you to defend him. I know him well enough.'

'But it's true! Why doesn't anyone want to hear it?'

'So you're sleeping together.'

'Occasionally. Yes.'

Suddenly she started to cry. I have only seen Tulia cry on two occasions, the first when she came to collect Leni, Ivo and me from Hamburg while Papa lay on the sofa, drunk, and stared at the ceiling with a martyred expression. Not long after Mama moved to New Jersey. Not long after Ivo became a member of the Tissmar family. When we packed our things and Ivo sat on the edge of my bed, mute, making occasional, incomprehensible sounds and going to bite anyone who tried to touch him. She had shut herself in the toilet then, and wept. Loudly and uncontrollably. Now I was seeing her weep again, hours after I had stalked past her stark naked. She wept almost soundlessly; she didn't try to hide her tears, or cover her face with her hands; she looked straight at me and wept. I sat there, silent, drinking the unbearably sweet liqueur, not knowing what to do or say.

I considered why she was weeping, why she always fought so doggedly for Ivo's love and attention, why she always had to defend him, what it was that made her worry about him so much. What did she know? How effectively had my family been able to erase her memory of that afternoon? Did Tulia feel guilty, I wondered, as I looked at her flushed and reddened face.

'Your father … It'll break his heart.'

'I don't care. I don't care about any of that.'

'I'm frightened.'

'Frightened?'

'Yes, for him.'

'Why are you frightened for him?'

'He's not as strong as he always makes out.'

Of course she felt guilty! This feeling was apparently the only constant in our family, coupled with the trouble we all took to ignore it.

'But you're my little girl, you're … How could I not have seen it? How could I?'

'It's not about you, Tulia.'

'No, but perhaps I could have done something, could have prevented it?'

'What? What do you want to prevent?'

'You two hurting each other.'

'Why do you think we will?'

She didn't answer. I looked at her, shook my head, and went back upstairs to bed. I couldn't sleep. I knew he had driven off in Tulia's car. I tried to distract myself with a book. It didn't work; I lay awake for hours, then put a pillow over my head.

Dawn was breaking when the duvet was suddenly pulled back, and before I was fully awake someone was dragging me out of bed. It was his hand gripping my wrist, yanking me to my feet. He was drunk, or high, or both. His pupils were dilated, and there were leaves in his hair, as if he had fallen over. I was still half asleep and couldn't muster so much as a word. He planted himself in front of me, held my chin so I was forced to look at him, and glared at me, full of hatred.

'You've ruined everything! You've ruined absolutely everything!' He started to shake me; he grabbed me by the shoulders and flung me back and forth. When he dropped me back onto the bed, I banged my elbow on the bedframe and let out a howl of pain. He left me lying there and stormed out of the room.

★

'I'm sorry.'

Mark was sitting on the edge of the bed. It was getting light outside. I said nothing.

'We should never have come to this. There's just one thing I want to know, Stella, then I'll let you go back to sleep. Do you still love me?'

I didn't answer.

'Stella?'

'I don't know. I don't know anymore.'

'You don't know?'

'No — I don't know anymore. Please will you go now? I'm so tired, I could sleep for ever.'

Mark got up and left. I put my head under the pillow and pressed down with my hands, as if it could keep the world around me at bay.

★

Theo put his hand over my eyes and kissed my forehead.

'I have to go to football practice. Papa's left already. Wake up!'

'Oh, sweetheart. What's the time?'

'Eight and then twenty.'

'Okay. I overslept.'

'No, we've got time until the little hand is just before nine.'

'True. Come on, we'll have something yummy for breakfast. What would you like?'

'Carrots.'

'What?'

'I'd like a carrot.'

'But Theo, we don't eat carrots for breakfast. We can eat them later.'

'But I want one.'

'Okay, okay, fine. Darling, may I ask you something?' I got up and went to the bathroom; Theo followed me in his Winnie-the-Pooh pyjamas and watched me turn on the tap and start brushing my teeth.

'Yes, you may.'

'What's the deal with the carrots?'

'What does that mean, what's the deal?'

'Well, what do they mean to you, why are you doing this?'

'Why am I doing what?'

'Well, you've been collecting carrots for quite a while now, and you don't want us to throw them away, even when they go mouldy, and you don't eat them, either.'

'That's not true. I do eat them.'

'That wasn't my question.'

'You've got toothpaste on your lip.'

'Yes, I'll wipe it off. If you answer my question, maybe we'll go and get an ice cream later, or we could go to the playground.'

'I don't know.'

Theo suddenly started to cry. I took him in my arms and tried to comfort him, but he didn't stop, he just sobbed louder and louder and clung to my neck. I carried him into the living room and sat down with him on the sofa. I kissed his face, his little hands, which he had balled into fists, and stroked the hair out of his eyes. How could I ever have thought I could bear to be without him, without his love, the feeling that I was indispensable to him, that he needed my arms, my lips, my shoulders to hold tight, to cling to, to kiss, to cry on? I hugged him tighter and tighter, and eventually he looked at me and frowned.

'You don't like Papa anymore, do you,' he said, and it was more a statement than a question.

'Whatever gave you that idea, sweetie? Theo, why do you say that?' I countered indignantly, and at the same time I was sickened by my feigned indignation.

'Because it's true.'

'But that's not the case at all. It's all just a bit difficult at the moment, we're ... well, how can I put it? It happens; all people have times when they like each other more, and times when they like each other less.'

'Do you sometimes like me more and sometimes less?'

'No, it's not like that with children and their parents. They always like each other.'

'Always always?'

'Yes, in fact they always like each other more and more. The way I like you. Every day I like you more and more, and one day my heart will be reeeeeally big because I love you so much.'

I started tickling him to chase the dark clouds from his face. He laughed and did a somersault on the sofa. Then we got up and I made a big breakfast. He seemed to have forgotten that he had asked for carrots, but the brown-tinged carrot beside the fruit bowl continued to make me uneasy.

I drove him to football practice. It was a sunny Saturday morning, and I sat with the other mothers and fathers cheering on their offspring from the damp wooden bench. I watched him; I was his mother again, participating in his life. From time to time he glanced over at the bench, at me, checking that I was still there. After practice, I helped him out of his sweat-soaked kit and put him in the car. I wanted to take him down to the river; it was warm, and I wanted to eat ice cream with him, to be a normal mother doing something nice with her son.

We drove down to the Elbe. On the way I bought a tub of ice cream with lots of different-coloured scoops, and although the sand was far too cold and the sun not really strong enough, we sat on the beach looking out at the water, at the shipping containers and the ships. There were people jogging past, people kissing each other, people taking their dogs for walks. And we were back in the middle of it all.

Theo soon found a couple of kids his age and started digging holes in the sand with them. Lighting a cigarette, I noticed a bruise on my arm from the previous night, given to me by my own husband, whom I had cheated on and deceived. The husband to whom I was lying; the husband I'd told I no longer knew if I loved him. I closed my eyes, and the smell of the water reminded me of Tulia, of childhood, and, above all, of the house near the port. The house that belonged to Emma, to Ivo. With its little garden, the narrow corridor with the bedroom at the end, the mysterious room where our parents played their dangerous game together. With the dark little kitchen where Ivo and I would make ourselves something to eat when we got hungry. Ivo could cook excellent omelettes, and I would butter slices of bread, always a bit too thickly, but the food we ate in that kitchen always tasted good. And the big black dog dozed at our feet and got the scraps we couldn't finish.

I didn't like dogs. I'd never told Mark. I didn't like them. The only dog I had liked and got used to was dead, along with his owner. Shot with a hunting rifle. He'd been lying at the feet of his dead mistress.

I only found that out years later, from Ivo. The dead dog had gone unmentioned, in view of the dead woman.

I thought back to an afternoon when Ivo and I had been playing hide-and-seek. It was my turn to seek. I usually found him very quickly, as the house wasn't especially big and I knew it well, but that afternoon I couldn't locate him anywhere. Until I found him up a tree, right at the top, holding a pair of binoculars. The branch he was sitting on reached all the way to his parents' bedroom window. The window was shut and the curtains closed, as they usually were when Papa and Emma were in there, but this time there was a little gap between them, and Ivo was staring at it through his binoculars. I knew he was doing something he shouldn't, and I begged him to climb down, but he ignored me, completely absorbed in what he was doing. I hauled myself up and sat beside him, overcoming my fear of heights and the bad feeling I had of bearing witness to something forbidden. Ivo's face was so tense, so focused, alien, and cold, that I couldn't stand being ignored by him a moment longer. Holding on tight to the branch with one hand, I grabbed the binoculars and looked through them.

I saw two shadows, two silhouettes, clutching at each other. My father was sitting on the bed with his back to the window, and Emma's legs were wrapped around his waist. I couldn't see her face as she was leaning slightly backwards, but I recognised her fingers, which were digging into his back. He leaned back further and further, moving sometimes faster, sometimes slower, and the impression conveyed by this tableau was one of great pain.

Ivo took the binoculars off me and started to climb down, quickly and skilfully. I followed, distressed, alarmed, and confused, far more by Ivo's remoteness and strangeness than by what I'd seen through the binoculars. From that afternoon on, Ivo would throw a tantrum whenever Papa went anywhere near him. He started clinging to his mother and whining all the time; he pretended to have stomach ache, to have grazed his knee, to have fallen over; he didn't want the food his mother made him, didn't want to do his homework, didn't want to play with me, didn't want, didn't want, didn't want. And I wept: in secret, in public, loudly, quietly, demandingly, pitifully, under my breath. I wasn't weeping about my father, or my mother, who more and more often slept in Leni's bed, or about Leni, who more and more often broke out in a rash and went riding less and less, as if punishing the pony for her parents' behaviour; nor about Emma, who more and more often sat at the table in the kitchen staring into space, as if the solution to all her problems were out there, in the garden, in the distance. The only thing I was weeping about was Ivo and his aloofness, his irritability, the fact that he had lost all interest in our adventures, in our games, in me.

After the weeping phase came, out of nowhere, the phase of me hugging Ivo, kissing him, taking his hand in mine; this was how I tried to banish the danger that frightened me, the gloomy atmosphere in the house. And Ivo relented: in stroking my cheeks and plaiting my hair, he forgave my father for doing what he did with his mother.

★

'Mama, look, a seagull!'

Theo ran towards me, scattering damp sand. The proud white bird strutted in front of him, nodding politely with each step. We watched it for a while, and Theo stood open-mouthed with excitement.

'Because carrots are for a happy home.' He didn't look at me as he spoke.

'What?' My thoughts were somewhere else entirely, with the gull, which was about to fly away.

'Because ... because. That's what it says on the calendar.'

'What calendar?'

'The calendar on the wall at Grandpa and Granny's. The kitchen calendar. And because it has tips for making your home nicer.'

'Carrots are for a happy home?'

'Yes. Carrots create a nice atmosphere in the kitchen. Carrots and oranges. But I don't like oranges.'

'Aha. And why do you think our kitchen needs a nicer atmosphere?'

'Well, not the kitchen,' he said, and ran off, to a red-haired boy who was moulding shapes in the sand.

★

Mark had left me a message saying something about lots to do and I'd rather sleep at Thomas's tonight and can you drop Theo off at my parents' tomorrow, they're going to take him with them on a trip to the North Sea.

After we had watched *The Lion King* on DVD for what felt like the fiftieth time, Theo went to bed. As Simba fought for his position in the animal hierarchy, I couldn't stop thinking about that bloody carrot in our kitchen. Later, I went into the study and sat down at the computer, the mouldy carrot still on my mind.

My inbox was overflowing. I ran a practised eye down the subject headers.

Leo: *Important! Read me!*

I skimmed the email. Leo criticised me, complained that I was irresponsible, wrote of the immense trust he had placed in me and of his disappointment, mentioned yet again that he had had high hopes for me and had been planning to put me in charge of the whole of Culture, but this couldn't continue, he couldn't be held responsible if I carried on like this. Now in particular he expected loyalty from me, he expected professionalism ... I didn't bother reading to the end. Instead, I composed a brief reply:

Dear Leo, thank you for your trouble, understanding, and patience. However, I feel that in my current state of mind it is impossible for me to meet your demands and live up to your expectations. I must be honest with you and inform you that, at present, I think the best thing for me would be to take some time off. If this is out of the question for you, and although I would be very sorry to do so, I will have to resign. As things stand, I believe this is the best way forward for us both. I am sure you will be able to find a

suitable replacement. I will therefore clear my desk over the coming days;
Nadia will certainly be able to make good use of it. I will come and see you
when I do, and we can discuss everything. See you then. — Stella.

I didn't know why I was doing this, but something within me was
rebelling, refusing to go on doing things I didn't want to do.

The next email was from Ivo, with no subject.

I've landed. It's warm, I feel good, things are great, as always when
I'm here. And I'm waiting. Attached is the ticket for the flight next
Wednesday, and all the other information you need. I'm waiting for you.
— I.

I closed the laptop and took a deep breath. I pretended I hadn't
read the email. I turned on the TV, zapped through the universe of
stupidity and obliviousness. But I couldn't forget. I saw Theo, who
had found the recipe for happiness in his home, his family, on his
grandparents' calendar. I saw Ivo, who used to plait my hair when he
was little, or pin it into a bun; I saw my father, with the small, slight
woman wrapped around his body as if chained to him, welded to him;
I saw Tulia's stricken expression when I told her that I needed Ivo;
I saw my sister with her three alpha sons, and the lube in its gaudy
plastic packaging. I saw myself going to work, and Leo's face when he
spotted a firm young backside. I saw my husband, who had wanted to
sleep with me and started weeping instead; I saw my mother, the way
she had sat on my bed back then and held my hand because she knew I
was slipping away. I saw myself in the seedy hotel room, next to Ivo's
naked, freshly showered body, lying on the imprint of an unknown
woman he chose not to remember.

And I screamed.

I screamed, as images from a cookery show flickered across the
TV, and the images made me and the world around me feel even
more desolate. What I was thinking, what I wished for, was absurd,
as absurd as people getting together in front of TV cameras to cook
while others sat in front of their TV screens gawping at meals they
would never taste, never prepare, never enjoy.

I opened the balcony door and went outside. I had seen him walk away, along this rainy street — he had disappeared as he always did, as he had back then, as he did every time he condescended to bestow that precious closeness upon me. Always it was followed by the phase of punishment. Of withdrawal, disappearance, in which I was aggressively eliminated from his life, wiped out, erased. I was painted over in his head with a white marker pen. He folded up all tents behind him, slammed all doors in my face, obliterated all traces just so I wouldn't think of following him. And always he left me alone with the thoughts that he had planted in my head. That I could never unthink.

★

I took out the folder he had left for me. Covered in stains, thick, fat, full. I turned off the TV and spread the notes, photos, scraps of paper around me on the floor. I sat amid the mountain of paper and searched for traces. Any traces that could dissuade me from what I was planning to do. And the more I pushed the thought away, the more I wanted to do it. As if my thoughts were the enemies of my wishes and feelings, and locked in a pitiless battle with them.

The photo of the man with the big beard appeared several times. Dates and places, none of which meant anything to me, were noted on them in Ivo's tiny, indecipherable handwriting.

Lado Kancheli. Born in Sokhumi, Georgia, 1963. Georgian musician and pioneer of the Georgian underground movement. Political activist. Trained in classical composition, specialising in guitar, at the conservatoires in Tbilisi, Georgia, and Moscow, USSR. Imprisoned twice for inciting insurrection against the regime. Co-founder of the Georgian National Party in the early '90s, which then came under the leadership of Zviad Gamsakhurdia. Officially left the party in 1992. During the civil war in 1992 he led a Georgian fighter battalion in Gali, Abkhazia. Lost family members in the war. Lived as a political refugee in the US for a while, later in Germany. Returned to Georgia; has lived there as composer and musician ever since.

★

I went through all the notes once more. It seemed that two years earlier Ivo had been commissioned by the BBC to make a programme about the Caucasus. The subject was the recent history of the region, in particular the three biggest Caucasian countries' relationship with Russia. These were Georgia, Armenia, and Azerbaijan; Chechnya also got a bit of airtime.

Ivo had always claimed TV wasn't his medium, but I knew from Mama that he had made programmes for the BBC and CNN in recent years, involving lengthy research trips.

Apparently the programme had been completed, but was never broadcast. What I couldn't work out was why Ivo had returned to the story two years on, or why he was concentrating on just one country this time — Georgia — and one person there in particular. People, individuals, didn't usually interest Ivo much, unless they were dictators or revolutionaries. He was interested in crowds and historical conflicts; he never saw things in isolation, but always in their historical context, in their chronological framework, in the context of world affairs. So I was puzzled by his fixation on the man with the big beard, who seemed to be neither a proper politician nor a proper artist. Who couldn't be considered either a victim or a perpetrator. Ivo loved radicality: radical views, radical attitudes, opinions. Going by his notes and records, it seemed that, as far as this man Lado was concerned, he had no strong stance, only questions.

The interviews Ivo had conducted with the bearded man didn't suggest radicality, either. They were epic; they chronicled things that had happened, yet adopted no clear position; they were critical of the regime, but barely engaged with the socialist past in any detail. There was nothing new, nothing that might have attracted Ivo or surprised him.

I made myself an espresso and went on rooting through the file. War photos. Brutal images that had nonetheless become mundane: of the wounded, the dead, refugees, children staring into the camera in fear and confusion. What was it about this man that interested Ivo, and why did he want me to go to Georgia with him?

My head felt as if it were exploding, but I couldn't stop. My morbid obsession with Ivo aside, something had been awakened in me, something I had thought long forgotten; something that, in the past, had driven me to type for hours, spend hours trying to reach someone on the phone, sit for hours in the library. Perhaps it was a primal instinct I had inherited from my father, a primal instinct he had passed onto Leni, me, and Ivo. A primal instinct originating, perhaps, in the desire to understand when there was nothing to be understood, when human understanding could only ever fall short.

I hadn't felt this drive for a very long time. Not since I had settled for writing mediocre stories for mediocre people: things that would upset no one and make no one particularly sad or happy. Neutrality dutifully maintained.

Around dawn I fell asleep on the sofa, papered over with Ivo's legacy.

16

That summer, when I returned from Tulia's, I rented a room in a shared apartment, with a man who had devoted his life to doing nothing and a woman who grew cactuses, cultivated cannabis plants, and really, really wanted to study geology, although she was already thirty-seven.

I studied, and spent most of my time in libraries or in the student magazine's makeshift editorial office. From time to time I would go to Abi's to cat-sit Xerxes, only arriving when Abi had already left, so I never ran into him, always taking the key from under the doormat and putting it back again.

I got to know a few women with whom I could go out, go dancing, and talk about men, but nothing distracted me as effectively as my books and my work. I wrote, and I talked to my father for hours; every weekend we arranged to meet in town for a meal.

After the day I walked past her naked, Tulia never mentioned either the incident or our conversation, and that was fine by me.

Ivo had dropped out of university, as I found out from Leni, who was in her esoteric phase at the time, having gone on a meditation course in India over the summer. Then, in the autumn, he got an internship with some very important newspaper in New York, and Mama wrote excited letters from America, praising him to the skies.

Sometimes, I wondered whether these eulogies to Ivo that certain members of our family so often felt obliged to make had something to do with their fear that he might one day feel he wasn't getting enough attention, wasn't loved enough, and so might start to lash out, and, in doing so, bring our house of cards tumbling down.

★

I didn't see him again until Christmas. Tulia had insisted we all come
to her, threatening to revoke our family membership if we didn't. Ivo
travelled back, Leni travelled back, and I drove to Tulia's with Papa
and his new flame, a not very successful actress. Ivo had brought a girl
with him, an English girl, whom they all flattered and fussed over as if
she were the Queen herself. Everyone found it incredibly thrilling and
exciting to see Ivo with a woman, and thus to find out more about his
taste and preferences. She was intelligent, extremely sarcastic, and had
endless legs. An art journalist, six years older than Ivo.

I hated her at first sight. Because she was no Lily from Munich
who would wait days and weeks for Ivo's cock, for little portions of
happiness that Ivo could serve her in bed at night, only to vanish from
her life again during the day. This one was his equal: she was strong,
she was clever. And she played with him, constantly challenging him
— all the things that Ivo really went for.

Leni had brought a boyfriend, too: a ghastly yogi who played
some sort of Indian instrument, whom she had met on her travels.
Apart from Tulia, I was the only one who had come alone, presumably
stinking of loneliness from a hundred metres away.

The Englishwoman, whose name was Bea, had brought exciting
presents, and told a stream of witty, entertaining stories about their
life, the life she and Ivo shared — they had met in New York —
ending her Christmas speech with the announcement that she was
learning German so she and Ivo could move to Berlin together.

Ivo didn't look at me. Or rather, he looked at me the same way he
looked at all the others; it wasn't directed at me. Tulia's narrow scrutiny
had not escaped me, though. Leni was grinning from ear to ear; Papa
was drinking, and groping his latest trophy. And I sat between them,
picking up the pieces of my future that I saw crashing down on me, a
future that didn't seem worth living, and I longed for Abi and our cosy
love, his solicitude, his support, and silently, I cursed Ivo.

After the opening of the presents, the usual drinks orgy began, with
Tulia's liqueurs and brandies. Bea seemed proficient at this as well. To

cap it all, the failed actress put on Anita Baker and demanded that all the couples dance. Papa danced with me out of pity; then, at the family's insistence, Leni and I had to perform some ancient dance we had learned at school an eternity ago, which looked every bit as pathetic and stupid as it had back then. I wanted to die of embarrassment.

I got drunk, put on the hat Tulia had knitted as my Christmas present, and went out into the garden to light a cigarette. I sat on the swing seat, listening to the noisy laughter drifting over from the house. I sat there and went on drinking mulled wine and chain-smoking. Nothing and no one would force me back into that hell.

And then he was standing next to me, asking for a cigarette. I handed him the half-empty packet without a word. He sat down beside me without asking. I automatically shifted away.

'You're looking good.'

His tone was cheerful, almost provocative. He stared straight ahead, poking the toes of his boots into the earth. Inside the house, Anita's sugary voice sang of love and human happiness, excluding all those currently sitting outside on a swing seat in the cold.

'You don't need to bother with platitudes.'

'How are you?'

'Just brilliant, thanks.'

'Are you still pissed off?'

'Pissed off? Is that what you call it?'

'Tulia didn't tell anyone.'

'Oh, please, just go back in. This is disgusting.'

'Disgusting? What have I done now?'

'You think I'm afraid Tulia will tell someone she caught me naked in the shower with you? You think that's my biggest worry in the world?'

'I don't think anything. I just asked you how you were.'

'Brilliant. I just said.'

'You've got to get over it, Stella. It won't do any good.'

'Oh, right. Get over it. Sure. I'll go to New York as well, pick up someone who'll help me get over it. All my worries, all my sorrows, all the people who've treated me like shit.'

'Don't be so sarky. It's easy.'

'Nothing is easy, Ivo, and I would be eternally grateful if you would stop behaving as if you were someone who'd never heard the word *problems*.'

'I'm fine. I'm in a good mood. Why would I put on an act?'

For the first time that evening I looked him in the eye, and at that moment I hated him. I got up and ran away. The prospect of spending the night under the same roof as him was unbearable.

I went arounds all the village pubs, hoping to distract myself, but found only one that was still open: a little bar in a guesthouse where I stayed till dawn, numbing myself with vodka. I had myself chauffeured home in a taxi, half dead.

★

I spent the months that followed in a daze. I studied, got bored, hated my life, hated the flatshare, the people, hated the streets, the city, my family, and the word *happiness*, which I considered an illusion.

My father recommended me to a few left-wing newspapers, and they let me write little reports for them that never seemed to be as radical, as eloquent, as biting, as succinct as Ivo's, which — unlike mine — Tulia cut out and kept in a white box.

I went on an exchange semester to New Jersey City University and lived with my mother. I let her cook for me and nurture me back to health. It was the first time in many months I didn't find myself thinking of Ivo every day and measuring myself against him.

Shortly before my departure — my mother had done all she could to persuade me to stay in America — I met Kasper, who was incredibly smart, loved James Joyce, and came from Bremen. He managed to engage me in conversation for longer than fifteen minutes, to drag me along to a rock concert by a band he worshipped, but no one else knew, to take me for dinner, read books aloud to me, show me the best pubs, and write a song for me that was off-key and very moving. And then I went to bed with him. And stayed in New Jersey longer than planned, which gave my mother hope that she might be able to persuade me after all. Kasper was taking university classes in aesthetics and Ancient Roman architecture, both subjects I had never heard of, and he amused me.

At the start of the new semester, I returned to Germany with Kasper and started to go back and forth, spending my nights in Bremen and my days in Hamburg.

Kasper was gentle, relaxed and clever; he knew things I didn't know and would never have got to know without him. Things like the fact that when the moon is full, you can experience emotional as well as physical ecstasy if you make love in the right positions; things like the history of Roman architectural monuments that no longer exist. Kasper was the best distraction I'd had in ages.

And so we stuck with each other, both of us knowing that, although this was not the love we wanted for ourselves, we had the will to make it so.

Then, one morning, I was unlocking my bike to go to a seminar — I was already late — and there he was, standing in front of me. Ivo. In an old leather jacket, his hair was a mess. He was smoking a filterless cigarette and biting his thumbnail. He was standing there as if he'd been waiting for me to come out. I jumped, and staggered back slightly. His eyes were red and he seemed to be having difficulty balancing. I left my bike where it was and went over to him.

'You okay?' was the first thing that occurred to me.

'I'm not feeling too good. Can we go to yours?'

'How do you know where I live?'

'You're my sister, Stella.'

'Since when?'

'I'm not feeling too good.'

I saw the colour drain from his face, and he started to stagger for real, as if he was about to fall over. I stood next to him, put his arm around my shoulders, dragged him up to the third floor, to the apartment, to my room, and laid him on the bed. My flatmates were out, and the apartment was steeped in the familiar quiet of morning. The low sun broke through the windows, creating a reverential atmosphere.

Ivo fell asleep immediately. I was looking for an aspirin in the kitchen; when I returned to the bedroom with a glass of water, I saw him lying there, blissfully, deeply asleep. I sat on a chair and looked at him. I looked at him for a long while, and the sight of him made me sad. I don't know why, but he seemed somehow incredibly vulnerable, incredibly alone, and incredibly young. As if, asleep, he was the young Ivo with the black dog and the sticky-out ears. The Ivo who played hide-and-seek with me and put my burning palms to his cheeks.

He woke up seven hours later. I was sitting in the living room trying to read, in between sneaking to the bedroom to check on him every twenty minutes. He stood in front of me, pink-cheeked, grinning contentedly, and said, 'I'm ravenous. Shall we go and get something to eat?'

I stared at him, taken aback. 'I can make you some pasta.'

'Oh, yeah. That sounds great. Will it be quick?'

'I'll do my best.'

While I cooked he sat in the kitchen, smoking, nervously drinking the remains of my flatmate's wine and watching me.

'What's the matter with you?' I asked.

'I drank a bit too much last night.'

'Drank? Are you sure you it was something you *drank*?'

'That's none of your business.'

'You almost collapsed! What are you doing here, anyway?'

'I'm visiting family. Tulia, Frank.'

'And me to finish off, so you can go home feeling good about yourself? That you went and saw everyone.'

'Don't be like this. I'm really not in the mood for you being catty.'

'I'm not being catty. It's just a bit weird for you suddenly to show up at my door and claim that you're visiting.'

'Shall I go? No problem.'

For a moment I thought how wonderful it would be if, right then, I could find the strength to answer in the affirmative; find the strength, just once, to tell him to go, and, most importantly, never come back. But I knew that, if I did, I would fall and fall into a bottomless pit for all the weeks and months of my life.

'No. You can stay.' I put a plateful of spaghetti on the table in front of him.

Later, I came out of the bathroom to find him stretched across my bed, weeping. I froze: I couldn't believe my eyes. He had been so confident and cheerful as we sat chatting about the press and his life with Bea in Berlin. I kept still; I wanted to give him time to calm down and sit up again. But he didn't calm down, and he didn't sit up. Slowly I walked over to him and sat gingerly on the edge of the bed. I didn't dare touch him, I just stretched out my hand, as if it impulsively wanted to touch him but had not received permission from my brain.

'What's wrong, Ivo?' I whispered, smoothing the bedcover with my fingers.

'I miss you so much,' he sobbed, like a little child, turning his back on me.

'You miss me? And that's why you're crying?'

'It's just so shitty, all of it; it's shitty and unfair. I miss you.'

'Ivo, what are you talking about? I don't understand a word.'

He took my hand and started kissing my fingertips, biting them gently.

'Do you remember what I said to you? In Munich? That we need to touch each other sometimes? That I need to feel myself inside you, to hold you. That's long overdue.'

I leaped to my feet. Everything inside me was trembling. His voice was calm again; he was able once again to talk about me as if I were an object that could be put in the corner and brought out from time to time, to make sure it was still there.

He got up and moved towards me. I retreated until I was standing in the doorway. He grabbed my wrist and pulled me to him, then lifted my chin and looked at me. And instead of giving him the slap he deserved, I kissed him.

I don't know what time it was when my flatmate knocked on my door and announced, in her usual bossy tone, that I had a visitor. We were asleep, and before I could even raise my head from Ivo's chest, Kasper was standing in the middle of my room, a bottle of wine in his hand.

'I thought ...' he began, then realised what was going on and fell silent. I covered my face with my hands, as if that would render me, or him, invisible; him, Kasper, me.

I remember it so clearly, even now: Kasper putting the bottle down very carefully, running his palm over the label. Still, I didn't look at him. Then he turned without a word and left the room. He even closed the door quietly behind him.

★

Theo waved to me when I dropped him off at Mark's parents'. To my surprise, they were still keeping up a polite front, but they eyed me suspiciously; their immaculate son had been in a bad mood for weeks because of me.

I got into the car and wondered what to do with my day, now that I no longer had a job, didn't need to look after my son, Ivo was gone, and all the friends I could think of would have told me to see a therapist, given the state I was in. Which was the last thing I wanted.

I drove around the city. Aimlessly, wasting time, in a car that was a gift from my husband. I stopped. I laid my head on the steering wheel. Cars drove past me, honking. I switched on the hazard lights. Neil Young's 'Long Road' was playing on the radio, and the sky threatened an angry downpour.

★

Ivo lived with Bea in Berlin and wrote for the big German magazines. Ivo earned money and Ivo took drugs. Ivo kept disappearing, and his girlfriend, who still only spoke English, would look for him, starting by calling all his relatives, including me. Bea had got skinny; her legs didn't seem so long anymore, her hair was dull and her fingernails ragged. She wrote little articles for the English tabloids, and as Ivo drifted further and further away, she dreamed of a baby with which to bind him to her. I even felt sorry for her when I saw her again, on Papa's birthday, and I despised Ivo for his apparent ability to destroy other lives as well as mine, effortlessly and without remorse.

Ivo's reports, on the other hand, got better and better. Ivo had money, bought Tulia an SUV. Ivo sent Papa first editions of books he wanted; Ivo remembered every birthday, organised meals in restaurants, and paid the bill as a matter of course. Ivo bought Leni and me plane tickets to Newark for Mama's sixtieth birthday.

After graduating, I rented a little two-room apartment of my own in St Pauli and got a job as an assistant editor at a publisher of literary fiction. I wrote for the Hamburg newspapers from time to time, as a freelancer. I became friends with a colleague called Sarah, who had beautiful green cat's eyes, liked sailing, and made me laugh.

Bea left Ivo, and the family mourned.

When Leni got engaged to a children's book publisher, Ivo showed up with a nineteen-year-old blonde whose breasts were so big that afterwards none of us could remember her face, let alone her name. Ivo came to Tulia's birthday high, which was not lost on her. He and Tulia argued on the patio while I danced to Anita Baker.

I had made a point of bringing an Anita Baker CD and a good-looking artist I had met at a private view where I had gone to write a profile of him. He painted, though he wasn't particularly successful. But he really was incredibly good-looking. I had the impression that all the women at the private view were staring at his arse rather than at the paintings.

And so, that evening, in front of everyone, I danced vulgarly and aggressively with my gorgeous new lover. The fact that they were arguing as I nibbled his earlobe made it all the more satisfying. Leni shook her head and cleared her throat. I grinned at her and stuck out my tongue.

No one remembered Anita Baker and that jolly Christmas party, apart from me.

★

I had been commissioned to research a feature in Berlin. I went by train and took a room in an old-fashioned guesthouse. I enjoyed the new faces and the distraction. On my fourth day in the city I bumped into Ivo, in a bar a colleague had taken me to which had just opened and was meant to be incredibly hip.

Someone tapped me on the shoulder; I turned and saw Ivo, who beamed at me and kissed me on the forehead.

'What are you doing here?' I blurted out.

'I should be asking you that.'

'I'm on a work trip. And I'd like to keep it a work trip.'

'Oh, you're still pissed off with me. Come on, I'll buy you a drink.'

'Nice try, Ivo.'

'Hey, Stella. I need to talk to you. I'm serious.'

And again, from one moment to the next his expression changed, and he grabbed my hand. I pulled it back and turned away.

I chatted with my colleague and his friends, while Ivo kept staring at me and grinning each time our eyes met. He was there with some weird-looking guys I had absolutely no desire to meet. I avoided him as best I could in a space of seventy square metres.

When I went to the bathroom, he followed me and planted himself in front of me.

'Why are you following me? I don't know what we have to say to each other.'

'Don't you want me anymore?'

'What are you talking about?'

I hated the way he was looking at me, the corners of his mouth a little turned down, his eyes sparkling and clear, his arms slightly held out towards me.

'Let's move in together. I'll come to Hamburg. I'm fed up with this shitty town and this nomadic life. Let's give it a go.'

'Are you on drugs?'

'No, I'm not, for once. Seeing you puts me in a good mood.'

'Ivo, this isn't funny.'

'I'm serious. I've been thinking a lot since Tulia's birthday, and I think: what the hell. I'll move to Hamburg next month, and if you're still just a teeny-tiny bit prepared to like me, then ...'

I turned and disappeared into the ladies.

★

A month later, Ivo really did move to Hamburg, not far from where I'd first slept with him. And bombarded me with phone calls. He didn't try to see me; he just kept calling, or wrote letters or little notes that he slid under my door. Then he started sending me flowers. Usually an orchid or three red roses. I never found out why it was always three.

Once the phone rang at two o'clock in the morning, and I knew it was him, and I told him to come. I didn't say hello, or his name, I just said: 'Come.'

A quarter of an hour later he was there.

Within a week I had packed my things and moved in with him. I didn't trust the change in him, his radical decision to be with me, to be close to me, but I was so happy that I would never have jeopardised that happiness by questioning it.

We made love morning, afternoon, and night. After a shower, before a shower, in the kitchen, in the bedroom, in the corridor, sometimes before we even reached the apartment, on the stairs. We barely talked, didn't eat much, and our work suffered. We hardly worked at all, and if I went in to the publishing house, or he had to go away to file a report, we would call each other and talk about when we would next be able to make love.

Leni was the first to start asking questions. One morning she dropped by unannounced and deluged me with questions about Ivo, which I did my best not to answer.

Papa also started visiting, and when he asked us to a family dinner at his place out of the blue, and invited Tulia as well, and she actually came, it was clear what awaited us.

I don't remember now whether it was Leni or Papa who made some stupid comment. Whenever I'd pictured a moment like this, as I had often done in the preceding years, in my imagination I was always the one who took up the cudgels against the whole world, for Ivo, for myself. I was the one who started speaking for him, just as I had before. But this time it was Ivo who stood up; he'd already had a lot to drink, and said calmly, 'We're together. That's why we're living together. Any more questions?'

A silence fell that seemed to last for ever. Only Tulia, who kept clearing her throat, made any sound. Leni started laughing — hysterically, as if she couldn't squeeze what she had heard into her brain, and was shielding herself from it with laughter. Ivo just strolled out of the room and left me there, feeling as if I had burst into a thousand tiny pieces.

Ivo had gone, and I had to defy the looks and unspoken reproaches from my family on my own. When I tried to leave, my distraught sister followed me into the corridor and grabbed my elbow.

'You'll kill him. You'll kill Papa. How can you do such a thing?'

'I don't owe you an explanation. I love him.'

'You love him? After what we had to go through, after everything that happened?'

'I want to leave now, Leni; please let go of me.'

'You're destroying our family.'

'This is just how it is. And believe me, if I could have chosen a different life for myself, I would.'

I took a taxi home, and before I had even put the key in the lock, I knew that something had been irrevocably lost. I just didn't know what. Ivo lay stretched out on the bed, eyes closed. On the bedside table was a little bag of white powder.

★

In the year and a half I lived with Ivo, I discovered that he loathed fruit muesli, that he liked to eat pears in bed at night after sex, that he still loved plaiting my hair. That he needed total silence when he was writing, and would even unplug the fridge because he said he couldn't bear the humming. I discovered that he watched me sleep in the morning, that he could kiss quite beautifully, as if with every kiss he were giving me a new beginning; that he was childish and moody, that he was a bad cook, but would always insist on cooking. I discovered that he exerted a magical attraction over other women, and repelled them in equal measure, because he could be so incredibly cruel and would strip away their defences. That he drank, a lot, and that he was constantly running away — from himself, from something I couldn't grasp, couldn't discern, couldn't name. That he was afraid of spiders; and that sometimes — not often — he would sit alone in the window seat, staring up at the sky, and his eyes would fill with tears.

I discovered that he had strange friends, and would disappear just like that, without a word, would go somewhere and sometimes only come back days later, with the usual grin on his lips, as if these vanishing acts were the most natural thing in the world.

I discovered that he had three different toothbrushes. That he would let me down, and sometimes could not abide it when I reminded him of himself. That when he got aggressive, he would smash things against the wall. That he had a violent temper, and could shout so loudly that it hurt my ears. That I was sometimes afraid of him; that he would bring home drugs, and people I had never seen before, claiming that they were old friends who were just going to stay a few days. I discovered that he would give me this closeness, would shut himself away with me in the apartment for days, postpone all his assignments, order food deliveries, drink wine with me, unplug the phone, listen to me for hours, tell me so many things; and I hated it all the more that then he would deprive me of this closeness by disappearing for days without leaving a message.

This went on for months. And for months Papa shouted, Leni badgered, and Tulia said nothing.

I became a ghost of myself, a creature marooned between the extremes of Ivo's love and his contempt.

★

One night, when he went out again unexpectedly without saying where he was going or when he was coming back, I followed him. I followed him to a club hidden away in a rear courtyard basement, where drugs were sold almost as openly as alcohol. A rock band was playing, and it was so jam-packed I could hardly breathe. I watched him snort one line after another, knock back vodka, talk to some guys I didn't know, and give a shaven-headed woman an intimate, never-ending kiss. I let someone persuade me to buy pills of some sort. I took one and washed it down with alcohol. I let someone else push me up against the cold wall and grope me.

At some point I found myself caught up in a fight. A man lay on the ground, groaning and bleeding from the mouth. Ivo had seized my arm and was dragging me up the stairs.

My head was spinning; I laughed. Ivo grabbed me and shook me repeatedly. I started to feel sick.

The following morning, when I opened my eyes, he was standing looking down at me.

'If you do that once more, you'll never see me again,' he said, and walked out.

I didn't see him again until three days later: three days in which I sat around in the apartment, crying and rubbing the cocaine dust I found on the washbasin and in the bathroom cupboard into my gums. He came home and took me in his arms. And I realised that, if I stayed in this unhealthy world, in the isolation of our apartment, it would always be this way.

17

We really shouldn't have let things get to this point. Perhaps we could go out together this evening, since Theo is with my parents. Karl's having a party. If you'd like to, let me know and I'll pick you up around eight. Let's start again. — Your husband.

He had always signed his letters to me like this. *Your husband.* As if these words defined him. Not his career; not being a father. The note was stuck on the fridge, pinned under one of Theo's dinosaur magnets. It almost cried out for forgiveness, a new beginning, an evening of reconciliation that would put everything to rights and give me a second chance.

But the note also reminded me of the plane ticket waiting for me in my inbox, which would be so easy, so quick to print out. The note reminded me that it was all a lie, that I should never have brought a child into this world with a man who always did everything right.

The note reminded me that I was infinitely alone.

I ran a bath and got in. The water was scalding hot and turned my skin red. I looked down at my body, my arms, my legs, my belly, where an embryo had once grown into a child and where a few stretch marks were still visible. I stared at my breasts, lying heavy in the water. At my feet, which were so like my father's, and which had always seemed so embarrassing, so obscene to me when I was a child; they were the reason I had refused to wear sandals. I observed my red, wrinkled knees.

I no longer knew what I was supposed to do with this body. To whom it belonged. In which direction to stretch out my limbs, move my legs. I slipped beneath the water.

★

'This is your left ankle. The little toe belongs to me; and look, your right nipple is practically begging me to adopt it. And this hair — yes, this dark hair, this belongs to me, too.'

I giggled as he touched my body, perched on the edge of the bath and looking down on me, sprinkling me with bath salt as if I were a carefully prepared meal about to be served to him.

'And — well, I'll have to leave you this elbow; you need that yourself, so I'll have to do without. But the tip of your nose absolutely belongs to me. No one else is allowed to touch it, not even you, do you hear? If your nose runs, or itches, or if it gets cold, you have to call me: my hand is at your service.'

He slid into the bathtub with me; it was too small for both of us.

'And what do I do with my bottom? It'll be sad that you don't want it,' I giggled, taking a puff of the joint he had lit with his left hand while rubbing shampoo into my hair with his right.

'Are you crazy? It goes without saying that it belongs to me, doesn't it? We don't even need to discuss it.'

And I giggled again and slipped beneath the water.

★

Then he started to take me with him. To his bars and basements. To his strange friends. He dropped acid, and I did, too. Ivo kept writing, going on business trips, while I was getting less and less done. Unlike me, he managed to completely separate his drug-taking from his work. If he had to do some research the following day, if he had to go to Berlin, if he had to interview someone or had a photoshoot, he would be there the next morning on time, looking great, not as if he had spent the whole night drinking and snorting coke and hadn't slept a wink.

One morning, Tulia paid me a visit. She came in without speaking, sat down at the kitchen table, and started unpacking her bag. Fruit and vegetables, and her jams; fish from the local shop in Niendorf, cheese and milk from her best friend's farm, and, of course, her plum liqueur.

She didn't say anything; she just started to prepare the food. I stared at her, tried to ask her why she had come, then gave up; I knew only too well how stubborn she could be.

'You two are causing me terrible pain.'

'Has Ivo been to see you? Has he complained?'

'No, he hasn't. He hasn't been to see me.'

'What do you want from me, Tulia? I don't need help; I feel good.'

'Good? Sure.'

I pounced on the food. The fish in cream sauce, the little pieces of cheese, sliced so neatly along with the tomatoes, and I realised that I was starving, that I hadn't eaten properly for days.

Tulia watched with satisfaction, and I lowered my gaze to the fish, as if it were the key to my salvation. She put her arm around my shoulders, and I concentrated even harder. Silently I looked at the fish, and silently the fish looked back, and it became clear to me that I was in a pitiful state.

Tulia sat on the sofa and watched me wolf down the food.

'Tulia, why … why did you never have children?' I asked her.

'I have all of you. That's more than enough worry, believe me.'

'But before there was us —'

'There've been many children I've had to adopt in my time. My sister, my husbands, my friends. Even my mother, when she got sick.'

'But children bring joy as well …'

'I've had plenty of joy in my life, sweetheart, believe me. Stella, you have to stop this nonsense, both of you. It won't go well for much longer. You're being naïve, thinking you can go back and put right something that cannot be put right. You've convinced yourselves that you love each other because you're desperate for your past to have a happy end. It's an illusion. You have to start living in the present; there's no point to all this looking back. Let it be. You're robbing each other of the chance, the possibility, of finding your own happiness. You have to go your own separate ways. This isn't love, it's some strange punishment you've imposed on yourselves. Don't be childish, Stella!'

Ivo came home. He was holding a small leather bag, and stopped in his tracks when he saw us.

'Tulia. I should have known, I could smell it as I came in. I'm ravenous.'

He inspected the fridge and the saucepans closely, and had soon warmed up his meal and served himself a plate. He sat down and began to eat without comment, throwing us the occasional curious glance.

Suddenly the question that, in all those years, I had never dared ask myself loomed up with physical intensity, filled the room, monopolised us, and began to shake our world. Because we both already knew the answer, and hated it.

★

As Ivo could not be dissuaded from the notion that I had asked Tulia to read him the riot act, he stopped talking to me. He disappeared again for a few days, and I found a letter among his things. I recognised the handwriting of my friend Sarah, whom I hadn't seen for months.

Yesterday was wonderful ... And I'd love a repeat of last night. I'll come to the Bombay on Wednesday — hope you'll be there. — Sarah.

I knew he'd cheated on me. I knew he would never give me what I wanted, not because he couldn't, but because he wouldn't allow himself to be happy for so much as a single day of his life.

I got dressed, put on make-up — something I hadn't done in ages — and went to the club Sarah had mentioned, which was one I'd never heard of.

I bumped into one of Ivo's friends and asked him to give me some coke. I snorted three lines one after the other and went onto the dance floor. There I met Michi the drummer, a twenty-six-year-old alcoholic I knew from Ivo's and my nocturnal odysseys. I draped myself around his neck and started dancing with him. I couldn't stop laughing; I didn't know why. Michi, disconcerted by my blatant advances, gave me a friendly hug and patted my cheeks. Eventually, having mustered enough Dutch courage, I dragged him into the men's toilets where I sat on the toilet lid, propped up my left leg and pulled down my knickers. It had taken three vodkas and three beers to get me there, Michi considerably less.

Afterwards, I stumbled outside. I sat down on the pavement and threw up. I stayed where I was. Everything was spinning and my limbs felt numb. My mouth was parched and my eyes were glazed. I was freezing. I don't know how long I was sitting there before he came. He'd been in the club. I hadn't noticed him, or he had arrived while Michi and I were in the loo. He sat down beside me, smoking and staring into space. Abruptly he got to his feet, took my hand, and dragged me to his motorbike. He put my arms around his waist and started the engine. We drove off, faster and faster. I started to feel dizzy; the lights blurred into a kaleidoscope. He shouted something, but the words were blown away and I couldn't understand.

On a bend leading to the main road that should have taken us home, we skidded. I landed in some bushes at the side of the road, which basically saved my life. Ivo bruised his kidneys. He had complex fractures, severe concussion, and internal bleeding. I had only minor lacerations and a broken arm.

★

'I'll come with you,' I told Mark on the phone, and hung up. I knew that this was my last chance. I got dressed and put on make-up, playing Marvin Gaye and dancing along as I laid out half my wardrobe on the bed.

Mark picked me up on the dot. He looked very relaxed and handsome in his black jacket, with a new haircut. I touched his wrist lightly as I got into the car. He nodded and smiled. I was really happy to see him, and, with him, to see our world restored. He took me to a club down by the port. It was crawling with TV presenters, journalists, producers, directors, actors. I hardly knew any of them, but they all seemed to know Mark, and vice versa. There was sushi, expensive finger food, and fancy drinks. Karl, Mark's friend and colleague of many years, was the originator of a highly successful political — and, above all, politically correct — TV programme.

I sipped a cocktail and listened to the swing band playing on the little stage. Speeches were given, entertaining and witty; various silly gifts were presented.

I danced with Mark, and whispered in his ear how much I regretted it all. That I would explain everything to him.

Later that evening I went out onto the terrace and looked down at the port. It was beautiful. It was soothing. The sight of water always gives me a sense of security. Two women I didn't know cornered me and engaged me in meaningless conversation. But I resolved to endure this bravely as well, to be friendly, appear nice, be interested — for us, for Mark and me. For our future together.

★

When I got out of hospital and went back to our apartment, the first thing I did was clear out the few drugs that were still lying around. I threw out old clothes, books. I threw out my old notebooks. I got myself a new phone number so none of my old friends could reach me. I tried to throw away the old part of me.

I forced myself to start writing again. I met up with people. I visited Leni every weekend and played with her children. I went with Papa to the Italian restaurants of which he was so fond.

When he was discharged, Ivo went back to live with Tulia in Niendorf. He didn't call.

The days when I wrote and managed to get newspapers to accept my first articles, and the days when I was effectively paralysed and just lay in bed staring at the ceiling alternated in quick succession.

He sent me a postcard: *I have to go away for a while or I'll lose myself. I'm scared. I need you so terribly it hurts. I don't want to make you unhappy. Don't be angry with me.*

But I was angry. I was so angry that, two days later, I went to Papa's house and took out all the sleeping tablets he had stashed in his bathroom cabinet. I was so angry that I got undressed, lay down on Papa's side of the bed, drew the curtains, and swallowed the handful of pills with a glass of water.

At some point Papa must have broken down the locked bedroom door and called an ambulance. They pumped my stomach and kept me in hospital under surveillance. Afterwards, I had to sign a form agreeing to see a therapist, which I went on to do for a year without disclosing anything I didn't want to disclose; I simply lied.

Papa called Mama. It was the first time he had spoken to her in all those years. She came to Hamburg.

★

With Mama, I went to the beach; we drove out of the city and sat in the sand. A summer without Newark: the summer without James, the summer without expensive presents and insincere solicitude. We went to shops, to the cinema, to the theatre. I bought myself books and started reading again; I devoured each book like a lunatic — no matter how good or bad it was, I read it in a heartbeat.

It was only several weeks later, when I had convinced Mama I could take care of myself again and had dropped her off at the airport, that I called Tulia and urged her to tell me where he was. At first she refused, but something in my voice must have persuaded her to give me his address in Berlin.

I took the next train. Equipped with coffee and cigarettes, I sat down on some steps in the lovely old rear courtyard outside where he was living, and waited for him. I waited for five hours.

In the twilight he walked straight past without seeing me. I called his name, and he turned. He looked older, sad, withdrawn. He didn't say anything, just motioned to me to follow. We went up to the fourth floor, to his apartment, which was virtually empty and smelled of lavender.

I sat in a kitchen furnished with little more than a serving trolley and a fridge, and looked at him.

'I don't want to see you anymore,' I said.

'So why have you come?'

'Never again, you hear? Don't you dare come anywhere near me ever again.'

'Yes.'

'I hate you.'

'Okay.'

'It is not okay. I hate you.'

'Yes.'

'Stay away from me. Avoid me. If we cross paths at some stupid fucking family get-together, act as if I were a distant relative and don't talk to me and don't even ask me how I am. Don't follow me onto the patio and don't sit next to me at table. If you see me in the street —'

'Okay. Okay.'

'Above all, never touch me again. Never again!'

'Are you quite sure about that?'

He moved towards me. I leaped up and stepped away.

'Yes, I am quite sure about that. I've never been so sure about anything.'

'All right, then.'

He stepped back and leaned against the wall.

'I'm not your plaything. I never was. I'm taking my life back. You have nothing more to do with it.'

I picked up my handbag and walked past him, my shoulder brushing lightly against his. He didn't move. I had already opened the door and stepped out onto the landing when he said, tonelessly, 'I love you.'

I ran down the stairs.

That was the last time I saw Ivo, until the day I was woken by Tulia's call.

Mark tickled me, and we kissed in the taxi like a couple of teenagers. He laughed as if the past few weeks had never happened.

We got back to our apartment, he opened a bottle of wine, and we went on drinking and dancing. Nuzzled against each other, we conjured up our joy, we danced a ritual dance to invoke our happiness.

At daybreak, after Mark had fallen asleep with an arm around my waist, I sat up abruptly and cried: 'I have to!'

Mark woke and gazed up at me, bleary-eyed.

'I have to go.'

'What are you talking about, Stella?'

'I just have to, Mark. I can't help it. If I don't go, I'll destroy everything, anyway. Just for a short while. But I have to.'

'You sleep with me, then tell me you're going to go to him after all?'

'I did try.'

'Oh, wow. This really is the icing on the cake! You've surpassed yourself. You're leaving me right after sleeping with me?'

'I have to.'

I kept repeating those words, staring into the gloom, while Mark got up and hastily put on his clothes.

'I've never had a choice,' I said again, but he had already left the room. And I thought of my son, collecting carrots and imploring God to make his mother the mother he wanted her to be.

PART II
HERE

18

My skin was burning, and my eyes were watering, and my lips were cracked, and even the beds of my fingernails seemed to hurt as the plane prepared to land. And I then set foot on the earth, this earth I knew nothing about, except that it was far away and wild. The furthest easterly point of my life to date had been Sofia, Bulgaria, where I had gone with my father for a weekend. That had been more than ten years earlier. For the past few hours I had banned myself from thinking. I had written a long letter and put all the thoughts I was capable of thinking into that: past ones, current ones, and, yes, perhaps even future ones, as if I could anticipate them all.

Now, I surrendered to the loud, wildly gesticulating crowd propelling me forwards. I showed my passport, I nodded, I shook my head, I did what others were doing, and I allowed myself to be charmed by the innumerable taxi drivers and porters who surrounded me at the exit. And then his hand pulled me away. It was hot and dry, and I had to take off my denim jacket. I followed him. We got into a mud-spattered Land Rover without exchanging a word. He offered me a cigarette. I took it. I pressed my parched face to the glass of the window.

'Thank you,' he said.

I looked at him; I knew I mustn't admit any doubt, but already I was doubting my decision.

'Thank you for coming.'

'I won't be able to stay long. I have to get back before he files for divorce.'

'He won't file for divorce. He'll hold on to you.'

'Leave it; I'm tired. I can't talk about Mark right now. You don't know him at all.'

'I know you.'

He stepped on the accelerator and rolled down the window. As the day grew brighter, the sky took on a purplish tinge. I would have punched myself if only I'd had the strength.

Instead, I asked, 'So, what now?'

'There's work we have to do here.'

The motorway stretched out in front of us. I closed my eyes and thought of Theo. I'd told him I would be back soon; hopefully I hadn't lied.

'By the way, did you know I had an inheritance?'

'What?'

'My father had money, apparently. Well, before … And I was given it when I came of age. By a lawyer in Switzerland. I never touched it. I just felt I shouldn't, because I didn't want anything to do with it. That it wouldn't be good for me. And suddenly, when I came back to Hamburg, I knew: now — now it's time. And now I plan on spending the money, and I plan on spending it with you. That does at least make sense, don't you agree?'

I stared at him, speechless, and bit my lip.

The smell of acacias and dust blew in through the open window, and the sky was heavy. Cypresses stretched along the side of the road. The city was old and hilly; concrete socialist buildings reared up between the old houses, confusing the overall picture.

It wasn't completely silent, not the sterile silence I was familiar with from Hamburg mornings, when I would wake before Theo to prepare his breakfast and get him ready for school.

We didn't speak.

At the top of a hill he turned into an old courtyard full of swanky cars. Laundry fluttered in the background, hung out to dry between two little apple trees; in the centre, a hose attached to a stone basin watered a rug laid out nearby, apparently for washing. How wasteful, I thought.

We climbed a narrow, spiral staircase; some of the wooden steps were rotten or already broken, and I had to be careful not to put my foot through them. At the top we walked down a long corridor with wooden floorboards that led to an old, unrenovated apartment with high ceilings and an unsealed parquet floor. It had wide windows and a little veranda, from which we could gaze down on the waking city. I felt curiously unsettled by the view — the countless church spires, the densely packed wooden buildings with colourful, ornate balconies at the front, the endless vines that twined about those balconies. I wanted to ask something, but my voice failed me; I was too tired, too overwhelmed.

Ivo led me to a large, but sparsely furnished room. An ancient bed that probably weighed a hundred tonnes stood like a throne in the middle. I stretched out on it and, after a while, fell asleep. Ivo left me there without covering me up.

★

My heart was fluttering the next morning as I walked to the bathroom, which was decorated with scratched orange tiles and a gilded mirror propped against the wall. Everything about this place seemed so impractical, so profligate, from the furnishings to the dripping taps and the toilet flush.

Ivo had put out a towel and a toothbrush for me. An old gas boiler was fixed to the wall, and I had to wait a quarter of an hour before the water was even vaguely warm. Then I climbed into the yellowed bathtub. Immediately the water seemed to make all my sluggishness magically disappear.

He had made coffee, in a brownish pot on the gas stove, and torn a loaf of soft, salty bread into pieces. He fetched a glass of honey and a big lump of cheese in a milky liquid.

'Breakfast *à la Géorgie*,' he said ceremoniously, with a loud laugh. We sat down at the round table and I tucked into the bread, which was still warm.

'The bread is baked in a clay oven that looks like a hole in the ground. They light a fire to heat the clay, then, when the walls are hot, they stick the dough onto them. It's only men who do it; they lean right into this purgatorial fire, and every time you think: how do they manage not to fall in? And in a couple of minutes the bread is ready. Anyway, I think it's amazing.'

'Yes, it tastes good.'

'It's crazy, the thing with the bread, isn't it? Yeah, a lot of things are crazy here. Okay, drink your coffee. I'll tell you a bit about it all. I know you expect that of me.'

'Correct. Go on.'

'I met Lado in New York several years ago. He lived there in exile for quite a while; I met him at some ridiculous event about political asylum. He was giving a lecture. We gradually became friends. Later he went to Berlin, taught some seminars at the university — as a political scientist, even though he's a musician. And he had — he has — a son, who's fourteen now, whom I came to kind of like as well. The boy was born here during the civil war, shortly before his mother and sister died. He's a great kid.'

'What does this have to do with you or me, Ivo?'

'I can't summarise it in a couple of sentences, Stella. It's complicated.'

'Spare me the clichés, okay. I didn't come here because I wanted a holiday, or to look after strange men and their sons. I'm in the middle of losing my own husband and son.'

'I don't want to tell you what needs to be done. I'm being honest with you, Stella. This all has something to do with us. I can't explain to you in words; you have to experience it, you have to get to know him, and you have to help me finish my piece. I'm not getting paid for this job, I'm doing it all at my own expense.'

'And what does any of it have to do with us? Nothing — absolutely nothing.'

'That's not the case, believe me. But I want you to work it out for yourself — what it has to do with us, and with you.'

I jumped up and went into the bedroom, where I lay on the bed and hid my face in the pillow. I'd made a mistake in coming here. I should have known. Ivo's ramblings made me aggressive; what he was saying made no sense — where was my place, my role, in this story? I dialled Mark's number on my mobile. He didn't answer. I sent him a text:

Please tell Theo I love him and I'll be back soon. You don't have to forgive me. You don't have to do anything anymore. I can't forgive myself. But please don't make Theo hate me. Tell him I'm on a work trip. Please.

Ivo came in and sat on the edge of the bed. I moved away; the thought that he might touch me made me unsure of myself, but I couldn't allow it, I couldn't allow myself to forget my anger and my guilt, not even for a few minutes. These two emotions seemed to be the last things I could cling to that offered me any stability.

'I have to remember. By any means possible. And you're the one who can fill in the gaps, the gaps in my memory. Maybe it's irresponsible of me to drag you away, but believe me, I'm thinking of you as well. You don't get it yet, but if you give me the chance, I'm sure you'll understand.'

I looked at him and nodded. No matter how much he hurt me, I would stay. I could hear in his voice that strange, defenceless tone that didn't belong to the strong, sun-kissed, successful Ivo he spent most of his life playing.

If only I had listened more closely at the time to what he was saying, had tried to decode it. But I was clinging to my pain, which blinded me and, at the same time, protected me.

★

We took the car and drove through Tbilisi. A place that seemed to be lost between something past and something still to come, something that had not yet happened. People talking loudly in an archaic-sounding language, gesticulating wildly; cars speeding crazily down the narrow streets as if on a racetrack; children, all playing ball, who had affixed seatless chairs to the walls of houses to serve as makeshift basketball hoops. Hordes of cats and dogs lounging around. Plants overrunning everything, and fruit on every tree, among the hanging laundry.

He turned up the radio, and I listened to the strange, hard language. It amused me — as if I had been transported to another time. Little by little my irritation subsided, and I felt something like relief, a youthful euphoria.

We parked in the southern part of the Old Town and went on from there on foot. The wide, greenish river stretched between harsh, rugged cliffs with houses and hotels built on top. Loud music and the clatter of cutlery came from the little cafés and bars that lined the cobbled streets.

We went into a restaurant furnished with tiny wooden tables. While Ivo ordered various dishes, none of which I knew, I pounced on the carafe of white wine that the waiter brought unasked. I devoured the unfamiliar food; all of it tasted delicious, which considerably improved my mood. Ivo talked about the country, about the first time he had come here. He sounded excited. I listened to him, and felt like a small child captivated by fairy tales.

★

In the early evening, we got back in the car and drove north. I didn't ask anything else, just peered out of the window. Lights flickered, and the river reflected the passing cars. I was so happy to lose myself in the lights, the greenish water, the strange smells, in Ivo.

'You know …' I began, lighting one of his Lucky Strikes.

'Mm,' he said, abstractedly, turning left, as the driver behind us honked noisily.

'I was just trying to imagine what would have happened if we'd stayed together, back then, you and I. If I'd had Theo with you.'

As if he wasn't listening, his concentrated expression didn't change; he just went on clutching the wheel. I wished I hadn't spoken.

Ivo and I had never discussed children. When we were trying to be together, children were the last thing we could talk about. In any case, I'd assumed Ivo didn't want them.

'What made you say that?' he said, finally, not looking at me.

'No idea. We don't have to discuss it.'

'Well, you've asked, so I assume you want an answer.'

'It was an observation, just speculation really, not a question.'

'As far as I'm concerned, if you really want to know, I didn't find the right woman for it. And with you —'

'Yes, it wouldn't have been possible with me. I know.'

'That wasn't what I was going to say. You need to be brave enough to hear an honest answer if you ask a question like that.'

'I just said, it wasn't a question, I don't —'

'Of course you want an answer! Fucking hell, Stella! Do you think I never asked myself this; do you really think I'm a machine, that I don't give a shit about anything?'

'Forget it — just keep your eyes on the road!'

'I think I would have curled up and died, from all the emotion and all the grief, if we'd ...' he said suddenly. Something inside me clenched; I turned away and hid my face in the darkness.

'I hated you, back then, for making a baby with some random guy just because he offered you fucking security.'

Abruptly, he fell silent, and parked by the side of the road. He was right: I couldn't handle his answer.

We were in a residential district of detached houses. Ivo rang at a black metal gate. I hadn't asked him where we were going. Someone yanked the metal gate open: a tall, thin boy with thick, black hair and delicate features. He was wearing a T-shirt with a Union Jack logo and black jeans. He flung his arms around Ivo and greeted him in almost perfect German, which completely threw me for a moment.

'This is Stella. And this is Buba, Lado's son, who I told you about,' said Ivo. I held out my hand. Stella, he said. Not: Stella, my sister; not: Stella, my stepsister; not: Stella, my girlfriend; not: Stella, my lover; not: Stella, my … The boy shook my hand shyly, and we followed him through a small garden with a tree stump in the middle, which was apparently being used as a card table. A light was on above the open front door; we walked through a tiny hallway into a big kitchen-living room. I liked its austerity, the stone floor and unpainted ceiling. The man with the full beard stood at the stove, cooking; he was gaunt, and looked much taller than in the photos in Ivo's file. He laughed, immediately gave me a hug, and greeted me in harsh, but grammatically correct German.

Soon the table was laid, the wine poured.

The boy, I noticed, was incredibly beautiful. Still imprisoned by his youth: the slight stoop, the nascent moustache, the bashfulness, erratic movements and still-childlike voice, none of which seemed to fit the rest of his body. But all this held the promise that he would grow into a handsome young man. He reminded me of Ivo, in a way — Ivo as a boy. Except that Buba's eyes were very different. They were so dark that the iris disappeared, and his thick eyebrows made his gaze seem forthright, proud. Whereas Ivo's eyes were always veiled in something no one could see or identify, the boy's eyes had already started to look the world proudly and directly in the face, and challenge it.

We sat at the table, and although I wasn't hungry, I ate, as the bearded man kept urging me to do.

'I've already heard so much about you, Stella, and now at last I meet you,' said Lado, raising his glass. Ivo followed suit, and I, too, slightly puzzled by this salutation, reached for mine. We clinked glasses and drank the wine.

★

Soon we were deep in conversation. Lado had lived in Berlin for four years. We talked about the differences between the cultures; he told us about his country, the political situation. Later, Buba fetched a guitar, and father and son struck up a song, which again I found a little unsettling. I wondered whether the two of them lived here alone, and concluded that this was indeed the case. And again I wondered what I was doing here, why Ivo had brought me here.

★

That night, back at the apartment, I lay alone in the enormous bed, staring at the ceiling. The window was open, and a soft, refreshing breeze drifted in from outside. The white curtain danced in the wind. I could hear noises in the distance, as if a television was on, and Ivo's footsteps echoing in the bathroom. I heard cars driving past; the wine had clouded my senses, and I felt free. I looked within me for the boundaries between past and future. I looked for the point of intersection. I looked for myself, or my missing piece. I looked for my words in his. I looked for my face in his.

He tiptoed barefoot along the corridor, towards the little attic room where he worked and would sleep while I was here, and which had a magnificent view of Tbilisi. The lost city, whose existence people only noticed as they drew near, because on the world map it appeared to have been forgotten; but, once here, it felt indispensable, for it seemed to hold the two worlds of Orient and Occident steady, binding them together. It swallowed both, yet was poisoned by neither. It transported oil for others, and allowed its water to gush forth, over all the rugs and all the plants and all the dirt that accumulated here.

I called to him. He came and sat on the edge of my bed.

'Promise you won't touch me?'

'Promise.'

'I want us to succeed.'

'Yes.'

'I don't deserve to be punished by you so badly. I did something terrible back then, but —'

'Ssh.'

'No, it's true. I did something terrible, and neither you nor I have ever got over it. We both did something terrible back then. But we were children, Ivo. We were just children! What could we have done? If you help me, I'll help you, no matter what with, or how, or what for. I'm here.'

19

After what felt like the tenth attempt, I was allowed to speak to Theo. He seemed furious with me, and was irritable and stern, but he remained polite throughout, as his father had raised him to be. I swore to my son that I would be back soon. I told him how much I loved him, told him he meant more to me than anything in the world. He said he was going to get his dog from his grandparents now; they'd reserved it, they were just waiting for it to be born.

'Theo?' I asked him, at the end. 'Can I ask you to do something?'

'What?' he asked, in Mark's voice — never an immediate yes or no, always carefully weighing things up. He wasn't doing it deliberately, I realised that, but I couldn't help hearing his father — Mark's voice, speaking through him.

'Will you look after the carrots again?'

'What carrots?'

'You know, the carrots from Granny's calendar.'

'Okay.'

'I'd really love it if you would. If you could save a couple until I get back.'

'Okay.'

'I love you, sweetheart.'

'Love you too. Come home soon, byyyyyye.'

Then: a vast emptiness. The dial tone on the line, which made Theo's *byyyyyye* seem even longer, more endless. But I kept listening nonetheless; I endured it.

The days were filled with stress, joy, excitement, *joie de vivre*, and melancholy. The whole country seemed to consist of an endless squandering of love, of money that wasn't there, of warmth, of everything that was lacking. As soon as it was there, it was given away, wasted, exploited. Nothing here seemed to last.

I familiarised myself with the roads; I took the car, always fearing I would have an accident, because nobody abided by any existing or non-existent traffic regulations. I met up with Lado while Ivo worked through his notes and videos, typed things up, and gathered material. I didn't know what I was looking for. And I became friends with Buba, who would sometimes touch my hair or smell it, then shyly glance away. Who ate an incredible amount, and played a lot of music; who was stubborn and clever when he wanted something. I went for walks with him and bought us ice creams. He showed me the secret places of the city he loved. The city behind the city.

We went to the cemetery high above Tbilisi that belonged to the heroes and great people of the nation, beside a church that looked out over the whole of the city. It was quiet there, quieter than anywhere else. We sat in the shadow of some bushes and drank cola. He wanted a puff of my cigarette, and I allowed it. He was my translator and city guide.

He had been born in 1993. In a seaside town, in Abkhazia, on the Black Sea coast. His mother, whom he couldn't remember, had been a Georgian actress at the theatre there. Lado had met her at the theatre while writing music for a play.

'They saw each other, fell in love straight away, and got married three months later. And then my sister was born. Mama was really good. I've got a video at home of a play with her in the lead; I swear it'll make you cry. She plays a woman who finds out that her husband has this lover, and then — well, you have to see what she does, I don't want to give it away. Anyway, and then after that everything got really heavy. Chaos. My father was already an activist — before this, I mean; he was pro-freedom and stuff. They were always secretly organising demos and printing leaflets in the basement. He went to prison. I wasn't born at that point. And he helped found this stupid fucking party. Today he says it was stupid, wrong, and so on. The others didn't care about the country; they wanted money and power.

It all went to pieces, anyway. They all fell out with each other. They had the same aims in the beginning, but, I mean, that's just how it is, everyone wants to do their own thing. I know exactly what that's like. And then the war came along. Russians and Abkhaz and Georgians, everyone against everyone else. That's when I was born. Papa says war is a means of self-preservation, that people need one every few years, and stuff. He says. Back then, if I'd been the age I am now, I'd have fought, too. Of course I'd have gone and shot those assholes. They threw out all the Georgians, but Papa says the Georgians didn't have a plan, they just set out and nobody knew what they were doing.'

Buba paused, gazing thoughtfully down at the city, which was cloaked in a hot cloud of dust. Birds were cheeping. The story he was telling reminded me of something I couldn't quite put my finger on, and I had the feeling that he could tell me more than his father or Ivo. I put my arm through his, as if he were older and I the one in need of protection. He liked to feel grown-up. He smiled, and asked me for a cigarette.

'The deal is that you don't inhale, okay?'

'Come on — I'm telling you about the war and I'm not allowed to smoke? I can handle it, you know.'

'What's the war got to do with smoking?'

'It's obvious!'

We fell back onto the grass, and he started telling jokes. I don't remember now why he did that or what they were about; they were crude and vulgar, and he found them very funny, and I laughed with him. I liked the way he laughed. Loud, uninhibited. All his big white teeth appeared and made his dark face shine. I reached out and patted his head; he made an irritated face, then laughed again.

★

'I found a woman at the cultural foundation who says she can arrange for me to access the national archive. There are war reports in there, and all the articles I need. She said that with a bit of luck I might even get to see video material. My press pass counts for more here than in Germany.'

'But I've got enough material already. What do you want to research on top of that?' Ivo stared at me in surprise and put down his pen.

'I have to do something as well. I thought you wanted me to find something out. Since you won't give anything away.'

'What exactly do you want to know?'

'There's some other reason for this trip, isn't there? And as you don't want to tell me what it's really about, I'll just have to rely on my feminine intuition.'

He stood up, to avoid my eyes, and went into the kitchen to make coffee. I followed him.

'So what's my part in this story?'

'Firstly, it's important to me that you're here.'

Tired from the afternoon heat, I had been painting my nails red to alleviate my boredom. He took my forefinger and put it in his mouth, the damp nail with its chemical smell. I pulled it back; the varnish wasn't dry.

I had turned Ivo into a substitute for my life, had put him in a position where he could do whatever he liked with me. In all those years, I had never wanted to admit it to myself, but here, in a far-off country, in these stories I couldn't decode, I would come to understand it with painful clarity.

★

The diffident brunette accompanied me to a desk. It was so incredibly cold in the gloomy national archive building that my toes curled, despite the heat outside. They had found an unprepossessing, very uncommunicative student of German literature to assist me. On the table lay three bulging folders and five video cassettes.

*

When I left the monstrous socialist structure seven hours later, I knew that Lado's wife had died in the bombing raids in Sokhumi. I also knew that Lado's daughter had died there, but not whether she was a victim of the executions, or the bombings, or what the circumstances of her death had been.

I knew that massive quantities of heroin were being trafficked through Abkhazia in 1992, and that the arms trade among the various separatist groups was valued at almost nineteen million dollars. I knew that Abkhaz and Georgians fired Russian-made bombs at each other. I knew that the UN only addressed the conflict at the very end of the war, and that the media kept quiet about it. I knew that the Georgian president at the time was accused of rabble-rousing and genocide against the country's minorities. That the Georgian troops consisted mainly of civilians who had been persuaded to fight, by way of money, weapons, drugs, or simply the prospect of fame and glory. I knew that, alongside Russian militias, Chechen guerrilla fighters under a man named Basayev were also involved in the massacre of Georgians in 1993, with many thousands dead and a quarter of a million Georgian refugees. It wasn't until 1994, after three attempts, that a ceasefire in accordance with UN guidelines could be agreed; one of the stated reasons for this was lack of coordination among the Georgian troops. I knew that the fifty thousand refugees who subsequently returned to their homeland were driven out again in 1998. But ultimately, after seven hours, I still didn't know anything. I would have preferred not to have seen the videos; I knew now why the student had politely excused herself and left the room when I switched on the video player. She knew what was on the tapes.

I wandered the streets, hailed a taxi. I didn't give a destination, just let myself be driven around the city as night fell. Eventually, I asked the driver to drop me in the Old Town, by the river. I went to the restaurant where Ivo and I ate lunch almost every day.

What was it that had happened to Lado back then, when he was a brigadier stationed in Gali? Why hadn't he been able to get his wife and daughter to safety, and how was it possible that Buba was still alive? Buba, who had been only a few months old at the time. Why was he alive, and why was his father alive, but his mother and sister were dead? I laid my head on the table, then called Lado's number from my mobile. I asked him to come. He seemed puzzled, but eventually agreed.

Half an hour later he was sitting at the table, looking at me uncertainly.

'Is everything all right?' he asked, in his heavy German.

'Yes and no. I was at the archives today, reading up on Abkhazia. Please tell me what this is about. I need to know. What do you both want? What are the two of you planning? What are *you* planning?'

'I'm going to Abkhazia in July, with Ivo. With his passport, he can get me a permit. I have to meet someone there. Someone who was there in those last days, at the massacre.'

'How did it come about that your wife —'

'She promised me she would leave town. I'd sent a car with two of my people. But she wasn't there. She'd just disappeared.'

'And Buba?'

'Buba was at his grandmother's that night. His grandmother is ethnic Abkhaz. My wife had an Abkhaz mother and a Georgian father. But she was *my* wife — everyone knew it. She would have had a chance otherwise. She refused to leave town before then, because her friends, her colleagues, her mother all lived there, and no one thought it would come to that. To that slaughter — mass slaughter, human slaughter.'

I wanted to ask about his little girl, but didn't dare. Instead, I asked, 'How did you end up going into politics?'

'It was time. Something had to be done. The pressure from Russia was increasing. We knew in 1989 that Georgia would demand to leave the Soviet Union. Georgia and the Baltic states were the hotspots back then; they couldn't stop the Baltics — Europe was too close — but here in Georgia we were cut off from everyone. That the Russians would start to put pressure on the minorities — that was something we hadn't reckoned with. When we took to the streets in 1989, no one thought it would lead to civil war. But they couldn't stop things falling apart. Back then there were a few smart people, a sort of intelligentsia, who wanted to achieve freedom without bloodshed, and I aligned myself with them. There were a lot of artists among them, many highly educated. The key people were soon got rid of, and those who were left quickly lost control of what they were doing. I just kept hoping for far too long, that was my problem. For a long time I thought: people will come to their senses, we have to stick together. I kept on hoping until I found myself in the middle of a war. I knew that children were going to die, children the same age Buba is now, so I couldn't stay at home. It was already too late by then. Listen, I studied in Russia, but I would never have believed the KGB could count for more than Tchaikovsky. But that was what my generation was like. A bit lefty, as much as circumstances allowed, and a bit rebellious, but only a bit. Wearing Levi's, listening to the Beatles. That was our revolution. There were lots of really good people around back then. But the hope — I was blinded by hope, and ...'

He broke off and looked at me. Then he placed his hairy hand on mine and said, almost inaudibly, practically in a whisper, 'Sometimes it's as if you're looking in a mirror and the mirror is shattered. Ivo is a blessing in my life. He's given me back so much that I thought was lost.'

I looked at him and felt pity; and I wondered why Ivo had sought out his story in particular to draw some kind of parallel with his own. What did all these war stories have to do with him? And wasn't it exploitative, unprofessional, and highly egotistical to seek out other people's stories for your own ends?

'Why are you going to Abkhazia? It's still dangerous for Georgians, isn't it?' I asked later, as we were leaving the restaurant.

'Ivo isn't Georgian.'

'But you don't exactly look European.'

'No, but I'll be travelling with Ivo.'

'Who are you planning to meet there?'

'Someone who knows why my wife didn't get in the car.'

★

When I woke up the next morning, Ivo had already gone out, leaving me a note to say that he wanted to take some pictures of Lado and was going to a local studio. He wrote that I should come to Lado's that evening; some friends had been invited over for a meal. I made myself coffee in the blackened pot and snuck into Ivo's room. Folders and photos were spread out on the table, countless newspaper cuttings from the 1990s, and pictures of Abkhazia and burnt-out Tbilisi shortly after the pro-independence demonstrations of 1989. I read copies of political articles from the German and American press that Ivo had neatly sorted in a file. I leafed through an English book about Georgian history from ancient times to the present day. Nothing that explained the story behind the story.

I lit a cigarette, and I went on searching. The dusty wind blew in through the open window and swirled up the ash in the ashtray. I turned on the ghetto blaster, which had been mended with Sellotape. There was a cassette inside. Anita Baker. I froze. I turned up the music. Never in his life would Ivo have listened to Anita Baker. I knew his records, his taste in music, his carefully compiled tapes from the olden days that he guarded and treasured. Music like this he would have dismissed as schmaltz. I fast-forwarded: it was the entire *Best Of*. I couldn't believe my ears.

Then I opened Ivo's laptop. I'd never done this before. It had never interested me; it was a work tool, nothing more.

Password ... I considered, entering all the terms I could think of: family names, places Ivo had lived. Nothing. I banged my fist on the table.

Then I started typing intuitively, randomly, lost in thought, and suddenly it made a little sound, and I was in. I sat up and tried to recall what I had entered. It was an M, and it was … It was EMMA. Emma. I gave a start, and realised I was so tense that I was sweating.

In the folder with the name 'Tbilisi' I found trivial information about the city, the country, Lado — Lado over and over again, but just pages and articles I'd already seen, nothing new.

Eventually I found a folder labelled 'S', and clicked on it.

Photos — countless photos from our childhood. All neatly scanned and saved. All carefully numbered. All with place and date. Pictures of Niendorf: Leni and me in the treehouse. Papa and me eating goulash in Tulia's kitchen. Easter 1987, in the garden, Tulia's fruitcake on the garden table. Newark, 1982: Leni, Ivo, and me on James's lap, Mama in the background, packing a picnic. 1983: Ivo and me at the beach, Ivo in red swimming shorts, me in a white cotton vest with sand in my hair, looking crossly at the camera. Leni and me making a doll's house in the barn, 1981. 1984: Ivo and me on a water slide at the indoor swimming pool in Niendorf. I remembered that day so clearly: I'd hurt my foot when another child slammed into me, and Ivo had comforted me all evening. Papa's birthday, 1987, at the house in Hamburg, with a woman by his side whom I only vaguely remembered. And then a photo, unlabelled, no date or location, in black and white. A picture I didn't know. Had never seen before. Even though I was in the picture. I didn't remember that day. I stared at the screen.

It was the garden of the house near the port, in winter. The black dog was visible in the background. The trees were bare. I was standing in the middle of the photo, with a pageboy haircut, the red scarf my mother had knitted me, and denim dungarees. I had a raincoat on, and my fingers were in my mouth. Right behind me, in profile, stood Ivo; he was looking not at the camera but at me. He was wearing rubber boots, which I still remembered clearly, and a baseball cap his father had brought him from Switzerland. The click, the camera, must have taken us by surprise. I am staring uncertainly into the lens, but Ivo is staring at me, as if he wants to warn me of something, as if he wants to protect me from the click. The look in his eyes is agitated, concerned, a look he had preserved all those years; a look that was full of fear, but also kept that fear hidden, rather than communicating it to the outside world. For a moment I closed my eyes.

Who had taken the photo? Papa, Emma? Why had I never seen it? Had I even realised we were being photographed? If Ivo had the baseball cap, and I had my raincoat on, it wasn't long before the end; if we were standing so close together in the garden, Ivo and I were already inseparable; if it was winter, then ... Then Emma would soon be dead. I printed out the photo on a page of A4 and packed it into my handbag, concealed in a notebook.

Why was he archiving us — why was he archiving me?

Ivo had a razor-sharp memory that never forgot a thing, never omitted a single nuance or a single detail, that in any given moment retained even what remained unspoken. So why was he painstakingly documenting his life like this? He had also saved a couple of articles I'd long since forgotten existed. There was even a wedding photo of Mark and me: me in a plain white cocktail dress and Mark in a black tuxedo, in front of the town hall. He must have picked up the photo at Papa's, or possibly Tulia's.

I sat in front of the laptop in bewilderment. I paced back and forth, sat down again, kept looking at the photos, closed the laptop, opened it again. It was about us. It was about me.

If Tulia were to be believed, the world was nothing more than a tissue of stories, individual stories of people, countries, civilisations and gods whose language we had not yet decoded. To a child, it was a fascinating idea: the world as a brightly coloured tangle of wool, different threads all woven together.

Sitting there in front of the 'S' folder, I thought again for the first time about Tulia's idea of how the world was put together. The way I saw my life in front of me in these folders: archived and captured by these photos, these dates and places, these people in the pictures standing near me or behind me or in front of me. What I saw in these photos was completely unfamiliar to me. It was as if I had discovered another room in a house I'd been living in for years.

Finally I switched off the laptop and went outside to sit on the tiny veranda. Children were playing in the courtyard, and music was coming from the second floor, an '80s hit. Someone got out of an SUV and shouted a strange-sounding name. In one of the neighbouring apartments someone was making chicken soup, and the simple, familiar childhood aroma made me smile.

★

I showered, hoping the water would cool my head a little, then walked aimlessly through the streets for hours, still thinking about the photo I had hidden in my bag. When I got tired, I hailed a taxi and went to Lado's house. You could hear the noise all the way from the street. I had to ring several times before Buba threw open the door. He flung his arms around my neck and wiggled his bum.

'Party!' he yelled in my ear, over the loud music, and beamed at me.

'What are we celebrating?' I shouted back, as we entered the house.

'Everything. No idea. The summer, or something?'

The living room was full of people. Some were playing guitar. Wine had been put out on the low table in big earthenware jugs. People were sitting on the floor, standing in corners. A young man in a Che Guevara T-shirt was excitedly telling a story I didn't understand. In the kitchen, a tall woman was preparing something on the stove. Ivo and Lado were nowhere to be seen. Buba took me by the hand and introduced me to every single person there. Most were artists, Lado's colleagues, but neighbours and acquaintances had also been invited. They seemed to be close friends of Lado's family, or else were there just because they wanted to party. Buba gave me a quick résumé, whispering the necessary information in my ear.

'The man over there with the horsey teeth is a really old friend of my father's. He has a little studio; lots of musicians go there. The woman with the big breasts is the girlfriend of that guy there; he's a sculptor, our neighbour; he's divorced and has five children. And the woman at the stove is Salome. She speaks German as well,' he said, leading me to her.

The tall woman turned and smiled at me apologetically; her hands were covered in flour. 'Nice to meet you at last,' she said. She wiped her right hand on a kitchen towel and held it out to me. 'I've heard a lot about you. We all know Ivo. And we've been waiting for you.'

I had been in that house several times by then, but I had never seen her, nor had I known that Lado had a girlfriend. Because she was definitely not just a friend; I could tell from Buba's tone. She said she just had to finish preparing the food and she'd be with me. Buba pulled me away, and we went outside to smoke.

'Is she Lado's girlfriend?' I asked, as he took a puff of my cigarette.

'She's his lover,' he said, rather irritably.

'Don't you like her?'

'She's okay.'

'She seems nice.'

'She's hot. That's what they all say.'

'Hot?'

'Well, you know.'

'Has she been with him a long time?'

'A really long time. She was with us in Berlin, and when we came back here, she came as well. But Salome was friends with my mother. So my father's known her a really long time, is what I mean.'

'I see. Then she must love you both — you and your father — very much.'

'No idea. Not interested. She'd be better off looking after her own child.'

'She has a child?'

'Yeah, a son. Older than me. But he lives with his father.'

I couldn't help thinking that anyone asking my son about his mother would get a similar reply. I felt a stab of fear and lit another cigarette in panic.

'Everything okay?'

'I was thinking about my son. He's in Germany.'

'Do you have a photo of him?'

I fished out a little set of passport photos I always carried in my wallet. Theo and me times four.

'Do you miss him?'

'Yes. But, you know, you shouldn't judge your father's girlfriend. Sometimes things are complicated, and you can't be where you want to be. I'm sure she loves her son just as much as I do Theo, or as much as Lado loves you.'

'How do you know she loves her son as much? You can never know a thing like that,' he said, his voice harsh. He started gouging the earth with the toe of his trainer.

Just then Salome came walking towards us. She had delicate limbs and stunningly long legs, emphasised by her simple skirt. Her dark-brown hair was cut in a bob, and she wore hardly any make-up, just a little mascara. She wasn't exactly classically beautiful; she had a Roman nose, and her eyes were slightly too far apart, but there was something very attractive about her, something unmistakably physical, almost provocative, and I thought of the word Buba had used to describe her: *hot.*

'Here you are!' she cried, joining us. The doorbell rang again and Buba darted off.

'You give him cigarettes?' she asked. I gave an embarrassed smile. 'Ah well — they always want to experiment with stuff at that age,' she went on, indulgently. 'He likes you. He's usually rather more standoffish with strangers. If you don't mind me saying. May I have a cigarette as well?'

She wasn't particularly at ease in the language, searching for words, but her deep voice made you listen, spellbound, no matter what she was saying.

'Sure. Here you go.'

'So, do you like it here?'

'There are a lot of things I find fascinating, yes, but I haven't really been here long enough to form an opinion.'

'I was in Hamburg once. It was too cold for me there.'

I smiled at her, and for a while we said nothing, listening to hear who had just come through the door. It wasn't Ivo.

We finished smoking our cigarettes, still in silence. I wondered what this woman did, apart from being so mysterious and hot, and what it was like to be the lover of a man whose wife had been found dead in their burnt-out house. I was curious, and — still thinking about the photos from the 'S' folder, Anita Baker, the ghosts in my head — I said, 'I'd like to know something.'

'Yes?' she replied.

'I wonder whether you know what they're planning.'

'I don't. I've stopped asking Lado about his life.'

Her voice grew quieter, and sadness shimmered through her proud demeanour. I would have liked to touch her; instead, I looked away and didn't say anything else.

Lado and Ivo showed up around midnight. They charged in, both a bit drunk and making a lot of noise, and started greeting the people sitting around the campfire, flinging their arms around their necks or giving them bear hugs. Ivo's exaggerated cheerfulness annoyed me.

A deep, smoky female voice began to sing. It was a sad song that reminded me of Portuguese *fado*, and the voice was the most beautiful thing I'd heard in ages. From a distance I recognised Salome, accompanying herself on the guitar.

I wanted to think of Theo, but I was thinking of Ivo. I wanted to think about my life, but I was thinking of his. And I wondered whether I would ever break out of my hell, learn to liberate myself and to run, towards the real life I had skidded past, scratching and wounding myself. The life I had never embraced as my own. Whether I could ever be free, free of this man, who at this moment, in my urge to run to him and demand answers to all my questions, I felt I hated.

It was Buba who found me. He sat down beside me and snuggled against my shoulder. He was carrying a plate of shashlik, he smelled of alcohol, and his cheeks were glowing.

'What are you doing here? Are you sad about your son?' he asked, and despite his height and his obvious desire to come across as grown-up, at that moment he seemed so young, so small, so vulnerable. And I envied him his youth, his ignorance, his freedom, and the potential to be open to everything, everything, absolutely everything in the world. He started feeding me little pieces of meat; he seemed to find this so amusing that he couldn't stop laughing. I ate and ate, just to make him laugh.

Salome sang, and Lado took over the guitar playing, which he did so expertly that I abandoned myself to the music and forgot everything else. It was such a pleasure to be able to let myself go, that night and the many other nights I spent in that house.

The last guests sat in a circle around the extinguished campfire, talking in the language that could almost make me angry by then, I wanted so much to understand it. Buba had fallen asleep on the sofa in the living room. I saw him lying there, open-mouthed, and covered him with a blanket. He was sleeping so blissfully, so happily, utterly childlike in his dreams. And I stood there looking at him, thinking of my son, and felt a kind of peace.

★

I went to the bathroom. I needed to pour cold water on my face; I felt so tired, so heavy, that it was as if I were seizing up, as if someone were filling my insides with lead. In the corridor, at the half-open door to Lado's bedroom, I heard a strange noise and stood still. I had to pass the door to get to the bathroom, and as I did, I glanced inside. I saw two shadows entwined on a narrow metal bed. Salome, gripping Lado's hair, and Lado, clinging to her waist. They were making love, but their love brought them no relief; in their togetherness they were alone, entangled, desperate, trying to forget. Salome was moaning, but not with lust, with a dull, brutal, lonely pain, and Lado was hiding his face in her neck as if to stop himself bellowing at the world.

I thought of the first time I had understood bodies entwined — bodies desperately seeking one another yet still alone, separate, distant, unable to permeate each other — as love. Of how I had identified the silhouettes through the gap in the curtains as lovers, and how, ever since, I had equated the pain in my spine with love. I thought of the first time I had slept with Ivo, and how I had given the name of love to the impossibility of making him mine. I thought of my love for Ivo that hurt and burned, that was desperate, harried, sweating, bleeding in its pursuit of closeness, that increasingly was turning into pain. Into the primal state of love. The impossibility of closeness, which I'd first seen as a child sitting on the bough of a tree, and had preserved as such in my memory. As had Ivo. It had bound us together for ever, this idea of love that was merely guilt, betrayal, pain, and loneliness, exchanged by my father and his mother. And we accepted it; we accepted it as love, we made it our own. We were young; we couldn't know that this could not be love, so contorted with pain, so chaotic, destroyed by the battle for closeness. We saw the image, and we lost ourselves in it.

★

I thought of the pain in my back, the pain I felt the lack of when I slept with other men. The pain that, to me, signified the closeness, the unavoidable, the uncontrollable, the frenzied in my life, that no one else apart from Ivo had been able to give me, not even the father of my son.

★

How had my father been able to go on living, after all that had happened? How was he ever able to touch a woman again, after his craving for love and the terrible subjugation of his own emptiness had cost another person their life? How could such a thing be called love?

I went on watching the shadowy bodies through the gap in the door as they tasted and smelled each other, pulled each other close and pushed each other away, each needing the other in order to transcend themselves, and it occurred to me that my love for Ivo was precisely this: the craving to transcend myself. That I should ask myself exactly the same question: how could it be love if it hurt and excluded others, if it let them be forgotten instead of remembered? How could it be love if my back needed scars in order to know it was loved? How could I describe what I felt as love if I misused others in order to forget, if I was prepared to deprive the person to whom I had given life of the very thing he couldn't do without: myself?

I stood there, ashamed, unable to move, paralysed by the tableau before me, spellbound, captive, as if I were six again, as if Ivo, holding on tight to the bough, were leaning aside to let me see. I saw how Lado kissed Salome, but his kisses were not for her; he overlooked her, needing only her lips for the kiss, only the kiss. I held my breath and clenched my fists.

How could I describe as love something that made me so lonely, so defenceless, so insecure, so egotistical, that deprived me of who I was? How could I stand there watching strangers make love? How could I forgive my father, and how could Ivo forgive me?

How could my son forgive me? Guilt seemed omnipresent. Guilt, even when you were unaware of it.

The colourful threads of the world.

The stories, woven into a fabric called pain. My pattern was just the continuation of my father's pattern, Ivo's pattern the continuation of his mother's. And I would bequeath my thread to Theo. That could not happen. The thought filled me with horror, and I put my hand over my mouth to stop myself from screaming.

And all of a sudden I realised, with absolute clarity, that what
Ivo was seeking here was his own story — the story he wanted to
rewrite.

20

We drove along the dusty country road. Buba kept taking a piece of raspberry-pink chewing gum out of his mouth and wrapping it around his forefinger. Lado was driving; Ivo sat beside him, playing one CD after another. Salome sat across from me on the back seat, staring at the scenery. We were heading for a small seaside village where Salome had rented an apartment. Lado told stories from his childhood, all of which had something to do with the sea, and Buba kept asking more and more questions. He wanted to know everything about the past that he had previously been spared, or simply not told. Ivo raved about a CD Lado wanted to record with Georgian musicians. Salome was quiet. I took photos of the lush green landscape rolling past. Buba, making plans for our week-long stay, suggested a swimming race.

'These two grew up by the North Sea. It's cold there; I'm guessing they're very good swimmers, so think about what that means, Buba,' said Lado, and Ivo laughed.

'Did you grow up together?' Buba asked. I turned my face away and waited for Ivo to say something, but he didn't.

'Yes. We did,' I said finally, hoping Buba wouldn't ask anything else.

'Neighbours?'

'No, we lived in the same family.'

'Are you related?'

'Ivo is my adoptive brother.'

'What does adoptive brother mean?'

'It means that Stella's parents took Ivo in,' explained Salome, who didn't seem comfortable with the direction the conversation was taking.

'But you're kind of together, aren't you?'

'Buba, that's enough now,' interrupted Lado.

'No, it's fine,' said Ivo suddenly, turning to face us. 'Yes, that's right. We are kind of together. We've known each other since we were very, very little, Stella and I, and even as children we already liked each other.'

The word *liked* made me want to slap him.

'We're not *kind of together*, Buba,' I said, and tried to hide my annoyance by stubbornly sticking my head out of the window into the wind.

★

In the remote villages, the roads were steep and bad and the views were staggering. Suddenly I could understand why people in this country seemed so indifferent to the mundane, surrendering themselves to everything that promised pleasure. After a bumpy five-hour journey, we finally arrived: a small brick house with a garden and swing that reminded me of Niendorf. The sea was just a few steps away, and green, thickly forested mountains rose up behind the house. The beach was empty as it was still out of season, but the water was warm and inviting.

Ivo and I got a twin room with a view of the mountains; Buba was allowed to choose his. There were two cats in the garden that we had been asked to feed, and Buba assumed the role of animal keeper with tremendous pride. And then we all ran down together to the beach. Swimming with Ivo had always been one of my absolute favourite pastimes; I had almost forgotten how childishly excited it could make me. We undressed quickly and sprang into the clear water.

★

'So, Stella, shall we relive the old days?' said Ivo, digging me in the ribs. I was still cross with him, and it spurred me on.

Lado and Buba wanted to be on the same team; Ivo and I were supposed
to be the competition, but I wanted to beat Ivo, so I pretended to agree
while secretly hoping I would leave him behind. We counted to three and
swam off. Salome, who had stayed on the beach, shouted something after
us in Georgian, but no one paid any attention. Buba yelled in delight, and
I dipped underwater. I could feel Ivo's quick, jagged arm movements
alongside me, and the warm salt water, unlike that in Niendorf, made me
swifter. The water healed everything, washed everything away, made up
for everything. I let it wash me clean, and, as always when I was in water,
I understood the point of baptism. It baptised me over and over again;
every time it made me clean, new. It forgave me. Every time.

Eventually Lado signalled that it was getting too much for Buba,
and they swam back. Ivo and I didn't turn around. We swam on.
On and on. We dissolved, forgot ourselves and swam away, as if the
answer to everything lay in front of us. I could feel the freedom in my
body, in my temples; my prison was gone, broken open.

I dipped under and surfaced again, and the sun blinded my salt-
encrusted eyes, and I knew I'd left Ivo behind. I always used to be the
weaker one, lagging behind Ivo, and now I had overtaken him. I heard
him panting and thrashing, but I knew I was in front; I was ahead of
him. I had done it. For the first time in my life, I had overtaken him.
Later, as we lay on the beach, I felt fifteen again. I felt good.

★

After dark, I went out into the garden to breathe the sea air and came
across Salome by the fence, her cigarette glowing. Wordlessly, I stood
beside her. She said nothing, just stared into the distance.

'Shall we go for a walk?' I suggested. I could see that something was
bothering her. She nodded, stepped forwards, and we automatically
headed for the beach. We sat down on the cool rocks and gazed at the
hushed, dark sea. She started throwing pebbles into the water; I copied
her, and we both laughed.

'You don't like me, do you?' she said suddenly, not looking at me.

'Where did you get that idea? You're wrong.'

'That's all right, then. I've been wondering what was up with you.'

For a while we sat in silence, both unsure what to say. Then she turned to me again.

'I have a child,' she said, staring at the ground. 'A son. He's fifteen. Lives with his father in Germany. His father's a computer scientist. I was married to him for a long time, though it was always Lado I ... But Lado married Nana, my best friend. We were neighbours, he and I; we grew up together. I was fifteen when he kissed me for the first time. On the street, on the way to a birthday party, and ... I thought he would love me. But Nana was different; she was at drama school, and came from one of the best families. She had everything. Lado wanted her. I knew before he told me. She could have had anyone, but she said yes to him. Life is absurd sometimes, isn't it?' She was talking more to herself than to me.

'She didn't even really know him. She'd just started her studies; she was the next big thing. She had everything. What was I supposed to do? I mean, he was my boyfriend. I'd always been there for him, I knew everything about him, and Nana — she was the spoiled little princess. Her father was in the KGB; she had no worries, no fears. He worshipped her. She was his ballerina. That was what he called her.

'Do you know the worst thing? The thing I can never forgive her for? That she never once acknowledged that she had hurt me. Marriage followed, then the child, a girl. You should have seen her, how pretty she was. The whole town would stop in the street whenever Nana was out with her daughter. And she asked me to be godmother, Maya's godmother, and I said yes. I said yes, though I never should have done. I looked after Maya when Nana was on stage and Lado was busy with his stuff. That girl was my unborn child, my ray of sunshine. They were often on tour in those days, and Maya would stay with me. Maya loved me. She called me Mama.'

Salome paused, then started throwing stones into the water again. Rings spread out across the surface, and little fishes flashed here and there. All around us was alarmingly quiet.

'I joined his political party back then as well; Lado and I, we were cut from the same cloth. The more successful Nana got, the more she grew away from her husband. That period, all the riots and upheavals, was not her time. Her father lost his position as an official. Nana feared the very changes Lado was trying to bring about. Then Lado was sent to prison, which in her eyes was a disgrace.'

'And then?' I ventured.

'Then? Then she started the affair.'

'An affair?'

'With a Russian officer. She met him through her father, who used to work in Moscow.'

'And?'

'And. Well, what is there to say? His name was Alexei, he was from Moscow, and he was based in Sokhumi. A boyish kind of guy, with jug ears. Barely twenty-five, I believe. Nana was fed up with the police searching her home, the prison visits, the political friends hanging around her house. It wasn't her fault; she wasn't the kind of Georgian woman who dances attendance on forty of her husband's friends at all hours of the day and night, serving them hundreds of dishes. It wasn't her fault she took a fancy to the boy. He was helpful, from a good family, knowledgeable about theatre. And she was afraid for her father, who had fallen out of favour. After all, she'd never really loved Lado. Of all her admirers, he was just the one who had impressed her most and adored her best.'

'And you — what did you do?'

'I married an old schoolfriend who'd been after me for years. I'd never taken him seriously. He was so patient and forbearing; he never reproached me, he even made friends with Lado, and he wanted a family, he wanted a child. I ended up doing to him what Lado had done to me. Like I said, life is absurd. And we lost everything. The war took everything we had: jobs, houses, possessions, our dreams, ambitions, desires — suddenly, everything was gone. Lado was in

Tbilisi. I was worried; I knew that if he found out about his wife's affair, there would be trouble, and I helped Nana — yes, I helped her hush up the affair; I was her alibi. It was Lado I wanted to protect; I didn't spare much of a thought for Nana. I couldn't understand her behaviour.

'Nana didn't believe our country was at war until it was already too late. She always said: it's just men playing games. She used to meet her Russian in secret, in the hotel where he'd taken a room.

'And then the shooting started. And didn't stop. Lado was in Tbilisi, my husband and son had left sometime earlier to stay with his relatives in Russia, and I was stuck in Sokhumi, with Maya and Nana. The first refugees had already left Abkhazia for Russia or Tbilisi. But as long as there was still a chance, we didn't want to leave. I was waiting for Lado, and Nana believed her Russian hero would protect her. He was supposed to cooperate with the separatists and pass on information of military importance to Moscow. I don't know whether he did. I just know that he was a young guy in love who'd got caught up in something that was too big for him, that had spun out of control. We were stuck there for almost six months. In Sokhumi. By then she was already pregnant with Buba. We'd moved into my little apartment, because the Kanchelis' house was too big, too great a provocation, because everyone knew who it belonged to. Suddenly Nana was the enemy — for the Russians because her father had ultimately sided with the Georgians, for the Abkhaz because her husband was fighting for the Georgians, and for the Georgians because she had an Abkhaz mother. By the end, she was hardly speaking. She would sit for hours staring out of the window; not even Maya could get her to talk. Occasionally, she would sneak out of the apartment and disappear for a few hours. And each time I had to prepare myself for the worst, for the possibility that she wouldn't return.

'It wasn't until just before they took Sokhumi, when so many people died, that Lado came home and begged his wife to leave the city, to go to Tbilisi, to take Maya away, but Nana said she would die if she were so far from her mother, her city; that her family's reputation made her untouchable, and protected Maya, too. Maybe in 1992 that was still true, but a few months later everything had been burned down, torn down, murdered, forgotten. No one gave a damn anymore about anyone's reputation.

'Not long after Buba was born, Lado came home and ordered us to leave. Before the world around us went completely crazy. Lado was stationed in Gali at the time, and he managed to get to Sokhumi by the skin of his teeth. It was a terrible time, and afterwards it only got worse. He came and said we absolutely had to leave the city in two days' time, in the early morning, because they were expecting a blockade.

'After Buba was born, Nana was like a different person. She dressed in her best clothes and didn't want to breastfeed the baby; sometimes she would disappear for days on end, and when she showed up again, she was drunk. I assumed that she was going to Russian parties, trailing around after Alexei like a dog on a lead. Lado had organised everything for us. His people were supposed to pick us up at dawn and fly us to Batumi in a helicopter. From there we would travel on to Tbilisi. I already had a ticket for the onward flight from Tbilisi, to my husband and son. Lado made me swear that I would get Nana and Maya into the car, by force if necessary, that I would do everything to make sure we got out of the city. He left Sokhumi and went back; he had to go to his men, he was supposed to lead them into the city the following night. To shoot, to set fire to the government building, to …' Salome sighed.

'The night before we were due to leave, I stood there with three suitcases, staring at Nana, who was putting on a smart dress. Lado had said they would fetch us at seven o'clock in the morning. I had Buba in my arms, and Maya was crying; maybe she sensed something. I asked Nana what she was doing, why she was getting dressed up. And she told me she had to say goodbye to him, there was so much she needed to say to him, she had to tell him that it had been wrong to sleep with him while her country was going to the dogs, that she couldn't be with him when her husband was fighting against him, that she couldn't talk to him about theatre when his country was sending weaponry into her country.

'And so I said: go, I know you have to, I'll look after the two of them, but please be back by five. And she said: I'll be back in two hours at the latest. Then she kissed my hand and disappeared.

'She didn't come back. Three o'clock, four, five. She didn't come. I was so worried I could hardly breathe. I woke Maya, picked Buba up, and went out into the street. Nana's mother lived quite close by. I rang the doorbell frantically, and put Buba into her arms. Suddenly Maya started shouting; she yelled and screamed that she didn't want to be there, she wanted to stay with me. She got completely hysterical. She was such a quiet, obedient child ... I didn't want to lose any time, so I just picked her up and ran off.

'Their grandmother was shocked and scared; she wanted to know what was going on. I said: I'll pick him up soon. I ran off, with Maya in my arms. I ran to the hotel where Alexei lived. They weren't there. I searched the streets. It was dark, not a single street lamp still intact. I ran along the beach promenade.

'I knew Alexei was often at the base, in the former theatre, which was now an administrative building; Nana had mentioned it once. So I hurried there. I thought that if Maya was with me, it wouldn't get dangerous. They wouldn't feel threatened, they wouldn't be violent. The city was asleep; it was such a peaceful morning, and if it hadn't been for a few bullet holes in the façades here and there, you might have thought it was a perfectly ordinary dawn.

'A young man was standing guard outside. I asked for Alexei. He looked at me suspiciously, then he ordered me to wait at the entrance and went inside. I didn't know then that all the soldiers stationed there had been summoned back to base that night, because they were expecting an escalation. Because they knew what was going to happen. Then he came back and said Alexei wasn't there. He had driven off in his car two hours earlier, the soldier said. I started to cry.

'I wanted to know if he'd been alone. He took pity on me and went back inside to find out. When he came out again he said no, his wife was with him. His wife, he said. What wife, I wanted to know. Nana, his wife, he repeated. I begged him to find out where they had gone. He kept repeating that he knew nothing about it, and reassured me that Alexei had to be back there at nine that morning. So I could come back again at nine.

'Nine o'clock — we'd never make it out of the city by then. I think I screamed; Maya got even more upset seeing me like that, and she started sobbing as well. I couldn't believe Nana had just stood us up — me, us, her children. After everything she had said, about the Russians, about herself; she couldn't just have forgotten it all again. Something had happened. I don't know — to this day I don't know. We walked back. I couldn't leave the city without Nana. I had to put the grandmother in the car with the children and let them go on alone. I had to stay and find Nana.

'I was just about to turn the corner near the house when Maya stopped and began to scream at the top of her voice. I asked her what was wrong; I tried everything I could think of to reason with her, calm her down. I'd never seen her like that. And then she told me: she told me that she'd told Papa, she'd told Papa that Mama had another boyfriend, that she went off with him sometimes, that he wore a uniform, but it was different to Papa's, that he sometimes gave Mama presents and that Mama always hid him and never brought him home, but that she, Maya, always stayed awake and watched him bringing Mama home in his car; that …

'I stared at her in horror, and before I could comfort her, she wrenched her hand out of mine and ran down the street as fast as she could. At exactly that moment, a big military vehicle with a Russian licence plate rounded the corner. It looked like the one Alexei sometimes drove Nana home in. Maya ran after it. She called out to her mother, and she ran and ran. Before I could catch her, she had taken a shortcut, scrambled over a garden fence, and leaped in front of the car. They couldn't brake in time. I heard the tyres screech on the asphalt. And then I couldn't see Maya anymore. Someone screamed, and I fell to my knees. It was those boys who called themselves the peacekeeping force. I knew before I reached her that she was no longer alive. She'd hit her head when she fell. I'd had no idea that she knew everything ...'

★

The sea was endless, the sky already starting to get light. A blue ray pierced the clouds and began to colour the horizon pink. I was clutching a little greenish stone, squeezing it in my fist. The cigarettes were finished. I glanced at Salome. She didn't cry. She stared at the horizon, and so did I.

'I bundled Nana's mother, and Buba, who was fast asleep, into Lado's car, and I stayed behind. I went with Maya to the hospital. It was almost empty. They only took her because she was dead. I didn't know where Lado was; I didn't know where Nana was. I didn't know where I was, but I knew I had to look for Nana. I didn't find her. The attack on the government building began that morning. The storming, they called it later. Lado didn't make it back to the city because almost all his men had lost their lives on the way there — and that, in turn, saved his. If he'd reached Sokhumi, he wouldn't have survived, that's for sure.

'The following night a man gave me a lift, a Russian whose car I just flagged down on the street. He said he was going to Gali, and told me to get in. We didn't say a word to each other on the drive. I don't remember what he looked like. In Gali he took me to one of the last Georgian bases and dropped me there. I didn't say thank you or goodbye. He drove on. Three days later I was put on a truck full of refugees. I didn't say a thing. They just took me with them. Just like that, no questions.

'In all those years I never told Lado what I knew. All those years we kept silent. Eventually he ended up in America; I went to Germany. I tried to stay away from him for a while. I didn't give him my phone number or address. I tried to live my life, but what is my life beyond him? I don't mean love, I don't mean what we once were, but those days and nights ... those last nights I spent with his wife and his daughter — I can't take them away from him. Do you understand?'

I put my hand on hers and pressed my lips together.

'I am that last memory that he still has. At some point he came to Berlin. I saw him, and knew I couldn't leave him again. He was so broken, so sad. I cooked for him, I did his laundry, I stroked his head when he drank himself into a stupor. I gave him money. I tried to love him the way I used to, but I couldn't do it anymore. I could see in his eyes that all he saw in me now was his adored wife's last months, and it made me ill. So ill that I left my family, my son, and came back here with him. And then, one day, I couldn't stand it anymore, being the dead woman, the one who no longer has any right to life, and I told him about Alexei. I told him something he'd already known for years.'

'Let's go in the water.'

'What?'

'Yes — let's go in the water.'

'It's cold.'

'No, it's not. Come on, take off your clothes.'

I got up and started to remove mine. Until I stood there naked, waiting, mutely beseeching her to swim with me. She looked at me, watching me, at first confused, uncertain; then she jumped up and began to get undressed. She had a strong body, a body that had withstood everything and had not been destroyed.

'You're a swimmer — you swim well, even against the current,' said Salome, as if she could read my thoughts. She ran into the water, and I followed her. It retained the warmth of the previous day, had not yet cooled in the early-morning chill. The water received us, tolerated us. The water was gentle and merciful; it had forgiven us, long before we were ready to forgive ourselves.

21

We ate fish and drank white wine; we played volleyball on the beach, which was usually deserted apart from a couple of backpackers or local kids. Ivo was distant, as if that afternoon in the sea had shifted, displaced something between us. I didn't ask him why. I needed time to put all the stories in my head in order, and I chose to be alone. Enjoyed being alone. I read books and articles Ivo lent me about the recent history of the country, but I was always searching in them for Lado, his dead, pale, ethereal, Shakespeare-loving wife and their beautiful daughter, and the austere Salome, whose name I let dissolve on my tongue like rich ice cream. I searched in them for Buba and Theo. I searched for Ivo, myself, my husband, Salome's husband, her son. And it was as if every figure concealed countless others behind it, like that Chinese army of the dead, standing in rank and file as straight as arrows.

At night, when Buba was asleep, we sat outside, smoking, drinking or passing a joint around, gazing up at the skies. Salome would usually sing then, with Lado accompanying her on guitar. I took Ivo's hand and brought it to my lips. He allowed me to, but didn't reciprocate my warmth. Then we lay down on our rickety beds, and I lay awake for hours, listening to Ivo's breathing. He didn't touch me. He ignored me, only spoke to me when absolutely necessary — he was far, far away from me, from this place, searching for something, I couldn't tell what. I kept thinking about the photo. The photo of the house by the port.

Just once I crawled into his narrow bed and pressed myself against him. There wasn't enough room for me beside him; we hadn't pushed our beds together. So I lay half on top of him. He didn't move. I knew he was awake; he was breathing heavily. I started to massage his legs, stroke his thighs; I pressed my breasts against his chest, touched his stomach. Still he didn't move. How I hated that about him, this coldness, this controlled remoteness, this unyielding stiffness he was able to maintain so expertly whenever he was evading me.

'Are you cross with me?' I whispered, touching my lips to the tip of his nose, which was hot and rough.

'I'm not cross with you.'

'But?'

'You don't trust me anymore. You poke about in things that aren't your business.'

I sat up and shifted away from his body. Had he found out that I'd been in his computer, that I'd found 'S'?

'You could at least tell me where your journey is headed.'

'The essence of a true journey, Stella, is that you don't know where you're going to end up. That's why we're here.'

'Ivo, what on earth is going on with you?'

He sat up and looked me dead in the eyes. The moonlight had transformed the little room into a mountain cave, sacred, reverently beautiful. I could see his eyes, tired, sunken, drowned in their own colour. I touched his cheek and he laid his face in my hand, suddenly yielding, and his eyes closed. He was back again, he was holding me tight, and I thought of how life consisted of moments like this, that they were what mattered; all the rest was just waiting. The little moments of closeness. Of forgetting, or remembering — perhaps they were the same thing?

'It never used to be about competing, for us,' he said suddenly, and kissed my shoulder. So it was that, after all: I had hurt him by swimming out on my own. Maybe that was it. In the past, I would never have dared to leave him behind. Perhaps Ivo had never been strong; perhaps he was only strong when I was weak.

'It was just a bit of fun.'

'No, it wasn't. You know that.'

★

We drove to Batumi, the biggest port on the coast, and went dancing. We sat in a beach restaurant and drank cocktails and partied — as if the country were one big village full of neighbours, its almost five million inhabitants all friends from school or kindergarten. As so often, Lado bumped into some acquaintances who were determined to invite us to eat and drink with them, seeing as we were friends. In the past few weeks I had had to get used to constantly being hosted by people who were far less well off than me, and I had stopped protesting. I resigned myself, went along with it. You had to accept all the litres of wine, the hundreds of dishes, the presents, even if you could hardly move from all the eating and drinking, and you had to express delight and enthusiasm, which wasn't always easy with such a copious amount of things on offer.

I knew that Lado just about managed to keep his head above water with a few composition commissions here and there; sometimes he even got commissions from abroad, which would keep him going for several months. I knew that Salome worked for an insurance company, but shared everything she earned with Lado and Buba. I knew that people were having to fight for their survival, that they lived for the moment, that words like *planning* and even *security* were alien to them, but nowhere had I met as many rich poor people as I had in Georgia.

'Tulia would love it here, don't you think?' I asked Ivo, as we returned to our table after dancing together. He wiped the sweat off his forehead and laughed, so liberated, so relaxed, so carefree; and I was relieved to see him so light-hearted. We laughed and laughed; I didn't even know what about. I glanced over at Salome, who had flopped onto a deckchair, and saw that she too was laughing. I saw the little lines dancing at the corners of her mouth, her dark eyes shining, saw her wrinkle her nose and the dimples deepen in her cheeks, and was glad.

The stars were twinkling in the sky, thousands of tiny glow-worms. They too seemed to absorb the joy of the evening, the way they glittered over the dark sea that stretched endlessly before us, and for a brief moment the whole world was bathed in happiness. Because I was happy, and could feel it with every pore of my skin. I was happy here, forgetting myself, forgetting everything, with these people who were so unfamiliar and yet, at the same time, so close. I ruffled Ivo's thick hair and glanced over at Lado, who was performing an improvised sabre dance with one of his acquaintances. Salome pressed her palms to her cheeks, which were glowing with pleasure and heat.

'What do you reckon, can the fish out there hear the music?' I asked her.

Salome started giggling again, more subdued this time, but still with the silliness of a child.

'Only Stella would ask a question like that,' said Ivo, laughing as well.

'Well, we are disturbing their normal sleeping hours!'

'A very German observation,' said Salome, winking at me.

The restaurant closed for the night, and we moved on. The sun was rising. Ivo put his arm around me and we strolled along the beach; the pebbles were cold, and I held my sandals in my hand. We saw ships in the distance; a few lonely lights shone on the water. The gulls screeched, and the little white houses on the seaside promenade looked harmonious and sleepy that carefree morning.

★

Buba's head was resting on my shoulder as we drove up the steep road out of town, through the long tunnel that led to our quiet village. I touched my head against his, his thick, black hair, and heard him breathing slowly, rhythmically. I smelled the salty aroma of his skin. I touched my forehead to his, and remembered Theo, when he was still a baby, and how I would take him into bed with me, even though Mark didn't want me to.

How he would start to crawl around on me, laughing at me. How he would fall asleep on my breast, and how, astonished at the sight of this marvellous creature that had emerged from my body and announced his arrival to the world with a mighty cry, I would lie motionless, afraid of marring his perfect happiness if I moved and woke him. Perhaps, ultimately, these are the moments that hold the threads together, the stories we should tell: not the battles, not who won and lost the world, not the cultural upheavals, the revolutions, the warriors and heroes, the kings and queens, the rulers and tyrants. No — perhaps, in school, they should tell us how someone laughed for the first time, screamed for the first time, what their first kiss felt like. Perhaps people should talk about and remember moments like the one when Buba dozed off on my shoulder and I felt happy and secure.

★

Later, I lay next to Ivo as he took a midday nap, and studied him: his face, his body. I tried to synchronise my breath with his, studied his fingernails, clipped so short it hurt just to look at them, his lips, his unshaven chin, his earlobes, his nostrils, the wrinkles on his forehead, his belly button, and thought that I wanted to commit him to memory for ever, wanted to remember for ever all that made him what he was. That I wanted to tell him how it felt to have his liver in my abdomen, his right lung, the left chamber of his heart; what it was like to have a twin. And I wanted to tell him that I had never regretted sharing everything with him, even if it was sometimes hard and I sometimes felt the lack of my own air, my own heartbeat, and my own pulse — but it hadn't mattered, it absolutely hadn't mattered.

I fell asleep and dreamed of a baby, of Buba's hair, of Papa picking me an apple in our garden, of Mark's hands warming my feet. Of Ivo's fingertips, which turned into crocodiles, and of a woman standing alone by the sea reciting poems, the wind whipping her hair, wearing a wedding dress and veil that seawater had turned wet and grey. Who had watery eyes, and was so weirdly pale you could see the veins on her forehead. Who kept reciting lines, like a prayer, in a language I didn't understand. Who had seaweed wrapped around her ankles. Who seemed to be waiting for someone; who was in despair. I dreamed that slowly, step by step, still reciting her lines and looking straight ahead, she walked into the sea. And I saw how, little by little, she was swallowed by the water until only her veil remained, floating on the surface. And when she had completely disappeared, I saw a little girl with unnaturally big eyes emerge from the water and call, 'Mama, Mama.'

'It's okay, calm down, it was just a dream,' said Ivo, putting a hand on my forehead. 'You were moaning like crazy! And you're dripping with sweat. Come on, let's make something to eat; I'm starving.'

★

After seven days in the dry heat, we drove back to Tbilisi. Still, now, I was confronted from time to time with scenes from a world that had been bombed to pieces. I would reassure myself, especially when feeling almost overwhelmed by the heat, that my world was a world full of uncertainty, but it was one without bombs.

I went with Buba to the cemetery above the city, and walked with him through the narrow alleyways of the Old Town. I wrote emails to Mark and asked about Theo. He sent two or three taciturn sentences in reply. Only ever the essentials. Now and then I was allowed to speak to Theo in the evening, although Mark would usually invent some excuse or other as to why Theo couldn't come to the phone.

Ivo disappeared every morning; he was working with Lado in the studio, he said apologetically, on the interview and the recordings. I didn't ask questions, didn't ask why he had once needed me here so badly. On the contrary: my time alone in this city felt like a gift.

I read, and lay in the rusty bathtub; I got to know the streets and their beggars, I got to know their stray cats and dogs. In the evenings I usually ate at the Kanchelis'. Salome and I never spoke again about the night on the beach. As if, after that night, there was nothing else to say, because nothing else could touch that story; as if she had said enough for both of us. I didn't ask any more questions, not about where my journey was headed, or when it would end; I didn't ask myself anymore. Only when I settled down on the veranda late in the evening to wait for Ivo, who was still off somewhere, always careful to cover his tracks, did I lapse into deep melancholy, because I couldn't wholly suppress the fear I felt deep inside, or the yearning for my son. Those were the moments when I thought about the fact that Lado and Ivo would be travelling to Sokhumi in July.

Today, thinking back on those quiet days, I still wonder why I didn't see what should have been apparent.

*

One very hot Wednesday, Salome called me and asked me to come to the Marriott. The bar was air-conditioned; a piano played quietly in the background. There was latte macchiato and Wiener schnitzel. Americans, Dutch, French, even a few Germans sat hunched over their laptops or reading the *Financial Times*. It was a place, removed from the life of the city, that was supposed to remind you of everywhere else in the world. Salome sat at a table, legs crossed, wearing a dark skirt and a blue satin top, and sipping a pineapple juice. She had put on a little lipstick; her dark eyes shimmered in the late-afternoon sun. From her appearance I guessed that she had come straight from work. Her thick hair hung straight as a curtain around her head, like an actress from the silent-movie era. She hugged me, and ordered two glasses of champagne.

'What are we celebrating?' I asked in surprise.

'Us,' she answered briskly, lighting a cigarette; she had asked the waitress to bring her a packet of Pall Malls as well. 'Also, I've been promoted, and am now rich.'

She laughed, and her teeth shone, astonishingly white. 'Enough to order champagne, anyway,' she added, winking.

I still felt the urge to touch her. To stroke her hair, her long nose, her cheeks. I lowered my gaze; I felt uncomfortable, staring at her like that. I drank the chilled champagne and thought of nothing. She talked about her work and her demanding boss, about the Americans who owned the company. She asked me about Ivo, about me, what I was doing with my days, how I was feeling, and after a while I started to wonder whether she was really so cheerful because she had been promoted, or whether there was something else going on. Her questions became more pressing, more intimate. I tried to sidestep them.

Eventually I blurted out, 'What's the matter with you?' — so loudly that a Dutch couple at the next table turned to look at us.

She fixed me with a searching gaze, as if she wanted to make sure I could handle it. Then suddenly, out of nowhere, the corners of her mouth turned down, she covered her face with her hands, and let out a deep, anguished sigh. For a while I wasn't sure whether she was crying. Then she looked at me, and her cheerfulness, her smile, her euphoria had abruptly vanished, and fear and despair had taken their place.

'I can't do this,' she murmured. 'Whenever you look at me like that, I can't help thinking … of that night by the sea. And today I just wanted to celebrate; work is so hard, and there's no reward, not really, and so I thought I could enjoy a little moment with you, for no reason. But when you look at me like that, I realise there isn't much to celebrate in my crappy life, that instead of sitting here drinking champagne I should just weep about it all.'

'But what's happened, Salome?' I leaned in towards her across the table and looked into her eyes, which were indeed filling with tears.

'It's just all a miserable lie. I do try, as best I can, and now I've gone and fucked up.'

'Tell me. Please.'

'I don't know. It's all of it at once.' She struggled to find the right words, speaking slowly, carefully. 'I feel as if I don't know what's going on anymore. I'm so empty, and I don't know what to do. I miss my son, who doesn't talk to me; I'm a terrible mother, and Buba, who should have been my son, doesn't want me; it's as if he wants to punish me for his sister's death. And his mother's, and because I claimed the right to love his father. What would have happened if I'd vanished from the Kanchelis' lives early on, if I'd looked to my own life instead of staying with them, instead of raising their child? If I'd just gone away, maybe they would still be together, maybe they would still be a family, and Nana would be alive, Maya would be alive. I can't get it out of my head. Lado will always be thinking of Nana and needing me to preserve this morbid connection with his dead wife.

'I let it all slip in the middle of a fight we had in Berlin. About Alexei, Nana, the years in Sokhumi. I reproached him, although … We never spoke of it again, until … until Ivo came.'

I lit myself one of her Pall Malls and stared at my fingernails — a little longer than usual, a little less bitten, a little pointy. I knew that I would never be able to forget what she was about to say, and I braced myself, asked my fingers for an answer.

'We settled here. Lado rented the little house. He was working, and at least for a while it seemed his life wasn't governed by his dead wife. I sensed that he needed me, that he was even prepared to give me a little of his constricted love. I was content; I couldn't expect more than that, and I've never been short of patience. I thought things just had to carry on like that and then one day we'd be a family, a real family, the family I deserved in life, that he deserved. I mean, is that too much to ask? Then came the phone calls from Ivo. I knew they knew each other from New York, that Lado thought highly of him, they were friends, and ever since then it's been different. Something in Lado changed — it changed, and I couldn't put my finger on what, I didn't understand it anymore. And then Ivo came here.'

'When? When was the first time he came to see Lado?'

'Last winter. In February. He stayed more than five weeks. Lado was like a little boy around him. And then Ivo started asking me lots of questions. He would meet up with me on my own, and I realised he knew a lot. About us. There were things Lado couldn't have told him. He often talked about Nana; he kept on asking me questions. At first I thought it must be to do with one of his reports, but then it began to feel weird. Don't get me wrong, I like Ivo, I know how much he means to Lado, how much he does for Lado, but it just felt kind of weird to me, all these questions. Although he was very subtle about it; he never asked directly, always in a roundabout way. And so to begin with I just told him stuff and didn't think anything of it, but after a while I didn't trust him anymore, and I realised there was something going on. Something they were keeping me out of …

'I watched them, I listened to every word, trying frantically to think, to fill in the gaps, to guess what it was all about, but I couldn't: I knew nothing, absolutely nothing; my head was completely empty.

'Ivo was sniffing around like a bloodhound, like a man possessed, on the phone for hours, interrogating people. I didn't know how much Lado was even aware of, how much of it was arranged with him, or at what point Ivo started acting on his own initiative. I tried to get something out of Lado, but he shut me out, acted as if there was nothing going on, or as if it had nothing to do with me. At some point I started to think that what Ivo was looking for here was something personal. I know, it's not a feeling I can justify, but I haven't been able to shake the suspicion.'

'He knows exactly what he's looking for,' I replied. 'He knew where the journey would take him before it even began, before he came to Hamburg to fetch me. It has something to do with him and with me. I can't quite figure it out. He doesn't usually get involved in other people's stories like this. I've no idea who he's trying to help, or if help is what he's trying to do. I feel like I'm almost there, I'm about to make sense of it all, and then some crucial piece is always missing.

Maybe I'll be able to explain it to you soon; I really hope so. But I still need to understand myself why he's so intent on having me here, what it is I'm supposed to see, to recognise.'

'It's frightening, isn't it, how alike our worlds are in their differences,' she said.

I wondered what she was getting at, but my brain had ceased to follow any kind of logic. We'd ordered more champagne.

'But do you think this is about you? Is he trying to show you something?' she began again.

'What? What could he want to *show* me?'

I thought of the photo. Salome looked at me closely for a while, then said, firmly, 'Think, Stella, think. What might he be looking for in our story? What might *remind* him of something? They're going to go and find Alexei. Ivo is the impetus Lado needed to dare to take this step, to go and track him down. I really hope it's to find peace and not to strengthen his anger — at himself, his dead wife, this messed-up world. We have to contact Alexei. He works in the Abkhaz government. He's some sort of diplomat now. And he has a Georgian wife, I believe.'

'Yes, that's where they'll go ...'

'Unless we can start another war,' she said sardonically. 'I'll try to reach Alexei. I'll try to explain it all to him. To warn him. Best-case scenario: they'll talk, and Lado will be able to put it behind him one of these days. Worst case: they'll come to blows, and then Ivo and Lado will definitely have major problems. Lado especially, I mean, with his history.'

I finished my glass of champagne as the balmy evening darkened outside.

★

We strolled down wide Rustaveli Boulevard. We walked on, on and on, until we reached Ivo's apartment. Salome cooked for us. Ivo wasn't there. We listened to Anita Baker, the only tape I could find.

'You're a very special person,' I told her, sitting on the little veranda as the city glittered and shone.

Salome smiled at me and tilted her head slightly. Then she just nodded, as if she knew everything before I said it.

Then I asked her to sing me something, and, without replying, she began. Her voice enchanted me; it always said to me that no matter how lousy life was, it would still be all right in the end.

★

I heard a rustling; he was getting undressed. I was barely conscious and didn't know what time it was or when I'd fallen asleep. He started unbuttoning my trousers; I was still fully clothed. He helped me out of my linen shirt and carefully set my bra aside. I opened my eyes and saw that it was already light.

'You were sleeping so peacefully,' he said. He wasn't sober, but he hadn't been drinking; it wasn't alcohol — he didn't smell of it. I moved over a little, and he got into bed, naked.

'Are you on something?' I murmured.

'Turn around.'

'We can't spend our whole lives running away,' I protested, as he pulled down my knickers. I was always amazed at how controlled he was, even on drugs. How rare it was for anything to throw him. How self-possessed he was, even though the high had made him sleepy.

'We're not running away, we're here ...'

He started kissing my body. Leaning gently over me, he moved downwards.

'I don't like it,' I said, as he pushed my legs apart.

'What?'

'All this secrecy, the way you're acting.'

His answer was to put his head between my legs.

★

I rolled aside, still taut, quivering, shaking, curled up like an embryo. I knew I had to pin him down, now, while he was stricken and fragile, if I was to catch him. He was breathing heavily, stroking my back. The first rays of sunshine pierced the sky and sliced across him. The fresh morning air streamed in through the window. I clutched the white sheet.

'I found the photo.'

'What? Which photo?' he asked sleepily. He was lying on his back, naked, satisfied, awaiting his reward.

'You and me, the day before your mother died. She took that photo. I remember now.'

As I said the words, the memory returned. Emma sneaking up on us and surprising us with the camera. I remembered that rainy day. I remembered every detail, every corner of the garden, every smell, every sound, because it was the last day I had spoken to Ivo. It was only after the trial that I had seen him again, in a paediatric clinic, where they brought me to him because he kept calling my name.

It was the day Ivo's father came home. The day Papa went shopping and then we all cooked together. Vegetable stew and fried potatoes. Afterwards, Papa and Emma went upstairs as usual, to the bedroom at the end of the corridor. Ivo and I played in the garden with the dog, who was called Pidy. I had blanked out his name, but I suddenly remembered now that he was called Pidy. It had rained; the ground was muddy. We ran and hid, only to be flushed out by the dog's barking. Me grabbing his black, shiny, damp coat, the smell of wet animal: I saw it all again in my mind's eye as if it were yesterday.

'The photo?' He sat up and hugged his knees. 'Where?' He kept repeating the word, as if he couldn't believe it. 'Where?'

'On your laptop.'

'How did you get into my laptop?'

'I guessed your password.'

'You nosed around in my files!'

His voice was harsh; suddenly, he seemed completely sober. I leaned against the cool wall behind the bed and covered myself with the sheet. My nakedness made me vulnerable. His nakedness, on the other hand, was like armour. He pulled his knees in tight, bracing himself for the battle to come — for it would be a battle. His eyes shone in the morning light, his muscles tensed, and I recognised that peculiar, extreme concentration in his face. I recognised it from the moments when, blinded by his fury, he was prepared to fight the whole world.

He jumped up, grabbed a cigarette, hastily lit it; the glow of it in the dim room made the sight of him even more disconcerting, more aggressive.

'You're playing some sort of fucking game, for Christ's sake. You know exactly where this is going; you're playing with me. You come back after eight years, get me to walk out on everything, even my son, and then hide everything from me! Who do you think you are? You've ruined my life; and yes, I'm blind and stupid to have believed you. To have followed you yet again. You've determined my whole life, you bastard; you've always geared everything the way you wanted it, controlled things, as if you thought you were God. You're not — I've told you that! I'm not playing along. Not anymore. My son is at stake here, and I love him, okay — even if, for you, love is an alien concept, I love him, and I don't see why I should give up everything I love for more humiliations, more disappointments.'

'Love, love — what are you talking about?'

'Stop it! You don't even know what love is. What you think is love is just a sick, egocentric addiction!'

As I grew louder and louder, he became more and more composed, quiet, thoughtful. He was listening attentively, mentally recording every word, and I didn't know whether this was the calm before the storm or whether he was surrendering before even throwing his first punch.

'And what crap is it that you're trying to get to the bottom of here, Ivo? Tell me. I'm giving you everything, I've got nothing left, I'm even living off your money now — I'm basically a kept woman.'

'Don't degrade yourself. I hate it when you do that.'

'Oh, really? And you know what I hate, what I hate about you? That you're so bloody complacent! That you don't give a shit how I am, how I feel. What about those eight years? What were you thinking?'

'You took enough sleeping tablets to kill a horse, may I remind you. You wanted to die, Stella, and I can't take on any more guilt. I can't.'

'I wanted you to love me, I didn't want to die! How stupid are you? Guilt? Guilt — bloody hell! I'm the guilty one, you know that: it's me. All my life I've been waiting for you to say so, openly, to judge me, punish me if you want, finally, once and for all, so there can be an end to this eternal back-and-forth!'

My heart was pounding wildly. I stood up, wrapped in the sheet, and went to the window to get some fresh air. I felt as if I were suffocating. The city, spread out beneath me, blurred before my eyes, and I had to cling on to the windowsill to stop myself from keeling over.

He came closer; I heard his bare feet on the floor. I stared out of the window. I would not survive his touch. I gripped the wooden sill so hard I got a cramp in my hand.

'It wasn't a punishment!'

He pressed his thumb against my spine, the tip of it damp and cold. I flinched.

'I've never wanted to punish you. It's never even occurred to me, you hear? You must never think that, never! I've tried everything, Stella, please believe me. I've tried.'

He tugged at the sheet, and it fell to the ground. I made no attempt to cover myself again. In the harsh sunlight, my white body — every vein, every pore, every scar, every scratch — was mercilessly exposed. He had known this body at six, at ten, at fifteen, at twenty, and now, at thirty-six. He knew its hidden places and its vulnerabilities, the bits that could drive me insane and the spots that calmed me down; he knew what my body attempted to conceal. It scared me that he was standing behind me, inspecting me, but I was firmly resolved not to lose this battle, not to let myself be appeased: this time, his touch would not change anything.

His fingertip crept along my collarbone. I began to tremble.

'My love is just like this, and I am like this; I told you, back then, when you took off your clothes at the beach. This whole time I wanted to prove to us that we didn't have to atone, that you didn't bear any guilt; I wanted to prove it to you and to myself. All my life I've been looking for evidence of this. Why won't you see it?'

He licked my earlobe and stroked my matted hair back off my face. His arm encircled my waist, and I looked down at his hand, his painfully short fingernails. I would get through this. I would not give in.

He put his hand on the back of my neck and pressed.

If I turned, fought back, he would hurt me. He bent me slightly forward and put his hand on my buttocks. I froze and held my breath. I felt a kind of nausea; I knew that his calmness, these deliberate movements, were not a good sign. I tried to breathe deeply to hide my fear.

'Why did you come back to Hamburg? Why? You knew what would happen,' I whispered, as he pushed my legs apart, gripping my head with the other hand so he kept pushing me further and further forwards, until eventually my torso was hanging out of the window. My nausea grew; I was afraid I might throw up.

'I didn't come back to Hamburg or anywhere else, not even here. I just came back to you, Stella.'

I bit my lip. I was determined not to scream. He was deliberately hurting me, and he knew I was fighting it. He was waiting for me to succumb, to soften. The windowsill was digging into my stomach and there were sharp pains in my ribs.

The sun shone at us, its light so merciless, so warm, so incompatible with my stiff back and my fingers, which had turned into rigid claws, with his cold hands and the unbearable pain he was inflicting on me. I didn't fight against accepting this just punishment. I wanted to weep, to denounce the wretched sun for shining so proudly on my defeat, but I didn't make a sound.

'To you. Because ... I ... love ... you. You'll probably laugh. Because I'm saying it to you now. But maybe one day ... I'll be able to explain. I can't yet. Not yet.'

He gripped my head, pulled at my hair.

'Because. Because you wouldn't understand. Yes, it's true, it's true, I've found something here that might be able to heal us one day — yes, when I say *heal*, I mean it, Stella. Because all this. All this is a sickness. That has ... afflicted us ... since ... since the ... afternoon my father came home.'

I felt no sympathy; as he was saying this, he was still pushing me further forwards, moving faster. Right at that moment, all I felt for him was contempt.

'I'll explain everything to you, everything. I didn't believe you'd actually come here, that you'd give me another chance, and —'

'Stop!'

'No, we can't stop. We're going to see it through to the end, okay? We can do it; this time we can do it.'

He spasmed, and sank down onto me. His chest on my back. I bent my knees and ducked underneath his body. In the bathroom I got into the tub and let the cool water run. The cold made me feel even more awake than I already was, and I scrubbed frantically at my skin; I let the water wash it all away: the night, the sun.

He perched on the edge of the bath, as he had done so many times before, but I paid him no attention; I went on washing manically, as if the water would make everything all right.

'It'll be over soon; it won't take much longer. We're going there now, and when I come back, it'll all be over. I promise you.'

I acted as if I hadn't heard him.

'I never punished you, you hear? Stella, look at me. I never punished you. If I punished anyone, it was myself.'

'I don't want to talk.'

'Stella?'

He put his hand on my back, and for a moment I considered pushing him away.

'I love you.'

'You've already proved that on numerous occasions. Thanks.'

'Stella.'

'Ivo. I can't help you if you won't tell me what's going on.'

'I can't yet.'

'Why not?'

'Because you have to see it for yourself. To get there by yourself.'

'But this doesn't make any sense.'

I leaned towards him and held out my hand. He sat there, crushed, exhausted, red-eyed, his lips cracked, his eyes cold. He clutched my hand and held it to his lips, kissed it again and again. I pulled him towards me, and he got in the bath. I shared the water with him, at that moment the most precious thing I possessed, perhaps had ever possessed.

'What are you intending do in Abkhazia? How will it help you?'

He didn't answer. 'I'd have given everything, to —'

'Leave it, Ivo. Let's go to sleep; I'm so tired.'

He covered his face with his hands and fell silent. I had got out of the bath and wrapped a towel around my waist. I stood in front of him, rooted to the spot, unable to move.

He just sat there, under the still-running water, hiding from the world like a little boy who holds his hands in front of his face and thinks he's invisible.

★

I fell asleep and dreamed of the pale woman, who had often haunted my sleep in the last few weeks. Beside the sea, in Tulia's house, in the unconverted attic. With the beautiful child. She and my sleep were becoming friends. Sometimes she looked like Mama, sometimes Emma, sometimes no one, and once she looked like me. But she always wore a wedding dress. The kind I would have liked to have worn, if I hadn't been nervous of splendour. And I secretly envied her her veil, too, which was always slightly damp and slightly dirty.

22

They were going there because of the man, the man who had cost Lado's dreaming wife and captivating daughter their lives, and perhaps knew nothing about it, or perhaps did. Who might have become a completely different person since then, or not. Who had simply fallen in love with the wrong woman in that time of war, or not.

Thinking about it made me feel nauseous. And this nausea, in turn, prevented me from preventing Ivo from going. Thinking about it confused me, made me agitated, fearful, upset. What was I so afraid of? What exactly was it about this journey that worried me? Apart from the fact that in Abkhazia, officially, there was still only a 'ceasefire' with the Georgians and going there could actually be very dangerous, especially for Lado, there was something else that frightened me far more than any specific misgivings associated with the trip.

I was going around in circles. I was making no progress; pieces of the puzzle were still missing and I couldn't see the full picture.

Did Ivo really believe he could correct his own mistakes through his friend? What exactly was Ivo trying to fix with someone else's story?

Because one thing I did know: Ivo was not seeking the same answers as Lado.

★

July had come, and Tbilisi was blisteringly hot. The city smelled of dust and asphalt. Parents left town with their children and fled to their villages and holiday homes, to the apartments they had rented for the purpose, to their grandparents or relatives. The heat was paralysing, and brought the city to a halt.

The phone calls with Theo were becoming increasingly difficult because of Mark's pitiless attitude towards me. I couldn't even blame him. I had to go back soon, to talk to Mark about Theo. I needed to fight for my son, but in this passive role I felt helpless: everything seemed impossible until I'd found out what Ivo was doing here.

I decided to wait for their return. All my pleas and attempts to persuade Ivo to let me accompany them had failed.

★

We sat at the kitchen table with a bottle of white wine. Ivo had showered, packed his rucksack, and sat down next to me.

'I'll be back in three days. There's no need to worry. We'll only be there for one day. The rest of the time we'll be driving — you know what the roads are like.'

I poured glasses of chilled wine for us both. Ivo put his hand on mine, and we fell silent. We drank, and said nothing. Said nothing, and drank. It was dark, and the night had made the heat a little more bearable. I listened to the cicadas and wanted to say something, but realised I had no words. I said nothing.

That night I held him tight and kissed his body. That night I didn't want to dream of the pale woman in the wedding dress; that night I didn't even want to dream of the sea. For the first time, I slept with Ivo without something digging into my body, without it hurting me, without causing myself pain. I loved him gently, carefully, almost like a child.

This is how our love would have been if our bodies had already been able to speak back then, in the garden, in the house near the port; this is how we would have been as children, pressed against each other, touching each other, discovering each other, never willing to hurt each other. This is how our closeness would have been in his little room, on the left-hand side of the corridor at the end of which our parents took off their clothes, sucked at each other, and licked their wounds like animals. Nothing stood between us, and this time not even the thought of Theo stopped me from being completely there with Ivo, wide awake and clear, as if in that moment the possibility of bringing them together had opened up in my life, because I believed in this possibility, wanted to believe in it, and clung to it.

At dawn I heard him moving around, but I was too tired to wake properly, as if my body didn't want to consciously witness his departure. He bent down, kissed me gently on the lips, and walked out of the door.

★

It wasn't until midday that I woke, my body sweating in the heat, and immediately sat up. I looked around: everything seemed the same, almost familiar by now. I got up, showered. I tried to distract myself, made coffee and a fried egg, turned the radio on, listened to the foreign language and the ubiquitous pop music that finds its way into the ether everywhere in the world. I hand-washed some clothes and hung them on the washing line on the veranda.

I wrote Mark an email telling him I was coming home. I made a few notes in my notepad, which was almost full. I plaited my hair. I put on make-up, although it was pointless in that heat. I wrote a letter to Theo in my head. I lay on Ivo's pillow and inhaled his smell. I put on one of his shirts that I found hanging from a heating pipe in his bedroom. I danced to Anita Baker.

I ate a piece of bread and honey. I went downstairs and bought some Lucky Strikes. I smoked. Then it got dark, and I sat on the veranda and waited until the lights came on in the city. I looked down at the courtyard and the noisy children, who had drawn chalk squares on the ground and were hopping about in them. I heard songs on the radio, all of which I knew.

I wondered where they were at that moment. How much longer they would have to drive. I banned myself from wondering. I found an old piece of Ivo's chewing gum stuck to the desk, peeled it off, and chewed it until it fell apart in my mouth. I stared at my feet. I stared at Ivo's shirt. I stared at the night. And then I jumped up and ran into the bedroom, searching for the phone, bumping into everything in my path, knocking things over. I called Salome. The cigarette shook in my right hand; my voice almost failed me.

'Stella? Where are you? Come round; I'm feeling kind of restless. Or shall we come to you? Buba's at his friend's. I managed to reach Alexei — he said Ivo contacted him months ago; he's expecting them. You see, it's all okay.'

'Is Buba …'

'What's happened?'

'Is he …'

'Stella, I can't understand you, you're whispering …'

'Is he … not …'

'Hey, what's happened, speak up before I go crazy! Did they call?'

'Buba isn't Lado's … He isn't his son.'

'What?'

'Does he know?'

'What are you talking about?'

'Does Lado know?'

'I don't know. How do you know?'

'I just know. It's about the children. Not Lado. I didn't see it. It's about the children. It was always about them. The fact that she told him — that Maya betrayed her mother, that she died, but another child survived — that Buba survived. I can't explain it to you — the children, the children, they were the central characters in this story. It was about them, not the adults!'

'Stella, please, calm down. I'll call Buba, I'll go and get him, and then I'll come to you.'

'No, not with the boy. No, I can't.'

'Stella, what does this —'

'It was Ivo's idea to go looking for the Russian. There's something he wants to know. Shit!'

I hung up. Salome called back, again and again, but I didn't pick up. I stood rooted to the spot; I couldn't even turn on the light. I stared at the darkest corner of the room. It had never been about Lado. It was the boy, who had shown me the city's secret places, who lay in the artists' cemetery with me, sipping cola and smoking covert cigarettes, telling me about his worries and about what gave him pleasure; the boy whose head I had stroked, who had played with my hair, whom I was so fond of, because it made me feel closer to Theo.

And it was the girl, who had drawn portraits of her family members, who had committed a betrayal the magnitude of which she could not possibly appreciate, could only sense, suspect, and who then fell victim to that betrayal. It was about her.

It was about us.

It was Ivo. It was Ivo who touched my hair and lay with me in the grass, who sang me songs and told me about his dreams. It was Ivo who spoke to me, with Buba's lanky body and too-deep voice. And it was I who uttered the devastating words that changed both our lives.

The clock, ticking on the wall, reminded me again of time, which had ceased to exist. It reminded me. It reminded me that he was gone.

I managed to move again, went into the kitchen, turned on the light, and considered what to do. I wouldn't be able to catch him up, not even if I left then and there. I started to howl. I screamed and screamed, I screamed the soul from my body, but it didn't help. I sat on the floor and pummelled the floorboards, scratched at them, crawled back and forth in search of a safe place, a place that could promise me hope. I left the apartment and bought a bottle of vodka. The people at the kiosk, who had me down by now as the weird German woman who belonged to the weird German man, stared at me. I marched back to the courtyard without saying goodbye. I ran back up to the apartment, taking several steps at a time.

I drank, and punched my forehead again and again: surely my brain would come up with something I could do to fetch Ivo back.

I had failed to see what was most important. I had been blind.

I drank from the bottle and turned the radio up so loud that my thoughts began to shudder. I lit myself a cigarette and sat down beside the old Soviet refrigerator, which was almost as loud as the radio. I pressed my palms to the floor, leaning forward again and again, tensing my body like someone praying in a mosque, trying to draw something together, to consolidate it into one single, clear thought.

I don't know how long I was crouching there before the picture began to fall into place. The radio had drowned out the clock, and I had long since lost all sense of time. My pelvis had begun to go numb. An old, resonant female voice was singing 'My Funny Valentine', and I found myself thinking of that cold day, clearly hearing every sound again, every rustle; I could actually smell it, every breeze bearing the smell of fish up from the port. The distant foghorns, the muddy earth.

★

It was extremely cold; a storm was forecast, and there were warnings of possible accidents. I even remember that Tulia had called that morning, before Papa and I cycled off towards the port, and ordered Papa not to drive the car, and to wrap us up warm, which he had done. Off we cycled, me in a red scarf into which Mama had knitted her guilty conscience, and the rubber boots my father had brought back for me from East Germany, which he always put me in whenever Mama wasn't there. I was looking forward to seeing Ivo; I was looking forward to spending time with Pidy, and to the apple cake Emma usually baked on cold afternoons like these. I was looking forward to an ordinary, familiar day.

Papa was very preoccupied that afternoon, and after he had done the shopping and we had eaten (no apple cake); after Emma had, for some reason, taken the only photo that exists of Ivo and me in this period, they went up to her room. After a while, exhausted and covered in dirt, we climbed up into our tree. Ivo showed me the horizon and talked about ships.

Back then he wanted to be a sailor, and I would always beg him to take me with him, though he would always say that girls weren't allowed on the high seas. But I wouldn't give in and kept pestering him, utterly convinced that I could change his mind. I couldn't imagine anything nicer than a life like that. With dangers and whales and dolphins and sharks, with seasickness, and pirates who attacked our ship, which we defended with our sabres and our knives. With sailors' caps and telescopes, great waves beneath our feet, and the endless horizon in front of our eyes. Our dream, Ivo's and mine, to which we clung, in which we ventured forward and fought on.

Suddenly, I heard the sound of an engine, and a moment later a dark-blue Mercedes turned into the drive and stopped outside the garden gate.

Ivo's mouth fell open and his lips formed an incredulous 'Papa'. And I was about to rejoice with him, at Pidy's frantic barking as he raced to the gate and sat behind it; I was about to climb down from the tree with Ivo to go and greet his father; perhaps I even would have done, if his expression hadn't suddenly altered to a grimace of desperation.

I clung to the thick branch and held my breath, made myself as small as possible, as if I were trying to hide. Ivo had sat bolt upright and was pressing himself against the trunk of the tree. He stared ahead, as if hypnotised, waiting for the gate to open at any minute. The bedroom curtains were drawn. When Pidy started barking, a curtain was pushed a little to one side and Emma looked out of the window. I heard rapid footsteps on the stairs.

Ivo loved his father; he raved about the summers when they drove down to visit him and went for long hikes in the mountains, and although to this day I don't know who the man really was or what he was like, I knew that he was a hunter and owned a gun cabinet that was always firmly locked.

Love could lie and betray; it could hurt and deceive. In the months in the house by the port I had learned this lesson very well.

And so I feared the love of this man who was about to open the gate and come in. Who would deprive me of the right to see Ivo. And so, in those few moments of waiting, I began to hate him. I already hated him before he entered the garden. I hated him for his love, which deprived me of mine.

I heard the front door open; then I saw my father, carrying his jacket, run out of the basement door into the garden and towards the back gate. Emma stood on the steps in shock, a hand over her mouth, watching him as he started to look for me, unable to call my name. Then she looked up, this small, fine-boned, bewildered woman with the clouded eyes, and she waved to us, to Ivo and me. But we didn't move. I was afraid of going, and afraid of staying, too. I was suddenly desperately afraid that we would have to go away for ever now, meaning that I would be forced to give up Ivo. And so I decided to stay.

In those seconds between Emma looking up at us and Papa disappearing, I chose Ivo, and looked away. Papa waved at me frantically, Emma whispered my name, and I saw Ivo's eyes. His eyes were begging me to stay, not to leave him, and I shook my head. Then the gate opened, and the tall man with the thick moustache entered the garden. He greeted Pidy cheerfully as he juggled all the bags and boxes he was bringing from the car. A moment later Emma ran to him and kissed him lightly on the lips. He put his arms around her waist and held her for a long time. They spoke, but I couldn't hear what they were saying.

'He wasn't supposed to come for another two days — two days. Another two days,' Ivo whispered, looking at me. Clinging to the branch, I tried to hold his hand, but the man started calling him, and Ivo let go of the branch and quickly climbed down. He ran to the man, who hugged him and lifted him up like a little child. Emma whispered something to Ivo, and as the couple went into the house, Ivo came back to the tree and called to me to come down.

I was afraid to move, and could no longer hold back the tears, so I began to cry. Very slowly I made my way to the ground, and suddenly I was even more frightened. My father had gone and left me there, and although I knew I had stayed of my own accord, that I had done it because of Ivo, because he had begged me to with his eyes, I couldn't accept it.

I had to follow Ivo into the house. I was introduced to the man as a school friend of Ivo's who had come round to play. The four places at the kitchen table were explained away by saying that my mother, supposedly an acquaintance of Emma's, had dropped me off. The man ate what was left of the meal, talked about his drive, how happy he was to be home, and handed out presents to his wife and son. Finally we were sent to Ivo's room, and shortly after that we heard the bedroom door at the end of the corridor slam.

*

Ivo sat on his bed and stared into space. He said nothing. I said nothing. I bit my fingernails. We didn't feel like playing, and we'd left Pidy outside in the garden.

We heard a curious squeaking sound, and Emma's voice, which soon gave way to quiet sobs. We heard the man's voice, and the bed groaned loudly and ominously beneath the weight of two bodies. It was a sound we were familiar with, but this time the sound had something terrible about it. A brief gasp, another sob. A few minutes later an object fell to the floor, and the man raised his voice. I glanced at Ivo, who had blocked his ears and was crying, shaking his head and rocking back and forth. I tried to touch him, but he pushed me away and I tumbled onto the floor. The voice grew louder, more unbearable. Emma's did, too. Something else was knocked over. I crawled back to Ivo and tried to touch him again. All his self-control seemed to have vanished; I saw a frightened little boy, who stared at me with eyes swollen from crying, and began to hit me. Emma screamed and screamed.

Ivo kicked my knee, and I fell. He sat on top of me and pulled my hair. I scratched him, tried to get his face so he would let go of me and I could breathe again, but he was bigger and stronger. He squeezed his legs tighter and tighter around my body, and I began to cough. The coughing turned to gasping, and I screamed.

But Emma's cries from the other room drowned me out, and beneath Ivo's blows I eventually fell silent. As I managed to free myself and crawl away, the desperate screams next door reached a continuous crescendo, becoming one long, endless wail. Ivo stood, his face twisted, holding his breath. For a moment I saw the decision to run into the other room flash across his face, and immediately afterwards I saw the fear that held him back. Then he looked at me, huddled on the floor, and anger blazed up in his eyes again, and he flung himself on me. He punched me in the face, and I felt something warm and wet run down my lip. I put my hand to my mouth and wiped it away, grabbed the little orange chair that had so often served as the ladder to the forbidden things in this house, and started to lash out around me. The toy cars fell to the floor, then the Mickey Mouse torch, our craft materials, our drawing books, Ivo's stack of comics. Ivo stared at me, aghast. The corners of his mouth turned down and his eyes shone in the faint, early evening light.

'I hate you,' he said, looking me in the eye. 'I hate you. This is all your fault. It's your fault, and I never want to see you again.'

As he said this, my fear returned, along with my pain, which embedded itself in every part of my body. Nothing had ever hurt me like those words. Nothing until then had ever rocked my life like the way he looked at me. And yet I stood there and looked back. I bore his hatred.

'Tell him. Go on, tell him. Tell your father. Tell him. Tell him, if you're brave enough — tell him who I am. Then you'll get rid of me.'

I shouted it over and over again, until he came up to me and put his hand over my mouth. When he was sure I had stopped, he let go of me and stormed out of the room.

★

It was already dark when I was woken by a woman's soft hand. I had been asleep on the floor in the wreckage of Ivo's room. Emma smiled at me. Her eyes, as usual, were kind, and veiled, as if she were guarding a secret.

'What on earth have you two been doing?' she asked, stroking the hair out of my face. She sat down on the floor beside me and took me in her arms.

'Where's Ivo?' I asked.

'Ivo's gone out with his father. I'll drive you home. It's late already. Come on, let's wash your face.'

'I don't want to go home.'

'But you have to, little one. Your papa's waiting for you.'

'I want to see Ivo.'

'That's not possible right now, Stella. Look at me, and listen. Things will be a bit difficult for a while, but then everything will be all right. It'll be all right, we just won't be able to see each other for a while, and you won't be able to see Ivo for a while either, but you'll come back here soon, okay?'

'How long will it be difficult for?'

'I don't know, darling. I don't know yet. Not all that long. Difficult times feel as if they last a long time, but they're not really all that long. Come on, up you get, and we'll drive you home.'

'But you don't know where we live.'

'Of course I do, Stella. I know.'

She took me into the bathroom and washed my face. Then she put some ointment on my bottom lip, which was split, and whenever she leaned towards me I saw tears in her eyes. Everything in the house felt so familiar and peaceful. The plates in the kitchen, still on the table, unwashed. The water bottles in the hallway. Pidy's bowl. Ivo's slippers in the corner, and my bike helmet, which Papa had left behind.

'Here, look, your helmet,' said Emma, as if my look had reminded her. My flowered helmet. My mother had bought two, for Leni and me, and we often fought over them because we couldn't always tell them apart.

We drove through town in the big Mercedes. I sat in the back, with my seatbelt on, staring the whole time at Emma, who seemed to know exactly how to get to our house. It was very late, the streets were empty, and the wind was picking up, growing stronger and more irate. Before we got out of the car she took a pair of sunglasses from her bag and put them on, although it was pitch-dark. She took me by the hand and we stood outside our house like a couple of strangers. She rang the bell once, briefly, and I waited for my father to open the door; but it was my mother who opened it, and a moment later Leni ran out of the bedroom in pyjamas and stopped behind her. And so there we stood — Mama and Leni on one side, Emma and I on the other. As if Leni were Mama's daughter, and I were Emma's child whom she had to leave with this other family for a little while. I couldn't see her eyes behind the dark glasses, but when she saw my mother she took a step back. I didn't know whether they had ever seen each other before. I could tell from Mama's expression that something wasn't right. She didn't smile, as she usually did with people; she didn't ask her in, and she didn't proffer her hand. After a while, when she had peeled her gaze away from the woman in the dark glasses, she knelt down in front of me and took me in her arms.

'Oh God, Stella. My girl. Oh God, I was so worried. What happened? What's happened to —'

'I'm sorry. I couldn't bring her any sooner,' said Emma quietly.

'What's happened to your lip? Oh my God!'

Mama seemed to be freaking out, and although I kept expecting Papa to appear in the doorway, he didn't come. He wasn't there. And somehow I knew that that was unforgivable, that he ought to have been there, that something was going terribly wrong.

'I fell over,' I said, before Emma could say anything.

'You look like a boy!' gloated Leni, giggling. Mama told her to go to her room.

'Didn't her father say anything?'

'He just called and said he'd bring Stella home later. Well, I don't expect anything else of him. So — now we meet.'

'I'm sorry.'

'Stop apologising. That won't help now. Just go. Go back to your family.'

Emma let go of my hand and stumbled backwards. She kept on staring at our tiled hallway, the little light switch in the corner, my mother's socks, her pinned-up blonde hair, our school satchels on the chest of drawers. The Tissmar family photo.

She turned and ran to the car. The slam of the metal door: the hard sound of disappearance.

As she stepped on the accelerator, I turned, wriggled out of my mother's arms, and ran after her. I ran and called out to her, I kept on calling her name. I ran and ran, and I heard my mother call my name, I heard her footsteps in the dark behind me.

Go. Go back to your family, my mother had told her; but I was her family, too — she couldn't just leave me behind like that. Because I already knew you can't leave anything behind just by stepping on the accelerator.

She stopped at the traffic light before the main road, preparing to turn right. I climbed over our neighbours' fence that marked the last front garden before the road and jumped onto the pavement. The street lamps blinded me, and just as I got to my feet and was about to run in front of her car to stop her, just as the traffic light turned green and I was about to run out into the main road, my mother grabbed me by the scruff of my neck and pulled me back. I don't know how she managed to catch up with me without taking the short cut over the fence.

The other girl ran, too.

That girl died.

I survived.

My mother caught me.

Salome didn't make it. The war got there first.

The silence had buried everything beneath it. Years, decades, life and dreams.

I survived.

Mama took me in her arms and squeezed me so hard I couldn't breathe. I was screaming the whole time. I screamed as loud as I could. *I told Ivo to tell him, I told Ivo to tell him, I told Ivo to tell him.* Until eventually my mother put her hand over my mouth, picked me up, carried me down the street and into the house.

She put me in her bed, took off my clothes and pulled up the blankets, and she didn't stop crying the whole time. But she didn't ask any questions; she didn't prevent anything. My father didn't prevent anything, my mother didn't prevent anything, I didn't prevent anything.

Mama kissed me again and again and hugged me tight. After a while she lay down beside me and wrapped me in her arms.

★

I put the vodka bottle on the ground and hid my face in my hands. The radio was still blaring, and I turned it down a little. I needed the noise, confirmation that I was still alive, that there was still a here and now. I wanted to sob, to force all these images out of me, but nothing came out, not a sound. I pressed my hands against my body, as if I could squeeze them out, but it was no use. I had bitten my fingernails until they bled, and I took another swig from the bottle. I stubbed the cigarettes out on the floor, right in front of my feet. I sat there in a heap of ash.

★

How could I have been so blind as to overlook the children?

And how, how could he have known all that? I had never told Ivo about that night. I had never told him anything about how I had run after his mother because I already knew I had done something irrevocable, because I already understood that I had set something irreversible in motion when I accused Ivo of being a coward if he didn't tell his father about us. Even though I couldn't imagine Ivo betraying me as I had betrayed his mother, I still knew that what I had done was unforgivable.

I had never told Ivo that, in my panic, I had revealed my betrayal of Emma to my mother. I had never explained to Ivo why I had urged him to speak those poisonous words.

Perhaps he had guessed; perhaps it was my mother who at some point had broken her silence; perhaps it was merely coincidence and the putting together of things to make a whole that had prompted Ivo to come back, that had prompted him to bring me here. To unpick, in front of me, someone else's story that would clarify my own, that would catapult me back there and resurrect everything we had tried so desperately, all those years, to forget.

But not even that night, not even in the flood of memories, in my urge to wipe it all out, did I realise what he was trying to do, what he hoped to do for me by forcing me to remember.

★

The following morning Ivo's father shot his wife, and the dog. With the hunting rifle from the cabinet that we were never, never, never allowed to touch, that was kept firmly locked.

On the evening when Emma drove me home, he collared Ivo and took him for a walk beside the Elbe. He cross-questioned his son, and his son gave him answers, told him everything he needed to know for him to shoot his wife the following morning. He tried to kill himself as well, but couldn't summon the courage, and eventually called the police. When Ivo came home from school there were flashing blue lights everywhere, in the garden and on the street. People were staring at the covered body as it was loaded into the ambulance; people were staring at the man as he was taken away in handcuffs; and people were staring at the little boy who stood there, shell-shocked, literally dumbfounded by it all.

★

Sitting on the floor, drunk, suffocated by my misery, drowning in self-pity, I asked myself why I had never managed to forgive us. Why I had never asked him for forgiveness; why I was bound by this wretched, sticky guilt. Why, for heaven's sake, I had never told him that I would have laid down my life to take back those words, the words that had cost his mother her life; that I had run for my life to try to stop her; that, looking back, I would have been willing to accept his hatred just so that *she* could go on living.

And as the radio offered up a smoky voice to the ether, I realised that I would have been willing to let him go, to release him — from me, from my guilt, and from his. That I would have endured it — I would have endured my heart, my body, my unwritten future, so his mother could live, and so he could have a different life from the one he got as a consequence of my love. For the first time, I admitted the thought that he might never have loved me if I hadn't stayed that afternoon, if I had simply followed my father home. And when I accepted this thought, when I swallowed it whole and unchewed, I crumpled like a rag doll.

23

When Salome arrived and started frantically ringing the doorbell, I had been sitting on the floor for nearly four hours and the bottle of vodka was almost empty.

I was sober. Despite the vast quantity of alcohol I had consumed, my mind was completely clear. So clear it almost hurt.

'What's the matter with you?' Salome sat down at the table and looked around.

'Where's Buba?'

'He's staying at his friend's. What's happened? You've been drinking.'

'My mind has seldom been so clear.'

'They'll be back the day after tomorrow. Please calm down. I was really worried about you when you rang.'

'Yes, yes: they'll be back soon, everything's okay, please don't worry.'

Did Salome really think I was drunk and overreacting, or had she simply not wanted to hear what I could tell her? I no longer had the strength to decide, and lay down on the bed. She came and lay beside me, probably because she felt duty-bound to take my mind off things. I fell asleep within minutes.

★

'I know you can't answer right now, but I want to tell you that I'm sorry I told you to tell your father, back then. Please, forgive me. There's something else I want to tell you, too. I want to tell you that it wasn't that one afternoon that first bound us together. Because it was only possible for that afternoon to happen as it did because I stayed with you, and you with me. Of our own accord. Because it was what I wanted, and it was what you wanted. Which means it wasn't that bloody afternoon, Ivo, that shaped everything. No: that afternoon made me realise *that I want to be with you, to stay with you*. I would give you the choice: if only I could turn back time, I would have run off, I would have jumped down from the tree and left with my father. And in doing so I would have spared you everything that followed. If I could do it, I would. I chose you, without knowing that this choice would destroy everything. But you did the same. And yes, Ivo, we were children, we feared for our dreams, we feared being torn apart, we feared for each other. But — yes, but. That's all I have to say.'

*

I left a voicemail message and hung up. Salome was sleeping on Ivo's side of the bed. The clock hands read eight. I went to the bathroom and washed. I looked pitiful: the dark circles around my eyes had become black holes. I brushed my hair and made myself a coffee. Despite my monumental drunkenness of the previous night, I was clear-headed and full of energy again after the short sleep.

I spent the day at the market with Salome and Buba. We did some shopping, then later we cooked at Lado's house and played cards. Buba had some friends over, and Salome and I waited on the boys like a pair of chaste old maiden aunts, laughing at ourselves.

Lado had called, and had said only that they would be setting off for home that night. Salome seemed relaxed, and I also managed to hide my unease. I fell asleep on the living-room sofa, befuddled by good food, house wine, and the sound of the television in Buba's room.

*

They were due back late in the evening. By then I had tidied up, done the laundry, distracted myself with inconsequential activities, sat on the veranda, and eaten vanilla ice cream straight from the tub. The heat no longer felt as oppressive, and something inside me seemed infinitely light, infinitely free and calm. As if something had been overcome. I looked down at the city and really felt I could imagine making a completely fresh start. A fresh start for Theo, for myself, and perhaps for Ivo, too. I could imagine turning my back on Europe for a few years and moving here. Visiting Mama, and starting to write again — real writing, unvarnished, unorthodox. I could imagine being free, a free agent, a freelancer. I could totally imagine living in this apartment and growing flowers on this balcony. Theo and Buba would become friends, I would learn the strange language and its songs, I would find myself again. Here, liberated from all constraints, free of my responsibilities, ready to move on.

★

This is what I was thinking when my phone rang and Salome told me they were dead.

★

Alexei had known, back then, that his Georgian lover was married to the enemy, to an enemy leader, in fact, and had given birth to his, Alexei's, child. She had confirmed this on the day that she was going to leave, to go back to her husband, and had implored Alexei to let her go. That night, Nana had begged him, and he too had begged her: not to go away, to show him his child at least once, to consider starting a completely new life with him. She pictured the poetry evenings and ceremonial halls, saw herself wearing her Desdemona costume again, thought of the Russian's gentle, benign, young love, and for a brief moment she thought this could be her future. Only for a moment: just long enough to go to his apartment and stay with him till dawn, to comfort his broken heart with a little closeness.

But he wanted to keep her with him, and promised her family would have unimpeachable protection if she stayed. He promised he would drive her to Batumi himself, in his car, in a few days' time. He promised absolute protection for her children, for her friend; he even guaranteed it for her husband. They would all reach Tbilisi unscathed. And he kept his promise. He even managed to make sure that Lado survived. Lado, who lost his entire brigade and survived, not knowing he owed his life to his wife's lover, the biological father of his only son.

Ivo had found all this out. He had been corresponding with Alexei Nevsky for weeks.

Back then, the Russian had promised Nana he would let her and their son go if she stayed with him just a few more hours. Nana stayed. She stayed, and by staying she secured her family's survival. She stayed, under bombardment, knowing that total occupation was imminent.

Then Salome left Sokhumi. A few days later, Nana and Lado's house was set on fire. It was the day Nana had gone back. Alone, unaccompanied by the Russian, without his protection, because he hadn't thought of her, he had forgotten that she was the one who needed it most. He never found out exactly what happened to her. For three days he searched for her, and at the end of those three days he could barely identify her burnt body. It was only weeks later that forensics established for certain that it was Nana.

She had simply left his house and gone back to hers. And that was where her body was found, three days later.

It was war.

It was a wrong time.

The Russian had kept his promise. He had given up his biological son. He had left the husband his son, in exchange for his dead wife.

Ivo wanted to bring peace: this was what he had promised to himself, the Georgian, and the Russian. Ivo wanted to make amends.

He wanted to ask strangers for forgiveness. For me and for himself. He was asking his dead mother for forgiveness by giving another dead woman the truth. He wanted to bring Lado to the man he so hated, whom he blamed for the death of his wife, but to whom he owed the son who had given Lado a second lease of life. This was what Ivo had wanted, just as he would have wanted my father to stop his father, to tell him the truth, to perhaps prevent the unthinkable. He wanted to give Salome the freedom to leave, to return to her family, because she wouldn't need to stand in for Lado's memories anymore. And he wanted to give me the freedom to decide: to go or to stay, of my own free will, unconstrained by the memory of a single afternoon.

He had wanted to give Buba the possibility of a future without guilt, the kind he would have wanted for himself, more than anything in the world.

He had persuaded unfamiliar people in an unfamiliar country to break their silence. He had asked them questions, he had searched and found, he had wanted to connect their past and present, because he wasn't able to do it for himself and his family.

And perhaps he wanted to tell the story of a little girl who ran for her life in a time of war, because she believed she had summoned death. To tell the story of another girl who ran to try to prevent something she couldn't prevent anymore.

Perhaps he had tried to force me to realise this: that when Emma drove back that night to the house by the port, my mother could have called her husband to account. That my father, after fleeing his lover's husband, could have driven home and waited for Emma and me. That he could have gone to Ivo's father and told him he desired his wife; that he should have taken me with him that afternoon, against my will, even if it meant forcing me, even if it meant dragging me down from the tree and carrying me off in his arms. Through the basement. Into the street. Outside.

Perhaps the reason Ivo wanted to uncover this other story, to tell it, was simply to make me see that those factors were just as responsible for our guilt, our failure, as the war in Salome and Lado's story, in Maya and Buba's, in Nana and Alexei's. That we both made the mistake of assigning the guilt to ourselves alone; that this was a mistake, and that all our attempts to punish ourselves, to make the adults accuse us, had come to grief because they were always met with silence. That our anguish may have had its origins in, and been triggered by, that afternoon, but not our closeness, not our longing for each other, not us. That we couldn't be made to bear the guilt of having chosen each other.

Perhaps.

★

The Russian had grown old with the years. He was still an administrator, in a crisis zone; he too had no real home. This was what Ivo had written in the folder labelled *Nevsky*, where I found the remaining pieces of the puzzle. He had married a Georgian woman, who lived alongside him, silent, hurt, in the shadow of a dead woman.

We, too, had lived in the shadow of a dead woman.

The Russian told Ivo his story. Ivo had corresponded with him for months; he had saved everything in the folder, and the Russian had written a lot, everything Ivo needed to know, as if he had been waiting for a stranger to come one day and deliver him from his silence.

And Ivo heard another story, the story behind the story — his story.

I assume that, at their meeting, Alexei Nevsky told Lado the truth: about Nana, his wife, and the day she didn't get into the car. All that Ivo had learned from him the Russian also told Lado. Then, sometime later, they got into their cars. I know that Alexei Nevsky got into his car as well. I know that they were not far from the beach promenade, the endless quay that was the first thing to be rebuilt and repainted after the war, the many bullet holes superficially plastered over.

I know that Lado took the wheel, and I believe Ivo only let him do so because he believed the truth Lado had just heard would bring him, if not happiness, then peace. Why had Ivo forgotten, why had he forgotten that the truth doesn't always heal — that it can also kill?

I know that Lado calmly switched on the engine, calmly turned the steering wheel, slowly drove off, let the Russian go ahead, and then, after positioning himself in the left-hand lane, abruptly spun the wheel and cut in behind Alexei Nevsky's green Lada Niva. I know that he kept his foot on the accelerator and sped straight at the green car, that the Russian lost control of his vehicle, skidded, and that the car slammed into the stone wall of the promenade before smashing through and hitting the sand six metres below. Ivo's Land Rover didn't go through the barrier, but rolled several times before coming to a halt in the middle of the road. I know that a white Mercedes crashed into the right-hand side of the Land Rover without braking, and that this cost Ivo his life.

Alexei Nevsky lived for another three hours before dying of his internal injuries. Lado lived only a few more minutes. Ivo died instantly; his heart stopped beating on the spot.

The driver of the Mercedes was a Frenchman. He survived the accident. He was in the country as an international observer for the UN.

★

I had to identify them both in the morgue in Sokhumi. Salome couldn't get a permit to travel to the city where she was born. The bodies were transferred by plane to Tbilisi.

Lado was embalmed so people could mourn him and say their farewells in a three-day ceremony, according to Orthodox tradition. I had Ivo cremated. It was only after I had collected his ashes from the crematorium that I called Germany. For some strange reason, the first person I called was my father. For a long time he said nothing; I couldn't even hear him breathing until he finally let out a sound like the cry of an animal. I heard him weeping, and tried to remember if I had ever heard him weep like that. He wept so uninhibitedly, so loudly, so entirely without restraint, that for a fraction of a second I forgot that this was my father, the man who had first deprived this boy of his mother, then made him live another life, a life with him and me. I said nothing. I did not try to comfort him. Before I hung up, I said that I would be coming to Hamburg in four days' time with Ivo's ashes in my suitcase, and that he needed to organise everything by then and tell everyone, including Mama in Newark.

As I said it, I meant those words as punishment for all that he had done. But when I hung up, I knew that Ivo had not wanted any more apportioning of guilt, and I knew that when I saw Papa I would tell him the truth, even though the truth could kill.

★

Hundreds of people gathered for Lado's funeral in the house with the tree stump in the garden. His coffin was laid out in the middle of the room where I had eaten, drunk, and laughed so often. Black-clad women — professional mourners — sat in front of it on chairs. Salome, in the middle, rocked back and forth, her face rigid, chewing her bleeding lips. Men stood in the entrance; Buba, in black, leaned against the wall and stared at the open coffin where his father lay. Father. As if nothing had happened: peaceful, restored, so others could mourn him. So the horror of the moment when his car rolled over was no longer apparent. So people didn't have to see what he saw in his final seconds.

I observed how the people in the room formed a circle around the coffin, sobbing, whispering, groaning, hugging relatives. I noticed the photo that someone had put up beside the coffin. A picture of Ivo. A picture I had never seen before.

Ivo in Tbilisi. In one of the winter months before he came to Hamburg to fetch me, to make me remember. It made me smile. I smiled because he was so beautiful, because in the photo he looked so happy, promising so many things, uncovering so many secrets, making so many people happy. And I was one of them. I looked at him.

★

In that time I didn't shed a single tear. I was mute. I was present. I tried to support Salome, who didn't sleep a wink and kept vigil by Lado's coffin like a faithful guard. I tried to hug Buba, to keep his rebellion, his anger, his despair in check when he started yelling or banging his head against the wall. I tried to be there.

I don't know where it came from, my inert staying power. My superhuman fortitude. My competence and vigilance. I didn't sleep, I didn't eat, I didn't drink, and yet I didn't keel over.

I made it through. I faced the days as they came, with such emotionless clarity that I sometimes wondered if I was actually still alive, or what miraculous strength one develops in such close proximity to death.

I arranged the buffet for the funeral reception, I organised Lado's gravestone, I took Ivo's smashed laptop to a repair shop and got them to save the data that could still be saved. I booked my flight. I phoned Papa and gave him instructions for the scattering of Ivo's ashes. I dealt with Ivo's belongings.

Four days after Lado's funeral, I flew back.

24

The farewell would be at Tulia's. Some wanted a grave in the cemetery in Niendorf, others a grave beside his mother's in Hamburg. Everyone wanted a share of Ivo. I had decided to scatter his ashes at sea. I clutched his urn and wouldn't let anyone near it.

I wouldn't allow anyone to comfort me, touch me, pity me. Ivo's pain was sacred to me; the pain he had bequeathed me was the only thing that belonged to me alone; it could not be shared. The only time I wept was the day I saw my son again. I opened the door, and Theo ran to me, tears streaming down his face. I took him in my arms and was silent. I couldn't say a thing, not a thing — what could I have explained to him? My decisions? My going away, my return? Mark stood in the kitchen, watching us from a distance. I knelt on the ground while my seven-year-old son hugged my neck and sobbed. He didn't know what had happened, but I knew that one day I would have to explain everything to him, my inability to be the mother he wanted me to be. I didn't know how, but I knew that by then I would have worked it out. And then, when he told me he had saved the carrots, I began to weep.

For a long time I sat with Mark at the breakfast bar, which I'd always thought hideously bourgeois, long before Ivo said so, when he visited me that first day. I didn't speak: there was nothing I could say to him. My eyes ached and burned. I put ice cubes on my eyelids. I still don't know if he can forgive me — I don't expect that of him — but my pain, Ivo's pain, allowed him to give me back my son; a part of him, anyway, that I would have to win back, conquer, fight for, but at least I could see from his face that he wouldn't try to stop me.

★

Tulia sat on the swing, staring into the distance. I sat down with her and put my hand on hers. For the first time, I noticed a white streak in her raven hair. She suddenly seemed old and fragile. For the first time, I saw her as the old woman she had already been for years. I could hear the sea. And without me having to speak, she seemed to know everything. Perhaps this old woman with the white streak in her hair was the only one who had forgiven us. All of us.

'Your mother's coming tomorrow. Tell your sister to pick her up from the airport. I don't want her having to drive up here on her own,' she said, and cleared her throat. Then we smoked a cigarette and gazed into the distance together. Gently, I touched her hair, and her forehead. She pretended not to notice. I stroked her hair, her forehead, her cheeks, and didn't look away. I looked at her. I saw her, and I saw the pain that, from now on, through Ivo, I would share with her for ever. With her alone. Only her. The woman who had raised us all.

★

It was just us. As I had wanted it. The family. The family that never was. Tulia, Leni, Mama, Papa, and me. We sat on the beach and gazed at the sea. After a while we got into one of the rental boats and took it out. Nobody spoke as I held up the urn and scattered the ashes on the water.

It was the last great freedom I was able to give him. I couldn't do any more.

Later, we all sat in the garden and drank the wine I had brought with me from Lado's. For Ivo.

We drank to Ivo.

My mother, my father, my sister, and my grandmother. No *buts* and no *kind of*. As if Ivo had made us a family again.

I hadn't told them much, just the essentials, and were it not for the expression in Tulia's eyes, which told me she saw through my half-truth, perhaps I too could have believed it was a traffic accident. A banal, absurd, utterly senseless traffic accident.

But at that moment I realised that one day I would tell the story. I would tell the whole story, everything Ivo had wanted to tell.

★

I'm flying back in August. I'm flying to Tbilisi. To Salome, to Buba. To another family that I will explain with *but* and *kind of*. I will take with me the data recovered from Ivo's laptop, and I will finish his report. I will live with Salome and Buba in the house where we all spent the summer days together, where we sang, talked, laughed, and hurt each other. I won't tell the boy the truth: that he lost two fathers at the same time. And I will tell Salome only half the truth, only what she needs to know in order to move on, no more.

★

Mark and I will divorce. We haven't actually said it yet. Having shared eight years of his life with me, having had a child and raised him with me, Mark is trying to remain neutral and objective, not to make things difficult for me, but I know that that's where we'll end up, by autumn at the latest. He will tell me that it isn't working between us anymore. But I am no longer afraid that I will lose my son — to whom I have made the promise that, for him, I will always be the mother that I am, though not the one he might perhaps like me to be.

I will visit the Frenchman who was driving the company Mercedes, whose name is Gérard; he took a leave of absence after the accident, and I speak to him on the phone from time to time, because he feels guilty and needs someone to talk to, because he can't go back to the life he led before, just like that. I will explain to him that it's not his fault. I will make sure he is not mentioned in my report.

Because the guilt has to end. It has to be erased. Although I know it's not possible, I want to try. I want to try, not least because Ivo tried.

★

And so here I sit, a few days before my departure. On the beach in Niendorf; our beach, from which we would swim out into the cold water. On the sand, which is cool and damp, because it's been raining for two days.

I sit here, where I so often sat with you; I sit here, where I offered you my naked body for the first time, as a gift, one I didn't know how to wrap and you didn't know how to unwrap, and I look at the water. Our bay, Ivo. Our place, where no one comes, because it's too cold, because there are too many boats moored here, the sand is too frosty. I sit here, looking at the sea, and for some strange reason, one I cannot explain to myself, I am not sad, not hurt, not lonely, not dead.

★

I look at your face, so pale, so peaceful, and still feel the old, familiar feeling, and mistrust it even as I feel it. I wonder how it can be that I still feel this closeness. Even now. I will never be able to explain this feeling to anyone; worse, I am not supposed to feel it, given what happened, in view of the future, *my* future. But this is how it is right now, and I am slowly accepting it, this sensation that seems to outlast everything else.

I have the sheet of paper in my hand, the picture of us. Before that afternoon; before the moment when we became what we became. I look at you, and I am grateful to you, for everything you could and could not give me.

I sit here and look at you while the sea strokes my hair, the hair you loved to plait that, in a moment, I will cut off, because somehow I must take my leave. Not of you — no: of myself. Of what I was, and can no longer be. I think of how the wind will carry my hair away as it did your ashes. That perhaps out there, at some point I cannot see or discern, we will meet. The remnants of us, or perhaps our beginning.

I will finish what you started. And I have stopped looking for explanations.

Perhaps the closeness is not pain, Ivo, as I always thought it was. Perhaps it isn't an us, either, but a you and a me, building bridges, always failing, always continuing to try. Perhaps.

I cut off the first strand, the second. I cut off the tips, then the scissors I took from Tulia's kitchen move further and further up. The hair falls, and the wind blows it away, almost to the water. I see the wind carry off single strands, and I am glad. Yes: I am glad to have less and less on my head.

I wish that the truth were this: that your quiet, sad mother accepted the love of my cheating, irresponsible father, that they could have been simply happy. Two happy people. For moments, at least. And that we children could have had nothing to do with any of it.

Ivo, I know that you left because you forgave me.

You've done it, Ivo.

You turned the end into a beginning.

My love for you is like an exquisite wine that I tasted and now want to drink all the time, but cannot find again, because perhaps it has all been drunk. My love for you is like a biblical painting, of guilt and forgiveness that never come. My love for you is like nothing but you.

My hair is cut off; every single strand is being borne away on the wind. I am almost bald, and it is almost gone, but I sit here receiving the wind as it lashes my head.

Have you ever considered that there is only a single letter between *live* and *love*?

The sea is dark. The sun has disappeared behind a veil of clouds. My head is shorn, and I am able to receive your thoughts directly.

Your death cuts me in two. But it gives me a new life. A life with no right, no wrong, no *but* or *kind of*.

I come to you shorn, I come to you naked. I am here, Ivo, beside

the sea, and I am someone now, even without you. I am myself, Ivo
— without that afternoon, without your love, without my family that
never was, without all that lay and lies before and after.

I am gentle; I am soft as wool, and my inside is silky smooth, as if I
were a baby, a foetus, secure, wanted, untouched by the world.

You told me so often that I had forgotten who I was, and perhaps
it is actually true. And perhaps I never knew it. Until now. Until here.
And perhaps I only realised it when I stopped fighting this gentleness
in me. But I know that I am not you, not anymore.

My head is naked now. I defy the wind.

And just as I am not afraid of the solitude, the silence, the questions
that will come after all of this, that perhaps are encapsulated in the
word *future*, I am not afraid of this realisation. I will have to weep. All
that I cannot process I must push out of me, and there will be no one to
hold my brow — I am aware of that as well. But what does it matter?

I look at your face. You are beautiful. You are as beautiful as ever,
and I find myself smiling. I look at your face and think that I am
grateful to you, for this gentle closeness and this terrible alienation.
That even though this closeness is a feeling I can never share with
anyone again — I let it go.

I look at you.

.